NEW WORLD

INFERNO

JENNIFER WILSON

OFTOMES PUBLISHING
UNITED KINGDOM

For Annette and Dawn
Because dedications are better than capes—
they won't fly in your face or suck you into a plane.

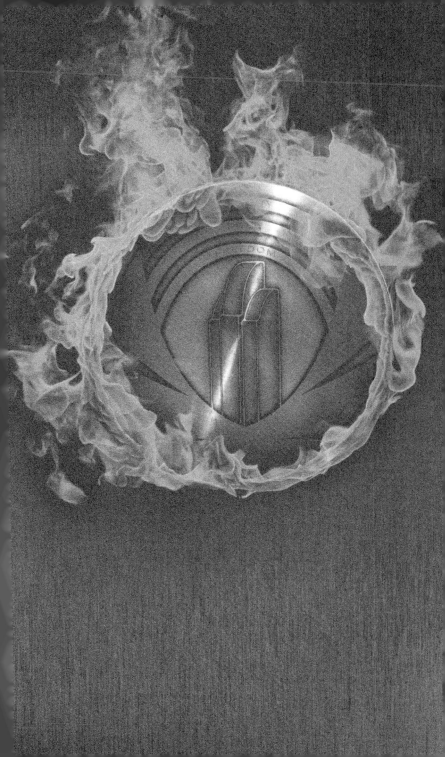

PREFACE

THERE IS THIS strange moment before war begins, a moment of peace, of hesitation and calm. It's almost like watching water the instant before it breaks a dam. For one split second the rebellious liquid brims at the edge of its enclosure as if questioning its resolve. A single drop will bead at the rim, holding its brethren back, as if trying to stop the inevitable. For that one moment there is a flicker of hope that the water won't spill over, that the chaos won't ensue, and that it will recede. But the truth is, it's *always* a false hope.

Too many things have been set into motion.

Too much pressure has built behind the dam and regardless of how much you pray for that water to stay within its confines, it's going to overflow the wall and the bedlam *will* come.

War is like that droplet. Always on the verge of breaking out, even though most of us refuse to see the signs. We close our eyes as it clings to the edge, praying the walls won't be breached, that our precious worlds won't be affected. But they will be. For when it does come—and it will—all you can do is try not to get swept away in the

1

flood.

1. HOME

THE WHISPERED STRING of profanities barely reaching my ears cut off under yet another deluge of gunfire. Chunks of brick and mortar rained down, nicking flesh in stinging bites.

"Damn it!" Archer's voice was audible this time even through the onslaught of bullets. Her vocabulary was becoming exceedingly more colorful with each shot fired. Feet tucked beneath her, the lanky ex-Wraith shouldered her rifle and began to rise. Without hesitation I lashed out. Grabbing her good forearm so tightly she flinched, I shook my head, my eyes screaming at her to shut up and sit down. Her loud mouth was almost as good a target as a moving body. Wrenching the captured arm away, she shook her gun at me, but paused in her now elevated crouch.

"You have a better idea?" She hissed, wincing away from another bullet that was a little too close for comfort. Her long dark fingers flexed greedily around her rifle.

"Let's start with you *not* getting your head blown off." I yanked at her again and this time she sank back to the ground. The jet-black barrel of her gun vibrated with the tension emanating from Archer's death grip. Another explosion of debris assailed us.

"What the hell are these pricks doing out so late?" She growled, covering her face with what remained of her partially amputated left arm. She jerked her head backwards indicating the dilapidated building on the other side of the disintegrating barrier we were crouched behind.

We had been five blocks from the clock tower, five blocks from food and shelter when the air was suddenly riddled with flying bullets, sending the five of us scattering like cockroaches.

"At least they're firing at *us*." I snapped.

Hidden in the shadows of a large electrical box twenty feet to my right, I could barely make out the sandy head hovering in the darkness. Lower, widened with fear, two brown eyes stared back at me. Triven and Baxter's arms were thrown wide shielding the little girl as they watched helplessly from their shelter. A bullet tore through the wall next to my right ear, searing the tip. Involuntarily I flinched back, clutching the side of my head. The bodies across from us lurched, and then crept forward in the sallow moonlight.

NO! STAY! My hands flashed out, bloody palms signing commands. Mouse's sign language was paying off in a multitude of ways. While no words were spoken that could give away their location, the message was clear. Fascinating how a person can shout without uttering a word. Miraculously, Triven listened, staying behind their rusted metal box, but as he shifted Mouse behind him into Baxter's arms, I knew it wouldn't be for long.

"We have to move." My words were for Archer as I glowered at Triven's shadowed form.

"Ya think?" Archer's tone was pinched with sarcasm. I ignored her.

"How many did you count before we took cover?" I asked. The ringing in my ear dulled my voice. I groped it, hands coming away slick. Not good. Why did head wounds have to bleed so much? I had counted two guns glinting in the darkness and based on the rhythm of the rounds, that sounded like an accurate calculation. However, as neither of us was about stick our heads out to get a better look, conferring with Archer seemed like the next best option. She hesitated, looking as though she was considering jumping up again. I kicked her boot, earning a glare.

"Two. I think there were two, but maybe three."

I nodded. Three we could handle.

There was a soft scraping noise to our right. The toe of Triven's shoe barely slipped passed the electrical box before a rain of bullets sparked the metal barricade and seared the ground around them. As Triven dove to cover Mouse, Baxter leaned out around them catching my eye for the briefest second. That was all I needed. Pointing two fingers at him, I gestured to my eyes and then the building our snipers were shooting from. He barely nodded before I was scrambling to my feet. Hands pressed to the tar rooftop, I crouched.

"Ready?" I barked at Archer, grabbing a large piece of dislodged mortar off the tattered roof.

"For what?!" She fumbled with her rifle, startled by my sudden movement.

"GET READY!" I screamed at the top of my lungs so Baxter could hear too. I chucked the debris to my right and as soon as the bullets lit up the roof following the distraction, I took off in the other direction. Rubble ground

5

beneath the soles of my shoes as I launched forward. Archer's startled cry resounded in my wake as I launched past her.

"Prea!" Triven's shout was filled with reproach, but I was already sprinting.

Come on! I thought, *follow me you bastards!*

I made it two strides before the Tribesmen fire began to trace me. Their bullets sprayed in my wake, trailing my steps as a smug smile pulled at my lips. Though I could not see them in the darkness, I could hear the bullets whistling through the night, see the sparks on the ground as they leapt at my feet. "NOW Archer!"

I felt more than I could hear Baxter and Archer moving to their feet. Seconds seem to stretch, then it was our shots puncturing the night as we returned fire. The bullets raining down on me ceased for three beats. What little glass was left in the building across from our roof shattered, tinkling as if fell, spraying the streets below.

"ONE DOWN!" Baxter's deep voice broke through the gunfire.

My legs pumped, fire burning through the muscles with each stride as my eyes stayed locked on the building's edge.

One still alive and ten feet to go.

A bullet snagged my hair, the stench tainting the air. Several of Archer's favorite words sprung from my lips as my legs pushed harder. I did not survive The Minister merely to die on this rooftop tonight.

Five feet.

Archer cursed as the gunfire stopped. Twisting, I saw her step out from behind our blockade, rushing toward the front of the building, gun raised. A body was falling from the building across from us. The woman's tattooed-covered arms flailed uselessly like a broken bird as she plunged toward the pavement below.

"Mine!" I hollered over my shoulder. *Don't kill her, not yet.*

Without hesitation, my legs thrust forward, launching me over the side of the building and plummeting down into the alley below. My hands caught rough surface after rough surface, slowing my progression with each stinging contact. The tendons in my shoulders screamed. *You've gotten soft,* the voice in my head whispered. As if proving the point, my feet landed with a thud, jarring my knees as they absorbed the impact. Three months ago that would never have happened. I cursed the stiffness of my joints and pushed them onward, ignoring the pain that caused me to limp the first few steps. Instinct took over, coercing me to slow at the mouth of the alley. I knew Archer was standing over me, watching my back, but still, one did not step out onto the streets of Tartarus carelessly. Glass speckled the cracked street, like glittering lethal confetti. Each piece glimmered as I shifted in the shadows, the Milky Way of this damned broken city. I wondered idly if that's what the stars had once looked like in the sky, when you could still see the stars, that is.

The crystalline path flared out, swirling around the unmoving shadow sprawled across the street from my alley. The Taciturn woman lay splayed on the black pavement, a halo of glass glittering in her auburn hair. It was almost angelic if not for the unnerving position of her limbs. One leg in particular stuck out at an odd angle, protruding sideways at the knee, and then there was the ominous dark pool leeching out from beneath her animal skin jacket. The fur itself appeared to be bleeding.

I hadn't heard her body hit the ground, but my mind could imagine the wet sounds of flesh splitting open, the crunches of bones breaking. I repressed a shudder—surely, she was dead.

Still my gun rose, trained on the motionless head as I approached. Not even my Sanctuary grade boots could remain completely silent on the wreckage that filled the streets of Tartarus. Each crunching step was excruciatingly loud in the hushed wake of the gunfire.

Ten paces away, I froze. *Impossible…*

The woman's chest rose and fell. It was ragged and shuddering, but the Tribe member was breathing. Unbelievably she had survived not only the fall, but also the two bullet wounds oozing from her chest. Tough chick. Regardless, without medical attention, she would be dead within minutes.

One swollen brown eye cracked open, roving the dark night before it fell hatefully on me. Despite the blood streaming from her chest tainting her tattoos crimson, a guttural snarl parted the Tribesman's lips. The barrels of my gun did not leave her face. Feet crunching, I closed the gap between us. Our eyes flickered warily, silently scrutinizing the other. Fascination sparked in my mind as I watched her face furrow in confusion. As the woman's eye wandered over my slight frame, colorless clothes, she could find no Tribe markers. No sign of alliance. A smirk split my lips as I remembered my own shock at discovering there were not only five Tribes roaming Tartarus.

"Do it." The Taciturn snarled, the words bubbling up a froth of red spit. Both her arms were limp at her sides, one twisted into an impossible angle. Even in the dark I could see the fingertips were turning blue. A memory of a dark alley, a heat-seeking bullet and a scared little girl flashed through my mind. Doc's serum had brought me back from worse.

The snake skeleton tattooed on the woman's face twitched, winking at me. She is the enemy… or at least she *was*. My finger yearned to pull the trigger, to rid the world of one more violent Tribe member. But that wasn't why I was here. That wasn't what Ryker had asked of me.

Leaning over the woman, I spoke in hushed tones. "What if I saved your life tonight? How would you repay me?"

She coughed up a foamy laugh. "I would kill you."

"Survival of the fittest." I smiled humorlessly at her. The Tartarus way. "And if I killed you?"

Her words were becoming harder to make out as her lungs labored to breathe. "My family would avenge me."

The word took me back a moment. Her *family*? "You mean your Tribe?"

"Your skin would make a lovely addition to our leader's coat." The words were slurred, but still held the gravity of their threat. She tried to laugh again, to appear unafraid, but as her shuddering breaths became desperate gasps, a shot of fear crept into the Taciturn's eyes.

Despite the bravado, in the end we all feared death. She was no different.

Good, fear was something I could work with.

"Fortunately for you, *your* hide serves me better alive than dead." With a flourish, I pulled a green vial from my vest pocket, swirling it above her good eye. The barrel of my gun never left her face as I crouched over her. Smiling devilishly at her, I uncapped the syringe and held it over her struggling heart. "This is going to hurt like hell."

"What are you?" Her question hung in the air. Her eye stretched wide with apprehension.

I knew what she meant, what answer she was looking for, but I belonged to no Tribe. Thanks to my parents, thanks to Ryker, I was one thing and one thing alone.

"Damned." I said, plunging the syringe into her chest.

The reaction was to be expected. A cry escaped her lips as the green liquid pushed free of the clear vial and began coursing its way through her body. It was fascinating watching Doc's regeneration serum work when not on the receiving end. Tissues began to knit themselves back together in a spider web of scabs and raw flesh. The minor breaks began to reset, the swollen yellow skin deflating to its natural pale color. The larger breaks—like her leg— remained unhealed, but she would survive until we could set them for proper recovery. The girl could be an asset, and if not that, then at least good for bartering. Gratitude slowly replaced agony as the Taciturn's body relaxed back against the pavement. Her hands unfurled as the muscles relaxed, no longer in excruciating pain and a genuine smile crept to her lips. In the absence of her cries, I could hear glass crunching in the alley behind me. My eyes flicked up for a millisecond towards the sound and the instant I saw Triven's approaching face, I knew I had made a mistake.

His lips twisted in a shout of warning just as a blade buried itself into my bicep and a single gunshot pierced the night.

2. BETRAYED

A SHARP HISS escaped through the gaps of my teeth as I struggled not to wince. The girl's brown eyes were still staring at me even though we had abandoned her body over twenty minutes ago. Open, glassy, dead. There was a single bullet wound that had been lodged in her forehead—an angry third eye weeping a solitary bloody tear. I glared at the figure sitting in the shadows across from me. Her knee was bouncing rhythmically as she watched Triven clean my wound.

"You know a little gratitude might be nice!" Archer threw her good hand up, glaring back at me. Popping up from her seat she began to pace. "I just freaking saved your life and you're looking at me like I ruined your day. Soooorry!! Next time you feel suicidal, let me know and I won't step in to save your ass. I'll just let the rabid Tribesman stab you to death, okay?!"

I glanced down at the floor, biting the side of my cheek to keep from screaming back at her. As mad as I was at Archer for shooting our first possible recruit—or prisoner, depending on whichever would have been more promising—if I had been in her shoes, I would have made the same choice. That was one truth I never questioned in this world of kill or be killed. I would always choose *my* people first. Alliances be damned.

The four of us were holed up in the clock tower's main room, bathed in the green light flickering in through the soiled faces of the decrepit timepiece. We didn't dare light a torch, but instead stayed in the shadows cast by the city's numerous fires blazing outside. On cue, another explosion tremored in the distance, its blaze of light illuminating Mouse's wide worried eyes before dulling to another flickering flame. I could almost feel the heat on my skin, despite the gooseflesh prickling my arms.

The others had better get back, *soon*.

Baxter had separated from us shortly after we abandoned the now useless bodies. We were to wait here no longer than two hours for his return with Arstid, then if they didn't show, we were to move onward without them. The idea of seeing the leader of the Subversive—of seeing Triven's mother again—was making my scalp prickle. I had a feeling despite the fact I had brought her son home alive, the new discovery of my lineage wouldn't warrant a warm welcome. She already blamed my parents for her husband's death, how was she going to feel when she found out I was The Minister's only remaining blood heir?

An involuntary grunt escaped as Triven pressed a sizzling compress to the uneven wound in my left bicep.

"You should let me use some of the serum on it." Triven said. The cloth in his hand came away crimson, but the bleeding *had* slowed.

"I'm fine." I told him for the tenth time. "Besides it's already clotting and it was a clean enough cut, just sew it up. I'm not wasting any more of Doc's healing serum."

Archer scoffed in disgust as she glowered at a spot in the floor. "*Now* you want to be stingy with it? Save a stab-happy Taciturn, no problem. But heal someone on *our* side? Naw, let's just sew the arm up and see if it turns green and falls off later. I mean, *I'm* pretty amazing with only one hand, so maybe you'll be good with it too." She waved her amputated stump at me. "I'm sure I could round up some of my ex-Tribe members and see if any of them are game to help speed that process along for you. On the other hand— pun intended—maybe it's a good thing you're too tough to use it yourself. It's not like we're in *short supply* or anything here!"

"Are you quite done ranting?" Triven rolled his eyes at his old friend when she finally paused.

"Give me a minute to catch my breath." Archer said, continuing her incessant pacing. I got the impression she wasn't a big fan of confined spaces.

"What do you mean *short supply*?" I derailed her train of thought before she could start again. This time her steps faltered. She looked at each of us in turn as if a guilty admission had slipped from her lips. She chewed on the words carefully for a moment before finding the right ones.

"There was a fire in Doc's medical bunker."

A flurry of questions exploded from both Triven and I simultaneously while Mouse's hands flew.

"Was anyone hurt?"

Maribel?

"Who started it?"

Is everyone okay?

"What happened?"

"Is Doc okay?"

Explain!

She held up her hand to quell us. "Only some of Doc's serum survived and not the strongest stuff unfortunately, but the real problem is that his equipment to manufacture it was completely destroyed. He brought all of it with him from the Sanctuary and without that tech he can't make more. What we have is all we may ever have." Her dark eyelids slipped closed for a moment. "Two were killed and two more were severely injured."

"Doc?" His name clung to my throat like sandpaper.

"No," Archer paused, waving her hand dismissively. "He wasn't there at the time. The council was in meeting."

"Who then?" Triven blurted out. I tried to build up a wall between my emotions and the names that were lingering on Archer's unwilling tongue. A scrap of bandage wound between Triven's fingers at his side, the only sign of anxiety on his otherwise stoic frame.

"Nixon and Cas were helping out in the lab when…" The subtle shake of her head spoke volumes. These were *not* the two that had lived.

Triven hissed, while Mouse's hand flew to cover her gaping mouth. Tears shimmered in her eyes. To me, however, these names meant nothing, just two more Subversive members I had successfully avoided. Triven caught my quizzical look and responded and sighed. "Father and son. Our most recent additions, before you. Nixon was a rarity, a Scavenger who loved his child more than the Tribe life. Cas was only nine."

"Seven." Archer corrected solemnly.

I reached out and pulled Mouse to my side protectively. "Who survived?"

"Veyron and Arden were there, healing from the attack in the alley. They're alive, but they both suffered a lot of burns and with the limited supply of serum... Well, some say they are lucky, but I'm not sure they feel the same way."

"But they're alive?" My heart sputtered a little faster. They were maybe the only other Subversive members I cared for since being abducted into their underground society. The last memories I had of them were bloodied faces drowning in a sea of Ravagers. I assumed that like my parents, I had lost them to the most feared Tribe in Tartarus. But they were *alive*. Relief washed through me, healing wounds I hadn't realized were open. Marred or not, they were still alive. My friends. It wasn't until this moment I realized that's what they were. Friends.

"Who?" I asked. Mouse squeezed my hand silently echoing my question.

"We have ideas, but..." Archer's mouth pinched as if she had already said too much. "Maybe we should wait for Arstid. They should be back soon enough."

An understanding glance passed between Mouse, Triven and I. Soon enough wasn't good enough, not when time was against us. We needed answers *now*. Triven stood, walking toward her to coax more words from his disinclined friend. "The more we know *now* the better."

"*Maybe* it's better if we don't wait for them at all." The words fell from my lips before I had intended to let them go.

Triven's hazel eyes fell on me reproachfully as Mouse raised her eyebrows in surprise, but it was Archer who responded first. "What is *that* supposed to mean?"

Though I refused to look at Triven, my words were for him too. "All I am saying is it seems a lot of things have gone wrong within the Subversive and all of the ones I have personally witnessed seem to involve your leader. The raid on the Ravager's warehouse, the night we breeched The Wall—those ambushes weren't a coincidence."

"Yeah, well there were quite a few of us who were there those nights, myself included. You going to accuse me next?" Archer bristled. "Or maybe it was Veyron or Arden. Hell, he only burned off half his face in that fire. Maybe that was all part of the master plan?!"

"Who requested they stay in the infirmary?" I asked.

Archer's lips pressed tight, giving me an answer despite their silence.

"Go ahead, *tell me* it wasn't her." I avoided speaking Arstid's name, sneaking a glance at her son. Hurt rimmed his eyes, but I could tell it wasn't merely what I had insinuated, but the fact that I was right about some things. He could see the gaps, the holes where she could have betrayed them. Triven's jaw worked, grinding down the thoughts he didn't want to believe. Still he came to her aid, "My mother may be many things, but she would never turn on her people."

I wondered if he heard the lack of conviction in his own words.

"Yeah *and* she's not the one wasting the last of our medical supplies healing the enemy." Archer said, folding her lean arms over her chest. The fingers of her right hand tapped impatiently as her stump twitched with a mirrored phantom movement. "Why the hell did you do it anyway? She was the enemy!"

A stiff silence hung in the room causing Archer's eyebrows to reach impressive heights. Triven's eyes wandered from Archer's face to her arm before sliding back to me. The corner of his mouth contracted into a frown. I knew then that he was thinking the same thing I was. She was an ex-Tribe member. Left for dead by her own kind. If we—children of the Sanctuary, born free of the Tribes— had abhorred the idea of uniting the Tribes, how would those betrayed and exiled feel? To the other Subversive members, these people were not simply murdering Tribe members. These were blood relatives who had left them to die in the streets. Kinsmen they had escaped from, and now we were asking our people to call these monsters allies once more. It would be like asking me to side with Minister Fandrin. The contents of my throat turned to cement.

"*Well?*" Archer twisted the word expectantly.

While shame stole our voices, Mouse found hers. Index finger raised, the child pointed to her shoulders in turn, and then in a downward arching motion that only moved her wrist, she closed over her finger into a fist before finally making a sweeping gesture at the room around us. Archer's brow creased in confusion. "Sorry kiddo, I didn't catch that one."

Irritated Mouse huffed. Triven translated without looking at his old friend.

"We need them."

"*Excuse* me?" Archer scratched at her ear as if she hadn't heard him correctly.

"WE. NEED. THEM." I over-annunciated, speaking a little louder than necessary. A strange smile tightened her mouth as Archer's dark eyes searched mine, looking for the joke she was obviously missing.

Laughter bubbled to her full lips, too chirpy to be sincere. "You mean we *need* them *dead,* right?"

"On the contrary my trigger-happy friend," I spoke gingerly this time, willing the words not to be true. "We *need* them *alive…* we…" The words faltered unwilling to come out. I remembered all too clearly how furious I had been when I found out what the Sanctuary's rebels had wanted from us and I didn't want to be the one to unleash that rage in Archer. Especially not when her rifle was still clutched in her hand. I didn't know her story as to how she escaped the Wraiths or how she had lost her hand in the process— Triven never divulged anyone else's tales. It was one of the reasons I trusted him with many of my own. Now however, I wished I knew more about what led Archer to the Subversive's ranks.

This time she laughed in earnest, her booming voice echoing off the dilapidated walls in way that made all of us cringe. My eyes shot to the door, wary of who else might have heard.

Unlike myself, Triven was willing to shoulder the burden. His words came out gently, like telling someone their loved one was dead.

"We need to unite the Tribes."

All signs of mirth slid from Archer's dark face. "You *need* to tell me what the hell happened over there. *Now.*"

ARCHER SLUMPED TO the ground as if her knees suddenly consisted of water. The rifle was still clutched loosely in her hand, making her look like a child clinging to a lethal safety blanket. What little color was left in her face had tinted green and for a moment, I thought she might vomit. My feet reflexively drew away to avoid the potential mess. We hadn't told her every gory detail—Triven had breezed over the extent of my torture, which was fine by me, living through it once was enough—and my lineage had been carefully omitted, but for the most part, she now knew what we knew. There were rebels inside of the Sanctuary. They had already started a war and were bringing The Wall down in just over than two weeks, *and* they needed us ready and waiting for that moment with the Tribes in tow, otherwise we were all dead. In truth, even with the Tribes on our side—which was an impossible task in itself—our chances were still slim. Passion cannot always trump the sheer force of weapons, and The Minister's army had a substantial amount of force. Without the Tribes, we were out-numbered and out-armed. With them, we had new enemies at our front and old enemies behind us. The question was, could we put centuries of hate aside long enough not to kill each other first? My hopes were not high.

"Shit." Archer stared unfocused at my feet. I knew that feeling, all three of us did. Her throat spasmed, her own words threatening to choke her, but still she didn't move. I had expected an explosion, an uproar that would make the Ravagers look gentile. I had braced myself for that. But *this*? This pale silent response was not what I had anticipated. In fact, the longer Archer stayed silent, the higher my anxiety rose. Triven eyeballed his friend with similar trepidation.

It wasn't until Mouse cautiously left my side, her delicate hand cupping Archer's wan cheek, that the warrior girl began to thaw out of her trance-like state. Sluggishly the tense muscles relaxed until the gun fell loose from her fingertips. Archer's hand closed over Mouse's, enveloping the ivory skin in ebony. She stared at the little girl I loved before looking at each of us in turn.

"This is a death sentence." Her voice was flat as it echoed my own past words. "Either way, we're screwed."

My shoulders sagged under the weight of her words.

"It's better to die fighting for what you believe in." Triven's words were powerful, but lacked true persuasion. This was a devil's errand. We all knew it. Triven and I had merely passed into the stages of acceptance already.

With a spark of sudden madness, the fire in Archer's eyes rekindled as she glared at him. "I *won't* help you." The words were soft, laced with an underlying fear I had never heard in her alto voice.

"Archer—" Triven cajoled, but she cut him off, pushing Mouse's hand away.

"NO Triven. You *can't* ask that of me. *You* of all people know my hand didn't simply fall off on its own." Triven cringed as she waved the vacant stump of her left arm at him. "*She* took it from me, nearly killed me. Shit, she would have succeeded if you hadn't found me. I *never* want to see that woman again. You can't ask that of me!" His slender body shot off the floor, trusty rifle back in hand. Her index finger flicked the trigger and though it wasn't pointed at anyone, yet, I moved Mouse back to my side. Archer's feet began to stomp the soiled floor, tiny clouds of dust erupting as she prowled.

"Woman?" I asked Triven, pulling Mouse closer.

Archer halted mid-step, pointing the barrel of the gun at me as she gesticulated each word. "My. *Mother.*"

Lowering her weapon, she shook her missing hand in my face.

Her mother?

Oh…

It was her mother who had taken her hand.

Archer must have seen the dots connecting and horror registering on my face because she snarled, turning her scowl back on Triven. The gun leveled at his chest and Triven's hands rose in defense.

"I *won't* help! THIS…THIS *PLAN* IS SHIT AND YOU KNOW IT. I WILL KILL HER FIRST—" She was screaming now, all sense to keep quiet lost. If she didn't accidentally shoot us right now, someone else would certainly hear her and come to finish the job.

"I'm the heir to the Sanctuary!" I'm not sure what made me say it, but regardless the effect was what I wanted. Archer froze, her head swiveling toward me.

"*What* did you just say?" Shock hushed her tone, but it was too late.

The damage was done.

Someone *had* heard us.

All eyes turned to the door as heavy feet descended. Scrabbling, I dove for my handgun lying discarded on the cot while shoving Mouse to the floor. My fingers grazed cool metal as a tattoo-covered man burst through the door, the barrel of his gun aimed at my face.

3. SCARS

THE TACITURN WE killed tonight had been true to her word. Her Tribe *would* come to avenge her—we just hadn't expected it to be so soon. Our guns turned on the intruder as the shadows spit a second person through the darkened doorway. Both Triven's and Archer's guns shifted to the newcomer, but I stood transfixed on the first Taciturn man before me.

His tattoos were clear, even in the dull jaded light. What had held my attention, however, had not been the ink induced marks, but the young man's face... or what was left of it. A sickening tapestry of angry red flesh and sinew had woven itself over half of his once handsome features. The scars had devoured an eyebrow while the left side of his lips had been pulled taught into a permanent grimace. The man was nearly unrecognizable except for his eyes... Then he spoke. The face was all wrong, but the voice I would have recognized anywhere. It was the same one that had shared many dark nights with me in the Subversive's holding cell.

"Phoenix?" He spoke as if afraid to say my name aloud.

The gun went limp in my grasp. I stammered, my voice was suddenly small, "Arden?"

Arden's face moved in unfamiliar ways beneath his scarred mask. There must have been nerve damage. Still the expression of shock was unmistakable. It seemed as if he was equally surprised to see us alive.

My old cellmate crossed the tower's floor, seeing only me. Despite my desire to look away, he was all I could see. Shame eroded my thoughts as I urged my eyes to blink, to look away from what had become of Arden's face. I shouldn't have stared. I should have focused on his hands, his shoes, anything else, but instead my gaze remained frozen on my friend's ruined face. For an instant, I could smell smoke from the fires that had marred him, the scent stinging with each step that brought him closer, as each scar came into sharper focus. I choked down a sob. I hadn't done this to him—not directly—but I *had* left him in that alley to die all those weeks ago. If I had fought Maddox harder, maybe I could have saved him from this fate. I could have... I could have...what? Brought him with us? *To what?* My conscience whispered to me. *To die like Maddox did? To get tortured like you?*

It was as Arden's arms wrapped around my stiffened frame and my traitorous eyes finally blinked, that I realized I *should* look at him. Not at the scars, but at *him*— the good man beneath the disfigurements. At the friend I had once thought I lost. Over Arden's shoulder I could see Triven trying to recover his own poise, his gentle features tainted by shock and pain for our friend.

Was that same look on *my* face?

Letting my muscles relax a little into his touch, I squeezed Arden back, silently vowing to never avert my eyes from my friend's face again. He deserved that much. Scars can disfigure a man, but they don't have to change him.

Even so, I was grateful for the additional seconds of composure when Arden stooped to help Mouse out from beneath the cot. Tears blurred her eyes as well, but instead of pulling away in disgust as most children would have, the tender girl gathered Arden's face in her hands. His eyes widened as she gently caressed the patchwork of welts and leaned in, placing a single kiss over the spot where his left eyebrow had been. Pain mingled with gratitude swam in his undamaged eyes as he leaned in, kissing the crown of her dark hair in return.

Missed you. Mouse signed to him.

"Missed you too kid." Arden said, the right side of his mouth pulling into a smile. The left refused to follow suit.

My gaze wandered to Archer as Triven took his turn embracing our old friend. The flames of rage had dimmed in her eyes, but with a curt nod, she made it clear our discussion was not over—merely postponed. I made a note to relieve her of her rifle before that particular chat resumed.

I had nearly forgotten our second intruder until Baxter spoke, his usual note of playfulness gone. "This isn't the time—"

"Where's my mother?" Triven interjected, glancing past Baxter into the barren hallway. The fact that he had addressed Arstid as his mother didn't go unnoticed. Had he actually missed her?

It was in that moment reality dawned on me that I had not simply imagined the smell of smoke on Arden. In fact, the scorching perfume clung freshly to both men. How had I missed the cloud of anxiety that had enveloped the room upon their arrival? The gun gripped tighter in my hand.

"There was another attack tonight—from the *inside.*" A tremor shook Baxter's last word.

Arden continued in his wake, "There was an incendiary bomb. It took out our entire support system." The good side of his mouth pulled down to match the ruined one.

"What are you saying?" Archer whispered, the hush of her tone sending fresh chills up my arms. We knew the answer in the pit of our stomachs. All of us did. Still it had to be said aloud. It had to be made real.

Even though they were expected, Baxter's words set the world on end.

"The Subversive's bunker has fallen."

THE SMOKE FILLING the night seemed thicker now. Choking the air out of my lungs.

The *Subversive* has fallen.

The Subversive has *fallen.*

The Subversive *has* fallen.

Those words echoed over and over in my mind as we ran. It seemed unreal, like another toxic-induced hallucination courtesy of The Minister's torture and Ryker's drugs. Only this was real. This was the world we had come back to. We left a city in the throes of a brutal power struggle and we had returned to utter pandemonium.

Our safe haven was gone.

Nineteen more of our own were dead. Add in the man and his child in the infirmary, and that put the Subversive's death toll at a whopping twenty-one citizens. For perspective, only five had died in the entirety of the last year. Now more than twenty-one in a matter of months. This was the most devastating loss their people had seen in nearly a decade, since the long-ago night the tunnel was caved in on the Sanctuary's original escaping rebels. Since the night of my own parents' deaths.

I could hear the others running alongside me on the skyline, could sense their energy sparking in the dark, but I felt oddly removed. Both Triven and Archer had gone sickly pale at the news, even Mouse's already slight frame seemed to deflate. I could feel the agony radiating from their moving bodies. See it in the stiffness of their strides. Hear it in their strained breathing. I could empathize, even feel it to an extent, but my pain was not theirs. As they mourned, a selfish voice whispered in my ears. *At least the ones I love are safe.* Disgust quickly followed the momentary relief, but even so, it was not strong enough to overshadow the relief I felt that Mouse and Triven were alive. I had come to respect many of the underground haven's citizens, but I had not grown up with them, I had not loved them in the same way. I didn't know many of the people in the Subversive, and in truth it had never truly been my home. But it was theirs. For the first time, I felt like an outsider to Triven's grief. I had lost people, but not my entire world, not my way of living.

While my companions grieved the loss of their people, I grieved the loss of our only safehold. Without the Subversive bunker, we had nowhere to hide, no steady food supply. Our small army was already faltering. As I watched my friends run—their ordinarily sure feet stumbling with anxiety—I doubted they had even begun to consider the loss of their home, their minds still drowning in the loss of their friends. If we couldn't unite the Tribes, if we couldn't breach The Wall in time, we were dead. It was no longer merely a possibility but a fact. Without food supplies and fortified shelter, we were sitting prey—waiting to be picked off one by one.

As everyone else's minds quieted with desolation, mine flew into overdrive. Twenty-one corpses left eighty-five survivors from the Subversive's bunker—fourteen of which were children. With Mouse and I added to that, there were now eighty-seven people. Eighty-seven hungry mouths that would need to be fed, to be kept alive... *Shit.* There was no way we could protect that many people, feed them all, hide them.

My feet stayed their course, running with the pack, but the desire to change course, to go in the opposite direction was overwhelming. It was alluring, primitive even. Being back here brought the need for self-preservation slamming back to the forefront of my mind. The sting of fear that had always poisoned Tartarus' air made my skin crawl with a thousand bugs, whispering a warning that I was going the wrong way. That I would die if I followed these people. The rogue girl inside murmured in my ear. *You're better off alone...* But even as she spoke, her words died away. I wasn't her anymore. Ignoring the ache burning in my feet, I pushed harder, taking lead of the group.

The Subversive's survivors had scattered, fleeing into the very city they had hidden from for so many years.

Thrust into a place that was actively hunting them for being traitors *and* adversaries. In desperation, the Subversive's members took to the only safehouses they knew of, *mine*— well the ones I had told them about anyway. There were seven they knew of, and eight more locations I had not divulged. Still, it was not enough to keep everyone safe, and with a traitor in their midst I had no intention of revealing my other safeholds.

The Old World school, however, was one of the places I had told them about and this was where we were headed. It was the largest and most accessible location and while this meant it could house the most people, it also meant it was the least safe. Baxter had sent the majority of the survivors there and though Arden had offered to go round up the others, I refused, saying we needed his keen eye with us. The truth was I had left him behind once before, and I would never do that to my friend again. He had suffered once for my betrayal. I would never let that happen again. Something in his eyes told me he understood.

As our shadows flew across the skyline, my instinct began to claw its way out. Survival mode 101: fight or flight? That was the question. Fighting could give us freedom, but flight gave us better odds of survival. Not all of us of course. I could not hide an entire community of people, but I could hide Mouse, Triven and myself. The question was, would Triven agree, or worse, could I even ask that of him? A part of me knew if I asked, he might say yes. It would be the ultimate act of selfishness, the paramount act of betrayal and abandonment of both worlds. I wanted to. God knows I wanted to, but as I watched Arden leap the rooftop gap beside me, I thought of what I had said to him back in our cell a lifetime ago. He had asked me if I thought I would run given the chance and tonight my answer still rang true.

"I'm afraid that chance has already passed."

If I wanted freedom, genuine untainted freedom, then we would have to stick together.

Raising my hand, I signaled to the others to slow our little procession. The school's derelict building looked silent, dark and untouched just as I had left it. Normally this was a good sign, but not tonight. There were no guards on lookout, no sign of movement, not a single indication of our people. A chill ran down my spine. Had the others made it there? Was this an ambush?

"Triven..." I whispered, glancing at the broken windows, searching for a glint of a gun, a shadowed face.

Nothing.

Next to me, Archer gripped and re-gripped her gun, her sharp jaw tense.

"They're there." Triven spoke. His voice was husky, breath ragged from the five-mile run.

"Baxter?" I asked, my eyes still scanning the building.

He stammered, "I—I don't know. We split off to get you. Arstid said they could handle the evacuation, but..."

"They are here." Triven's voice was firmer this time. His eyes were sharp, rebuffing the possibility of any possible contradiction.

"Okay." I nodded to the street below us. "Okay... We will need to enter from the ground level. There is a hatch on the back corner—"

"We know." Baxter spoke, gently reminding me.

"Right." I shook my head. Of course they knew, I had told them how to access it. I changed mindsets. "I should go in first and check the building out. If it's clear—"

"*We* will go in together." To my surprise, it was Archer who cut me off this time, although everyone else didn't look too far behind in voicing the same opinion. Even Mouse's hands were hovering, ready to protest.

Keeping my voice low, I let the intensity rise. "How do you know the Ravagers aren't waiting inside ready to kill *all* of us? *I* know that building better than anyone else. I know where the vents lead and how to get in there unseen. If this is another trap, I can take care of myself. There is no point risking all of our lives." I glanced at Mouse meaningfully and was rewarded with a terrific glare from my tiny friend. Triven, however, looked down at her, the crease in his brow deepening. As much as he wanted to believe his people were in there safely waiting for us, he knew I was right. This could be a trap.

He signed in resignation, "Phoenix and I will go in. If it's safe, we will signal for you." Our three vocal friends objected noisily while Mouse stamped her tiny foot, but Triven merely held up a hand. "We need to ensure the safety of at least *some* of us. There is too much at stake."

Both our gazes fell heavily on Archer and Mouse. They knew what must be done. They knew our mission and despite Archer's scowl I knew we could trust her to tell the others if we didn't return.

"If we're not back in fifteen minutes—" I began pointing to my father's watch hanging from Mouse's neck.

"Come in guns blazing." Baxter caressed his rifle, a smile pulling up his lips.

All playfulness disappeared as I corrected him, finishing my sentence.

"*Run.*"

THE STREETS WERE silent as Triven and I moved to the shadowy building. I could feel eyes watching us, though it was hard to tell if they were friend or foe. Still, nothing moved but us. On the horizon, the first brushstrokes of dawn were painting the sky, disrupting the lingering blackness. We had maybe forty minutes before the night sky would no longer give us shelter under its veil.

Dead ivy hung over the secreted vent. The brittle stems appeared untouched, showing no sign of having let fifty odd people pass through. Triven seemed to be thinking the same as I swept back the vines, instructing him to hold them. Like mine, his eyes traced the ground for footprints or broken creepers, and like mine, his eyes found nothing. Carefully, I pulled the rusted vent from the worn brick wall and with a nod climbed into the pitch-black shaft. In the wake of losing all visuals, my other senses perked up. Despite Triven's careful hands and cautious movements, the sounds of the grate shifting back into place and his knees sliding to catch up to mine seemed painfully loud. I knew it was only because I was not the one making the noises, but still it caused my ears to twinge.

We moved forward as fast as we dared. Time was of the essence, but not worth being careless. The space was tight, but not as small as many of the vents I had explored over the years. Triven's wide shoulders would have no problem navigating these, brushing the sides occasionally yes, but not impaired. We couldn't stand, but at least it was manageable on all fours. It was the vents you had to belly crawl through that were the worst. Darkness distorts time and what were probably minutes, felt like an hour. Eventually a waft of cooler air brushed my cheeks. The fresh oxygen swirled in my nostrils bringing with it the scent of decay and long-forgotten parchment. This was the scent of the school I fondly remembered. It was almost as good as the library's.

Triven's hand brushed my calf, pausing as he realized I had stopped moving. His long fingers closed gently over my leg, reminding me he was there—that he was ready. It was an oddly grounding sensation, comforting even.

Carefully reaching to my left, my fingers found the loose grate I already knew was there. Before sliding the cover aside, I unholstered my gun. Hearing the quiet slip of metal on fabric behind me signaled that Triven had done the same. I flexed the calf under his hand. *Ready?*

He squeezed back. *Ready.*

The grate moved without a sound, my expert hands knowing when to pull and where to release. Muscle memory was an amazing thing. I peered into the room beyond waiting for a sound, searching for movement in the shadows. It was nearly as dark as the vent itself, the grey linoleum floors barely visible. As with our approach outside, no sign of life could be seen. Methodically, I moved forward, gun sweeping the seemingly empty room.

Throat tightening, I slid one foot out from beneath me, the soft sole landing noiselessly on the floor. As my heel touched, another disturbing thought crossed my mind.

What if this wasn't an ambush? What if the Subversive members never made it here? What if they hadn't gotten this far? What if they were already dead and we were hunting ghosts.

Please let this be an ambush.

If it was, then maybe—*maybe*—Triven's people were still on their way, maybe they weren't dead... yet.

As that thought spilled free, I straightened and froze. The cool tip of something round met my temple and despite the utter darkness, I knew exactly what it was.

The muzzle of a handgun always felt the same.

4. AMBUSH

DESPITE THE OBVIOUS intent of the assailant, the trigger had not yet been pulled. That was their first mistake. The second was putting the weapon within my reach.

Whipping my neck forward, I raised my left hand. The back of my fist slammed into the weapon forcing it and the owner's hand into the wall as I pivoted. My wrist twisted, palm slapping the weapon as I pinned it. My right hand followed its gun seeking a target, but it was quickly met with resistance. Bony fingers captured my forearm, keeping my weapon at bay. Despite the slenderness of the clammy fingers, they were surprisingly strong. It was a reminder that while people here were grossly underfed, we fought harder than any of the Sanctuary's citizens. *And* we fought dirty. I slammed the assailant's hand into the wall twice, hard. A shot fired as Triven's knees thundered inside the vent. If he stuck his head out now it was going to be blown off. Shoving one foot in the vent's opening, I found Triven's chest and kicked him back. As his body tumbled inside, the force threw my attacker and me backward. Metal clattered against the ground, our guns sliding just out of reach as our bodies tangled. Two swift punches cracked my mouth, the third narrowly missing my ear as I twisted away in the blackness. My own blows only landed twice as I aimed for the largest target I could find. Bare knuckles cracked against bone, maybe a shoulder, then a jaw. It was nearly impossible to fight a shadow in the dark. Finally, my fist sunk into softer flesh, driving hard into the body colliding against mine. There was a huff followed by a choked wheezing. I had hit the stomach. Lunging at the noise I tackled the hunched body to the ground. I could hear the person's head crack against the floor and took advantage of his temporarily dazed state. Floundering for my gun, my fingers instead found something heavy. The object grated against the floor, snagging on my rough fingertips—a dislodged brick. It scraped as I dragged it off the floor and prepared to strike the lolling head beneath me. I barely noticed the flicker of light filling the room, nor Triven's face as it blossomed into view. Nor did I see the shock of white hair. Instead, it was Triven's shout that broke the spell.

"Stop!" His voice boomed in the otherwise deserted room.

Gripping the brick I was about to smash into *her* skull, my arms froze, hovering over my head. The woman beneath me now had a cropped white head of hair and while her face had aged grievously since I last saw her, those spiteful honey colored eyes were unchanged.

"Mom?" The word fell from Triven's lips with a sense of desperate relief.

At the sound of Triven's voice, Arstid's struggling ceased. Her head swiveled, tears welling as she lit on her only son's illuminated face, a torch light glowing in his hand. With a burst of strength, the woman shoved me off her. On shaking knees, she blundered toward Triven, pausing before reaching him. For a moment, neither moved, as if afraid the other was a mirage. She broke first. With a violent lunge, Arstid collapsed into her son's unfurling arms. Her head pressed to his shoulder before tilting to examine his face. I wondered what changes she would find there.

"I thought I lost you..." *Too.* She did not speak the last work but I could hear it. Her husband was long dead and she had already begun to mourn her child as well.

"Where are the rest of the survivors?" Triven asked his mother, soothing her shaking arm.

"Here. They're here, down in that bunker-type room. It was my watch. I'm sorry I thought maybe you were Ravagers, that we had been betrayed again..." Her words were painted with disbelief. "The others?"

Her eyes turned back to me, but the love that was there a moment ago for her son, had vanished. It was obvious her apology was not meant for the both of us to share. I glared back, still not entirely sure this wasn't a set up.

"They're waiting for our signal. We weren't sure it was safe." Triven stepped back from his mother, her arms lingered, reluctant to let go. I wiped the trailing blood from my bottom lip, concealing a vindictive smile as she did the same with her nose. It had a little crook to it now.

"I'll get them." I said, moving toward the vent without waiting for a response. Despite my dislike of the woman, I needed to cool off and Triven deserved a moment alone with his mother. Even if I didn't trust her, he did, and besides of all the people left in the Subversive, *he* had nothing to fear from her. Arstid was many things, but she was not my grandfather. Family still meant something to the woman.

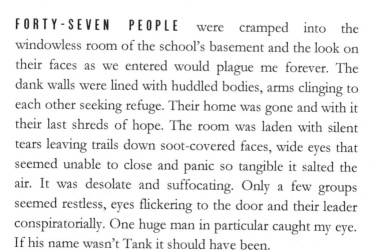

FORTY-SEVEN PEOPLE were cramped into the windowless room of the school's basement and the look on their faces as we entered would plague me forever. The dank walls were lined with huddled bodies, arms clinging to each other seeking refuge. Their home was gone and with it their last shreds of hope. The room was laden with silent tears leaving trails down soot-covered faces, wide eyes that seemed unable to close and panic so tangible it salted the air. It was desolate and suffocating. Only a few groups seemed restless, eyes flickering to the door and their leader conspiratorially. One huge man in particular caught my eye. If his name wasn't Tank it should have been.

While the three of us were greeted with expletives of shock and relief, Archer, Baxter and Arden melded into the gathering crowd seeking faces they had not yet seen. People embraced Mouse and Triven like the family they were, and while I received a few hearty handshakes and tentative pats, there was still a hesitation between the Subversive members and myself. Still, it was nice to be welcomed and even nicer to see the hint of fear in their eyes. Fear the stories of my legend had put there. Unlike the rebels, these people did not witness my torture, they didn't see the broken girl temporarily caged inside, nor did they see a lost friend. These people saw the rogue, the girl that had survived these streets. If only I could see her with such clarity again too.

As smiles faltered revealing desolation, reality set back in. It dawned on me that this was our lives now. The brief celebration was over and while we had survived, others had not and the fates of more still were unknown. This is what it would be like every time we reunited. The vicious cycle of war had begun. Until it ended, we would be doomed to relive this moment over and over, or until *we* were one of the missing faces.

I stayed in my old hideout long enough to watch Mouse reunite with her once jovial friend. Maribel's scrawny arms enveloped her friend instantly and while a smile forced the girl's lips upwards it did not quite make it to her eyes. It was as if the light inside her had dimmed. Even the golden ringlets adorning the child's head appeared to have lost some of their bounce. The girl's voice alone seemed to have survived the tragedy of tonight's events. Though it was quieter than I remembered. Everything about these people was quieter than I remembered. Still it didn't take long for the questions to begin flooding the conversations. They wanted to know what happened, what it was like inside The Wall, what happened to Maddox and Bowen, how we had survived... This onslaught of questions never stopped.

That's when I left.

I made an excuse of starting the first watch, but really I wanted to get away, to breathe my own air. To be able to think. It was wrong of me to leave Triven there alone to answer all of the questions, but if irritated, he showed no sign of it. Instead he handed me an extra rifle with the promise of coming up soon to relieve me. His mother glared at this, her bony claws digging into his arm, pulling his attention back to his people. When Triven turned away, her gaze fell away and she nodded curtly at my left shoe before turning her eyes back on her only son. The movement was so quick and fleeting, I might have been hallucinating. Stifling a snort, I had a feeling that was the closest thing I would ever get to a thank you from Arstid Halverson.

THE MORNING BREEZE felt cold compared to the hot air of the overcrowded safe house. Chills feathered my spine, prickling down my arms, but it was nice. Despite the exhaustion creeping in, my mind was still churning, reeling over the past few months' events. In one night we had gone from needing to achieve the impossible, to needing to achieve the impossible *while* babysitting the Subversive members. Less than a day back and already everything was going wrong.

A masochistic part of me wanted to wallow, to relive everything that had gone awry, to drown in the dark memories shadowing my mind, but what good would that do? We needed a plan—we *needed* to look to the future. The people on this side of The Wall needed a leader and in some perverse twist of fate, it was supposed to be me.

The sickly sun had risen low in the sky now, spreading its sallow color across the skeleton city. The city was always the quietest at this hour. We who prowled the night were hunkering down to make way for those who claimed the daylight. Plumes of some still burning fire clouded the atmosphere. I watched in fascination as they lazily twisted a path toward the sky, evaporating in the morning air.

"Home sweet home." I muttered. The burden crushing my chest lightened a little as I surveyed the broken buildings. Automatically, my attention drifted to the goliath wall separating the two worlds I had been claimed by. Both worlds were my past, present and future, and yet, both were lacking. They were fragments, sewn together in an attempt to make me whole. Both worlds had created me, both had destroyed me and both had given me hope. I wondered what was happening beyond that Wall. Was there even a war left to fight or were the rebels already dead?

My fingertips grazed the rectangular shaped object that suddenly felt like it was burning a hole through the thigh pocket of my body suit. Zipped carefully inside was the tablet Fiona had forced on me in Ryker's absence. Scanning the city again before averting my eyes, I pulled out the device. As soon as my fingers brushed the glassy surface, the screen flickered to life and staring up at me in his immaculate Sanctuary uniform was Major James Ryker.

5. SOUVENIRS

RYKER'S FACE WAS smug, but slowly his usually coy smile faltered. My breath hitched, he wasn't dead.

"Ryker?" I questioned, waving my hand at the screen. Two beats and my heart sank. There was no recognition in his eyes. He couldn't see me. This was just video like the others I had seen, a recording. On cue the screen glitched, rewinding itself a half second before playing again. Ryker's voice emanated from the device speaking to me from the past. The volume was low, forcing me to pull the screen closer to my face to hear his words. I squatted on the roof clutching the screen as I hid from the possible eyes below.

"Hey Princess." I glowered at his unseeing face. "If you got this, then I think you already know shit went wrong." His Adam's apple bobbed before he continued. "Hopefully I'm not dead, just detained—because let's be honest, the world needs more pretty faces like mine."

"Pompous ass." I mumbled. My thoughts scattered. *Was he a* dead *pompous ass?*

"Hell, maybe we're both dead and there's no point to this stupid video." He seemed to sober up, our thinking patterns syncing. "If you *are* dead, then this video is a complete waste of my time. Knowing you though, if you survived my escape plan, you're probably glaring at this screen wishing *me* dead." His mouth twisted self-righteously. His genius escape plan mainly included getting shoved into a human oven and then nearly being suffocated before dropping out into an abyss of human ash. Yeah, I should have wanted him dead—except that he might actually be…

He paused, chewing thoughtfully on the corner of his lip, his bright blue eyes as penetrating through the screen as they were in person. "You're not dead though, are you? I know you, Prea. You could probably survive a second Devastation." He rolled his eyes. "Look, whatever happens, you have to stick to your side of the deal. There are thousands of people in here counting on you, whether they realize it yet or not. This world needs to change and you *must* help it. *Especially* if I'm dead. You and I both know—but other people need to *see* what Fandrin is made of. And the Tribes, they deserve a place in this new world too. I know you said they are monsters, but they're humans too. We need them to fight together and in turn we must allow them a victory. We are all trying to survive and it's time we started doing it together. The Wall has entombed both sides; if it doesn't come down we will *all* die one way or another." He leaned in closer to the monitor. "I *need* you standing there on the other side when it comes down. This new world *needs you*." The military leader had emerged, all straight lines and harsh tones. Gone was the playful air I so often detested.

"Once outside of The Wall, I doubt this device will transmit to our side and the battery life will dwindle, so use it sparingly. If you got out when you were supposed to, The Wall will be coming down sixteen days after your escape. The clock is ticking Princess. No pressure, but if you fail we may *all* die. And if you're *not* standing on the other side when The Wall comes down, then you had better freaking be dead." He hesitated before adding. "*Don't* be dead."

He leaned forward and the screen froze, his face focused on something off to the side. That was it.

A tempest of emotions swirled in my head. I flicked the screen causing Ryker's motionless face to recede back to black, but the dull click of my nails did not reflect the anger percolating under my skin. I tossed the device relishing in the clatter of noise it made before sliding to a stop at a pair of black boots. I flinched. How long had he been standing there?

"Ryker could have gotten lucky. He could still be alive." Triven did not meet my eyes. He knew what I had been watching.

I shook my head. "If Fandrin's got him alive, then Ryker is anything but lucky. Trust me, *I* would know."

Triven stooped to pick up the discarded device, but not before his face contracted with guilt. I immediately regretted my words. They were honest, yes, but cruel. Triven knew what I had endured while in my grandfather's imprisonment. He saw what that man did to my body and my mind. I would never forget it, and in some cruel selfish way I didn't want him to either. I didn't want to be alone in that hurt. But that wasn't fair. Triven had suffered—was suffering—in his own way. The twist of his features, the hollowness that echoed in his eyes was proof. He had blamed himself for what had happened to me. I had forgiven him, but still sometimes when my guard was low, that venomous snake called hatred would raise its head and lash out. Anger likes to spread. In fact, it seemed to thrive on infecting others. It wasn't rational or right, but it wasn't always easy to keep in check either. I couldn't scream at Ryker, so Triven became the target.

Ever the better person, he didn't take the bait. Instead he sat down next to me, his long legs extending far beyond my own. The screen was still clutched in his gentle hands. I took a deep breath. "I'm sorry. That was uncalled for."

His chin dipped slightly, but that was the only acknowledgement he made toward my misplaced angry words. "We thought Archer, Veyron and Arden were all dead too."

Sharp rocks filled my head as I leaned into him, my temple dragged down by the weight to rest on his shoulder. "People die."

"Have hope."

"Be realistic." I countered, raising my eyebrows.

He actually laughed, "I'll try, if you will."

"I hate him." I nodded at the screen in Triven's hands. The words were mostly true, and it felt good to say them out loud. I did hate Ryker—for torturing me, for bringing back a past full of ghosts I had thought were forgotten, for rescuing me, for asking the impossible and for possibly sacrificing himself to ensure our escape.

I also knew in part, Triven needed to hear those words. He knew my relationship with Ryker was complicated and that I didn't harbor the same feelings as the rebel leader did for me, but still, Triven deserved the reassurance.

As his arm wrapped over my shoulders, squeezing gently, I knew it was the right thing to have said. For both of us.

"He's alive, Prea." Despite my harsh words, despite both of our frequent distaste for Ryker, neither of us wanted him dead. Punched in the face occasionally, maybe, but not dead.

"Ever the optimist, are we?" I asked. Triven's hands swept the screen, dusting it off as he began to replay the message.

"No… In my experience, people as stubborn as him are hard to kill." His hazel eyes tilted in my direction before glancing back to the screen, a strange expression crossing his handsome features.

Triven's eyebrows rose as he watched the video. "He really is a pompous ass, isn't he?"

I snorted, "*My* words exactly."

Our shared laughter faded.

What if he is dead? The unspoken question hung between us.

When the video stopped, Triven's finger flicked across the screen, turning the device off before handing it back to me. Not wanting to touch the physical reminder of our impossible situation I shoved the device back into my pocket trying to ignore the overwhelming weight it now seemed to carry and rose to scan the streets again. Triven's broad frame shadowed mine.

Together we looked out over the empty streets, both of us lost in our own thoughts. A purple smoke unlike the other blacks and greys that painted the skyline furled and unfurled its translucent violet tendrils as they wound their way along the rising breeze. The undulating plume swirled then abruptly rolled in on itself, doubling back against the nearly invisible force field. It was mesmerizing to watch. The smoky cloud halted midair, before sliding upwards toward the murky sky. As it moved, crackles of electrical lightning sparked whenever tiny ash particles hit the electrical barrier. Not even the vapors could penetrate The Wall.

"Sixteen days." Triven's deep voice broke the growing silence, grounding me back to reality.

I nodded, focusing on the source of the purple smoke.

"Did you tell *her*?" I asked, my eyes on the faded water tower.

"No. I thought we should do it together." Triven's fingers reached for mine, easily sliding into their now familiar place. They squeezed lightly.

"Archer?" I squeezed back.

"She's held her tongue."

"For now." I amended.

"For now." He agreed. His chest rose with a stuttering breath, releasing as I leaned into his shoulder. My head pressed to Triven's collarbone, his chin dipping to rest on top of mine.

This was it—the last moment of calm before the tempest.

"You know, this is the first sunrise I have seen *here* in nearly five years." The words felt disjointed, threaded loosely with the plan weaving itself in my head.

A purr emanated from his chest and neither of us moved, prolonging our stolen moment. I clung to him, knowing that in the end, I would have to be the first to step away.

The time to unite the Tribes had come, but a few things that needed to be taken care of first.

"I've got a plan."

"And?" Triven's sandpaper cheek snagged in my hair.

"And you're not going to like it."

6. LOYALTIES

ARSTID WAS WAITING for us when we returned, arms crossed, eyes narrowed in my direction. I rolled mine in response. It was nice to see not everything here had changed in our absence. Her narrow shoulders held square, but there was something off about the way her pointed chin jutted up. Then I saw it, the subtle shift of her feet. It was something a hesitant fighter would do. The stoic pillar of the Subversive was unsure of the future, of herself. At one time, I would have laughed at her discomfort, relished in it even, but not today. Not when it was taking all my focus to conceal the same in my own body language. An unexpected thought flickered to life. *Had she even wanted leadership, or had it been thrust upon her shoulders like it had mine?*

"We need to talk." The commanding tone of her voice cut the air. "*Now.*"

The thought soured. *Maybe she had wanted it.*

"So we do." I halted, mirroring her stance. A frustrated sigh came from my left. Though I didn't spare a glance in his direction, Arstid's eyes shifted to her son.

"Shall we?" Arstid's fingers unhinged from her arm, gesturing to the door behind us.

Several people I recognized from old council meetings began peeling themselves from the flaking walls and sullied ground, but my feet remained rooted.

"This will do fine." I nodded to the room around us.

The council members' eyes darted to the other citizens scattering the room, falling heavily on the children. My eyes only found Mouse's. The girl's mouth turned up approvingly, with a curt nod of encouragement. At her side, Maribel's eyes were round with equal parts eagerness and anxiety. Arstid's chin rose higher, her taut mouth falling open to object, but I cut in.

"There's a traitor among you." Bodies stiffened as an invisible vacuum sucked the oxygen from the crowded space. My eyes scrutinized the faces, trying to memorize them, before turning back to their leader's icy glare. "Is everyone here? Is everyone accounted for?"

Murmurs of confirmation buzzed as people counted their loved ones. I could see Baxter's lips twitching out numbers as he counted each head. Arden's eyes were simultaneously hopping from Subversive member to member doing the same.

"We're accounted for." Arstid spit, but it wasn't until Baxter and Arden both nodded in confirmation that I continued.

"Starting now, *no one* is ever alone." Several onlookers started, but others nodded in agreement, eyeing their once trusted companions with suspicion.

"I will NOT have you spreading a seed of mistrust among my people!" Arstid protested, but worry had flashed across her features.

"That *seed* was planted long before tonight." I leveled at her. The woman's shoulders shook, whether from rage or fatigue I wasn't be sure.

"Arstid…" Arden's voice emerged from the shadows behind her. "Phoenix is right." A pain twisted Arstid's face as his scarred hand slid over her trembling shoulder. Arden's voice dropped to a whisper as his other hand traced the welts now fabricating his new face. "This wasn't an accident. You know that."

Her fingers wound apologetically over his as her gaze fell to the floor in defeat. She didn't need to look at him to know what he was referring to. Despite the ice queen's cool demeanor, not even her frosty glare could completely hide a guilty conscience.

My eyes narrowed.

Averting the attention from his mother, Triven stepped forward addressing his people. "We're not saying to turn on each other. The traitor may be in this room, or out there with the rest of *our* people. We are saying to watch out for each other, to protect each other. There is strength in numbers."

"We can't stay here!" A woman cried, the rising panic finally overflowing. Her hands grappled at the front of her shirt like it was choking her. "What if this location has been leaked? What if the traitor is out there and already exposed us?! We're easy pickings here!"

"We have to help the others!" Another voice bellowed, a tall man standing alone in the back. His loved ones were obviously not here.

A swirl of anxiety scattered in the room's growing light, spiraling out and grabbing hold of any vulnerable heart in striking distance. A charmer in a cage of vipers, Triven's hands rose, temporarily quelling the fear. "We are going to get them. There is a place we can hide everyone," his eyes shifted to me questioningly. I knew he did not agree with my plan, but still he continued. "We're moving out tonight, I know there are lot of questions but we need you to trust—"

A sea of shouts drowned Triven's last words. The desolation that had kept these people imprisoned finally given way. Undiluted fear, anger and hate soured the room like a fine poisonous fog. Mistrust had been brewing since we had left, and it was finally boiling over. No, not just boiling over, it was devouring them.

"You just said we can't trust anyone!"

"We will starve out here!"

"Why should we trust *you*? You left us!"

"My family is out there!"

"You can't hold us here!"

"You still haven't answered…"

"How do we know *you* didn't do this?"

"Or *her* for that matter?!"

"I'm not going back to a Tribe. I will kill everyone in this room before that happens."

"Maybe *you're* the traitor!"

Wave upon wave of terrified verbal vomit spewed out, the noxious fumes contaminating the room. Voices clamored, their volumes growing as panic took hold of the crowd. My eyes darted to the windows as my fingertips brushed the hilt of my holstered gun. If these people didn't shut up, if they didn't listen, the Tribes were going to find us and then we were all dead. We needed these people under control and we needed it now. A few shell-shocked citizens still lingered on the floor cradling themselves, but the majority of the once docile group was now converging on us, and it was apparent their leaders no longer had control of the situation.

Shoulders jostled me, jockeying for their voices to be heard. The sea of bodies morphed, pulling and pushing us in its wake. Mouse's slight frame had disappeared into the sudden swarm while Triven became the dam blocking the door. Though he held strong, it was clear he was losing ground. On the other side of the tide, a head of silver hair could be seen twisting to those around her. The crowd pushed closer, my heart rate escalating with their intensity. Both Triven and his mother tried to calmly restore order, to subdue their people, but their empty raised hands did nothing to pacify the ex-Tribesmen. Archer pointed her rifle into the middle of a man's chest while Baxter was climbing onto the lockers to try and reign in the escalating chaos from above.

This was not going according to plan. In fact, the entire situation was a fiasco. Damn it, we didn't have time for this. These were supposed to be the civilized people, the rational ones on this side of The Wall.

Shit. Shit. Shit. The word pulsed with each heartbeat.

Then one man caught my eye. He was the largest and the loudest of the group, steamrolling his way through the center of the throng. I vaguely remembered seeing him upon our arrival, though I had paid him little attention then. It was "Tank". Though I had not taken the time to learn all of the Subversive members' names or faces, his was *certainly* one I had never seen before today. I would have remembered this one. A mohawk of dark dreaded hair hung to his tree-trunk-waist. His nose, much like the rest of him, seemed oversized, but when compared to his bugging eyes and enormous skull, it seemed rather proportionate. But the part I would have remembered, the part that I couldn't have been forgotten, was not his size, but the *markings* on his face. They weren't tattoos, but scars. Fine deliberately puckered pink lines spiraled from his temples down his cheeks. A dark patchy beard covered most of it, but what was visible, was striking. I had seen those markings occasionally before. He had been a Wraith and only their deadliest warriors had borne those marks. While no one dared touch the man, a small group shadowed his steps, rallied by the man's intensity. Round face reddened with rage, the behemoth's eyes were set on Triven who was still blocking the door. His intention was clear—move or be moved. The barrel-chested man only had to clench and unclench his oversized hands twice before I reacted.

"ENOUGH!" I roared over the chaos and as the man's fist rose toward Triven's face, I let my knife fly.

7. FUSE

CRIES BROKE OUT, cutting through the pandemonium as a thin red line split the front of the ex-Wraith's shirt.

He froze, staring down in shock before fingering the blossoming crimson stripe on his chest. The man's face lifted, burning a deeper red than his shirt front. His eyes widened before narrowing to slits at the sight of the barrel of my handgun suspended under his flaring nostrils.

The blade had barely nicked his chest, but the edge was razor sharp. I made sure of that every morning. The hilt was quivering in the wall next to the temple of a motionless wide-eyed woman. Aside from the man's rage fueled breaths, the room had gone utterly silent.

I used the hushed moment to cock the firearm and level it directly at his heart. It was an unnecessary action, as the gun was a semi-automatic, but it got the point across. *Move and I shoot you.*

"Were you *trying* to kill me?" The man snarled through stained teeth.

"You're still standing there, aren't you?" Triven's hand brushed the lower part of my back as I spoke, the brief contact whispering to tread carefully. "You're lucky I didn't shoot you in the face. If I hadn't been worried about giving away our location, I might have. *Although* that may not freakin' matter anymore, seeing as all of you idiots might have already done that for us!" My glare swept the room, pleased to find a few remorseful faces. "Are you *kidding* me?! What the *hell* is wrong with you people? Did you forget where you were? Have you already forgotten what it's like out here? Who you are in *this* world? We are not inside your precious concrete tunnels anymore. You are *not* safe out here. Away from *this* group," I gestured to the room, "you are nothing but traitors, *deserters*."

"*We* know better than anyone else what it's like to be alone out there, rebel." The man sneered, jabbing a sausage finger at the door behind me. Others nodded their heads in agreement.

"Really?" My eyebrows rose accusingly. "*Really?* After you defected, how long did you survive on your own before the Subversive found you? A few days? A few weeks? Maybe a month if you were lucky?"

His mouth opened then clamped shut. Heads stopped bobbing.

"That's what I thought. You don't know shit about what happens out there when you're on your own. You won't survive a day, *Wraith*." I spat the last word at him, knowing it was a low blow. Several other faces flinched.

Rage ran off the man in sheets. I could taste it. Smell the urge to strike me.

"Grenald…" One of his trailing shadows warned him from behind, eyeing my steadfast firearm.

Arstid's voice carried over the crowd. "Maybe the council should—"

Raged pulsed through the crowd, but I was the first to speak.

"No, no more councils. These people need to make a decision, on their own, *right now*. Within the concrete walls of the Subversive I followed your rules. But we *are not* there anymore. That world you built is *gone*." Arstid recoiled from my unapologetically harsh words. "We're in *my* world, in *my* home and I make the rules this time. I'm going to do my damnedest to keep *all* of you alive, but the truth is, no one is safe here. Especially not on your own. If you want my help, you're going to have to trust me. Trust *us*. Trust each other. If you don't, there's the door." I nodded toward the exit. A few stray eyes twitched longingly to the open door behind us. "But, walk out that door and you're done here. This world is about to change forever and if you leave us now, good luck. We won't be coming to rescue you *again*. The war you have all wanted so badly is here. And things are about to get a lot uglier before they get better, but I can promise you this. It's better to fight it *together* than to die *alone*. We have seen what we are up against. Believe us or not, I don't really care. But for the first time ever, Tartarus needs to be a united front. Prove to me that those concrete hallways weren't the only thing holding you people together. Prove that there is still decency in the human race and unite. *Unite...* or get the hell out."

Several people stared opened mouthed, and it dawned on me that these were the most words many of them had ever heard me say. And a there was weight in my words, the air was heavy with it. In the stunned silence, the pattering of small feet echoed to my side before stopping. Mouse's fingers squeezed mine, her silent pledge one of loyalty. More surprisingly was the second set of steps following closely behind hers, and while I never took my eyes off the huffing giant towering before me, I caught a glimpse of unruly blonde hair bouncing next to Mouse. There was stirring in the room full of human statues. Some made their way to the front, to our side. Seven people in total—Arden, Baxter and Archer were among them. Though Archer looked less than happy about the situation, she still stood tall next to Triven's shoulder.

All other movement in the room had ceased. No one dared breathe, much less move. My threat clung to the silence, dripping from the ceiling, plastering the walls. It was an ultimatum, but still, I was not their leader. I wasn't even one of them—not really. Questioning eyes fluttered to each other, before falling on their leader's weary face. One word and Arstid could undermine me completely. One word and her people would turn on me. One word and we had already lost the war.

Arstid's eyes softened as they fell on her citizens, before landing hard on me.

My stomach dropped. Her glare said it all. It was over before it had ever begun.

Drawing to her full height, she closed the gap between us. Grenald took a tense step back at her approach. With a twisting grace, Arstid spun away from me, effectively inserting herself between my gun and the giant. The barrel now aimed at the middle of her own spine as she faced Grenald. I knew I should have lowered the gun, but I didn't. Instead my finger tensed on the trigger. Then she spoke, sealing my fate.

"These people, *your people*, kept you alive, helped feed and clothe you, gave you a *home* in a world that turned its back on you." She gestured to everyone in the room. To the community that had flourished despites the odds. "We are *not* a Tribe. You are *not forced* to be here. We are your friends, your *true* family. The Subversive saved everyone in this room and if you cannot trust us now, then you have no business being here. But know this. Turn your back on us now—when we *need* one another the most—and Phoenix is right, we will not be there to save you again."

Grenald's face flushed deep purple as his lips contorted into a snarl. With a scalding exhalation, the ex-Wraith shoved past Arstid, his broad shoulder clipping her bony one as he stomped to the door. Those nearest scattered from the raging bull's path. With a roar, a colossal fist slammed into the frame, sending shockwaves rattling through the door, but instead of exiting, the man turned, planting his broad back against the wall next to the opening. Fingers folded, his hands clamped down upon his partially shaved head. Sparks flew from his dark eyes, but still Grenald stayed. And it seemed that with the furious titan now guarding the door, any other thoughts of desertion evaporated.

The city's law of survival was reflected on all of their faces. The same words that haunted all of our dreams.

Join or die.

These people weren't a Tribe, but they were still children of Tartarus. The desire for survival still burned in their blood, coursed in their veins and pulsed in their hearts.

Together we were a band of survivors. Alone we were dead.

When no one else moved, I reholstered my gun and retrieved the knife from the wall. "Okay. Everyone get comfortable, it's going to be a long twenty-four hours."

FORTY-SEVEN PAIRS of curious eyes followed me as I moved through the dimly lit space. Several people scattered as I shooed them away from the metal cabinets they were huddled against. None spoke. Listening to that many people breathe, their tongues held by fear, anger and grief was torture. Their silence was oppressive. It made me wish a fight had broken out. At least that would have relieved some of the tension.

The atmosphere was humming with unasked questions, but mercifully the stunned people kept their mouths shut. Judging by several glances at my sheath, I assumed it was out of fear that I would throw a knife at them too. Which, in all fairness, I might have.

Mouse's hand still clutched Maribel's swinging idly between them as they followed me through the rows of lockers. Eyeing me suspiciously, Arstid trailed close behind. Her glare was burning a hole in the back of my suit. She had sided with me only a moment ago, but that didn't change months of mistrust. Nor did it clear her name in my book either. We were allies now, but not friends.

At locker number two-hundred-sixty-two my feet halted. It was the number of pages in my father's favorite book in the edition I had nicked from the old library. The latch was cold, its rusted surface untouched for nearly a year. The hinges protested as I popped the handle, but the faded blue door swung open. A waft of dusty air caressed my cheek as it opened and I smiled. Stepping back to reveal the contents, sheer pleasure warmed my chest when Arstid's eyes popped wider.

"Is that what I think it is?" Her voice was hushed.

Several onlookers pressed closer to get a better look, Grenald's massive frame prominent in the cluster. Triven and Baxter had flanked him, ready to subdue if necessary.

Reaching in, I snagged a silver MRE pouch and launched it at Grenald's stained chest. "Consider this a peace offering."

He frowned at the packet dwarfed in his gargantuan hands. For a moment, I thought he might crush it, but instead he turned, handing it to a small boy cowering next to him. The child's eyes warmed and the giant's cleft chin dipped in my direction. *Peace offering accepted.* I mirrored the ex-Wraith before catching Triven's eye, letting my gaze linger.

See, I'm playing nice, it said and based on the quirk of his lips he got the message.

Beckoning the girls closer, I grabbed two more handfuls of the silver ration pouches. "Start handing these out to the other *children.* Make sure everyone shares."

I scanned the growing crowd as the girls sought out the other children, daring someone to try and claim a meal from them. It seemed I wasn't the only one concerned. Archer materialized, her rifle resting prominently on her shoulder. She began to trail the girls as they handed out the food to the other kids. Her glare alone was ward against any selfish thought. Still, no one bothered Mouse or Maribel, instead they were watching me.

I moved methodically, carefully selecting each numbered door. Several were meaningless numbers burned into my mind by necessity, others bore more significance. The address of a favorite character's home, the page which held a favorite quote, the days counted since I came to this hellish city—each locker held different things, each one seemingly random. The clusters of people skittered as I waved them aside to gain access to each closed door. Gasps rose from the Subversive's members as they watched the contents being unearthed. Bags of freeze-dried food, bottles of purified water, blankets, books and lanterns. Even Triven's eyes widened with each new unveiled warehouse stash.

"When you told me you had supplies hidden here, I assumed a few dirty blankets and a bottle of water." Triven eyed the purified water as he handed it off to a weasel-faced man who bore the signs of once being a Scavenger. The missing teeth and yellow pallor that never seemed to entirely fade always gave them away.

"I thought you had learned not to underestimate me." I smirked as his ears flushed pink.

"Apparently, I needed to be reminded of how enterprising you are." He winked a hazel eye and it was my turn to flush.

To my utter surprise, no one rushed the exposed supplies, but instead gathered closer together clinging to each other in hope. It seemed with the emergence of supplies, the panic that had so forcefully gripped the room moments ago had subsided, for now. But even as the provisions were handed out, I could see the worry blossoming again. My stash was never meant to feed such a large group of people. They knew it wouldn't last.

I pushed a handful of food packets and water bottles into Triven's open arms.

"There's not enough for everyone, they're going to have to share and ration themselves. This all needs to last the day."

Surreptitiously, I slipped five silver packets into the satchel now slung over my shoulder. They were promptly followed by six books, an oversized shirt and two water bottles. Only Triven's keen eyes caught the light-fingered action. His eyebrows rose but he said nothing.

"How many are we going to take with us tonight?"

We had never solidified this part of the plan, sidetracked by the mob situation that had nearly derailed us.

Tightening down the satchel's strap, the numbers started ticking through my brain.

"Ten at most, anything else will risk too much exposure." I eyed the members of the Subversive, counting off the key players we had mentioned on the rooftop before stopping on one member in particular. "Bring Grenald."

Triven's brow creased as he handed the supplies off to a maternal-looking woman to continue doling out. As she moved away he leaned in closer with the pretext of helping me tighten my shoulder strap. "You think he can be useful?"

"I *think* we should keep him close." My gaze flickered to meet his. Triven's breath was warm on my cheek, making it hard to pull away. "There is one more locker."

I nodded over my shoulder for Archer and Baxter to follow us. In the back corner of the room, near the hidden vent shaft I had spent many nights sleeping in, was locker four hundred and twelve.

When the door popped open, Baxter let out a low whistle and despite herself, even Archer eyed me appreciatively. Three handguns, one rifle, ten clips, and seven throwing knives layered the faded blue interior. Before I had met these people, before I knew what it was to rely on someone else, I had always kept stashes of weapons near each of my hideouts. It was stupid to travel with this quantity of weapons on your person. The weight alone would only slow you down, and flaunting that many weapons definitely made you a more desirable target. These had been my reserves, my safety blanket. Like everything else hidden here, they too had been slowly filched from the Ravagers' warehouse over the period of six years.

After taking two of the knives for my own collection, I shut the door and leaned against the cool surface.

"Make sure these are delivered into the right hands. The hunting party will need the majority, but the others will need protection too. I watched Grenald and his pack of followers talking near the now closed door. "Maybe don't hand these out until the last minute."

"So does this mean you're going to tell us what the hell this freaking plan of yours is then?" Archer followed the trajectory of my stare before stepping into my sight line, forcing me to see only her exasperated face.

"Can you keep your shit together this time?" I countered.

Her eyes threw fire at me.

Baxter leaned over my shoulder, his head inclined at Archer. "Of course she can keep it together, I mean look at the glare. Very reassuring."

He grinned when she punched him in the arm, clearly not amused. Baxter dug his pinky finger into his ear, clearly unfazed.

"It's time." Triven's hand brushed mine as he drew me to the center of the room again. "You ready?"

"Not really." I said honestly. "Do we have a choice?"

"Not really." He echoed somberly.

8. BLOOD

SUSPICIOUS GLARES FOLLOWED us as we emerged from the locker bank. People were taking in my pack, the way it hung heavily from my hip.

"You're leaving?" Arstid's eyes flickered from me to her son. The room fell into utter silence, even the precious silver food bags stopped crinkling.

"*Archer* and I need to go see someone." Archer's left eye twitched, but other than the minuscule movement, she gave no hint of surprise. "Another rogue. If you want to keep your people safe, we're going to need help. I have a few f-friends." No one missed the stutter in my words. The use of the word friends sounded strange even to my own ears. "I can't promise they're going to help us, but we need to try. We can't stay here."

Heads bobbed in agreement, looking at their sad meals and the stained walls. Grenald folded his thick arms, but didn't say anything. Nor did those around him.

As my mouth suddenly filled with cotton, Triven took the reins, sensing my unease to keep speaking. "We're moving out tonight and are going to need volunteers for a hunting party. Supplies are low and only the most able-bodied are welcome to join us. Who *are* of age." He amended, shooting a glance at Mouse. "But, as badly as we need supplies, we will also need people to stay here and help protect the others."

It was easy to tell those eager to go on the hunt, their feet already carrying them closer. There were more than I had expected, to be honest, although many would not be viable volunteers. Still, their gumption surprised me.

Triven raised his hands, stalling them. "We're going into the Ravagers' food warehouse. Phoenix knows the best way in, but I can't guarantee anyone's safety."

Several people faltered, fear crept into eyes, but still they remained steadfast. Fists flexed, jaws set. They were not backing down. How was it possible that these were the same people who had dissolved into full-blown panic only moments ago? Odd that fear could make a person lose their mind one instant and gather courage the next. It was funny like that.

"Good," Triven smiled half-heartedly at his people. "We'll go over the plans after everyone rests. We still need someone—"

"I will stay here and watch over the others." A slender woman with lean muscles clutching a toddler to her chest stepped forward. Despite her obvious mothering nature, her weathered face was set in a determined line. One set of her fingers clutched the little boy, while the others caressed a sidearm on her hip. She met my gaze, she wouldn't let anything happen to my Mouse or the others.

My heart throbbed. She reminded me so much of Veyron. I hoped our missing friend was still out there, still alive. Selfishly, my guilty conscience *needed* her to be alive.

"Everyone grab some food and a little shuteye. We'll meet in two hours to make a plan." The groups began to disperse with Triven's words. Those eager to get started however, stayed close with no intention of resting.

Archer sidled next to me.

I began checking my weapons. "Grab what you need. We're leaving."

She tapped her rifle pointedly. "Ready when you are."

"Fine." I turned back to Triven. "You know where you're taking them?"

His lips quirked. "For the tenth time, I've got this. Besides, Baxter knows this city nearly as well as you these days. He'll keep us on course."

At the sound of his name, a boastful grin lit the sniper's face. "I doubt anyone knows this city like P here, but I sure as hell am getting a feel for the skyline. Don't worry," he slapped Triven a little too hard on the shoulder. "We'll be wherever you need us."

Shaking off Baxter's hand, Triven leaned in closer, sweeping his lips across my cheek as they sought my ear. "Be careful."

I knew he wanted to tell me to stay, to remind me that separating was a bad idea, but Triven held his tongue. We were in agreement despite our selfish desires to stay together. I needed someone here to keep an eye on everyone. No one was to be left unguarded at any point, not until we knew who could be trusted. I needed him to be our eyes, while I found a more secure shelter. Plus, Archer deserved answers, answers only I could give her. We needed her on our side and I was leery she would explode again. That couldn't happen here. Not in front of these

71

scared, angry people. The group was teetering on a knife's edge and someone with Archer's influence could tip the scales with a simple nod of her head.

Triven's hand closed around my forearm, fingers squeezing, speaking volumes. I returned the gesture as he straightened, squeezing so hard it hurt. "You too."

His gaze followed mine to Grenald. The man watched us shrewdly. But the giant's glare finally fell away when mine did not.

A small hand tugged on my pant leg. Fear colored Mouse's features, pulling her shoulders inward. I bent wiping a smudge of dirt from her cheek.

Together. You promised.

"You're right, we need to do this together. That's why I need to get Archer on our side. Right?"

I guess so. Her face fell, seeing reason.

"We *will* meet you soon."

Hurry.

I hugged the child to my chest, her frail arms clutching me equally tight. "Always." I took hold of Mouse's shoulders, peeling her away from me. As always, the child seemed to take a small piece of me with her. "Watch over the other children. They're not all as brave as you."

The girl's shoulders lifted, chest inflating with pride. Her sharp chin nodded seriously as she backed into Triven's waiting hands.

Reluctantly, I turned away, ready to beckon our one-handed friend only to find Arstid whispering in her ear. The older woman stiffened at my gaze, squaring her shoulders as I approached. Deliberately, Arstid was blocking our only exit.

"You realize this buddy-system of yours applies to you too? Archer doesn't leave your side."

"Duly noted."

"Where *exactly* is it that you're going?" I half expected to see icicles clinging to Arstid's tongue, her tone was so cold.

"The fewer people that know, the better. I think you understand why."

Her mouth pinched.

"Triven knows and I suppose he can fill you in after we leave, if you insist. At least that way if anything goes wrong, we'll know who is to blame for a betrayal."

A sneer twisted Arstid's mouth, souring her words. "Keep your eye on her."

Archer smiled wickedly. "With pleasure."

"Like mother like daughter." Arstid spat as she plowed past, her shoulder colliding with mine.

I bit my tongue smothering the words. "You have no idea…"

Not daring to steal a glance backwards, I headed for the door with Archer on my heels.

"You better have packed some answers in that bag of yours." Archer lowered her voice. She checked the safety on her rifle as we entered the empty hall, rather dramatically snapping it off. "I'll shoot you if I think you're lying to me."

"I wouldn't expect anything less from you, Archer. But for now, get your head in the game. We're going to see The Healer."

73

"**WE'RE STICKING TO** the streets?" There was a hint of a whine to Archer's tone. I was coming to learn her irritability was often a smokescreen for fear. "You *do* realize it's broad daylight out, right?"

My feet continued their serpentine path through the battered street. The map of the skyline played through my head, giving my steps purpose. Tartarus seemed different from down here, strange in the daylight. The sun was not bright—certainly not by the Sanctuary's standards—but it still cast an unfamiliar light to the city I had grown used to seeing in shadow.

I intentionally ignored Archer's irritated questions.

"So, what did Arstid say? To shoot me in the back? To keep an eye on her favorite little rogue? Or maybe I'm due for a little *accident* on our outing."

"Something like that. Interesting how she seems to sense you're a *liar.*"

I hesitated in the mouth of an alley, twisting so she could see me roll my eyes.

"I never lied to you, Archer." Her eyebrows rose and I amended my statement. "Not about anything important."

"Sooo I'm supposed to believe that you 'just found out' your lineage is from the people who happened to banish us here?"

"Yes." I turned my back to the streets, facing her straight on, daring her to question me.

Her eyes probed my face.

"You're either a hell of a liar, or about as damn stupid as they come."

I glared at her. "I'm not a liar."

"So, stupid it is."

"You *do* remember I saved your life once." I turned away and scanned the streets, letting out a low curse.

Three Scavengers were prowling an alley. Picking through the rubble for unknown treasures. Fortunately, they hadn't seen us yet, their feet still lazily heading our way. Archer and I pressed ourselves into the dwindling shadows.

"We need to take shelter until they pass." I hissed, signaling Archer to back up.

"Like I said, *stupid.*" Her voice lowered to barely a whisper, but she moved.

I could hear the vindictive smile in her hushed tones. Squelching the urge to shut her mouth with my fist, I nodded at a gaping hole in the wall halfway back down our alley. Unlike the approaching Scavengers, our feet made no noise against the asphalt. The canvas of my bag slipped into the shadows just as their filthy stench rounded the corner, our breath held, feet frozen. If they came down the alley we would have to kill them. The room we had slipped into offered little shelter, and while there was a crumbling set of stairs visible in the corner, we wouldn't make it there before being seen if they followed.

Their steps paused at the mouth of the alley, not pursuing but not leaving either. Scraping noises and guttural grunting echoed down the alley walls and through the hole as they dragged something metal into the streets, undoubtedly digging for rotten goodies. While it was obvious they weren't going to come our direction, unfortunately it also appeared they had no intention of leaving anytime soon. The rats were settling in right in the middle of our path.

We would have to wait them out.

The Scavengers weren't the most fearsome Tribe, but they were one of the most feral. They tended to swarm like parasites and if these three caught wind of us, the entire Tribe could descend within minutes like flies to a carcass, ready to pick us clean.

My companion's expression curdled, still she followed as my feet picked a line through the rubble toward the stairs. Careful not to dislodge any of the wreckage, we moved in a series of advances and pauses, listening to every movement made outside. As we settled ourselves in on the second floor, safely hidden from the Scavenger's view and ears, what little patience Archer had, evaporated.

"We should have taken the rooftops." A flush was creeping up her throat into her cheeks. Her leggy frame was posted sentinel-like by a blown-out window. Her body was buzzing with tension, long fingers thrumming on her rifle's hilt.

Doing my best to appear calm in contrast to her agitation, I sat on what looked like an overturned bookcase. "The roofs in the daytime are not safe. Especially not in this area, they're too low and make you an easy target for a sniper. It's safer on the streets. More places to hide." I gestured at the building around us.

"We're moving at a snail's pace."

"Of course we are. Why do you think we left when we did? Trust me, it wasn't because I wanted quality time with you." My fingers idly doodled patterns into the dust collected on the metal surface beneath me.

"Please, everyone wants more quality time with me. I'm a ray of sunshine." Her dark eyes glared at the streets below, her rifle shifting threateningly in her hand.

"Obviously."

She opened her mouth ready to snip back, but a clang from outside silenced her. We stiffened, but as the sounds of a squabble rose through the windows we both relaxed. Apparently, the rats had found a tasty morsel worth fighting over. Keeping hidden, Archer leaned forward, watching them quarrel below us. I stretched on my perch to see for myself.

Two of the Scavengers were brawling over a glinting object. Both men were emaciated, but power packed every punch thrown. The third party member, a younger girl, watched mildly entertained, chewing on what looked like raw rabbit leg. My stomach soured as her teeth grated over the bone, scraping off every last morsel.

"You seriously want to join up with these asshats?" Archer was eyeing them with disgust. The girl gave a little cheer as the taller man overpowered the other, knocking the smaller man flat.

I slouched, pinning my gaze on Archer. "I don't *want* to do anything, but we're starting a war. Everyone is going to have to do things they don't want to."

"I'm not helping you."

"You've made that painfully clear."

Her was jaw set, eyes throwing knives. "Do you want power? Is that why you're doing this? You want to lead your own army?"

I snorted, trying to suppress a laugh. "Please, I would make a crap leader. Killing people, fending for myself—that I'm good at. Leading a group of murderous thugs, not so much. Let's see… Current recruitment tally—two Taciturns found, two dead—Great start!!"

"In all fairness, I was the one who shot those two." She looked more proud than remorseful. I didn't respond, letting the silence hang between us.

Finally, she sighed.

"So, you're seriously the heir to the Sanctuary?" Archer looked somber, a tinge of fear swelled in her eyes when I nodded. "That man who tortured you…"

"Is my g-grandfather." My tongue swelled around the word, unwilling to let it out.

"And he's the one you want to kill."

"He's the one we *must* kill."

She swore, rolling her eyes up to the crumbling ceiling. "Let me see if I got this straight. You get to raise an army to kill your sadistic family. While me, on the other hand, *I'm* being asked to *beg* my murderous bloodlines to join your little shindig. Doesn't really seem fair, does it?" Archer's lips curled up. "Really Phoenix, how would you feel if *I* asked *you* to partner up with Fandrin after everything he did to you?"

The color drained from my face. I braced myself, preparing to stomach a lie, but the words falling out of my mouth were truth. "I *hate* that monster with every fiber of my being, just like you hate your old Tribe. *But* somethings are bigger than *us*. Thousands of lives are at stake here. If we can't put our own crap aside, it's our loved ones who will suffer. Do you really want them to die because you couldn't get over your own family bullshit?"

Archer's gaze fell away, closing before meeting mine again. "This is a *monstrous* thing you're asking of us."

"Sometimes monstrous things must be done to kill a monster."

She took a shuddering breath. "Is he really *that* terrible?"

"Let's just say, I'm sure he makes *your* mother look like a saint."

Archer chortled darkly, "You haven't met her."

"You haven't met *him*."

She worried her bottom lip, eyeing me speculatively. "I'll help you with the other Tribes, but I want nothing to do with the Wraiths."

"Because your mother took your hand—"

"Because she's their leader now." Archer swallowed, the words grinding through her clenched teeth. "Grenald told me, he defected after I did. Taking my hand tipped power in her favor. My left hand gave her the throne."

There were no words I could offer of comfort and I knew Archer wouldn't want to hear them anyway. So, I told her the truth. "Well, I guess we can agree both of our families suck."

"To say the least... Apparently homicidal bloodlines are all the rage these days." Tremors shook Archer's right hand as it tightened on the gun, thinking of her own family. "But why keep it hidden? Everyone will find out eventually. If The Wall is really coming down like you claim, they *will* find out who you are."

"Eventually, but hopefully not until they've already judged me for who I am and because not my genetics. It's the same reason Triven doesn't readily tell people Arstid is his mother. I mean, how many of your friends know who *your* mother is?" I glanced at her disfigured arm.

"Arstid is the only one, not even Triven knows," she stared down at the streets. "Obviously, a few of the other deserters too, but they've held their tongues. We don't talk about our pasts in the Subversive. Our pasts stay in the past."

Her eyes finally met mine and I knew we understood each other. These were not secrets to be shared. In confiding in one another, we had armed the other. Archer knew she couldn't divulge my secret without her own being shared and vice versa.

"Look, I can't promise you anything. But no one wants *that man* dead more than I do, Archer," my words were sharp. "And if it takes gathering the Tribes to bring him down, I'm going to try."

Archer's shoulders had relaxed a little, the tension of the last twenty-four hours having faded, but her brow puckered. "I won't help you with the Wraiths. I'm sorry, but I can't. I will do what I can to help with the other Tribes, but not *them*. Not her."

"That's fair."

Pushing off the wall she moved fully into the opened window. "The rats are moving out."

"Then so are we." I rose, checking the window for myself before heading back to the steps.

Archer hesitated at the top. "They will find out. When The Wall comes down, our people will find out who you are."

"I know." I paused but didn't look back. "You too."

"Don't remind me." I heard the double click as she checked her safety again. "Let's go meet this Healer of yours."

9. TRANSACTIONS

THE WEATHERED ROPE felt oddly familiar. I gave it a little tug for good measure. Despite Archer's presence, the old woman had tossed down the ladder at my whistle. Which unnerved me more than if she had shot at us.

Was it The Healer up there waiting for us?

I glared up at the dark opening in the water tower base. The distance was greater than I had remembered. A fall would be deadly. I glanced at the space where Archer's left hand should have been and she bristled.

"I've *got* this."

I nodded speculatively. "Fine, but if you fall off and die, that's on you. Oh, and for once in your life, keep your mouth shut when we get up there."

"*Or* what?"

"*Or* she may kill us both."

"I suppose you're going to tell me to leave my gun down here on the ground too."

I snorted. "On the contrary, your finger had better not leave the trigger and if it does go south, make sure you're the one to shoot first."

This should have been easy. I had climbed this rope nearly a hundred times, and yet this was different. I was different. I had never liked the idea of being trapped in The Healer's water tower, but as we ascended toward the open hatch, images of my cell in the Sanctuary flashed into my thoughts. No windows, one door, and walls that seemed to slowly close in on you. My breath was rapid and shallow as droplets of perspiration clung to my forehead.

"Pull it together." I growled to myself. I could see Archer eyeing me, but amazingly she held her tongue.

True to her word she was keeping pace with me, linking her left elbow through the worn rungs as her hand moved to the next. I thrust myself up the last few steps, propelling my body into the darkness above. When my feet landed, the knife at my hip was already drawn. The air was stifling and the usual fire burning low in the corner was the only light. The metallic echo of my feet on the tower was still ringing when Archer's head popped through the opening.

She recoiled, "Smells like something died in here."

I could have kicked her.

"Tings die in 'ere all da time." A familiar cackle rose from the gloom, followed by a withered hand and a magnificently maintained pistol. It was steady as a rock in her thin hands. "Pull up da rope."

Archer bent and began the laborious process of gathering the rope and closing the heavy hatch. As she rose, her rifle slid from her back holster, the movement so fluid one might have missed it in the dim light. The Healer, however, narrowed her eyes. Nothing escaped her milky lenses.

"Speakin' o dead tings, I tot you were a gonna for sure, guuurl." Her beady eyes swept me from head to toe. "Maybe a part o' ya did die. Tings different wit ya. da ol' Healer can smell it."

Her crowing laugh reverberated in the space, making us cringe. Archer's grip tightened on her rifle, mine on my knife.

"Tis good to see ya child." She said quieter now, but her gun did not lower. "And not alone." The Healer eyed Archer appreciatively. "Dis ya lady?"

Archer snorted. "Please, she would be lucky to have a girl like me."

Another bout of laughter split the woman's face and her gun lowered slightly, though her finger was still on the trigger.

"I like dis one. Even more mouthy dan ya."

Archer's nose twitched against the pungent aroma but otherwise no one moved.

"What ya want den?" The old woman's gaze fell hungrily on my bag. A gnarled hand gestured to the table in the center of the room. Avoiding what looked like dried birds' feet, I dumped half of the contents from my bag onto the stained surface.

"Mmmm…" The Healer purred as she took in the treasures. "Ya been busy."

"We need healing salve. As much of it as you can make."

One hooded eye narrowed at me. "Ya planning somethin' child?"

I shrugged, "Good investment."

The woman shuffled forward to better inspect my offerings. Archer shifted behind me.

"Ow much ya need?" She spoke to me, but was watching Archer, scrutinizing the girl.

"How much can you make in the next eight hours?"

The cracks in her face deepened as she frowned. "More dan one girl can carry."

"That's why I brought a friend." I dumped the remainder of my bag on the table and she gave me a gap-toothed grin.

"Clear da table. We go' work to do."

THE HEAT IN the tower had become overwhelming. My shirt clung to my skin, the stench of my own body odor repulsive as it mixed with the herb-infused air. Archer hovered near the hatch, gun still in hand. Her skin glistened as she mopped her brown forehead with her arm. Her attention never left the old woman. My hands were cramping, aching nearly as bad as my back when I finally stoppered the last jar. The hours had passed in a haze of violet smoke and boiled herbs. The results weighted down my bag. The sting of its strap biting into my shoulder was well worth the stash inside. When the final container disappeared into the bag for Archer, The Healer finally settled back onto her stool, wiping her crooked hands on the filthy layers of her skirt.

The old woman had been careful. Despite my vigilance, she'd added ingredients I'd missed. I knew no matter how hard I tried, The Healer's potions could never have been replicated.

The jars clinked as I slid the bag from the counter. Archer held out her damaged arm, tilting her head so I could slip the bag over her shoulder without having to let go of her rifle. The Healer was fingering through the things I had brought her, barely paying us any attention.

"Let's get the hell out of here." I read Archer's lips, her words so quiet I couldn't hear them.

Without a glance at the old woman, I bent and yanked the heavy hatch open. A blast of cool air struck my face, clearing my head and chilling the sweat that clung to my skin. It was wonderful.

Archer shivered next to me in pleasure as the air reached her too. Darkness was falling, transforming the city back to the nightscape I knew. I scanned the ground carefully before kicking down the rope. It slithered, hissing against the floor as it fell. Reluctantly I stepped back into the haze and tapped Archer, signaling her to descend first. She didn't need any coaxing. Archer's rifle was re-slung over her chest as my fingers gripped my own handgun.

I glanced down for a split second to gauge her progress and started at the sound of moving feet. The Healer was poised in front me, tongue licking her thin lips as she watched me.

I didn't trust her. I never had. We had offered support for each other, had a kind of symbiotic relationship, but it had ended there. Still, she certainly could be useful. I could maybe even save her life. The problem was in her trading. If I asked her to join us and she refused, then what? If she says no, must I kill her? She traded with too many people. She could leak something to the Ravagers, she could ruin us all. Or I could say nothing and just leave her here... probably to die.

Her wiry grey eyebrows rose. "Hold ya tongue girl."

Was it possible the old nut was clairvoyant? Nevertheless, I nodded, heeding her warning. She was telling me what I needed to know. *I am not to be trusted with your secrets.* Her only side was her own. The Healer was a tradesman, not an ally. She would not side with us or anyone else for that matter.

"Good trade?" I asked, knowing this was most likely the last I would see of the old woman.

"Good trade."

Without another word, I lowered myself out of the hole in the floor and let go of any notions of saving a woman who didn't want to be saved.

Archer had paused halfway down the rope, one arm laced though the rungs while the other pointed her rifle at the opening. Relief smoothed her brow when I emerged. As my feet began to move so did hers.

When I finally met solid ground again, night had claimed the city and Archer's gun was sweeping the perimeter. The rope tugged free from my hands and rose quickly back to its owner.

"To the roofs?" I could hear the edge of relief in Archer's voice.

"To the roofs."

The progression was slower now. But despite our cautious movements, every step caused the jars in our bags to clank and each tinkle of glass threatened to giveaway our position. We paused at the opening of an alley, scanning the streets surrounding us. They were quiet, a little *too* quiet for my liking. I poised to move but Archer caught my arm.

"Why did she trust us to stay up there with her?" This had obviously been plaguing her and I understood it. People didn't trust people out here. It wasn't in our nature.

I stepped back, keeping watch on the streets as I answered. "It has nothing to do with trust. The woman may be old, but she's not senile. Physically, I did most of the heavy lifting for her just now. Plus, that tower of hers? It's wired to blow at the touch of a button. If anyone tried to cross her, she would blow them to kingdom come without batting an eye. If I had to guess I would say born Adroit."

"Damn."

"Impressed?"

"A little, yeah. That old bat is either crazy or a genius."

"I would go with mostly genius."

Archer shrugged as though she thought the former.

I started to move before she could object again. We could debate that later. If we didn't move, we were going to be late for our rendezvous.

Tethers dangled behind us as we scaled the building. Methodically tied at the other ends, the bags from The Healer sat on the ground, waiting to be hauled up. My hands never faltered on the pocketed concrete wall when we reached the access point. But more impressively, neither did Archer's. It was fascinating to watch. She moved in lunges and tugs, relying on her legs to propel her upwards until her hand caught her next hold. I slowed in fascination, until I caught her teeth glinting in the dark as she passed me. Suddenly this was a race. I plunged my hand into the next hold, yanking my body upward and overtook her in two moves. The win was mine, but as my right hand landed on the roof's ledge a split second before hers, it suddenly broke away with nothing but a handful of crumbling brick. Gravity jolted as I fell back, a scream strangled in my throat. My left hand kept hold in its pocket. The sharp edges scraped skin from my fingertips as I slid to a halt. The tendons in my shoulder howled as I was yanked toward the earth. For two heartbeats, I swung there, dangling in shock before my feet began to scramble for purchase. Then a hand was in my face, fingers thrust toward me in offering.

I hesitated.

Archer was leaning over the building edge, arm outstretched to me, chest heaving, and her grin spectacular.

"Trust issues much?" She wiggled her fingers.

"Pot. Kettle." I said, staring pointedly before I grabbed her hand allowing it to pull me up. It was an Old World saying that had always stuck with me.

"Touché." A hint of a smile tugged her lips.

"I let you win." I shot back at her as my feet settled beneath shaking legs.

Her gun leveled at my chest in response. "I said I'd shoot you if you lied to me."

I spread my arms, giving her a larger target. "If you can fire a gun as fast as you run your mouth, then I suppose I had better watch myself."

Archer genuinely smiled, a snort of laughter huffing from her chest as her gun fell away. "Let's make a deal, Phoenix. You try and be honest with me and I'll try not to shoot you."

I rolled my eyes but returned her smile. "Deal."

She leaned casually against the roof's partition as I pulled up our lines. The heavy bags clinked as I hid them in an air shaft to retrieve later. I would send someone back after we raided the Ravagers' warehouse. Right now, the weight would only slow us down. I scanned the buildings around us. The last rays of the sun had disappeared.

We had been late, but so were the others.

Picking up on my growing tension, Archer left her post to join me on the roof's ledge.

Her mouth opened, but the words were swallowed by an explosion that rocked the air. Waves of heat assaulted our exposed skin. We hit the ground, arms covering our heads, but the shrapnel never touched us. It was too far away.

Blinking off the shock, I found my feet were suddenly beneath me again. A mushroom cloud ballooned between the rooftops as a flickering light licked broken walls and suddenly I was sprinting. Careening towards it as fast as my legs could carry me.

"What?" Archer's winded voice barely carried to my buzzing ears.

"The warehouse is under attack!"

Understanding bloomed and Archer's strides were lengthening, almost overtaking mine.

Our only hope for food was going up in flames.

10. RETRIBUTION

IF THE FLAMES hadn't been guiding us to the warehouse, then the screams would have. I scrambled to a halt two roofs over from my access roof, stunned. The front of the Ravagers' warehouse was engulfed in flames, the brick and metal façade quickly searing to black. Still, it was whole. The explosion hadn't targeted the building, but the guards outside of it. A crater had been blown out of the ground, dead center on the path where the Ravagers made their round. I had watched them walk that route hundreds of times. Apparently, I hadn't been the only one studying their patterns.

What I assumed to be a Ravager was staggering blindly around the deserted street. His *or her*—I could no longer tell—entire body was consumed in flames, arms flailing like a flightless bird and useless against the blaze. It transformed the person into a living torch, illuminating the night as it floundered. The screams were so high-pitched they were more animal than human. It was as the body collapsed to the ground and the screaming stopped, that I finally saw what littered the pavement around it.

What I had thought was burning rubble began to take shape and what had looked like a smoldering support beam had grown fingers. I stopped searching for the other two guards that performed rounds. They were there, well, *parts* of them at least.

The smell of burning flesh made me sick.

Archer's hand pressed over her mouth, clearly trying not to gag. Then her head whipped back, the stench forgotten. "Someone's coming."

Her gun was raised as my knives broke free from their casings. I crouched, ready to let them fly.

Shadows emerged from the smoke, guns raised. Immediately I rose pushing Archer's rifle aside.

"Triven." The relief in my voice was thick.

His expression spoke the same words. *You're alive.*

We reached for each other's hands, squeezing as they connected, then quickly letting go.

Ten others emerged behind him, breathing heavy, eyes fixed on the mayhem before us.

"Did you?" Triven stiffened as he took in the bodies.

Before I could respond, the side door to the warehouse burst open.

I hissed, sinking to my knees and felt the others follow suit.

Three silhouettes had emerged, weapons in hand. They charged to the front of the building. The first Ravager stopped, nearly tripping over his still smoldering comrade. The others faltered, colliding with the first. I could see the metal adorning his face glinting in the firelight. In unison, their pierced heads turned to the burning building.

The biggest man turned, shoving one of the Tribesmen with such force the smaller man was momentarily airborne before slamming back down to the ground.

"Get Hendrix, NOW!" The man was literally foaming at the mouth. Specks flying as he screamed.

The curvier figure reacted first. She took off down the street leaving the third man to scramble after her. A guttural roar split the night, making us flinch. The lone Ravager flew into a rage, kicking his dead Tribesman on the ground, then launching a handful of dirt at the growing wall of fire. A chunk of the building's exterior crumbled off, devoured by the flames.

I stared up at the hazy night sky, wishing for the first time that rain would fall. Toxic or not, it could still put out a fire. Though the building had barely been damaged by the explosion, the fire was going to take it to the ground. But the sky gave me nothing. If we were going to save any supplies inside, we had to move now.

Pulling the handgun from my hip, I trained it on the Ravager's chest. At this distance, it was better to aim for the larger target than the obvious kill shot of the head. The trigger pushed back slightly as I flexed my finger. I could feel the others watching, but no one moved to stop me. We all understood. One life to feed our starving people.

Exhaling slowly, I began to squeeze. But before the hammer engaged—before I could fire—the Ravager took a staggering step back directly onto a landmine. The click was barely audible, then he was gone. One second the Ravager stood before the burning building, the next he was raining down around us. Triven's arms wrapped over my head pulling me down as the explosion shook our rooftop.

"Adroits." He yelled over the ringing in my ears. One thing was sure, at least we knew they were already long gone. That Tribe never stuck around to watch their handiwork.

A mist of dirt rained down, smattering us with softer, squishier bits I tried to ignore. As the onslaught slowed, I pushed myself to my feet. A heavily pierced ear glinted near the toe of my boot. I edged away from it, refusing to look down again.

"We have maybe fifteen minutes before the others return with reinforcements." Something crashed inside the warehouse. "Maybe less time before the building caves in. We need to move now."

A giant shadow blocked my path. Grenald. "You can't be serious? You want us to go into that burning building?"

"We *need* food. Do you have a better idea?" When he didn't respond, I pushed past him. "You're wasting precious time. Move."

The others trailed me to the access roof, fear rolling off them. The smoke was denser here, choking the air and stinging my throat.

"Get the ladder from under the vent and make a bridge." I coughed the order to no one in particular, but of course Triven was the first to respond. Grenald and two others moved to help him.

"Water!" I barked at Archer. She dug in her small pack, tossing me a half-empty bottle. Stripping off my over-shirt I began hastily ripping it into strips and dousing them with the little water we had left. Baxter quickly caught on and did the same with his own shirt, throwing me the scraps as he cut them. I paused once to whisper in his ear, pleased when he nodded in understanding. After making sure everyone had a piece of cloth, I tied mine over my mouth and nose, then watched as they did the same. "Two of you need to stay here. Shoot any Tribe member that shows up." Archer and Baxter stepped forward, our best snipers at the ready. "Good. The rest of you will follow me. Grab anything you can get your hands on, but remember the preserved goods will last longer. You have ten minutes and then we're getting out."

I stepped up on the ledge, my toes on the first rung when another fiery crash boomed from inside the warehouse.

"Make that five." I amended and was moving towards the blaze.

Though emitting heat, the warehouse roof was solid beneath my feet. I pressed the back of my hand to it. Warm but not hot. The ladder creaked as others crossed, but I didn't spare them a glance.

The glass pane moved with ease, and I took no time being cautious with it. Every second was precious and evidence of our intrusion was moot at this point. After all, the fire would cover our tracks. Sliding though the open window, a blast of heat scorched my eyes as I jumped onto the exposed beams. The metal was beginning to sweat from the growing temperature of the blooming fire, but at least it wasn't wood. The Ravagers were brutal and not known for their intelligence, but at least they didn't choose tinderboxes for their storage.

The front half of the warehouse was ablaze. Racks were being swallowed in leaping flames, the contents of their shelves shriveling to ash. The layout rushed through my mind. The front housed most of their dried meat and perishable foods, worthless, but the water was near there too.

Hands thrust a rope into my face, breaking my focus. It was quickly followed by Triven's half-masked face. His eyes were bright with intensity, a reflection of the flickering flames danced on their surface.

"I'm right behind you." His hand brushed mine as I took the rope.

My feet slid as I crossed the beams at a run. Careful to drop it at the farthest point from the flames, I flung the rope over a thigh-thick pipe and tied it off to the beam. Trusting my work, I leapt onto the cord and plummeted toward the warehouse floor. My palms burned despite being carefully wrapped in my sleeves. The rope jerked as someone else climbed on and I cinched my boots, slowing the fall just enough to cushion the landing.

I took off, shouting instructions and gesturing wildly at the far back corner of the warehouse. Praying someone heard and understood. Hundreds of MRE bags littered the shelves there. Those were our focus, but I was headed to what we needed the most. To the water and consequently, to the growing fire.

Heavy boots followed mine and I didn't have to look back to know who it was. The warehouse blurred as tears filled my eyes, fighting the stinging smoke. Even beneath the saturated mask, my nostrils blazed with every breath. Desperate for relief, I gasped through my mouth, choking on the heat.

Still, I ran.

The flames were licking the racking two down from the water, but for now the bottles remained untouched. As my arms rose to clear the shelves, Triven's bag appeared below, held open to catch the precious cargo. I began sweeping the shelves, filling his pack with as much weight as I thought he could carry. I could barely see him through the tears streaming down my face and our voices were crippled by coughing fits, but we moved on. When bottles began to hit our feet, we switched. Our hands clashed as we fumbled to get his pack over his shoulders and replace it with mine. My numb fingers nearly lost their grip on the bag as the first armful of bottles hit, the weight taking me by surprise.

Shouts were coming from the back of the warehouse and the flames were creeping closer. It felt as if the skin on my back was blistering with the heat. I longed for the heat suits we had left in our packs. Even covered in the ashes of the dead, I wanted them now. Suddenly the stench of singed hair enveloped me and I was being thrown to the ground. Hands pounded down my back and up the base of my neck, before rolling me over.

I heard Triven retch, before choking out the words, "Enough! Go!"

We struggled to our feet, clinging both to our bags and to each other as we blundered toward the shouts. Blinking back tears, I could see the behemoth Grenald shouting to us, waving us to the rope. The ground abruptly shook, knocking Triven and me to our knees and the giant man rushed at us. A large piece of the roof had crashed onto the racking we had just left. Abandoned bottles of water smashed beneath its mass, the racking now mere scrap metal. The flames leapt toward the exposed slice of sky above, relishing in the oxygen, feeding on it.

"Move!" I coughed out, pulling Triven's arms up with mine. The weight of the water was slowing us down, the lack of oxygen starving our lungs. My eyes burned, though I couldn't tell if was from the smoke or sweat pouring down my forehead.

"Idiots!" Grenald thundered as he met us. The weight of my bag was suddenly gone. Then Triven too was moving with easier. He retched again, but kept moving forward.

Grenald's hands worked quickly, knotting the end of the rope around our bags, then signaling for them to be pulled up. I looked up, following the rising sacks. Two men were perched on the beam, hauling the bags as a woman handed others out the open pane.

"Is everyone out?" I gagged, glancing around the warehouse. Triven buried a coughing fit in his elbow, eyes scanning the half-destroyed room.

"We're missing one," Grenald barked, hacking against his own mask.

"Who?" Triven squinted through the thickening smoke.

"Cortez."

"There!" Triven fingered a shadow emerging from the smoke. Like us, the woman was floundering under the weight of her bag. The two men ran toward her, one reaching for the bag, the other for the girl. But my feet didn't move. I had seen something. Another shadow. No… another man.

Three aisles to their left, a man was clutching a cloth over his nose with one hand while the other shoved handfuls of red bags into his pockets. I had seen him in the school, he had been with Grenald's pack. Oblivious, an ember hit his shoulder. My eyes rose to the ceiling above him.

I hurtled across the space, arms waving, trying to shout a warning but nothing came out. The man looked up at me, startled as I plowed toward him. But it was only when his eyes followed mine that he realized his mistake.

I watched the horror dawn on his face. Then my hands were colliding with his chest, shoving him away. But I was not fast enough, and despite my speed, despite the intensity of our collision, the slab of falling ceiling crashed down over us and my world went black.

11. TRAPPED

THE LITTLE AIR left in my lungs was crushed from my body. Terror pulsed in my veins. Something in my chest had cracked under the fall, but the impact of the debris had not killed me instantly. It was, however, asphyxiating me. If I didn't wriggle loose soon, if my lungs couldn't get the room to expand, I was going to suffocate.

No, I *was* suffocating.

Only my fingers moved, straining on the concrete. I couldn't feel the man I shoved.

Was he under here with me?

Had I pushed him free?

Flexing every muscle, I shoved against the weight bearing down on me.

Nothing moved. Not even an inch.

Firelight crept in through a crack in the wreckage, but I couldn't turn my head to seek its source. I couldn't breathe, couldn't scream, I couldn't *do* anything. Only my fingers obeyed. The nails scraped feebly at the ground.

Then fingertips found mine, winding over my hands pulling at my wrists. My shoulders screamed under the strain, but I didn't move. *Pull harder!* I wanted to yell, but no air came out. Then the hands were gone. *NO! NO!! Come back!*

I clawed at the ground again, the pain in my chest was excruciating. My lungs were going to burst. I had read about people drowning. Was this what it was like? Was this what it felt like to slowly have your life drain away? This was worse than the fire, worse than the torture Fandrin put me through. This was worse than being crushed to death.

Suddenly, the slab groaned around me. The pressure shifted, first pressing harder against my left shoulder, then it was gone. White spots popped in my vision and hands were pulling me, dragging me away. There was a crash of something being dropped and then Triven's voice was in my ears.

"Is anything broken?"

I gasped, unable to respond.

"We don't have time, move her!" Another voice shouted over his.

More hands were pulling me to my feet. The black in my vision began to recede, pulsing at the edges of my sight. Grenald and the woman they had called Cortez were shouldering the man I had shoved.

Running ahead, the woman ducked out from under the man and began to tie her bag to the rope. She motioned for retrieval, but there was no one above to pull it up this time. The others had already scrambled to escape, the roof's structure no longer trustworthy.

"How the hell are we supposed to get up that with all this?" Cortez glared at the rope, then at me. The woven cord had begun to smoke, but it was the dark plume of black smoke filling the ceiling that worried me more.

"The door!" Grenald shouted, pointing to the side door we had seen the Ravagers exit earlier.

I was already shaking my head no.

"It—locks. Needs—key." The words struggled to form, each breath was excruciating.

"Screw keys." Cortez yelled. Yanking her bag from the floor, she charged to the door, but three steps later flattened herself to the ground. We all did.

The door pinged, sparking as bullets riddled the handle and the hinges. My hands searched for my knives, for my gun, for any weapon.

The Ravagers were back.

Three heavy kicks assaulted the thick metal. The final blow sent the perforated barrier crashing to the ground with an ear-splitting clang. Smoke sucked through the opening and a familiar voice emerged from the darkness followed by Baxter's soot-covered face.

"Well don't just lay there!" He turned, training his gun back on the alley.

Triven's arms pulled on my waist and I stifled a scream of pain. We blundered to the door as more ceiling crashed around us and then we were out. Coughing, covered in grime and shaking, but we were out. We were alive.

Cortez staggered against the opposite alley wall and Baxter was there, taking the sack from her hands.

"And they say chivalry is dead," he smirked at her, then let out a sharp whistle. Three ropes dropped down, nearly hitting us as the smacked against the wall. Loops were knotted at the bottoms. Grenald was quick to shove the foot of the man he was carrying into a loop. Forcing the man's fingers to grab hold of the rope, Grenald then gave the cord a tug and the man was suddenly lifted upwards. Soaring over our heads and disappearing over the side of the building.

Doubling over, Cortez let out a shaky laugh. "I don't recall you holding any doors."

"Please," Baxter scoffed, helping Cortez to the second rope. "I don't just *hold* doors for the ladies, I blow them off their hinges."

Her laughter dissolved into a coughing fit and then with a tug, she was being pulled away too.

Triven shoved me toward the last line, helping my feet find the sling. The first rope fell back down next to us, and then ground was gone and I was being pulled toward the skyline.

Hands found me at the roof's edge, tugging me over. I rolled, splaying on the cool surface. Yanking the fabric away, I pressed my face to the tar, letting it soothe my hot skin. Coughs spasmed my body and I clutched my ribs trying desperately to minimize the movements.

A body hit the ground next to me.

Triven's face was black except for two trails of pink flesh where tears had washed his cheeks clean. He crawled toward me, stopping to gag twice. I pushed up, closing the last foot between us, one arm still cradling my torso.

When his breath returned, Triven's hand pressed over mine. "Broken?"

I nodded, still looking for my voice.

Archer's face was suddenly there scrutinizing us.

"That better have been worth it." She muttered. "Can you move?"

I dipped my chin in confirmation.

"Good, the Ravagers are coming and we need to go." She pulled me to my feet, whispering in my ear. "You do make a crap leader."

I started to laugh, but then flinched. "Told you."

Someone handed me a bag and I was being pushed forward, but I shoved back against the guiding arms.

"Baxter?" I searched for the sniper.

The entire warehouse was now engulfed in flames, silhouetting our rag-tag band. Still, it wasn't enough.

"Baxter?" I called again and his face swam out of the crowd. I lowered my voice. "Is it done?"

Instead of answering, he checked his wristwatch and grabbed my shoulder. On cue, the building shook around us and while everyone else started, we turned calmly to the fireball emanating on the other side of the Ravager warehouse.

Triven was at my shoulder in a heartbeat, his eyes wide. "The passage?"

It was the only remaining way into the Sanctuary. The Ravager's private supply tunnel. I smiled as the flames climbed higher. "The rest of this city has starved long enough while these monsters flourished. It's their turn to go hungry. Nobody in, nobody out. It's time we leveled the playing field."

The bag on my back felt lighter as I patted the canvas fabric stretched tight with food.

Clutching my ribs, I turned away from the blaze.

"Let's go get Mouse."

DESPITE BEING COVERED in soot, faces smeared with dirt and ash, all the grime couldn't smother the smiles blooming on the Subversive members' faces. We had escaped with not only our lives, but enough supplies to feed their people for a few months—not *well*, but no one was going to starve. As our group began inventorying the haul, I couldn't find the heart to tell them the night was not over yet, nor that the food supplies would be irrelevant if we're all dead in fifteen days.

Our group had split shortly after vacating the warehouse sector. Three people were left behind to guard our spoils under Baxter's watchful eye, while the rest would head back to the school to gather those still taking refuge there. I wanted to go inside to gather Mouse in my arms and personally escort her back to the rooftops, but Triven had insisted we stayed roof-bound as sentries. I knew it was because he wanted to tend my wounds before phase two of our plan, but that knowledge didn't keep the scowl from my face.

"Archer will get them out safely." Triven focused on his work while I watched the street below.

We hung back from the group, letting them celebrate our victory for a little longer while Triven played doctor. I held the singed edge of my shirt up to my chest with one hand as Triven's fingers probed my rib cage. In my other hand, Archer's rifle kept a steady aim on the streets below.

Despite his tender touch I winced, causing the barrel of the gun to twitch. Every breath I had taken since nearly being smashed to death was accompanied by tiny knife stabs.

He frowned. "You broke at least two of them, probably four, and bruised the others."

The skin under his hand had already turned a deep bluish-purple, the edges rimming with yellow. The grotesque color was striking against my pale skin. Everything hurt like hell, but it appeared I had at least not punctured a lung. I tried to focus on the diminishing flames burning in the distance, but the distraction did little. My focus swiveled back to the streets.

There was no movement from the vent. Archer and two others had disappeared through the opening nearly ten minutes ago and every ticking second since had been torture.

"I've seen worse." Grenald's deep voice grumbled as he appeared behind Triven. I yanked my shirt down, but he scoffed. "*Please*, don't flatter yourself. Let's have a look then."

I curled my grip tighter around the hem, but Triven's fingers grazed mine, encouraging me to lift it again. "Grenald worked with Doc a lot. He might be able to help."

Slowly, I lifted the fabric, glaring the entire time. Leaning down, he let out a low whistle. "That's a beauty for sure. We don't have any serum on hand, so this is going to have to do."

He tossed a red pouch at us that Triven caught with expert hands. He turned the bag over, inspecting it. "What is this?"

"*That's* what I was taking when you saved me." The man I had pushed out of the way tentatively walked over to Grenald's side. He flinched, looking at my exposed skin. "Medical kits. They're not as good as Doc's, but they can still save some lives. I thought you of all people deserved one after what you did."

"You do see the irony that she wouldn't *need* that if you had just left the warehouse when I said to." Grenald rebuked the man, but without any true malice. In fact, it was the most soft-spoken tone I had yet to hear from him.

The second man ignored Grenald. "Name's Otto by the way and thank you for saving me. I didn't get the chance to say that properly before… and I'm sorry about that." Otto eyed the blossoming bruises.

Normally, I would have shrugged off his apology, but the movement would have hurt like hell. So instead, I did nothing. I wasn't sure what made me save Otto. Why my body had sprung into action so quickly, and then again, I did. In the milliseconds that had passed before the ceiling crashed down, I had thought of Maddox. Of how he had saved me. Of how he died. Of how I had watched him die.

The men shifted uncomfortably under my gaze.

"We're *both* grateful." Grenald cleared his throat. He was fingering the cut on his chest. I watched in surprise as his other hand reached out and the men's hands found one another, grimy fingers intertwining. It was then I understood why some of the anger had eased from the giant's eyes. I had saved the man he loved. Otto elbowed him in the side, and Grenald's hand fell from his chest wound. Apparently, I was to be forgiven for the knife throwing incident earlier too. Sort of.

Triven opened the red packet producing gauze, wrappings, two blue pills and a jar of something orange. Grenald pointed to the wrappings. "You should bind her ribs up as tight as she can tolerate. It's the best we can do for now. The blue pills might help with the pain too, but unfortunately there's not a lot that can be done."

"Thanks." I reached for the wrappings only to have Triven gently slap my fingers away.

"Stay still." He commanded.

The first pull of the bandages was the worst. I held my breath to keep the pain under control, and tried to smooth all the muscles in my face. Grenald and Otto began to back away. Eyes looking anywhere but my bruised skin. They stopped when I spoke.

"Any news from the other survivors?" *Of Doc, of Veyron?* I hadn't had the chance to ask this yet.

Otto let go of Grenald's hand, stepping forward again, oddly eager to continue our conversation. He crossed his arms, burying his fingertips in his armpits as if fending off a chill. "Not yet, but it's early still in the night. We may need to send out scouts to look for them."

"Once we get the rest of them to safety, we'll send out a party for the others." Triven spoke, trying to keep his focus on my bandages. I wondered if the others noticed the way his eyes worried my face on the word "safety".

I glanced in the direction of the hidden vent again. "I should've gone with them."

Grenald looked as though he felt the same.

"You *needed* to get this taken care of." Triven said. He paused, the tail end of bandage taut in his hands. "Ready?"

I tightened my grip on the rifle, locked my elbow over the roof's edge and nodded.

Pulling as hard as he dared, Triven cinched the wrappings tighter and secured them in place.

"That will have to do." Concern knotted his brow.

It wasn't perfect, but they did feel better.

Dropping my shirt, I placed a hand to his cheek. "I'll be *fine*."

He knew I wasn't only talking about my ribs, but about what was to come next. His jaw tensed, but Triven didn't say anything else. I had warned him he wouldn't like my plan. He knew the risks, but he had still agreed. I had promised these people a safe place to stay and I was going to do everything in my power to make that happen. Broken and bruised ribs be damned.

There was a scraping sound below us, barely audible, but we had been anxiously waiting for it. Praying for it. We snapped to our positions. Triven, Grenald and two others began lowering ropes while the rest of us took watch. Our guns scoured the streets ready to shoot anything that moved.

My scope swept back to the school, watching their backs. The Ravagers should still be busy with their fire, but that didn't mean the other Tribes weren't restless tonight.

The vent's cover had been moved aside. The narrow tip of a handgun emerged followed by Archer's willowy limbs. Slowly, cautiously, more people began to filter out, eyes alert and wide with fear. Then a child with brown hair appeared from the shadows, and there was a tugging at my heart. In her hand was a knife, drawn and ready. In fact, most of the older children were carrying weapons, even the light-hearted Maribel clutched what looked like a small dagger. Mouse paused, staring at her best friend, and I could read her thoughts from here. Her friend's blonde ringlets were a beacon in the dark. Reaching up, Mouse pulled Maribel's hood over her head, tucking in the stray locks. She then took the knife from the girl's hands, readjusted Maribel's grip and mimicked a proper thrust with a stabbing motion. Maribel gave a shaky nod, but the girl had gone paler.

I wasn't sure if I was proud or horrified.

Other children around them began adjusting their grips too, mirroring her instructions, but unlike Mouse, the weapons looked foreign in their small hands. Their grips were awkward, fearful even. If anyone fell while running, it was obvious they would be more likely to impale themselves than to harm others.

I took a tight steadying breath.

Guns drawn and the children corralled in the middle, the group began moving. Their pace seemed terribly slow, the seconds stretching into minutes. The children were pulled up first, some in small groups of two to three, others cradled by their parents. My gun never left its watch, finger poised to fire, not even when the small hand touched my shoulder. Despite the bandages strangling my ribs, I took a deeper breath. Mouse was here.

The child's fingers tightened as Grenald pulled the last rope.

"Everyone's up." Archer was panting as they pulled her over the ledge, her boots the last to touch down.

Shouldering the gun I twisted, gathering Mouse into my arms. Kissing the top of her head I turned to Triven. "You're sure they can make it?"

"They don't have a choice. Can *you*?"

"*I* don't have a choice."

Before I could second-guess myself, I pushed against the bandages holding me together, against the pain, and I began to run.

The Healer had already turned me down. If The Master did the same, blood would be shed and people were going to die.

12. MASTERED

THOSE WHO HAD stayed to guard the stolen supplies sagged with relief when we arrived, Baxter's grin widening to the point of being painful as he welcomed our group. The journey, though a short distance, had not been an easy one. We moved in stints like an ever-rotating wheel. Split into groups of four, those most able-bodied would run ahead, scouting the city until the next leg had passed them. They would then take up the rear, slowly rotating back to the front again. For two miles, this process continued. I was careful in choosing our path, selecting the buildings with the least exposure, the ones that offered us the most shelter. But with that protection came other risks, especially for the children. Most of them rode in the arms of an adult, or clinging to their backs. But as the adults became tired, the jumps became more strained. Feet slipped and shins were scraped. In several instances where the gaps were significantly wider, I had watched—gut clenched—as several kids were thrown from one rooftop to another, always landing in waiting arms on the other side. No child was ever dropped, but the sight was enough to turn anyone's stomach.

We had made it two miles and not a single life lost.

Then, on the third to last jump, we lost one.

I had been at the back of the pack, completing my fifth rotation when he fell. I could see it in his leap, knew that he wasn't going to clear the gap. The man was thinner, older than the others. His legs had been shaking when he pushed off the ledge. Then there was a flail to his arms and I knew.

He didn't even cry out.

His chest had slammed into the ledge of the other building, arms and legs clawing for anchorage. I had launched myself next to him, twisting back to grab for his hands. But as I reached, the man did something that shocked me.

He let go.

There was no fear in his eyes, just acceptance. I had lunged, but he was gone. His eyes had closed as he fell to the streets below, a serene smile lighting his lips as his arms opened wide, welcoming death. I looked away then, squeezing my eyes closed just before his head smashed into the concrete. I wished I could unhear the gruesome sound that had followed. When I could finally open my eyes, I had pointed my gun at the body below. If the fall had not killed him, then a bullet to the brain would be a kindness. He made his choice, there was no need to suffer for it.

But no bullet was needed. The man was gone.

I looked back toward our group then. Should I tell someone?

Grenald stood three feet behind me, his eyes on the space where the man had just disappeared. He pressed an open palm to his chest then moved it as a fist to his forehead. A salute of farewell. Hoisting his bag higher on his back, he had shaken his head and turned to follow the others. The message clear. There was no point in telling them, not now. So, I too moved on. My feet carried me to Triven's side, Mouse riding safely in his arms. I didn't leave there until we found the rest of our group and even then, I stayed close to them. My anchors.

The man's death had shaken me. He had simply let go, stopped trying. Less than a year ago, that could have been me. I was ready to let go. But things had changed. *I* had changed. I was still willing to die, but for very different reasons.

There was no time for mourning. I pushed away the memory of the old man's face and focused on the task at hand. A few bottles of water were handed out, passed and shared between the tired group. They needed to rest, to eat, but they wouldn't get either. Our lookouts kept watch, but even with their keen eyes, this place would not be safe for long. The fire that had consumed the Ravagers' warehouse was all but out and that meant they would be seeking revenge for their losses. Soon.

Triven offered me a water, glaring as I tried to shove it away. To placate him I took a sip before passing it to Mouse. It was liquid heaven, the cool water soothing my scorched lungs, but as it hit my stomach the muscles clenched, threating to throw it back up.

To take my mind off the twisting pain, I grabbed a shard of metal off the rooftop and began drawing in the ash collected there. The Subversive members were quick to gather around me watching the city materialize. The maps were locked in my brain. The streets laid out in a perfect grid, the lines creating the footprint of my skyline. At the center, I drew an X marking The Master's lair. Seven blocks over I drew a circle.

"We're here." I tapped the circle, then pointed to the X. "We need to get there."

Arstid stood at her son's side, her breath still short from the run. "Are you going to tell us exactly *what* is *there*?"

"Shelter." I left it at that and turned to Arden, who half-smiled at me encouragingly. I began to trace a line across the buildings, marking our route. "I will lead the way. When we reach this point," I tapped a building three away from The Master's. "All of you will need to fall back. The rogue we are seeking doesn't enjoy company. He will fire on us first given the chance, but I think I can reason with him—"

"You *think*?" The motherly woman from the school basement stiffened with concern, latching onto my poor choice of words.

"I mean I *can*. He *will* listen to me." *I hope.*

Worry heightened the pitch of Arstid's voice. "And if he won't?"

"Then we will kill him and take the place by force." I lied. If The Master wouldn't see reason, we were screwed.

AS WE HAD gathered our stolen supplies, saddling those most capable with the heaviest load, I had felt Triven watching me. Watching for any sign of pain, hoping for an excuse not to let me face The Master. I had given him nothing. Now, though, I was thankful he was running behind me. I could feel the color draining from my face, the pain pulling at the corners of my mouth.

Five buildings out.

I held up a hand signaling the others to slow. They did. For the most part.

Legs pumping harder, my hands began checking my weapons, inventorying each one. Saving the supplies from the Ravagers' warehouse, gathering the others—easy. Convincing the man I had called The Master—the man Triven knew as Xavier—to take in eighty-seven traitors was another story.

It was hard to feel particularly optimistic at the moment. Yes, I wanted The Master to take us in, to give us shelter in trade for food, but Triven and I had asked him before to side with us and been turned down. If he did the same now, we would have to kill him. *I* would have to kill him. If he didn't kill me first.

On a good night, I stood a chance, but this was not a good night.

My throat burned, my lungs were screaming, my ribs were splintering and my limbs had begun to shake with fatigue. But my ears still heard the first knife and my exhausted body snapped into action.

The knife clipped my shoulder as I dropped. I slid feet first, drawing my knives as the silhouette of a man materialized on the next roof over. Tucking my legs under me, I propelled myself upright again. Two leaps found solid surface and then I was launching myself over the alley and across the rooftop as my hands flicked out. The shadow vanished, dodging the deadly projectiles. My feet barely landed before another knife whistled past my right ear. I tucked, rolling to a halt at the shadow's feet. My neck pulled taut and every muscle in my body froze. The man's hand extended, a knife held firmly at my throat, the blade kissing my skin.

"Sloppy." The Master chided, pushing the knife closer.

"Arrogant." I replied, twitching my hand. The barrel of my gun tapped his inner thigh aiming at his groin. He smiled, but didn't pull back his weapon.

The Master's eyes flickered up, then narrowed.

"You've brought strays." His knife pressed deeper. There was blood now.

"I've come to make a deal." I jabbed the barrel of my gun further into his crotch and the knife's pressure receded a little.

"And what do I get out of this *deal?*"

"Revenge."

The Master's gaze sparked with curiosity, then the blade was suddenly biting at my neck again.

Footsteps were approaching and I knew their guns were already drawn. I held up a hand in warning and the footsteps stopped.

Don't shoot, we need him, I silently warned them. *Triven, don't let them shoot him.*

The Master eyed our party crashers suspiciously. "What's your deal then child?"

"Take these people in, train them and I will give you Fandrin."

"How about *I* make you a deal?" His eyes burned. "Beat me and I will do as you ask. I win, and your strays are left to die in the streets."

He spoke the words loud enough for the others to hear and protests were already echoing back.

"Deal." I agreed.

"No!" Triven shouted, but I was already in motion.

Simultaneously leaning back from the knife's blade, I kicked out in a sweeping motion and took The Master's legs out from underneath him. His body slammed to the ground with an impressive blow, but he was not down for long. Then again, neither was I.

Arching back, The Master rocketed forward onto his toes. The momentum carried him forward and he used it. In one swift kick the gun was ripped from my hand. I heard the metal sliding across the roof but had no time to search for it. His arms flashed out, alternating between a glinting blade and claw-like fist. My feet danced away, arms raising to block each blow. He followed, hands and feet chasing my every move. The blows were powerful, calculated.

He was faster than I remembered or maybe I was slower. My body buzzed with adrenaline, the pain was ebbing, my head clearing. There was a glint in The Master's eye. This wasn't about winning, about beating me. He was actually trying to *kill* me. He wanted to set an example for the others watching. No one was to ever ask for his charity. This wasn't the man who I had paid to train me. *This* was the rebel who had survived by remaining alone and by killing those who threatened his way of life. And right now, I was the primary threat.

While he was yet to land a solid strike, I knew I was wasting precious energy. If I couldn't retaliate soon, the match would be over in a matter of seconds and *we* would lose. All of us.

I set my stance as his fist plummeted toward my face again, but this time I moved with him. My arm rose first deflecting his blow, then hooking onto it. My elbow kinked locking over his and I twisted, throwing all my weight forward. Head tucked, feet pushing, my body flipped forward yanking The Master's with it. His body went airborne, first sailing over mine then crashing down beneath me. A huff of air was forced from his lungs as The Master's back slammed into the ground and I had him. My hands twisted around his wrist, yanking his arm back at an impossible angle. He thrashed but my legs were already wound around him. One knee encircled his neck, my thigh crushing down on his larynx as the other pinned his torso to the roof.

His legs jerked trying to dislodge my grip, his free arm grappled with my leg, punching it fiercely, but I refused to let go. Instead, I flexed back, stretching my body to its greatest length and pulled harder on his arm as my legs thrust him further into the ground. His tendons were stretching under my hands, both the elbow and shoulder dangerously close to dislocating. A scream of pain and determination escaped my lips as my ribs protested the strain. Fire bloomed along my left side and I twitched. The movement was infinitesimal, but it was a fatal mistake.

The Master didn't hesitate. Rolling toward me, his left arm thrust forward popping me once, hard in the ribs. My entire body seized with agony. My grasp went weak and suddenly he was gone.

I rolled three times gasping for air, tears streaming down my cheeks. Hands pressed beneath me, I tried in vain to push my body upright. Every breath was coming in short stabbing wheezes. My shoulder collided with something cool and hard just as a hand wound in my hair. It yanked my head up and a knife slid beneath my exposed throat.

But before it could slice, a gunshot cracked and the ground two feet from my nose exploded.

Triven was advancing, his gun raised but shockingly he hadn't been the one to fire. His mother stood on the roof's edge, gun aimed at us. A small wisp of smoke emanated from its barrel. Even more stunning was that they weren't the only two to have moved. More than half of the Subversive's members had crossed the roof's edge and were surrounding us, weapons at the ready.

How odd.

"Don't Xavier." Arstid's words were laden with hatred.

The Master glared at her, pulling back harder on my hair. I cried out involuntarily as his knee pressed into my back, pushing down on the broken ribs. Another shot and this time Xavier flinched as the bullet clipped his shoulder.

As the pressure of his body lifted just enough, I flipped over, the pain excruciating. He froze, knife still at my throat. The others stopped moving. Clasped in my hands was my lost gun, the barrel aimed squarely at his heart.

"It's a draw." I wheezed.

"Then you lose." Malice flashed in his eyes.

They lose. That's what he was saying. I had not bested him. Triven's people, our people would not be given shelter. He would not help them.

If I pulled the trigger, we had nothing. Finding the way into Xavier's lair without his help was all but impossible. I had tried. That was one of the many reasons he was called The Master.

We needed him, but he had no need of us.

"My life for their safety." I blurted out. It was a desperate offer, a disingenuous one. The Master had never been gentle with me, never forgiving in his lessons. But he hadn't killed me in the six years we had known each other. I was banking that he wouldn't change that tonight.

I spun the gun on a finger, offering it to him. Xavier snatched it away without even blinking.

Footsteps shuffled somewhere nearby again and he raised my gun. A bullet sparked the ground less than an inch from Triven's toe.

"I wouldn't." Xavier warned him, the gun twitching in his hand.

Triven looked murderous, but I held up a hand compelling him to stay put. *Trust me.* I silently pleaded with him. Arstid's fingers grasped her son's shoulder, restraining him. Behind them, Baxter's rifle was pointed at Xavier's head.

"Kill me and they'll shoot you." I warned him.

"Life has gone on far too long already." He glowered. "I warned you that I didn't want to be involved and what do you do? You bring the damned fight to my doorstep."

"I am bringing you people in *need*. The same people you abandoned six years ago."

He didn't flinch.

I lowered my voice, ensuring only he could hear me. "The Wall is coming down, Xavier."

His pupils widened and he leaned in closer. "You should never pick a fight you can't win. I thought I taught you that."

"Some fights are worth losing to stand up for what's right."

The pain in my ribs was swallowing me again. Sweat gathered at the nape of my neck, my breaths becoming more labored.

"So, you're willing to die for what you believe in? To save these people?" The tip of his knife hovered above my left eye socket.

We weren't just talking about our deal any more, this was bigger than that. He wanted to know what I would risk for my beliefs.

I thrust my bare throat at him, daring him and secretly hoping I had been right before, that he wouldn't kill me.

"Yes." I proclaimed and I knew then I had been wrong.

"Stupid girl," he snarled and plunged the knife down.

13. WALLS

BLOOD FLOWED DOWN my face, pooling in my hair.

I blinked.

Feet were rushing us. But not a single hand fell on Tartarus's Master. No one was stupid enough to touch him, though every knife was drawn, every gun cocked.

Xavier leaned in closer and hissed, "You. Owe. Me."

Then the weight of his body was gone.

The knife stood embedded in the tarry rooftop, its blade slicing deeply into my left cheek. But I was alive.

The black grip disappeared beneath a hand, then the knife was yanked free. The warmth on my cheek began spreading faster. Triven's face hovered above mine. Archer's familiar outline stood over us, her trusty rifle aimed at what I assumed was Xavier's chest.

"Can she move?" Archer didn't bother looking down.

Triven's fingers moved to my throat, checking my pulse. I twisted away.

"I'm fine."

Leaning a little too heavily on his arms, I struggled to my feet, planting them wide. Every movement was agonizing, but necessary. I needed to stand, needed to prove I was okay. I needed Xavier to see me stand. I took two unsteady steps away from Triven's arms and mercifully didn't falter.

The Master's expression was one of perfect ease despite the multitude of weapons aimed at him.

"Well?"

"Well what?" Even the vibration of my own voice sent a tremor of pain through my chest.

I stopped breathing.

"Are you coming?" Without waiting for a response, Xavier turned and leapt over the building's edge to the next rooftop.

Wasn't this our goal? What we had wanted? I started to follow.

"You've got to be freaking kidding me." Archer protested from somewhere behind me, but I could hear her feet moving forward.

"Don't take your gun off him." It sounded like Arstid, though her voice was suddenly much farther away.

Still, they were all following him.

Following me.

I took two more steps and then slid into oblivion. I remembered the ground rushing up to meet my face and hands catching me. Then there was nothing. Not even pain.

SOMETHING ITCHY AND moist was stuck to my face. It pulled uncomfortably at the tender skin. But that discomfort was nothing compared to the lightning bolts exploding from my chest.

People were talking.

We were no longer on the rooftop. Something akin to a bed cradled my body and the room was definitely an enclosed space. The sounds were harsher here. It also smelled faintly of copper, heavily inked paper and dust.

The Master, Xavier, had taken us in.

The voices were hushed, but still each syllable stabbed like an icepick in my already throbbing head. The words echoed, lingering uncomfortably in my ears.

I kept my eyes closed.

"Why didn't you tell me it was Xavier?" The disdain in Arstid's voice draped over her words.

"Would you have come if I did?"

There would be a crease between Triven's eyebrows now. It always accompanied his well-practiced frowns of irritation. I had—after all—caused many of those frowns myself.

"He's a *traitor*."

"The same could be said about us."

"He abandoned us!"

I took a shallow breath. "He just saved all of our lives. If he didn't take us in, we wouldn't have lasted the week."

The words fell off my tongue, slurring as they came out.

There was the sound of moving fabric, and something warm cupped my unharmed cheek. I barely heard Arstid excuse herself, saying something about getting clean bandages. I'm not sure Triven even noticed her leave.

"How's your chest?" he asked.

"Never better." I winced.

Triven harrumphed. "And the ego?"

"Let's say it makes my ribs look pretty damn good."

A throaty laugh hummed next to my ear.

"Will you open your eyes so I can check your pupils?" his voice was sugar-sweet and I knew I was in trouble.

My lids slid back slowly and I came face to face with the crease line I had envisioned seconds ago.

I smiled.

He did not.

Triven's fingertips pulled back my eyelids, watching the reaction in my pupils. As he studied my face, I studied his. Dark circles had pooled beneath his eyes, the whites rimmed with red veins. Even his cheeks looked gaunt.

"How long has it been since you slept?" I wanted to reach for his face, but the pain assaulting my torso stopped me from moving.

"How long has it been since *you* slept?" He shot the question back at me, his attention moving to my cheek. Careful fingers pulled the sticking bandage away.

My eye twitched.

"Um, about sixty seconds ago."

He paused, leveling me. "Passing out and sleeping aren't the same thing Prea."

I repressed the urge to stick out my tongue. "Have you really not slept in over twenty-four hours?"

He shrugged, "I dozed a little while we waited to join you and Archer. I'm fine."

It was my turn to glare. He ignored it.

Finishing his inspection, Triven sat back on his heels. His mouth was pinched. I couldn't begin to imagine what I looked like right now. After the fire and the fight, I felt like one giant bruise.

As if reading my thoughts, Triven pulled a small black case from his pocket. Inside was nestled a syringe of green liquid. The two slots next to it stood empty. "You should use this—"

"No." Despite the pain, I placed a hand over his, closing the case.

"We don't have *time* for you to heal naturally. You need to be at full strength."

"You have no idea how tempting that offer is. But my wounds will heal. If I use that, I could be stealing someone else's life."

"Prea…"

"What if it were Mouse's?"

Pain flickered in Triven's tired eyes. I pushed the case down and he let me, for now. Triven set the box aside, his eyes turning to the ceiling.

"I told you I could handle this."

Triven still didn't smile, but the crease eased. "You're a real pain in the ass, you know that.

"You love me."

"Sometimes." The corner of his mouth turned up finally.

"My plan worked though."

"I wouldn't call this," he motioned to my battered body, "A total win."

I inhaled and recoiled from the pain. "True, but it wasn't a loss either."

His hand found mine, squeezing gently. "No more crazy plans, deal?"

"I can't make any promises." The words came out playfully, but I wasn't joking. I couldn't make him that promise.

Triven knew it too.

"Fine," he resigned. "Then next time *I* get to be the punching bag."

I grabbed my ribs as they pierced me again, "Deal."

A shaggy head of brown hair popped into the doorway. Otto grinned when he saw I was awake. "They're back."

Triven nodded, thanking him.

"Who's back?" It came out winded despite my best effort.

"We sent out a recovery group. They went to find the others."

I glanced up at Triven. "How long was I out?"

"Nearly twelve hours."

"We lost a whole day?" The pendulum swinging over us seemed suddenly closer.

"*You* did, but *we* did not. A hunting party went out in search of the other Subversive members shortly after we landed here. And it appears they're back."

Otto's smile widened. "Not a single person lost."

I smiled back at him, it was hard to resist Otto's charms.

"I guess it's time to answer some questions." I muttered, though neither of us moved. Triven and I simply exchanged a hesitant glance.

We knew this had been coming. There were no more excuses now. No longer was there a dire need to find our people food or shelter. To conceal our plans in case of a traitor. If they were all truly here and accounted for, that meant, like us, the traitor was trapped within these walls. There was no way out of here without The Master's knowledge, without his guidance. That was part of the reason I chose this place. I hated the idea of keeping a betrayer fed and warm in our midst. But the best place to keep a traitor was under your thumb, plus a traitor cannot whisper secrets where there are no ears to hear them.

Triven rose to his feet. I struggled to follow him.

Otto hesitated. "Do you need help?" He eyed me hesitantly.

"No," I spoke before Triven could accept Otto's offer on my behalf, and began to force my body upright. Triven's hands were instantly there. Careful to keep the pain from my face, I pushed my way onto weak legs. As soon as the room stopped tilting I took a tentative step. My legs wobbled, but held. Triven's arm slipped around my waist and though I wanted to prove I was fine, I needed the support. Otto stood awkwardly in the doorway, a hand half-raised to help.

"You don't have to come." Triven lowered his voice.

I pulled myself up taller, using the pain to shake off the intruding exhaustion.

"Can you gather everyone in the main room? Xavier too?" I leaned further into Triven the longer I remained standing. Hopefully he didn't notice.

Triven pressed a lip to my ear. "Tap twice on my hand when you need a break."

His fingers drummed on my hip. I pressed my fingers tightly over his, refusing to let them tap.

WE MOVED SLOWLY but steadily, fueled mostly by my stubbornness. When we finally reached the main hall, I was panting from exertion. Still, I made it on my own two feet.

Arstid was waiting for us outside the gilded double doors to the main room. She seemed surprised to find me not only standing, but not healed.

Many were already gathered in the marble room, huddled against pillars, sprawled on the dull floor. Some were animated, chatting as they reunited with their lost friends. A slow hush fell over the room as we entered, creeping its way to the corners until every eye was turned our way.

I scanned the crowd quickly, finding the dark shock of hair I had been seeking. Doc Porters sat inspecting the scraped knee of a child. His face lit up then fell as he assessed me. Reaching for a black bag, Doc shifted, ready to come inspect me next. I gave him the slightest head shake accompanied with a smile. *Later*, it said. He nodded and settled back to the child.

Triven walked me along the edge of the room. Partially because there was a long counter I could discreetly lean against for support and because the center was now too full of bodies. I had once thought this cavernous room of The Master's to be oversized, but now it seemed small filled with so many people.

We reached the midway point of the room and despite my earlier resolve, I tapped Triven's fingers twice. He didn't react, but merely stopped as if this was the exact point we were heading for the entire time. Careful to keep his hands low on my hips, he turned me toward him and lifted. I braced myself against his chest hiding the pain as he slid me effortlessly onto the tall counter. Though no one else undoubtedly noticed, he hesitated there for a moment, allowing me a beat to compose my face before stepping away. Sweat clung to my brow and beaded down my spine. The short walk had taken more effort than I had anticipated.

I looked out over Triven's shoulder, willing my eyes to focus properly. When they finally did, my heart leapt only to sink back.

Surely it hadn't been an illusion.

A wisp of blonde—the tail of a ponytail—had just disappeared behind a marble column on the other side of the room.

"Veyron?" I wheezed, pushing Triven's shoulder.

He followed my gaze, but any sign of her was now gone.

It had to have been her. The height of the woman had been about right and I knew no other person who wore his or her hair so defiantly long. But why then had she turned from us? I wanted to hop off the counter and chase blonde hair I had seen, but someone more important caught my attention.

A child was barreling through the crowd. Her eyes bright, Mouse flung herself into Triven's waiting arms and after a satisfactory hug, she wiggled until he set her on the stone counter next to me. There were dividers spaced on the marble surface, but the two of us were small enough to squeeze between them comfortably. Mouse was elated to see me up and moving, but was still careful not to touch my purpled skin. Ignoring the pain, I leaned into her, letting her know it was okay to touch me and relishing in the warmth of her body.

"Missed you kid." I smiled at her.

She looked at the people gathered in the room, at their tired but hopeful faces.

You did good, but you're an idiot.

I laughed, stopping quickly as it jarred my ribs. "Yes. But I'm *your* idiot."

Mouse grinned and leaned in to kiss my good cheek.

I took her hand in mine.

Archer startled us as she hopped over the back side of the counter and slid up next to us. She leaned against the partition, swinging her long legs.

"Baxter says that's everyone, but he couldn't seem to find that Xavier guy. Do you think he and his crap attitude vacated?"

She looked optimistic.

I skimmed the room, and there, in the darkest corner of the ceiling, was a glint of silver. The flicker was barely visible in the dim light, but I knew it was a knife being idly flipped. I didn't need to see his face to know Xavier was watching me.

"No. He's here."

Archer cleared her throat awkwardly. "Well, looks like you three got the floor." She clapped me roughly on the shoulder. I choked on the pain and Triven shot her a murderous look. Archer pulled her hand back, but managed not to look repentant. "Oops, right sorry… Welllll, good luck with this."

She quickly jumped down from the counter and made her way to the back of the room.

"Coward." I muttered. Though I couldn't really blame her.

The room was nearly silent now. Eyes darted from us to Arstid who still lingered by the door. It was clear she was letting us take the lead, though whether it was because her last involvement went *so* well or because she actually trusted us, I didn't know. Attention quickly turned to Triven as he began to address his people.

"For the past forty-eight hours, we have kept you in the dark. That was unfair. It was not my—*our*—intention to lie to you. Or to hide the truth. But after what happened in the Subversive, our first priority became getting all of you to safety. Our people have suffered great losses in these past forty-eight hours and it is with heavy hearts that we now find ourselves here. Phoenix risked her life to make this happen, to give you a safe place to hide, but we also must apologize. Our actions were not completely selfless. We also wanted you fed, warm and safe so you could hear us with open minds."

Murmurs began to buzz. Nothing in Tartarus was ever free, everyone here knew that.

"As many of you know, Phoenix, Mouse and I spent the last month trapped within the Sanctuary. What we found there was shocking. We were lucky to survive. Bowen and Maddox, sadly, were not so fortunate." Many in the gathered crowd mimicked the same motion I had seen Grenald do when that man let go on the rooftop. Hand to their chests, then to their foreheads. "The stories my mother has told us for years are true. The Sanctuary is not the utopia we had once hoped for."

"And we're supposed to take your word on this?" A thin man leaning against a pillar called out. His arms were folded skeptically.

"No," Triven said. "You're here to decide for yourself."

He pulled the tablet from his pocket and handed it to Mouse. Her fingers flew expertly over the screen until a projection shot out onto the wall behind us. Several people gasped, while other crept closer, entranced by the moving images. Mouse tinkered with the volume, but even with it at its max, the crowd had to become absolutely silent to hear the accompanying audio.

The video was a compilation of images. Scenes that were stolen from security cameras, from people's homes, from the streets, from a hidden camera on Ryker's lapel. The Rebels had wanted to create a piece of propaganda favoring only the negative sides of the Sanctuary, but both Triven and I were against it. Our people deserved to know the truth, not a one-sided story. So many things were corrupt and horribly wrong with the world Fandrin ordained his utopia. But many other things were better than what we had here. I wanted our people to see all of it. To decide what they wanted to fight for. Some people needed to fight for hope, while others against a villain. Whatever their reason, we needed them to fight.

The video continued and no one spoke. It showed happy families dining together and others being executed together. It showed children being stolen from their parents and beaten into loyal soldiers. It showed there were surpluses of food and safe homes, the parts of a thriving community it was indented to be. Then it showed my torture and the orders that came from Fandrin's own mouth.

I could feel Archer's eyes on me during this part. I refused to meet her gaze.

The video laid everything out for our people to see. Good and bad. The hopeful and the tragic. Only the Rebels themselves were cut from the film. It was one thing we had all agreed upon. If we had been caught, if we hadn't escaped, their anonymity must remain absolute.

When the clip finally stopped and the wall behind us went dark, the hall remained still. Even the flickering of Xavier's knife could no longer be seen in the shadows.

Many were looking at me. I said nothing.

A tentative voice shattered the spell holding everyone's tongue.

"How does this affect *us*? We can't do anything about what is happening there. The Wall—"

"*The Wall* will no longer be an issue." Shockingly it was Archer who responded.

"What does that mean?" Several people shouted twisting in her direction. She instantly clammed up.

"So you're asking us to start a war with The Sanctuary?" A woman called out. Though I couldn't see her in the crowd, she was louder than the others.

"No, we are asking you to join a war that has already begun." Triven spoke in the direction of her voice. "Yes, we went to the Sanctuary seeking intel, thinking we could *start* a war, but war was already there. It has been for a long time. The Rebels Arstid once was a part of long ago—they survived and have been biding their time. The day we left, they made their first move in almost seven years. It was what enabled us to escape, and it was the tipping point in a revolution."

"I still don't see how this affects us." Someone else shouted.

I finally found my voice, though it was not loud.

"In fourteen days, The Wall is coming down, and the Rebels have asked for our help in assassinating The Minister. To burn his rule to the ground and build a new city, together. Tartarus will no longer be our cage."

"We saw the army in that video. We're not enough." A man yelled.

"You're right. *We* are not." I dared a quick glance at Archer. "But with the Tribes we can be."

There were two beats of stunned silence. Then came the explosive reaction we had been fearing.

"Listen! In fourteen days, The Wall is coming down. We need to—" Triven's words were lost in the mayhem.

People were screaming at us, at Arstid, at anyone near them. A few were even making their way to the doors. Though how they expected to find a way out was beyond me. Xavier had turned this place into a maze.

There were people crying hysterically, holding themselves tightly and a few were making their way toward the three of us. Though whether it was in support or to kill us for our proposal, it was hard to tell.

I automatically pulled out my handgun, taking aim.

One man was less than three feet from us, knife drawn, when I jumped. A gun had gone off, but it wasn't mine.

14. HONESTY

THE SHOT BOOMED, echoing off the polished surfaces, coaxing out cries of surprise. Everyone ducked reflexively as bits of the ceiling showered down on us. Pulling Mouse painfully to my chest and sheltering her head, I glared in the direction of the gunshot.

The shooter was impossible to miss.

Grenald stood with his wide shoulders coated in bits of white plaster. His shotgun was still raised high above his head, finger still on the trigger. Those closest to him were backing away, all except Otto who had pulled his own gun and was eyeing anyone who looked like they might interfere.

The room had gone absolutely still. Those leaving had paused in the doorway.

The giant leveled the rifle in my direction and Triven moved to step between us, but I laid a hand on his shoulder.

"Wait." I whispered. There was a dip to his wrist, a laxity to Grenald's grip. He wasn't *aiming* at me. He was *pointing* at me.

Grenald's voice boomed, and as before, people listened. "In the past two days alone, Phoenix has risked her life to get you food and shelter. Not to mention the fact Triven has personally helped bring most of us into this community after we defected. Hear them out. We owe them that much."

He looked to Otto, who bobbed his chin in support.

Part of me wanted to laugh. Apparently saving loved ones' lives earned you loyalty. Had I known the power it yielded over people, I might have started doing that sooner. Well, maybe.

I had hoped Triven would talk as breathing was taking most of my focus, but his people were looking at me.

Sighing, I pressed a hand to my aching ribs. "Look, I'm not asking you to join hands and skip off into the sunset. I'm not even asking you to get along with them. Hell, the less we actually have to do with the Tribes, the better. All I am asking is that for a little while, we point our guns in the same direction instead of at each other."

"And you think you can get the Tribes to agree to that?" Arden called out from the back of the room.

"No, not really." A few people started at my honesty. "But the chances of succeeding in uniting them are much worse without your help. I know you hate them. You all have your own reasons, and every one of you has a right to hate the Tribes. But I don't have that luxury anymore. I have taken on worse odds on my own before and I can do it again." I took another short, pained breath. "You can stay here and pretend that nothing exists beyond The Wall. That this is the only way of life. Or you can choose to fight for a better one. Either way it's still *your* decision. Triven and I made a promise, but we didn't make any promises for you."

"And how do you know it will be better if we choose to fight? If we help you gather the Tribes?" It was the mother who had been with us at the school. Wen, I thought I remembered someone calling her.

"At first, it probably won't be." Arstid finally spoke from the doorway, her tone authoritative. "It wasn't when we started the Subversive either, but it *got* better. So many things are broken on both sides of The Wall, and the Rebels are right," She glanced at me, undoubtedly thinking of my mother. "Nothing is going change if we don't fight for it." She hesitated before adding, "Don't you want a better world for your son? I certainly do."

Triven flushed, but gave his mother an appreciative look before adding to her speech. "We're not asking all of you to fight and those who do choose to join us, we aren't promising everyone is going to survive. People are going to die—your friends and family... We're not promising a victory either, only a chance to fight for what you believe in. For a choice in the future you want."

"Far from it. In fact, if all you care about is your own life, it's better that you *don't* join us." I added.

"And what if we value our children's lives?" A man called from the left. A little girl stood between his feet clinging to her father's legs.

I looked down at Mouse. "Then you fight."

Triven kissed the top of her head, before carefully brushing my cheek. His expression was strained. He hated to ask this of them as much as I did, but the touch was a gentle reminder we were in this together. "Both sides are suffering. We starve out here, while their ample amounts of food are poisoning them. We kill to stay alive—to give our children a future—while their children's futures are stolen from them. In different ways, that Wall has imprisoned both our worlds."

Several people glanced back at the blank wall where the video had been played, undoubtedly trying to recall everything they had just seen.

We were on the verge of winning some of them over. I took another desperate stab to further open their minds.

"Minister Fandrin is a liar and a manipulator. I won't be him. I won't lie to make you fight with me. But this war, it isn't *mine* or *yours*. It's ours. *All* of ours. Everyone in this city *and* in the city on the other side of The Wall will be affected. Whether you choose to fight, or not. Personally, I want a say in my future.

"The Rebels have asked a terrible thing of us and now I am asking that same terrible thing of you. I know that. But I'm not asking you to fight for *me*. I am asking you to fight for yourselves. Beyond that wall is an army trained since they were children to sacrifice themselves for their Minister. They have better weapons than we do and their skills far outmatch our own. The only thing we have on our side is the element of surprise. Alone there is little we can do to impact the outcome of this war. But if we can get the Tribes to fight against the Ministry too—come at them from every direction—we may stand a chance."

"And what if the Tribes turn on us?" A man with a half-tattooed face asked.

"Expect it." I answered without hesitation. "They might. The Tribes are a loose cannon. I'm not expecting to control them, merely to light the fuse and point them in the right direction. I can only hope they do more damage to the other side than our own. I never intend to fully trust them and neither should any of you."

Many deflated with relief, which surprised me. I had never had high expectations of the Tribes' involvement and hearing me admit that somehow soothed them. Most people wanted happy tales spun to comfort them, but for some reason, these people found more solace in my harsh honesty. I had never been the person to have a sunny disposition, it just wasn't how my brained worked. I was built on facts and mistrust, and that would never change.

Triven seemed to sense the shift of emotions as well and went in for the kill. "We will answer every question you have to the best of our ability and then you can make a choice to fight or hide. We will not retaliate against those who choose not to fight." This was both a promise and warning to those who might not feel the same.

"Unfortunately, though, those unwilling to fight must remain here until The Wall has fallen. With the recent events, we cannot risk our plans being sabotaged." Arstid's words were final.

Hands began to raise with questions, but before Triven could call on any of them a coughing fit wracked my body. I doubled over, nearly falling face first off the counter. Triven steadied my shoulders as Mouse clung to my arms. When I was finally able to straighten, tears were streaming down my cheeks and blood splattered my hands and lips.

Panic filled Triven's eyes and Doc jumped forward from the crowd, black bag clutched to his stomach. "I propose that we vote to use one of the remaining healing serums on Phoenix so she can move forward in her plan.

So she can continue to lead this revolution. Those inclined to agree, say aye."

I began to protest, but Triven's shout drowned me out. "Aye!"

Shockingly it wasn't only his voice echoing off the high ceiling. Over half the room had agreed.

It dawned on me at that moment, I had somehow become a leader in this revolution. A thrill of hope pulsed through me and at the same time, I wanted to vomit.

IT TOOK NEARLY the rest of the day to sort out all the Subversive members' questions about the Sanctuary and our provisional plans. In the end, more had chosen to side with us than I had expected. A small group of seventeen chose to abstain from the fight. Some because they refused to work with the Tribes and others because they didn't believe things could be better. I couldn't blame them for their choice.

Even though the majority of people had agreed to fight with us, only five had actually offered to help gather the Tribes, and each was unwilling to be involved with their own ex-Tribes' acquisition.

It was a mess.

In the end, we ended up with Archer and Grenald—both ex-Wraiths, Arden and Otto—both ex-Taciturns and Elin—an ex-Scavenger barely my own age. Not a single Adroit had offered their help, their nature of not getting their hands dirty still ingrained apparently. Not even Baxter offered his usually ready gun. I supposed we all have our limits, this was his.

Arstid had wanted to be involved with the planning too, but we all agreed it was better that she stay neutral in support of her own people. Though I hated to admit it, we needed her to be their voice of reason and that meant not being aligned with the Tribes in any way.

Triven had tried to look hopeful as our little group assembled, but I knew we were screwed. No one slept well that night, even one of Ryker's little white pills didn't keep all of the nightmares away.

The plans were rough at best. We had agreed that after the incident at the Ravager's warehouse, it was most advantageous that we go after the Adroits first before they blew up all the other Tribes. Generally, Adroits didn't venture out into other territories seeking casualties, but apparently things had changed. Several dead Ravagers could attest to that.

Elin, the ex-Scavenger, felt confident he could get us safely into their territory. He claimed to have scavenged that area regularly before he found the Subversive—or they found him, more accurately—and knew where most of their bombs were hidden. Or at least how to look for them. His green eyes radiated confidence.

The goal was get in close enough to take an Adroit or two hostage and use them as leverage. We would require two things from the hostages. To spread the word to their leader of what we were doing and not to die in the process. As a Tartarus rule, Tribal hostages were never taken and then released. This act would be our first peace offering.

The question was, what message to send back with the freed hostages? Ultimately, we had to speak to the

Tribes' leaders. If we couldn't get them on board none of the other members would follow. They were not egalitarians. Archer wanted to send a threat that we would blow them all up if they didn't fight for us. Otto thought it was better to give them a semi-false hope of gaining access to the endless amount of supplies in the Sanctuary and freedom from the Tribal lifestyle. There were huge problems with both plans. One gave us soldiers under duress—making them more likely to turn on us—and the other offered a lifestyle they may not care about at all. Yes, the Tribes were all about survival, and yes, some of them may desire a more amicable way of life. But some of them liked it here. They thrived on the power and violence, and would never want that to change.

In the end, we settled on banking on their greed and basic desire for self-preservation. The captives would be sent back with a simple message. We were a rebel group that was going to blow up The Wall, invade the Sanctuary and take out the Ravagers. If their Tribe wanted in, then their leaders were going to have to meet with us. Then lastly and most importantly—and a total lie—was that the other Tribes had already joined our ranks to claim their profits.

The last part was juvenile, but we were relying on the Tribes' desire not to be left out. If the Ravagers, the largest and most deadly Tribe, were taken out, there could be jockeying to be the next big power in Tartarus. More supplies meant making that happen and getting the most supplies, meant working with us. It was the only benefit of the Tribes' distrust of one another. If the plan was successful with the Adroits, we would repeat similar kidnappings with the other Tribes.

Maps were drawn roughing out Tribes' territories and the best routes to each. Navigating the skyline was the easiest part, but unfortunately, unlike the arrogant Ravagers, the other Tribes were paranoid enough not to have easy roof access to their buildings. The Adroits were the worst. Surrounding their territory was a block-wide wasteland of blown-up buildings and spike filled crevasses. Their nest was at the center in what looked like an old factory of sorts. It had two massive smokestacks and I had always suspected it was where they sourced most of their explosive materials. The entire area always smelled of sulfur.

Unfortunately, it was also one of the few areas I knew little about. When your main goal for six years was staying alive, you didn't go to the areas that were known for blowing up.

We lost an entire day poring over the maps and plans. Everyone was stalling, we all knew it. But the clock was ticking and we had already lost two more days.

Naturally, I wanted to leave after nightfall, but Elin was insistent we move during the daylight, claiming he could see the traps better. The thought of being out in a known Tribal territory during broad daylight sounded like a terrible idea. But with the rest of the ex-Adroits refusing to help, we were left with few options.

I sent the others to gather the best weapons they could acquire and went to find Xavier. The stairs leading down to his vault were steep and I relished each easy breath while descending them. I owed Doc for his help. Not only in allowing me to be healed, but also for giving the choice to the Subversive members. Healing me was no longer a selfish act, but a gift given by those who trusted us. The serum he had wasn't as efficient as the most recent batch.

The bruises lingered, fading to ripe yellows, but my ribs had at least mended and although they still ached slightly, were no longer crushing my lungs.

Xavier was sitting on a pile of papers and glittering rocks in the corner of a steel-clad room looking his usual brooding self. He was using the tip of a dagger to pick something out from under his fingernails. My feet never made a sound and he never looked up, but The Master knew it was me.

"You seem to have quite the following up there kid." He pointed the knife tip at the room above us, then went back to picking his nails with it.

"For someone who said he didn't want to be involved, you're keeping a rather close watch."

He smiled darkly, still focusing on his fingers. "What do you want Phoenix?" He had never been one for niceties.

"Thank you for taking them in."

"And?"

"*And*, I want you to train them. Many have skills but they're rusty. I need them on point." I thought of the children running with knives, who were more likely to harm themselves then wield them for protection. I swallowed hard. "Even the kids."

He froze, glaring at me over the blade. "You're making a child army of your own now?"

I flushed crimson at the accusation. Actually, I had expected the comparison to my grandfather, but it still ignited rage. "Not in the least. But I also refuse to let those people—*even those children*—up there walk out into this without knowing how to defend themselves."

He tilted his head. "So you want me to train them, like I trained you."

I thought of the relentless lessons, the concussions and constant bite of his cane when I messed up. "Do that, and I will break your nose."

He scoffed.

"My ribs are healed and the last two times we met I bested you. You may be better than me in the long run, but I can still break your face before you take me down."

He laughed louder this time. "I almost missed that fire, kid. *Almost.*"

"So, you'll do it?"

"What's in it for me?" He reached down into his throne of junk and picked up a gold disk, rolling it idly between his knuckles.

"When this is over, we leave you alone. You'll be free to live wherever you want, however you want. And I will personally guarantee you're given whatever you need to make that happen."

"And if you get yourself killed, then who's going to pay me what I'm owed?" It was a serious question. A relevant one.

"I will make sure everyone knows of our deal. You won't walk away empty handed. And you can live out the remainder of your pathetic life as an angry old hermit. Do we have a deal?"

He tossed the useless coin aside, letting it clatter down a pile to the floor. "For now."

"You will only train the kids how to hold a knife and defend themselves. The defense basics—that's it. I don't want them sparring. I don't want them fighting."

With that, I turned to leave him to his sulking, pausing when he called out to me.

"Don't forget. You have twelve days and I'm kicking you out. *All* of you."

"Deal." I said over my shoulder. I prayed the Rebels would uphold their end of the bargain, or we would be trapped here, homeless, with four pissed off Tribes on our tails.

"Good luck!" he crowed after me. "Don't get yourselves blown up!"

15. FOOLISH

I STARED OVER the edge of the building at the destruction around us.

My entire resolve had spoiled in the two hours it took us to get here. Despite our caution, there had been three close calls with Ravager hunting parties. It seemed they were on the warpath since losing their food supplies. While the thought made me smile, it was also a huge inconvenience we hadn't originally accounted for. To make matters worse, they were hunting Adroits just like we were.

After closing in on two potential kidnap victims we found ourselves beaten to the punch. A block before we planned to descend on them, the Ravagers got to them first. I had had to plug my ears against their screams, choking back my own. In the end, once the Ravagers had had their fill, the kindest thing we could do was quicken their slow deaths. Archer eased their suffering with two clean shots. It was nearly twenty minutes before any of us was ready to move on again.

It had become painfully clear that while we had wanted to avoid getting too close to the Adroits' blast area, it was the only place the Ravagers were also unwilling to go.

Now, we crouched low over the crumpled edge of a half-blasted building, glaring suspiciously at the ground below. What could barely be called a wall stood across from us, providing what little shelter there was. Beyond that, there was nothing. I saw nothing but rubble and bits of torn metal littering the streets, but Elin's keen eyes saw more. His finger extended as he pointed out two triggers carefully buried in the dirt. They were barely visible, the oblong mounds blending in with the rest of the debris around them. Now that he had pointed them out, however, I could see two more further down the street.

"They're everywhere," Triven whispered next to me.

"At least nine every block." Archer agreed. "Shit."

It was three blocks to the Adroits' factory. We would be lucky to make it one.

"Maybe we should re-think this." Otto stared wide-eyed at the streets below us. I was inclined to agree with him. Something felt off and my instincts were usually right.

"No, no. I got this." Elin's voice sounded sure, though I didn't buy it. "We just have to make it to that building." He fingered a small cinderblock structure two blocks down. "They keep some supplies in there. We might be able to surprise a couple of them."

The approach there was completely exposed. I could see everyone else was thinking along the same lines. Even Arden's eyes narrowed at the gaping streets.

What was that Old World saying? Something about shooting fish in a barrel? The phrase finally made sense to me and we were about to be the fish.

Elin must have been gauging our doubtful expressions. "They never watch that area cuz the IEDs do the work for them." He tried to reassure us. "Trust me. I used to scavenge it all the time."

I still couldn't shake the sinking feeling in my chest, but maybe this was always what it felt like to trust others' plans.

"Grenald?" Triven turned to him, questioningly eyeing the rope he carried.

The huge man didn't seem keen on the idea either, but began unraveling it from his massive shoulders. Creeping to the edge of a hole in the roof, he slowly lowered the rope into the depths of the building. Lacing the cording around his lower back, he braced his feet against a wall and nodded at Elin.

The ex-Scavenger slid lithely down the rope first, with Archer quick to follow. I was surprised when she had requested to join us on the ground level instead of taking point in the roost. But Otto was a good enough marksman to keep watch for us, and despite missing an arm, Archer was exemplary at hand-to-hand combat. I thought maybe it was her way of trying to make up for not helping with the Wraiths. Personally, I would have preferred the latter.

My feet were already on solid ground before Triven had climbed onto the rope. Elin was waiting by a doorframe, scanning the alley. As Triven's boots zipped down the line, Elin pointed to his eyes then down at his feet lifting them in turn. *Step where I step.*

As Archer kept her weapon on the streams of washed-out sunshine leaking in through the building's many holes, I followed Elin. Gun and knife drawn. The slight drag of a right toe told me Triven was following.

Elin carved a calculated path through the alleyway, weaving toward the open street. Every footstep was placed with caution, falling exactly into his treads. I counted the IEDs as we passed them. Seven lined the alleyway alone. I paused as the sound of Elin's footsteps changed in front of me. I didn't dare take a step without looking down.

The young man had stopped in the middle of the street about twenty paces in front of me, a triumphant smile on his face. Elin's arms spread wide as if to say, "See I told you they don't watch this area."

For an instant, the emerald hue of his eyes glowed brilliantly in the green-tinged sun. Pride beamed on his face, then there was a crack, and the smile faltered. A snap of red exploded on Elin's chest and his body was suddenly being propelled backward. His knees didn't even buckle. The boy simply tipped backward from his heels like a falling tree. I could see the look of shock register on his face the instant before his body hit the ground. I never heard the click, but there was a brilliant light followed by a searing heat and an explosion loud enough to rattle my teeth.

The ground disappeared from under me. I was airborne. An outburst of heat scorched down the alley walls. My hand flew up automatically as I tried to twist away. The ground rushed up, knocking the wind from my newly healed lungs with a violent huff.

Rubble and body parts rained down in a mist of red. With my arms wrapped around my skull, I pulled the hood over my head knowing it would do little. The heavy thuds twisted my stomach as they hit the earth and bounced off my body. I was about to pull my head up when six more explosions went off in the street behind me, each following the other. One was so close, I could feel the shockwave ripple the ground. I now understood the pattern the bombs had been placed in, and why there were so many. One goes off and a chain reaction would ensue. The other must have been set off by what remained of Elin, or... or...

Dirt filled my nostrils, the grit spiked with an ammonic tang as I pulled my face up, desperately searching for signs of movement. A ringing deafened my ears as the last bits of rubble rained down, not that it mattered. I doubted anyone was stupid enough to call out anyway.

I wasn't facing the street anymore, but back toward the hole in the building we had just exited through.

Relief warmed my chest as I caught sight of a sandy head shaking itself fifteen paces in front of me. The soot had stained the golden head grey, but he was moving. Triven was struggling to his feet, his eyes screwed up against the shock of the blasts. There were a few scrapes on his cheeks, a larger one oozed from his temple, but he appeared whole. Archer was there in the fading smoke, pulling Triven up, her eyes turned in my direction. Behind them, Arden's terrified face poked out of the opening. The dark dust deepened his already prominent scars. Bruised and scared, but they were at least alive.

Elin had been wrong, the Adroits did have snipers. The haze gave us some shelter, but it was quickly dissipating. We had to get back under the cover of the building. Planting my elbows underneath my chest, I began to push myself upright and froze. I thrust a panicked palm at all three of them as they picked their way toward me and then made a chopping motion at Triven. *Stop!* Maybe I even said the word aloud too, but it never pierced the ringing in my ears.

We had been blown off our carefully selected path.

Triven froze immediately as he saw what I had seen. Pulling back on Archer's arm, he pointed down. Less than a hand's length from my nose was an undetonated IED. Everyone's attention flashed to the ground. Cautiously, I pushed myself back onto my heels, away from the live bomb. As I rose, a piece of gravel crunched under my boot, causing my entire body to seize.

I closed my eyes. Breathing no longer seemed second nature. *It's nothing, you're fine.* After taking two shaky breaths, I began searching for my earlier footsteps in the dirt. They were faint at first, but grew more visible the father I got from the blast zone—*from Elin*—the small voice in my mind whispered. I tried not to think of the look on his face as he fell.

I shook my head, "Focus!"

Triven remained perfectly still until I reached him. Archer's rifle bounced around the mouth of the alley, waiting for a target to appear. When one didn't, she finally gave up and made her way after us. No one spoke.

Was it possible the Adroits didn't know the rest of us were here? Had they only seen Elin? Or had they thought the other explosions had taken care of the rest of us?

As we made it inside, Grenald's ashen face appeared in the hole above us. I shoved Arden to the rope first. Once atop he could help Grenald pull Archer up faster. Heat was rolling off our one-handed companion in waves, her long limbs trembling. She refused to meet my gaze and part of me was grateful. It wasn't until she was pulled halfway to the roof, that I turned and pressed my face into Triven's chest. A few tears squeezed their way free as his hand pulled tightly at the nape of my neck. I couldn't tell if it was just me shaking or both of us.

This had gone horribly wrong.

I had let Elin take lead against my better judgement, and now he was dead. Another Subversive member killed because of my actions. We weren't any closer to gathering the Tribes and if we didn't get away from here fast enough, we could all suffer the same fate. A hand's width and we *would* have been dead.

Once all six of us were back on elevated ground, we ran. We ran and we didn't stop, not until the smoke was miles behind us and the stench of the explosives had faded away. When we finally took shelter on the top floor of an abandoned building, I doubled over and vomited. Guts still clenching, I moved away from the pile of sick. I straightened, trying to stretch the cramping muscles and was immediately met with Archer's fist as it shot toward my face.

16. FAULTS

"**ELIN IS DEAD** because of you!"

Shocked, I barely had time to turn my head. Archer's fist grazed my cheekbone, clipping my left ear. Her long arm snapped back, thrusting forward twice more in quick succession. Both times narrowly missing its target.

"What the hell, Archer!" I yelled.

As the shock of her attack wore off, anger flared. How *dare* she blame me? If she and the others hadn't refused to help us, to share the secrets they knew about their ex-Tribes, then this would have never happened. I wouldn't be wearing Elin's blood like war paint. Before I could stop to think, my fists clenched and I fought back. I had expected her to retreat, but instead Archer threw herself harder into the assault.

She had nearly a foot on me, and as her body slammed into mine, a bony shoulder smashed into my face. We rolled, gathering filth from the ground. Dust came off us in clouds as we punched, kicked and snarled our way across the room. What I lacked in height, I made up for in rage. Incoherent words snarled from our lips, neither of us pulling punch.

Someone—Triven probably—moved to intervene, but Grenald's voice stopped him.

"Let them get it out."

And get it out we did. I landed a kick to Archer's chest, effectively throwing her backward. Springing to our feet, I drew back to punch her. Both our hands flew out and while my throw had more skill, Archer's arm was longer. Bracing myself for the hit, I froze, dumbfounded as she struck me. Not with a fist as I had expected, but with an open palm. The sharp snap sliced through the air and someone behind me gasped. The action was so much more demeaning than any punch.

Archer stiffened, seeming surprised by her own actions.

I took advantage of her hesitation. My palm struck with an equally impressive sound. To her credit, she took the returned slap. Never flinching. Blood rushed to her cheek outlining my handprint on her bronzed skin. The sting on my own cheek a sign that we matched.

She heaved, stepping so close to me I had to crane my neck back to see her face. "I thought you said you *knew* the Tribes."

"I *DO* know them—as much as any outsider can know! But I was never one of them, unlike *some* people!" I stepped even closer to her, leaving no room between us. Archer stood her ground but straightened, distancing her face from mine. I continued, breathing heavy. "*Maybe* if we actually knew someone who had been in the Tribes, this might be easier! Hell, we might even survive this stupid mission. But wait… too bad we seem to be fresh out of ex-

Tribesmen. *Right*, Archer?!" I slammed my body into hers, shoving her back a step. "I mean, it's not like *you* know anything that could have saved Elin's life. Right?! It's not like *you* could have led us to another Tribe or anything!" This time I shoved against her thin shoulders. She staggered.

Twice Archer's mouth popped opened, and twice nothing came out. Tears were brimming on her thick lashes. She tried to blink them away.

I was right and she knew it. I wasn't completely guiltless in Elin's death, but neither was she. Her refusal to help with the Wraiths killed him just as much as my ignorance about the Adroits.

"If all of you continue to refuse to help with your own Tribes, others are going to die." I dropped my voice. It wasn't a threat. It was the truth. "We can't continue to do this blind. You *have* to be involved."

Archer shifted on the balls of her feet, refusing to look at anyone. Her right hand groped at the stump abruptly ending her left arm. The others' gazes fell away with their own guilt. Only Triven still watched us. Grief distorted his features, pulling them down. He hated all of this as much as I did.

A long finger leveled at my face. The tip quivered between my eyes. "Fine… FINE! But I swear on The Wall, if she… if you…" Tears fell freely from Archer's eyes now, fueled by a hundred emotions. "I will make *everyone* regret you ever asked me to do this. Got it?"

I slapped her finger away.

"*Fine*."

UNCOMFORTABLE DIDN'T EVEN begin to describe the rest of the run back to Xavier's. Though only Archer and I had quarreled, our exchange had greatly affected the entire party. A cloud of regret and guilt followed us the entire way, the loss of Elin's life haunting our steps. We were coming home emptyhanded and a man short. I wondered if any of the others would even bother showing up to our next attempt or if this was the first nail in the coffin.

Honestly, I didn't want to do this either. Not now, not ever. I never thought this plan was a good idea. This was what I had tried to warn Ryker about. I was not a leader and after today, it seemed obvious I was going to fail him.

Archer said that she would help us with the Wraiths but that was only one Tribe. Though they tried to hide it, I saw the others' faces when we got back. The way Arden looked at me tore at my heart. I had let them down. We were going to fail. Everyone knew it.

Xavier had been waiting for us when we returned. I could see him counting our heads, taking in our battered appearance. He said nothing. He didn't have to. I had expected him to look smug, pleased even. But there was a dark twist to his features. Disappointment maybe? Wordlessly he led us inside, then disappeared again.

As soon as we got in the building, I split from the group like a coward. Not wanting to see Arstid's face pinch with anger, the way Doc's would fall. Watching the last seconds of Elin's life had already been too much. With it came all the ghosts from my past. My mother. Father.

Maddox. Elin would join their ranks now. Destined to haunt my dreams with so many others.

When Triven found me hours later, hiding in the room filled with crates we had used as our meeting quarters, my attitude had only further soured. A pile of splinters scattered the ground under the crate I perched on. The tip of my knife dug relentlessly into the lid again, prying more slivers free.

"They're never going to trust me again." I didn't look up. The tips of his black boots stopped between mine. His hands landed gently on my shoulders. The knife stopped its digging, but I kept my head down. Slowly, Triven's hands slid up to my neck, his thumbs tracing my collarbones until they cupped my cheeks. A flush of heat followed every touch. Gently Triven pulled my face up until my eyes finally met his. They were warm, smiling in the gentle way only Triven could. A finger gently traced one of my bruises, courtesy of Archer. He bent leaning into me and stopping, as he always did, just before touching my lips.

I closed the gap, sighing into the kiss as it warmed me. Triven couldn't take the pain of today away, but his shared pain always eased mine. We weren't in this alone. When he pulled away, he took my breath with him. The kiss was brief, but spoke volumes of unspoken words. It surprised me that he was smiling as he straightened.

"Have a little more faith in our people." He kissed my forehead tenderly, pulling away when a gagging sound came from the door.

"Get a room." Archer snapped as she strode through the passage. "If you're done getting over yourself, we have plans to make."

I stared astounded as not only Archer marched into the room, but so did the rest of our recon team followed by Baxter, a weasel-faced man I recognized but didn't know his name, Cortez from the warehouse fire, and the very last one was Veyron.

My heart lurched as she entered the room. Even after seeing Arden first, after bracing myself for the damage done, tears welled at the sight of her. Like Arden, Doc's second-hand serum had healed the burns, making them look years old, not months, but the damage was still extensive. Her round face had not been disfigured as badly as Arden's, the scars not reaching her lips or eyes, but half of her beautiful hair had been burned away, taking part of her left ear with it. The scars shaved the left side of her scalp into a permanent partial Mohawk, tracing down her neck onto the little of her shoulder I could see. But instead of wearing her hair down to cover the damage, she kept it tied into a tight ponytail, forcing people to see what the fire had done. If the traitor was still with us, he or she would have to look at their handiwork every day.

I tried to find a smile, but Veyron's glare iced over as it swept past me. Not a single trace of friendship graced her expression. The message was clear. I was unforgiven and she did not want to be here. From the looks of it, Baxter wasn't too enthralled with the idea either. He took a seat on a crate nearest the door. The pressure of Cortez's hand on his arm appeared to be the only thing anchoring him.

Her own cheeks now showing signs of our quarrel, Archer hopped onto a box across from me. It creaked. Triven shifted to open the space, his thigh almost touching mine as he leaned against my crate.

"We had a little meeting without you." Archer nodded to the others. She slouched, whether actually at ease or faking it I couldn't be sure. "We all agreed that you suck at leading."

Triven cleared his throat and she smiled unapologetically.

"*But*, you were right." Archer stared down at her toes, all humor gone. "Elin's death was all of our faults."

Baxter stirred, his usual playful eyes solemn. He shared a glance with Veyron. "If we had helped you, he may not have died today."

"You don't know that." I countered.

"Shut up Phoenix, we're trying to make a point here." Archer reproached.

I forced my mouth shut, smothering a harsh retort. Triven covered the lower half of his face, undoubtedly hiding a smirk.

"None of us want to be a part of this." Otto looked to his friends seeking their approval of his words. "And we get it now that you don't wanna be either."

I bit my lip, hard. No, I didn't.

"None of us have the ability to unite the Tribes. We're all traitors." Arden's hand swept over his Taciturn tattoos as he spoke. "But you and Triven, you're neutral. It's unlikely, but you have a better chance than any of us."

"And you're obviously willing to die trying." Grenald nodded at me as if that fact made the situation better.

Cortez spoke for the first time. I had assumed before that the rasp in her tone was from the smoke, but it appeared it was just her voice. Deep and gravelly. "If The Wall is really coming down like you said, we want to fight for a change. We don't want to die here because we were too scared."

"Speak for yourself. I'm *not* scared of the Tribes. I'm pissed at them." Archer cut in, earning a group eye roll.

"What we're trying to say is that we'll get you as close to every Tribe as we can." Otto dipped his chin encouragingly.

"The rest is up to you two." Cortez added. Triven's leg brushed mine. "We won't be of any help when it actually comes to dealing with the Tribes, but we can at least try to stack the odds in your favor."

"Thank you," Triven said gravely.

"It's more likely that you're going to get yourselves killed." Veyron's voice was harsher than I remembered. Cutting even. "But this way, at least we can't blame ourselves for your deaths."

A chill followed her words.

"Okay," Archer settled herself in. "Let's figure out how to keep your stupid asses alive."

THE FIRST UNANIMOUS decision was that we couldn't stay here. Not while we were seeking out the other Tribes. We were lucky not to have been followed as we fled the Adroits. I was furious with myself for not thinking of it earlier. My months with the Subversive and then the Sanctuary had weakened my sharp mind. I had foolishly let myself become comfortable, complacent and forgot my number one rule about seeking refuge in Tartarus. Never stay in the same place.

If a Tribe had caught wind of us, we would have led them straight back here. Xavier's refuge was a fortress, but it was no underground bunker. There were too many exposed walls, too much to watch. If a Tribe wanted in, they would find a way. The assault on the Subversive proved that. Exposing ourselves to the Tribes was one thing. We would not expose our friends and families unnecessarily.

There were enough of my old safehouses scattered around the city to hide. Providing they hadn't been compromised in my absence. I was profoundly relieved I had withheld many of them from Arstid in my initial debriefings. With a traitor in the Subversive's ranks, any safe house I had told them about was compromised.

Taking on the Adroits quickly became our last priority. Both Veyron and Baxter rebuked us for the ill-advised attempt, though they looked nearly as shamed as the rest of us.

The Adroits would be on edge now. With the Ravagers hunting them and our explosive entrance, our ex-Adroits were certain the naked-headed Tribe would retreat into their factory, rendering them practically untouchable. Getting to them would now be the most difficult.

We schemed over our hand-drawn maps, the ex-Tribe members analyzing their territories while I plotted our safe houses. Together we laid routes and solidified plans. It was easy to tell that even *talking* about the Tribes bothered all of them. Arden's hands trembled as he and Otto went over the Taciturns' strengths and weaknesses. Both Veyron and Baxter grew paler by the moment when we spoke of the Adroits, and the weasel-faced man, Nos, and Cortez refused to look at each other during the

Scavenger planning. Even the formidable Grenald tensed when speaking of the Wraiths, his over-sized muscles flexing anxiously. It was solely under Otto's gentle touch that he relaxed. Only Archer showed no sign of emotion. To an outsider it might appear as a sign of strength, but I could read her now. The lack of emotion meant she was ablaze beneath the calm façade. The harder her jaw set, the more I knew she was barely holding it together. It was unbelievable how much they had all held back. How much of their pasts they had tried to bury since joining the Subversive? But I knew better than anyone, ignoring the past doesn't make it go away. It's always there haunting your every step, feeding your every decision, whether you know it or not. With each of them, however, once the carefully sealed lids had been popped, the information flowed out in crushing waves.

With the ex-Tribesmen finally opening up about their own, it became painfully clear we could not approach them all the same way. Each Tribe would have to be dealt with very differently. Each one needed different motivations and threats.

The Adroits respected intelligence and cunning. Threatening them with a bomb and then offering one as a gift could help seal their alliances. The Wraiths who behaved more like a pack, would need to be threatened as a whole. The Scavengers would be the complete opposite. They would have to be sought out independently to spread the word to as many of them as possible. Though they were a Tribe of one name, they acted as individuals and would choose to join us as such. The wild cards could be the Taciturns. They respected stealth and violence, and their most current leader wasn't known for his mental stability.

The man was a time bomb, impossible to read and equally lethal. Stories of his cruel insanity preceded him. I could feel Maddox's hand tightening around my throat as I recalled the story about his brother and how the leader now wore a vest made of his brother's hide. The Taciturns would be impossible to control and with spies placed in other Tribes, it would be even harder to take them by surprise. Baxter had suggested killing the current leader in hopes of a more amicable one taking over. I could see reason in that plan. We all could. If it came down to murdering one insane tyrant to kill another, I would pull the trigger myself.

When we finally left our room, physically and emotionally exhausted, plans were ready to be set in motion and not one of us looked pleased. The Wraiths would be first and we would move out tonight.

17. ADAPT

MOUSE WAS WAITING for us in our closet-sized room. She sat on my makeshift bed of paper and singed blankets. My father's watch twisted in her fingers.

You're leaving again. She scowled at me.

I moved to sit next to her, Triven flanked her other side.

"To keep you safe. To keep everyone here safe."

I'm coming.

Triven leaned in closer, pressing her between the two of us. "Not this time Mouse."

"We need you here." I added, knowing—like me—the little girl needed purpose. "You have more skills than the other kids. I need you to look out for them. Help them learn to defend themselves."

I don't want to defend. I want to fight! She threw her fists hard as they crossed in an X in front of her, accentuating the word fight.

Apparently, Xavier had kept his word. I knew training had started today and obviously Mouse was displeased with the type of training she was receiving. We had talked about this before while in the Sanctuary. Though not much younger than I was when abandoned in this city, Mouse seemed too little to be trained the way I had been. To have to fight the way I had. I didn't want my life for her. I had let her watch us train the Rebels, but a line had to be drawn there. I didn't want her engaging.

I tried to hug her to me. "Mouse, I'm tired of arguing about this."

For the first time, she pushed me away. *So stop arguing.*

My exasperated sigh was echoed on Mouse's other side. Triven composed himself better than I did. "Mouse, there won't be a need for you to fight."

You're fighting.

"We're older than you."

You were my age when you started.

A sour taste puckered my lips. I knew she would throw that stone. "*I* didn't have a choice."

I do! My choice. I love you both, but you're wrong. I should learn.

"Mouse…" Conviction was slipping from Triven's voice.

"No." I said more firmly this time.

Then I go with you.

"Definitely not."

"No."

We spoke over each other in agreement.

Tears were blooming in her deep eyes. Though her lip quivered, Mouse didn't let a single one fall. She jumped up, turning to face us. She had grown so much, her brown head now significantly taller than ours as we sat below her.

I have to learn.

"Why?" I pressed her. A part of me feared it was because she wanted to be like me.

Her next sign sent a chill down my spine.

Brother.

Gage.

A snarl ripped up my chest. Yes, Gage was a reason she would want to learn how to fight. How to defend herself and possibly kill others. Kill him. Her brother was a psychotic sadist. Both of us had fallen prey to his tactics, both had barely lived to tell about it.

Fear, anger and determination flitted across Mouse's face. How could I tell her no when I was seeking revenge on my own family? When she had seen first-hand the skills I was refusing to teach her. She deserved to feel in control, to not be afraid of her brother. If training granted her that peace of mind, then who was I to tell her no.

Next to me, Triven's face held resolute. Though my stories of Gage painted a horrific picture, he had not met the boy. Had not personally seen the cruelty that burned in the young man's eyes.

I reached to Mouse's hand, pulling her toward me. She let me. Her knees folded delicately beneath her, putting us on the same level.

"He will never touch you again. He will never come *close* to you again."

Her jaw strained, pink lips smashing together as she braced herself for my rejection.

"But I understand."

Mouse's wide eyes popped with disbelief.

"You've got a right to protect yourself, to *know* that you can protect yourself."

Really? Mouse's hands trembled with anticipation.

"Really." I smiled at her gently. I could feel Triven's disagreement, but he didn't contradict me. Not in front of her.

The little girl threw herself at me hugging hard. I could sense her relief in the hug, that she needed this.

Thank you. She sat back on her heels. Her round face carried the weight of someone much older. It hurt to see it there.

She glanced at our bags, still half-packed in the corner. *How long?*

Triven tucked a stray hair behind her ear. "Ten days."

We had planned two days for each Tribe. One day of recon and one day to infiltrate. If everything went well, the last day would end with Triven and I in a room with four of Tartarus's Tribe leaders. The thought alone gave me palpitations. Then one final day of peace before The Wall came down. One day before everything changed forever.

The words *suicide mission* kept whispering in my ears. I smiled through the dark thoughts clouding my mind. Mouse needed to see hope on my face, so I gave it to her. It wasn't a lie if I didn't say anything, right?

Mouse was not so easily convinced.

Be careful. She pressed a small palm to both of our cheeks. I placed mine over hers, holding it in place. "I don't want you to train like I did. Do you understand me? You are not a Sanctuary cadet. You will *never* train like that."

Mouse nodded, her throat bobbing. Like me, she knew too well what it meant to train like a Sanctuary cadet. We all did.

You can do this.

"We're going to try."

ELIN'S BLOOD STILL flecked my jacket. I should have washed it off, but it was a morbid reminder of my mistakes. Our mistakes. Mistakes I didn't want to make again. Ten of us left The Master's seeking out the Tribes. I was going to come home with ten. With or without the Tribes behind us, I would at least do my best to bring them home. I owed them that much.

Archer ghosted to my side. Her hand kept rubbing what was left of her arm. A nervous tic that had started since she had agreed to help us.

"You're sure you want to do this?" She stared at the marble building across from us. Once upon a time it would have been beautiful, gleaming in the sunlight, a monument of the city. Now, it was a dilapidated skeleton like all the other buildings in Tartarus.

I had seen this building a hundred times over the years, knew this was the Wraiths' territory, but would have never guessed this structure was their base. I had never seen anyone enter or exit. Archer told us there were tunnels underneath, allowing the Wraiths to move unseen. And unseen they were. They were truly ghosts.

I couldn't answer Archer's question. Besides, she already knew the answer. I didn't want to do this. Neither of us wanted to be here. *None* of us did.

We had spent the entire last day canvassing the area, watching for movement. There was none to be found. But both Archer and Grenald were positive the Wraiths were there. Maybe they sensed them in a way the rest of us could not. Tethers from their pasts.

I stared at the tarnished dome capping the building.

"You're sure the oculus is still unwatched?" I had asked this question a hundred times in the last twenty-four hours and the answer was still not what I wanted.

"Two years can change a lot of things." Grenald seemed to shrink in the shadow of the building. Neither had set foot in Wraith territory for nearly five years combined. Things could and probably did change in that time, but we were hopeful they hadn't.

"They don't have any reason to think it's been compromised. As far as they know, the only ones who could talk are dead. That *we're* dead." Archer's hand reached back, feeling for her rifle. She tapped the muzzle, caressing her truest friend.

"An hour?" Otto stood close to Grenald, though he never reached out to touch him. His presence alone seemed to comfort the giant. A little.

We were all on edge. And with good cause.

Triven's hands gripped a little too tightly on the rope slung across his chest. My own hands automatically checked my weapons again. Three knives, two guns, an extra clip and one small but significant pack. It was the pack that bore the most weight. Both physically and mentally. Strapped securely to my back were three packets of Sanctuary food, a medical kit and a bomb that could take down the entire building along with everyone in it. I hoped we wouldn't have to use it.

"What if she's not alone?" Archer's breath was shaky.

"She will be." Grenald reassured her, again.

"But what if—"

I cut her off. "It doesn't matter. Something is bound to go wrong in there. We'll figure it out. Adjust." I paused. "The only thing that doesn't change—"

"If you're not back in an hour we move on without you." Archer pulled her rifle free now, clutching it to her chest.

"We're holding you to that." Triven swept the entire group, making sure they all understood. There would be no rescue mission.

Their silence sealed the contract. There were three faint pops six blocks down and a black smoke began to rise, filling the streets. It was our signal from Nos and Veyron. Baxter, Cortez and Arden were ready for us. It was time. The group moved to take their places. The minutes were ticking down. Starting now.

I stopped and turned to block Archer. "If we don't... *Promise* me that you will *move on*. That you will try, with the others?"

She hesitated, chewing on her cheek.

"Archer," I growled quietly, "I *need* to know someone will carry this out if we fail. Someone *has* to be there when The Wall comes down. Someone has to fight."

"Fine," she snarled. But as I pivoted on my heels to follow the others, she snatched my arm. Her fingers would leave marks. "I'll do it if I *have* to. Don't make me *have* to."

My eyes moved from Archer's grip on my arm back to her face. "Be careful out here too."

We didn't say the obvious. What we both were thinking.

Don't die.

She let me go then, as I pulled away. Without a second glance, Archer dropped to her knees setting up her vigil. Her fingers danced over the sights on her gun. Eyes checking the scope, then the streets. At least with her at watch, we were untouchable out here. For now.

Triven, Grenald and Otto were waiting for me on the roof ledge. The gap between our roof and the Wraiths' was nearly half a street. It seemed to yawn in the darkness, opening wider. The distance could not be jumped, but fortunately we had other means of crossing. Grenald slumped to one knee, balancing the air gun on his shoulder. Otto stood over him, a hand pressed to Grenald's other shoulder as his eyes focused on the western sky. There was spark of light in the distance. Baxter's signal. Otto's hand squeezed in response and Grenald didn't hesitate. With a quick pull of the trigger, an anchored projectile shot from his gun. A dark line tethered out behind it, whistling as it cut the night air. The spiked end hit the Wraiths' rooftop, but any sound of clatter was swallowed by a thunderous explosion emanating from signal Baxter had detonated.

Baxter, Nos and Veyron had done well. More plumes of black smoke began billowing through the streets mixing with the dust bombs already swirling there. The ex-Adroits had assured us the smoke would coat nearly half the city so there would be no red flags indicating the Wraiths were the intended target. Grenald and Otto worked quickly, yanking the line tight and tethering it. The moment Otto's head jerked, I was climbing on the cord. Interlocking my boots over the rope, I let my body swing down. My hands moved rhythmically, pulling one over the other. The line shook as Triven followed. Mercifully, there was no moon in the sky tonight. The black smoke undulated below us, its fingers reaching up to swallow us too. We were shadows sliding out into the night.

Grenald's shot had been perfect. The anchor had caught between two pillars of twisted metal, giving me enough room to set a steady foot on the building's edge before letting go. Triven's feet reached just after mine. We grabbed each other's forearms, bracing ourselves for the next part. The building's roof rose in stained arcing panels that stretched skyward. The dome's incline was not severe, but the metal surface was slick with years of acid washed rains. My first step was a jarring reminder.

Even with our boots—gifts from the Sanctuary— my foot slid back two inches. It wasn't enough to throw me off balance, but it was enough to send my heart racing. Triven's hand pressed against the small of my back reassuringly.

"Stay low." I whispered.

Thighs burning, backs hunched, we scrambled side by side to the top. Twice one of us lunged for the other, catching each other when our feet failed. Our boots cushioned our careful steps, the soles clinging precariously to the surface. Without them, we would have never made it this far. Only the soft swish of our suits spoke of our presence. I had beaten my suit, washed so many times it should have fallen apart, but it still smelled of ash to me. Of smothering flames and the dead. I hated pulling it on again, letting it cling to my skin, but it was another safety line. With hundreds of odds against us, this was one advantage in our favor. They were bullet-proof at long distances, fire repellant and helped control body heat. *But could they work against bombs too?*

The oculus was dead center at the peak of the dome, just as Archer and Grenald said it would be. We slowed, staying low as we approached the circular opening. No light filtered out, but as we got closer light could be seen flickering below. No glass covered the hole as we peered cautiously inside.

My stomach clenched.

The sheer height of the room was terrifying. I now understood why they didn't watch this point more carefully. Aside from being near impossible to reach, no one could survive a fall from this high up. And that was the only way down. The room below us was a cavern of ornate walls, sloping floors and lines of tattered chairs. Flecks of gold flaked off the surfaces along with peeling colors still rich in pigment. Many of the seats had been ripped from the floor, left overturned or broken to form over-sized beds of torn velvet and animal pelts. Tattered curtains hung on one side of the room, where the ground was elevated above the rest.

At the center of the raised platform was a throne made of what looked like bones and fur. A girl, maybe Mouse's age, lounged in the gruesome seat. Her leg was draped over the side of the chair and cradled in her lap was... No. I squinted, it was! She was holding a book. Not just holding it, but it appeared she was *reading* it. The sight was astonishing.

Still, it wasn't the unexpected grandeur of the building or the child that had shocked me.

At a quick glance, I estimated nearly three hundred people below us. That was almost double what Archer and Grenald had estimated.

There was a slow exhale next to me. Triven was doing the math as well. I placed a hand over his arm, meeting his shocked gaze. This didn't change anything. The plan was still the same. I pushed my back to him, feeling the gentle tug as he took what he needed from inside. When the pack cinched closed, I twisted on my knees to face him again. I steady myself to stand, but instead found my face caught in his warm hands. Before I could pull away, Triven's lips were on mine, hungry and frightened. Instead of stopping him, I pressed myself hard into his kisses. Neither of us was gentle and we reluctantly broke apart. His thumb brushed my lips as my fingers memorized his face. Every goodbye in Tartarus could be the last. Especially now.

Our hands slipped down each other's arms catching at the fingertips for one final squeeze. Then we set to work. Triven's hands flew in controlled, well-practiced movements. My attention stayed on those below, gun drawn. One sign of an up-turned face and our mission would end here. But no one looked up.

Triven pressed my shoulder when he was done and we were moving again. Careful to keep out heels down, we tilted back sliding down the dome in the opposite direction we had come from. The heat from the friction never penetrated our suits. The building's ledge loomed at the edge of the dome and we pressed our feet down harder. Panic flared for two heartbeats as we continued to slide before finally slowing.

We moved as quickly as we dared, tracing the edge of the dome. My mind ticked the panels as we passed them. On panel fifteen I found what Archer had promised us. Her own private escape.

A trapdoor.

It was small and the fit would be tight for Triven, but it was there. My fingers rubbed against the plate holding my hair back. The grease I had smeared there coated my fingertips and then I slathered it on the rusted hinges.

Waiting until Triven had his gun pulled and aimed at the door, I grabbed the handle and paused, unsure of what was waiting on the other side. Archer swore she was the only one to know about it, but things change. She might not be the only one anymore. Every nerve in my body spiked with adrenaline. This was it. Our last chance to back out. We could walk away right now and no one would blame us. We could survive the night. I could go home and see Mouse. This was the last chance I would get to walk away from this war.

With a deep breath, I pulled the hatch.

18. GHOSTS

DESPITE MY GENTLE coaxing and the oil, the hinges still protested from disuse. Every muscle went rigid. Waiting. Listening. Not a single noise followed. Either no one had heard us or they were waiting patiently for us to enter.

Triven's feet moved and mine snapped back to life in response. The space beyond was absolutely black, giving the illusion of an endless abyss. I thought of the height from oculus.

Archer promised, I reminded myself.

Threading my legs through the opening, I rolled onto my belly. The rusted edges scraped against the Sanctuary suit, but didn't pierce it. I clung frantically with my fingertips as my feet slid down the wall. Pulses of blood thrummed in my hands, my ears, matching the spiking rate of my heart. My body was nearly at full extension and still my toes found nothing. The metal bit into the pads of my fingers, then I let go. Swallowing a scream, I dropped into the shadows.

Air rushed from my lungs as my feet collided with a solid surface. I braced my head against the cold wall before quickly shuffling sideways. I felt along the wall, groping for anything tangible. A body landed with a quiet thump next to me and Triven's arms were immediately reaching for me. The tremor emanating from him steadied as our hands connected.

I counted our steps as Archer had instructed. On the sixth step, I raised my hand, finding the iron beam it was looking for. Pulling Triven level with me, I raised our joined hands until his too grabbed onto the cold support. I tapped the back of his hand three times.

On the count of three.

He pressed back hard once, then began the countdown in measured taps. On three we pulled ourselves up onto the beam. We perched for two beats. The darkness eased here. I could see shadows, trace the lines of the beams. I could now also hear voices carrying up to us.

Triven tapped my hand and pointed toward the right. A sliver of light slashed the darkness. Slowly, methodically, we maneuvered through the open beams. As we approached, the sliver of light fluttered. A thick curtain gently swayed, stirred possibly by a Wraith passing just on the other side. Seconds stretched on as we sat uncomfortably wedged amid the metal supports. People were talking, laughing and fighting somewhere below us. The sounds echoed off the arched ceiling, amplifying every noise. But there was nothing near us. At least nothing moving.

My knife slid from its sheath followed by one of its brothers. Guns allowed you to kill from a safer distance, but attracted unnecessary attention. Triven pulled his own. His eyes glinted in the seam of light. Buried in them was the encouragement I needed. Careful to move the fabric as little as possible, we slithered from our hiding place. Our toes found the rail on the other side of the curtain with ease. Archer's and Grenald's instructions were good. We were not in the body of the building, but suspended above it. An elevated platform hung above the stage I had seen from above. The light up here was just enough to see by, yet allowed us a place to hide. Grenald had said these suspended bridges were rarely used.

But tonight, he was wrong.

I felt the approaching steps before I heard them. The tiny vibrations reverberated under my boots. They were coming from our right. My head swiveled and I saw her. Wandering up the labyrinth of catwalks was the girl I had seen sitting on the throne. She was on a level lower than ours and the child's chin was tucked down watching the room below as she moved.

She hadn't seen us.

My heart clenched. She was only a child, but she was alone…

The perfect prey.

GO! I signed at Triven, pointing back to a shadowed corner. He moved without hesitation. As he melded into the darkness, I launched myself back over the rails and into Archer's curtained hideout.

The curtain fell still just as the child's steps rounded the corner. My hands were shaking. The uncharacteristic tremor was amplified in the tips of my knives. I quickly shoved them back into their sheaths, nearly nicking my thigh. Why did it have to be a child? Why couldn't it have been a warrior—*Stop it,* I chided myself. The beam of light blotted out as she passed and I forced my body to move.

The curtain whispered as I slid out. My feet hit the rails with flawless precision, toes touching just long enough for my hands to find purchase. With a lithe leap, I vaulted onto the platform landing an arm's length behind the Wraith child. Dark twists of hair whirled as the girl whipped around to face me.

She had startling green eyes that popped wide before narrowing to slits. Surprisingly, she did not cry out. Instead, she snarled. Her hand dug into the folds of her fur-laden smock, procuring a sharpened bone fragment. Before she could lunge, the shadow behind her came to life.

In a sweeping movement, Triven snatched the homemade weapon from her hand and slid his own knife under the girl's exposed throat.

"Cry out and we will kill you." Triven's tone was sure and lethal. The child stilled immediately in his arms. Repulsion tighten my throat at his threat, but I was thankful the girl could not see Triven's face. Strain pressed his brow. He hated saying the words as much I hated hearing them. At least he was the one to hold the knife, to make the threat I could not.

The girl was taller than Mouse. Her head thrashed against the middle of Triven's chest as I pulled the patch Doc had given us from my pocket and pressed it over her mouth and nose. Slowly the girl's body began to relax. Her eyelids drooped. I pulled the cloth away before she went completely unconscious. We needed a semi-coherent hostage, not one that looked dead.

Refusing to meet her gaze, I tried to ignore the constellation of freckles that painted her nose as I whipped a fabric gag into her mouth. With Triven's blade pressed firmly to her neck and Doc's suppressant coursing in her veins, I doubted she would scream, but it was not a chance I was willing to take. I then made quick work of binding her hands at her waist. The heat of her drugged glare burned as my fingers searched the folds of her dress, producing three more shivs. Her legs wobbled and the bones around the girl's neck rattled together. My hands forgot their work as I stared at her neck.

She had already taken a life.

Bones were not accessories freely given in this Tribe. They were *earned*. The child smiled behind the gag. Killer and proud.

Pulling away, I visually swept the ground below us. Not a soul turned in our direction. Though my heart was pounding, the entire disturbance had gone unnoticed. We were safe, for now.

Let's move. I let my fingers speak to hide the tremor lingering in my voice.

Keeping his knife near the child's chest, Triven lifted the girl with his other arm, pinning her to his torso. The child dangled there like a rag doll, head rolling, but her eyes scorched with rage.

Avoiding the flaming torches lighting the platforms periodically, we moved along the rails, darting in and out of the shadows. The catwalks offered us the perfect vantage point. They wove a spider web of tracks through the air, weaving around solid curtains and metal supports. From our perch I could see nearly every Wraith as they moved below us. Three times the whites of a Tribesman's eye flickered our way, and three times we dove to the ground. Each time, Triven pinned the girl beneath him, pulling the knife tight in warning. She did not betray us.

Cheek pressed to the black surface, I squinted.

"There." Two platforms over was a dead-end. The suspended track broke off midair, one of the railings dangling precariously from its side. A dark curtain hung near the end. Everything about the broken gangplank screamed deathtrap and was exactly what we had been looking for.

The girl's eyes widened as we made our way to the broken plank. It was possible this was where she was headed. There was no mistaking our trajectory now and she knew the Wraiths had a traitor. Not even Archer had known about this secreted entrance, but Grenald had. As one of the Tribe's once most trusted warriors, the giant had been privy to it. Archer's knowledge got us in the building. Grenald's would give us the element of surprise.

Taking the first step, every muscle tensed as the broken platform swayed. My eyes darted to the Wraiths far below us. The heavily draped room cast us into darkness, hiding the shifting platform from any wandering eyes on the ground. Still all it took was one Wraith and we were dead. Despite our careful movements, each step shifted the suspended walkway. Without question, subduing the child in Triven's arms had been the right move. One thrash from her and the rocking platform would alert the Wraiths of our presence. Luckily, she was small. Our original plan had not been to seek out a child, but I had to admit her size made the kidnapping easier to manage. Triven would not have fared so well shouldering a full-grown man.

My toes reached the splintering edge. Legs bent to absorb Triven's movements, I reached for the black curtain. As my fingers swept the stiff fabric, I glanced back. Triven's gaze had steeled.

There was no going back.

19. THREATS

THE HIDDEN PASSAGE was little more than a hole torn in a brick wall. But beyond the opening was a tiny room. Trying not to rock the platform I navigated the gap into the room beyond. It was the size of a small closet. The space was almost entirely encased in brick. The only variance was a rectangular patch covering the back wall. Faint light seeped through the fibrous material hinting at a room beyond.

As soon as I stepped onto the solid surface, Triven passed the girl to me. My back pressed against the brick as I made room for him. The darkened space was barely big enough for the three of us. The girl shifted as I moved, her head lolling back in my arms. She cast a spiking glare I refused to meet. As soon as Triven was on steady ground, I pressed her back into his arms. We forced the child to stand between us, Triven supporting most of her weight. As the knife returned to her throat, I turned away.

She was not my concern.

She *couldn't* be.

One deep breath. *Move.*

Pressing the tip of my knife to the dense material, I twisted my wrist. The taut material ground beneath the blade. Fibers frayed. A stream of light cut the darkness. The hole, no bigger than the tip of my knife, was small but enough. I would risk a lot of things tonight, but going into a room blind wasn't one of them.

The room on the other side was small, but lavish by Tartarus standards. Peeling red painted walls were covered with Old World paintings of long dead people in outrageous garb and the floor was almost entirely covered with fur. Bones of varying sizes and shapes hung in random groupings. Trophies. There was no ceiling in this room just as Archer and Grenald had promised. The shadowed curves of the dome were barely visible from my peephole.

Perfect.

Burning torches flickered in every corner, casting dancing shadows around the crowded room. Cracked mirrors lined the only wall space not covered by the decaying gilded art frames. It was there I could see our target. Reflected in the mirrors was a woman with ebony skin perched on a chair nearly as impressive as the one downstairs. The woman's midnight hair was braided in thick rows, each line ornamented with a trinket. The bones, feathers and bracken made a sort of crown. At her feet slept a four-legged beast, its steady breathing the only thing setting it apart from the other piles of fur. It sniffed in its sleep as though catching our scent. The woman shifted, her long limbs hinting to her stature. The metal in her hand winked as she dragged a stone over its edge methodically, sharpening the blade.

I saw it in the shape of her eyes, the twist of her mouth.

This was Archer's mother.

This was the leader of the Wraiths.

The material flexed slightly beneath my fingers as I pressed a hand to it. I flashed a signal over my shoulder.

Wait five seconds.

Triven stopped breathing in response and I exploded to life. The rectangular frame swung violently outward on its hinges, but made no sound. I burst through the opening, knives at the ready. My feet landed silently on the pelt-covered floor, but both guard dog and master reacted. The mutt's head snapped in my direction, a feral snarl ripping out its throat. The woman moved too. In a flash, I dropped in a low crouch. The blade of her knife skimmed the top of my head, clattering off the brick wall. I barely heard it hit the floor.

The Wraith leader rose, reaching for other unseen weapons. The dog clamored to its feet, taking stalking steps toward me. Every hair on the back of its spine was raised. Mine did the same.

"I wouldn't do that if I were you." I kept my voice low, eyes quickly assessing which of the two was the greater threat. Woman or beast? Wrist snapping out, one knife imbedded itself in the dog's path. Its snarl grew, but it stopped advancing. For now.

When the woman's eyes snapped from the knife back to me, my empty hand had already been filled with a handgun. Its barrel focused between her eyes.

For an instant, she looked ready to call out, to order her dog to attack, but then her eyes shifted. Triven had stepped out of the opening behind me.

The child stood precariously in his arms. Her eyes were alert over the gag. The leader shifted, then surprisingly sat back down on the empty throne. She faked her ease nearly as well I did. But the pulse hammering at the side of her neck gave away the pretense. The temptation to glance back at the little girl was overwhelming. But I pushed it way. Who was this child we had grabbed?

"They'll come running if you shoot."

The woman's voice was a surprise. Smooth tones, not matching the exterior at all. My voice sounded gruff in comparison.

"They'll never make it before I put a bullet in your head." I tilted my chin toward Triven and the girl. "Or hers. Maybe your successor will be willing to hear us out."

The woman smiled wickedly, as she held out a hand to the animal. The dog settled obediently back on its haunches, teeth still bared but subdued. Its yellow eyes never left my face. Neither did its master's. She shifted, sitting up taller and the bones around her neck rattled. There must have been nearly a hundred of them. My throat constricted. Which ones were Archer's? Watching me, her hand stroked affectionately over the trophies from her victims. Her other hand opened to me inviting me to continue.

"We came to make you an offer, Teya."

To her credit, she didn't flinch at my use of her given name. Instead she smirked.

"You break into *my* home, threaten *my* blood, and yet you dare say this is an offer?"

She was buying time. Teya's assessment of Triven and I had not gone unnoticed. Underneath the calm façade, I could see her puzzlement, the worry pulling at her lips. We bore no sign of another Tribe. No markings. If we disappeared tonight, she wouldn't know where to seek revenge. It was my turn to smile.

"Would you have listened otherwise?"

Her silence was answer enough.

"If we had wanted you dead, we would not be having this conversation." The dog snarled again. I did my best to ignore it. "But here we are."

"Here we are." Teya's voice was flat as she stole another glance at our hostage. I could see her weighing the options. Was this child's life worth sacrificing to take ours? I already knew her thoughts on child sacrifice, Archer was testimony to that.

"She'll be the first, but not the last..." The tip of my knife pointed to the ceiling. As Teya's head tilted back, I heard Triven press the trigger hidden in his palm. Teya's eyes darted to something hanging high above us and then narrowed. Without looking I knew what she was seeing. Suspended in the eye of the oculus was a white sphere. The light that had once been inactive was now blinking red at Triven's command.

"If detonated, it will level this entire block." Triven spoke for the first time. His voice was strained but steady.

"Adroits," Teya snarled, lurching to the edge of her seat.

"Sanctuary grade," I quickly corrected. Her eyes popped, but she said nothing, so I continued. Now or never. "But like the *other* Tribes, the Adroits have already accepted our offer." I paused, letting my lie sink in. No Tribe liked having the lesser hand. "We're bringing down The Wall and we want you to join us in overthrowing the Sanctuary."

"You lie." Teya no longer looked amused.

Moving slowly, I momentarily holstered my knife, pulled a food pouch from my bag and threw it at her. Regardless of whether or not she could read, it was clear the silver package was not from Tartarus. She turned the pouch over with long fingers. Contemplating more than the contents.

"And what do we get out of it?"

"Revenge. Food. Weapons. Take your pick."

She picked at the chair's arm. "And I'm supposed to trust you, that the other Tribes are willing to join?"

"No, you're not. In six days, there will be a gathering of the Tribal leaders. Show up and make your own choice. Don't show and deal with the consequences."

"Are you *threatening* me girl?" Teya eyes tightened.

"I'm warning, *not* threatening. If I were threatening you, you'd know." I smiled crookedly back at her. "I'm telling you what's coming and offering your people a chance to fight for yourselves. For a freedom none of us have ever known."

Teya's eyes sharpened with hunger. The beast growled low as she placed a hand on its mangy head. "And what do *you* get out of it?"

This was the question she had been mulling over. There was never a trade in Tartarus where both sides did not profit.

"A better future for my sister." I didn't hesitate on the word when thinking of Mouse. She *was* my sister and my child. My lifeline.

"*And?*" Teya's eyebrows rose.

"*And*, I get to kill the ruler inside their Wall."

"So, power." The Wraith eyed me suspiciously.

"I only want to destroy one man's hold on it, *not* to gain it for myself." The words rolled out easily as they were the truth. I wanted Fandrin's head on a platter as the rest of his corrupt empire went up in flames, but as for ruling after his death? Ruling was for more civilized people. *I* was not civilized.

Teya's head cocked with a twitch to the side, making her look more wild animal than human. Her eyes were keen as a hawk's. "You want the Tribes to unite?"

I nodded.

"Yet you clearly do not belong." She once again searched us for markings. There were none to be found.

My head shook slowly. "I've *never* been a Tribesman and I never will be."

The conversation was quickly coming to a close. I could see her patience was waning. Barely resisting the urge to step back toward the door, I tightened the grip on my weapons. Then understanding lit her dark eyes.

"You're the *ghost.*"

"Excuse me?" Her choice of words cut. That was what I had always thought of the Wraiths as—ghosts. I was nothing like them.

"You're the one we call the ghost. You haunt the rooftops. Rumored sightings, but no one has crossed paths with you and lived to tell about it."

My teeth ground together. Apparently, I had not gone as unnoticed as I had thought over the years. Neither had those I had killed in self-defense.

"I sought you once. Possibly to recruit. Or kill you. Pity, you're a hard one to find." Her teeth were stark against her dark skin.

"Well, here I am."

"Here you are." The hungry look filled Teya's eyes again. Her voice was alluring, reminding me of a Greek book I once read. A siren, that's what she was.

I thought of Archer's mutilated arm. Sweet talker but a monster, through and through.

"Six nights. When the moon is at its highest. The building will be marked with white smoke." I took a step back, feeling Triven move with me, the girl still clutched in his arms.

Teya launched herself upright. The beast echoed its master, a snarl ripping from its throat. Every muscle in her body tightened as her piercing gaze darted from me to Triven, then to the girl.

Triven pulled the girl closer, whether to emphasize his threat or purely on instinct to protect the child from this warrior woman, I couldn't be sure. Teya saw it as the former. Like the feral dog, her lips pulled back into a snarl. A subdued moan rattled out from behind the girl's gag.

Doc's paralysis was wearing off.

Taking a large sidestep, I slid between Triven and the Wraith leader, forcing her to stare at me, and only me. Taking another small step backward, I then forced Triven back into the covered portal.

Teya and her hound moved with us.

"Don't." I warned. "Follow and she's dead."

"Now *that* sounds like a threat." Teya spit.

"It is."

"Careful ghost girl."

I stepped back again, but she did not follow this time. Under layers of rage there was a hint of fear in her eyes.

"You have six days." I reminded her.

Her claw-like fists shook with anger, but the woman did not cry out and her feet remained steadfast.

"You threaten my flesh and blood to force my hand?"

Genuine shock broke my composure, if only for an instant. Archer had a sister. Dropping my voice so only she could hear, I hissed back, eyes narrowing. "It was *your* hand that shed your flesh and blood first, Teya. Not mine."

Confusion momentarily defused her rage. I didn't wait to see if understanding would eclipse it.

"Follow and they all die." I tipped the point of my knife to the oculus again. Though I doubt she had forgotten that threat. There was more than the loss of a child holding her in place. "Six days. Don't come, and hers will be the first of many lives you lose. Come and your people can fight for trophies of their own."

With a careful step back, I crossed the threshold into the hidden room.

"I am a Tribal *leader*—"

"You are a prisoner wearing a crown of bones. You *are not* free."

With a sweep of my arm I yanked the makeshift door closed and wedged the hilt of my knife between the frame and the brick, jamming it shut. If Teya wanted to follow us, she would have to cut through the barrier.

Triven was already back on the platform, hand held out to help me cross the gap. The child hung over his shoulder like a limp jacket. Her fingertips were twitching again. Dully fingering her wrists' bindings.

Doc's paralysis was *definitely* wearing off, fast. We had to move. Now. Teya may not follow us immediately, but if the girl regained control, she would alert every Wraith in the building to our presence.

"Leave her." I whispered in Triven's ear.

He didn't hesitate. Swinging the girl off his shoulder, he propped her up into a sitting position on the planks. The plan was to take her, to use our random victim as bait to lure Teya to the Tribal gathering.

I was changing the plans.

Triven skillfully tied her to the rail to prevent her from rolling off and I placed the second bag of food rations in her lap.

The child's eyes burned as her lips fumbled around the gag. Her throat jerked and for an instant I thought she would choke. With a gentle finger, I pulled the gag from the girl's mouth.

A lazy pink tongue poked around her lips. The words were barely louder than a whisper. Disjointed and slurred. But I heard them. The message was clear.

"Run." A lazy smile, "She's going to kill you."

We smothered the girl's growing smile with the gag again and we took her advice.

A cry broke out from the floor below, but we didn't look to see what had caused it. Teya let us walk out of her room alive, but bomb or no bomb, we hadn't escaped. She would be coming after us. This was merely a head start.

A dog howled. The mongrel's outrage triggered its brethren to join in the haunting chorus. A crash came from Teya's room, followed closely by a louder one. Either the warrior leader was breaking through the passage or her rage had gotten the better of her.

I was not going to wait around to find out. Grabbing Triven's arm, we bolted. We barely cleared three platforms, before ours were no longer the only feet running.

The metal stairs clanged with pounding steps but no battle cry rose from the floor below.

Was it possible that they weren't hunting us?

Unlikely.

Two more turns and we would be back at Archer's hideaway. Adrenalin hummed in my veins. The curtain—*our* curtain—fluttered farther down the catwalk.

One turn.

Twenty more steps.

A scream barely trapped behind my clenched teeth as an arm hooked around my waist and yanked me sideways off the platform.

20. VERMIN

PAIN SHOT THROUGH my shoulder as it slammed into the wall. Then the ground plummeted. I didn't have time to scramble for traction before my feet landed again on a metal surface. Triven's hand clamped down hard over my mouth, smothering a curse. His arms pulled tight, pressing me closer into his body and further into the shadows.

I knew better than to fight against his restraints.

He had yanked us from the platforms at the perfect moment. Where the rails had stopped and a huge support beam protruded. The massive support was hollow in the center like an iron "U" and it was here that he had pulled us down. A cross beam, barely wider than our feet, had caught our fall, rendering our noses almost level with the platform we had just vacated.

I counted the seconds as Triven's heart pounded against my back.

At seventeen, we both stopped moving. Stopped breathing.

Rattling filled the air. Bones.

Four sets of leather-bound feet clambered past. They were not running full tilt but their movements were clipped with haste—with a purpose. At that pace, they would find the little girl in under a minute and we would be utterly screwed. Fearing for her peoples' lives, Teya had not pursued us, but her warriors didn't know about the bomb and wouldn't hesitate to take our hands along with our lives.

The last sole had barely passed our hiding place and we were moving again. We hoisted ourselves back onto the plank, trying not to move it. As I slid back onto the hanging dais, I snuck a glance at the retreating group. Four men and three women moved like cats across the darkened platforms. Like Teya they had long limbs and lean muscles. And like Grenald, they bore the facial scarring of warriors. This was the Wraiths' most deadly hunting party.

Staying in a crouch, we backed away as quickly as we dared, not yet bold enough to take our eyes from the Wraiths. Nine now shared the raised space with us and hundreds were lying in wait below.

It wasn't until Triven's fingers squeezed my shoulder that I turned away from them. We were back at Archer's curtains. Urgency and fear hastened our movements as we slipped back into the darkness of the exposed beams. Then, as my hands tried to settle the fluttering curtain, the Wraiths' battle cry rang out.

What started as one voice quickly became hundreds. Cold sweat coated my skin as we flung ourselves—half-blinded by the total blackness—through the maze of iron supports.

Twice my feet slipped and once the stinging bite of metal slashed my palm, but we never stopped. Not when

Triven was pushing me towards the hatch, or when I was pulling him up. Not when we were back outside on the dome's smooth surface, or even when we hastily retrieved the deactivated bomb. My arms shook as we crossed the wire back to a distraught and waiting Otto and Grenald. The second our feet were on solid ground and the wire was cut, we were running again. None of us stopped, not until the Wraiths' cries could no longer be heard and my old safe house was miles behind us.

As my lungs burned and muscles pleaded with me to stop, I could only think one thing.

One Tribe down.

Three more to go.

ARCHER'S VOICE ECHOED off the walls of my hotel safe house. It was not one of the ravaged rooms with rotting beds and broken windows, but a storage room with a chute that dropped ten stories down to the basement. What had once felt like large space to me, was now cramped with bodies. We had berated by her at least thirty times in the past hour.

"I still can't believe you left the hostage."

Archer had refused to say child, girl, or Wraith. It was always *hostage*. I think it made it easier for her to disconnect. Which should have been easy for her since *she* hadn't been there. Despite her carping, I still stood by my decision and so did Triven.

"She would have slowed us down." I retorted, again. "We barely made it out as it was."

"She was our *leverage.*" Archer shook an open palm at the ceiling.

"She was a liability." I countered.

"They will never show up to your little meeting now. They have no reason to." Archer's words had bite, but her body slumped. She was finally giving up.

"They might not have anyway." Triven added and several other heads agreed.

"Well, they're definitely not going to now." Archer pulled a silver pouch from her bag, ripping the top open a little too aggressively and spilling something green onto her pants. She swiped at it, effectively rubbing more into the fabric.

"Look, it's done. We made a split-second decision. The girl stayed." What I didn't say, was that a part of me was under the impression Teya was more likely to come since we had let her child go. My actions made me an enigma in her eyes. And people had a hard time staying away from things that puzzled them. But how do you tell a child whose mother who tried had to kill her, had just let us go to save her *other* child.

"Whatever." Archer muttered, focusing all her energy on attacking the pouch balanced between her knees.

I poked at mine. Food was never easy to stomach after a night like tonight. Or with the nights to come looming over us.

Grenald had said nothing since our exodus. The giant was impossible to read, seemingly disappointed in our choice and yet relieved. The remaining six—though they said nothing—seemed relieved as well. Whether morally or because it was one less body to move and keep hidden, who knew?

The room was filled with crinkling and chewing. Despite her squawking, both Archer and Grenald too had visibly relaxed. Their part was done. The rest of us were not as lucky.

Nos finally broke the silence talking around a mouthful of food. "There's a huddle nearby. One-a the bigger ones."

I hadn't heard the term *huddle* until this mission started. Unlike most of the other Tribes, the Scavengers tended not to gather in one place as a whole, but in smaller groupings they apparently called huddles. The Tribe was still united as one, but since they turned on each other just as frequently as they did others, smaller factions had developed for protection. In a perverse way, they were almost like families. That is, families that procreated and were willing to kill each other.

The biggest problem this created for us, was that there was no true leader. No single person for us to convince. Since the Scavengers gathered within a sprawling ten-block radius, we could only hope to find a few of the larger huddles and hope they would spread the word.

Nos was from one of these larger huddles, but Cortez had been tight-lipped about hers.

I couldn't blame her.

Even with their instructions, we were better off hoping to ambush a Scavenger huddle rather than plan an infiltration as we did with the Wraiths.

Our team seemed more relieved by this scenario than the other plans, but it didn't ease my mind in the least. What they saw as an open assault with a multitude of ways to escape, I saw as a multitude of ways to be ambushed.

"I still think we should go after them tomorrow instead of just doing *recon*." Cortez, despite her obvious nerves, had already finished her meal. She was Subversive now, but definitely a born Scavenger. They never wasted a morsel.

"We talked about this already—" Nos was already on the defensive as though he had been expecting her to say that. The two had squabbled since our first meeting and hadn't stopped yet. Had I not been completely exhausted, I would have told them both to shut up.

"They might move!" She countered.

"Not if we follow *the plan*." Nos retorted, wincing at his own words. None of us liked *the plan*. But it would be an effective one.

"What if they don't come?" Otto asked, sounding genuinely concerned.

"They will." Nos, Cortez and I spoke almost in unison. I refused to look up from my meal.

They came for my parents, they would come for us too.

OUR RECON DAY had proved fruitful. To everyone's distaste.

The trap had been set to lure the closest and largest huddle to us. We would still be horribly exposed, but at least we were in a position to give ourselves the best possible chance at survival.

The alley we had chosen was ideal. It was almost a street's width and culminated in an impenetrable brick wall.

The mouth was the only way in or out. At some point, it may have been considered a courtyard even. Now, it was a cratered cement slab covered in trash and three bodies.

Two looked dead, and one was.

We hadn't killed the Taciturn who was sprawled face up on the ground near the opening to the streets. But the staged scene painted the picture that way. Our recon had procured the freshly killed body. A hit by the look of him. The bullet hole in his forehead and staring blank eyes were a gruesome bonus. Triven and I were collapsed face down in broken looking heaps on the pavement near the barricading wall. Both our arms were tucked under us at odd angles, concealing our weapons at the ready. Twice already I had to wiggle my fingers to keep the tingling at bay. The last thing I needed was a useless hand when the time came.

Nos had snared a sickly-looking rabbit as well and used its disgustingly warm blood to add to the gore. He had even wasted precious bullets, as a call to the surrounding Scavengers.

To a passerby, it was evident that a fight had broken out and all parties involved had paid the price. No question about it, if there were Scavengers in the area, they would be coming soon to pick our bodies clean. Very soon.

Archer and Baxter perched on the roofs above somewhere. Dutifully unseen, and equally deadly. Nos and Cortez were tracking the Tribe's movement, sending up noiseless smoke clouds to alert our snipers of their progression. Otto, Grenald and Veyron were perched above the barricade wall, looped ropes at the ready and poised to be lowered to us at a moment's notice.

A birdlike call echoed down the walls to us and my ears were instantly alert. The Scavengers were less than a block away now. Triven stopped breathing next to me. I desperately wanted to reach out to him, both to comfort and to seek comfort. But I knew any movement now would shatter my composure. Instead, I whispered into the cement.

"Together."

Like mine his response was barely audible, but it soothed my nerves.

"Together."

In some way, this had become our I love you. Meant only for us and Mouse. It was our bond. Our family. Our vow.

The Scavengers did not make the raucous noise like the Ravagers, but they were not approaching quietly either. Goading voices spoke in broken English. I had a sudden respect for Nos and Cortez. Both spoke eloquently. They sounded nothing like their ex-brethren. Lazy feet dragged as the group moved. I could hear the sound of something larger being pulled along with them, though I didn't dare raise my eyes to look.

My stomach knotted as the first of the Scavengers caught sight of our trap. There was a low whistle.

"Pickin's be good today." There was a chorus of cackling. Still not a single Tribesman rushed into the concrete courtyard.

Good.

Had they rushed us, this meant the huddle's Alpha wasn't among them, but their hesitation divulged he was. They would move when he signaled. Even rats had their pecking order.

As we had planned, they came to the dead Taciturn first. His skin would be cold, greying eyes focused on the green sky above. There would be no question that the body was dead. Hopefully they would assume the same of us as they approached.

Someone was walking toward us, his smell preceding his steps.

I held my breath.

In the wake of his movements, I could hear the other members of the Tribe descending on the body. Fights were breaking out, fabric was ripping and feral growls were echoing off the buildings.

Feet sidled next to me and I tensed. If they flipped me first, I would have to be ready. If they flipped Triven, I had to be sure to react at the same time he did. Timing was everything. Archer and Baxter could provide some cover if we moved too slowly, but it was better not to waste the bullets unless necessary.

Hands never touched me. But a filthy toe jammed itself under my shoulder and kicked up. I rolled with the force of its kick. My back pressed against the ground briefly before I popped up into an alert seated position. Both my arms flung wide brandishing two semi-automatic handguns—yet another gift from Ryker. The woman who had turned me over leaped back in surprise, squealing as Triven came to life in the next instant. Like a flea, she bounced back from us. But fear quickly turned to anger.

I gently squeezed the triggers on my guns and a red dot bloomed to life on the man I assumed to be the Alpha's head and another man who was too close for my liking. Crude weapons were drawn, but no one advanced. I took their hesitation as an opportunity to get to my feet. Triven rose with me in perfect unison. I swept the crowd of filthy Scavengers. It had been years, but still I searched for my parents' clothing among the group. The scent of blood accompanied the memory.

Every eye watched our weapons with hunger, not fear.

"Don't. I'll shoot you before you can take it." Triven barked, nodding at his gun. His tone emanated an authority that even raised the hair on even my arms. Whereas I had been the mouthpiece with Teya, *he* would be our voice with the Scavengers. Unlike Teya who favored powerful women, the Scavengers were a male dominated Tribe. They wouldn't listen to me, not unless I underwent some serious anatomy changes.

"More 'a us than you's." The Alpha grinned, displaying an array of rotted teeth.

He took a tentative step and the huddle moved with him. Four shots cut the air. Triven's and mine both bit the ground at the Alpha's feet while two more nicked the ears of the Scavengers closest to us.

Damn, Baxter and Archer were good.

The entire huddle halted its advance.

"You sure about that?" Triven threw the words back.

Jaundiced eyes searched the rooftops, but they would find nothing. A collective shudder vibrated through the group as they retreated in on themselves. Four Scavengers at the back peeled off from the huddle. Those were the Betas—the ones Nos and Cortez had warned us about.

They wouldn't fight us. They never would have. These people were deserters to their core. Even now, in an alley where we were clearly outnumbered, they would rather wait for the outcome than to be part of it. If their huddle survived this encounter, all the better. If not, then the Betas would come slinking back when it was over to pick their own huddle clean and move on with no remorse.

Rats, I thought with a disgusted tremor.

Unlike the Betas, the Alpha male had not moved. His barrel chest heaved beneath the matted brown layers. The multitude of filthy clothing had fused together with years of grime and sweat.

I held my breath, blocking their putrid stench. Triven's throat muscles clenched and I felt a pang for him. I could get away without breathing much, but he had to speak. His nose twitched.

"We don't usually take down livings, but there are always exceptions." The S's whistled out the gaps in the Alpha's teeth. His pink tongue pressed wiggling against the gaps, as if trying to escape the stench of his own mouth.

Triven's voice came out lower than usual, masking his nerves. "Kill us and you'll lose out on the biggest haul this city has ever seen."

Greedy, the huddle leaned in closer. My eyes wanted to dart to our friends. *Keep your guns ready.* I silently warned them. Desire had momentarily subdued their bloodlust, but it wouldn't last.

The Alpha's head twisted. "So, the undead came to make a deal?"

"More food, water and weapons than any Tribe has." Triven offered, tossing him a food pouch as I had Teya.

The Alpha's beady eyes dilated as he scrutinized the bag. He slapped back a few other Scavengers who had edged too close.

A gap-toothed grin accompanied his broken English.

"We listening."

21. PELTS

TWICE MORE WE made the same offer to other Scavenger huddles as we had made first to the Wraiths. And twice more, we couldn't be sure of the outcome.

Though rank enough to asphyxiate, the Scavengers had proven less threatening than we'd expected. They had never been known for their aggression. Generally not the hunting type, they preferred the role of buzzards. Easier to pick at carcasses than to kill.

Still, I had expected worse.

But on my whistles, our ropes came down and pulled us safely back to higher ground without incident. No shots were fired, no knives thrown. The only thing that followed us were hungry eyes. The only obstacle was having to move and restage the Taciturn body each time. Both Arden and I had refused to touch it.

Overall, it seemed too easy.

The Wraiths had not hunted us down—yet—and three huddles of Scavengers had listened to our offer. While we were still alive—a definite plus—not one had actually committed to joining our cause. They hadn't even committed to meeting with the other leaders. Four days had passed and it felt like the Tribes were slipping through our fingers like water. We could touch them, but they weren't in our grasp.

If this stupid plan didn't work—if I proved my initial instincts right—then we would fail.

Somehow it felt like we already were. New nightmares began merging with old ones. I was always standing on a rooftop staring at The Wall. My parents and Maddox flanked us. Blood poured from their wounds, filling their mouths and silencing them. Then The Wall would fall and though I tried to hold Triven and Mouse close to me, hands would always rip them away. Fire consumed us as the worlds collided and we were swallowed whole. Night after night, the dream came. But at least the screams were kept to a minimum. Mostly, because it was impossible to wake up screaming when you rarely slept.

I wasn't the only one with circles under my eyes. Archer had taken to sleeping with her rifle clutched to her chest. Cortez started chewing her nails until they bled, and Grenald had stopped talking almost entirely. I couldn't decide if I liked the giant better as a mute or if it only unnerved me further. It also hadn't helped that my last two hideouts had been a little tight for the bulky man. He had cursed me the entire way in and out of both.

Tonight's safe house was at least slightly roomier. The building was a maze of hallways with endless doors. There were twelve floors, each filled with vacant rooms of rotted furniture and broken windows. It may have been tempting for some to claim one of the tattered rooms as a safe place, but they didn't meet *my* standards. My safehold was on the top floor. Accessible now only through scaling the elevator shaft. There were no windows in the room and bare floor. Dusty furniture was stacked in random piles, but there were also crude mattresses. Much like so many of the other locations I had chosen over the years, it was a storage room of sorts. I chose them not as a source of supplies, but because they were generally better fortified than most spaces. One door that could easily be blocked and a rare window. Typically, unappealing to others. Very homey.

As we made our last scouting sweep of the Taciturns' territory, the thought of an actual mattress made me hasten my steps. At least tonight I would have a soft bed while lying awake.

Had the others beat us back there? I reached for my neck, searching for my father's watch before remembering Mouse had it. My hand fell away empty.

Our full group had broken off into tomorrow's teams. The Taciturns covered more territory than the Wraiths and getting to their leader was not going to be so easy. Arden and Otto had both described the Taciturn leader as an unhinged recluse. Zed, the leader in question, was known for killing anyone who he thought might betray him, which was apparently nearly everyone. He was the one who had skinned Maddox's brother for a new vest. I shivered, remembering the moment Maddox's screamed in my face the reason for his defection.

Since Zed apparently rarely left his hideout and could give a crap if we threatened his own, even getting to that monster would be a challenge in itself, much less trying to win his favor. There was only one thing about Zed we could count on.

His bloodlust.

This Tribe leader liked to make public spectacles of those who had wronged him. For a traitor's killing, he would definitely make an appearance. Despite my protests, our plan evolved from this knowledge. It was the riskiest plan and the most likely to get one—if not all of us—killed.

If getting to Zed necessitated getting caught, then Triven and I would allow ourselves to be captured, but this time, we weren't the only ones putting our lives on the line. If it was just the two of us, there was no guarantee we wouldn't be slaughtered on the spot. But with a deserter, an ex-Taciturn, caught with us... well, let's just say Zed would want to add to his wardrobe.

I avoided looking at Arden as we crouched behind a collapsing chimney.

I trusted him with my life, and although it was selfish, I was glad Otto had volunteered first. My friend had already been through so much. I also wasn't sure I could have handled both Triven and Arden there with me. But I still had half a mind to knock Triven out and leave him behind tomorrow. He had forgiven me for abandoning him and Mouse once before, but I knew he wouldn't if I left him behind again.

I wouldn't if the roles were reversed.

Triven's hand wound discreetly over mine as though he had heard my thoughts. His warm fingers squeezed gently.

I pressed back. No, he would not forgive me for that.

"They're moving on." Arden peered past the bricks to a small group of tattooed covered figures on the ground below.

"Then we should too." Triven's hand squeezed once more before letting go.

We had split up to better scout the area and though Otto should have been with us, no one protested when Grenald had demanded they not be separated. Frankly, I wouldn't have blamed them if they had secreted off to spend some time alone. The closer death loomed, the more we sought solace in those we loved. Especially if that loved one might die tomorrow.

The thought had crossed my mind many times in the past few days to do the same with Triven. Every night I curled up in his arms, pressing my back into his chest. But aside from those few restless hours, we kept our physical contact to a minimum in front of the others. Brushing hands, squeezing fingers, it suddenly wasn't enough and I wished Arden had gone with the others too.

It felt wrong letting Arden take the lead tonight, but as well as I knew the rooftops, he knew this area and the people that stalked it. His scarred face had been tense since we left the Scavenger's territory and the strain amplified as we ran. Though I could sense his relief at not being the bait tomorrow, there was something eating at Arden. His twisted lips seemed to pull down against the scars. But then again, maybe it was nothing. We were all twitchier than usual and none of us had been at ease since leaving Xavier's barracks.

Arden's feet moved in steady assured steps, but like mine, there was a haste behind their movements. He wanted to be out of here as badly as I did. Probably more.

Shoulders nearly touching, the three of us bounded across the gap to the next building and the stillness of the night was shattered.

Triven saw them first, but his cry of warning was too late.

As our feet landed on solid ground, the shadows suddenly leapt to life.

Arden was the first to fall. There was a glint as he pulled a knife, but it flew from his grasp as a pillar of metal crashed down on him. The towering vent shaft collided with Arden's lean body, knocking him flat and pinning him on the spot, his thrashing limbs were at least a sign that he was still alive.

My own fingers barely grazed the grip of my gun when a fist collided with the side of my face. Hands and knives seemed to come at me from all sides—grabbing, punching and slashing from every direction. Tattooed hands.

I blocked, trying to fight off each assault. Many of my own punches smashed into jaws, noses and stomachs, but too many blows were landing on me as well. I staggered. Two gunshots discharged somewhere behind me and I foolishly turned to look. I glimpsed Triven as his gun was ripped from his hands. Both of his arms were wrenched back at impossible angles as he was slammed face first into the tarry rooftop. Blood coated his forehead and leaked from his nose.

For one second his gaze met mine. Terror I had only seen once before—when I had left him and Mouse in a sewer grate—flared in his hazel eyes. Then there were hands in my hair ripping me back off my feet and into a wall of human flesh. My scalp blazed as a knife's blade bit into soft skin. In desperation, I snapped at the ink-covered arm holding me, biting hard enough to tear flesh. But an involuntary cry escaped me as the Taciturn yanked harder on my hair. Triven began to thrash against his own three captors, his eyes locked only on me. A woman's foot ground down over his head smashing Triven's face further into the ground. She pulled a gun, pressing it next to her heel on Triven's temple with a sneer. Tears stung my eyes. I had thought I watched him die once before. I barely survived it then, I would not survive it now.

Hands groped my body, relieving me of every weapon they could find. The same was quickly done to Triven, but Arden was left alone, his ex-Tribesmen enjoying his frantic thrashing. Blood filled my mouth as I bit my tongue to keep from screaming.

Taking a deep breath, I forced myself to calm down. There were thirteen of them. Four for every one of us, plus a small woman who seemed to be doing little more than enjoying the show.

The image of a female being run through with a blade writhed on the forearm flexed beneath my nose and she was not the only marking visible in the night light. Images of skeletons, reapers, flames, weapons, demonic looking creatures and bloody bodies covered every inch of our attackers' skin. What little skin was not exposed, was concealed by grey and maroon clothing. Taciturns, all of them.

Our recon had suddenly become the mission. I forced my breathing to steady.

This had been what we had wanted. Not in the *way* we wanted, but the result was still the same. Only Arden had unwittingly taken Otto's place. *And*, the others had no idea to come looking for us. We were on our own and if not careful—and lucky—in the next few minutes, we could easily be left for dead on this rooftop.

A line of fire blistered to life on my throat as the blade pressed against bare flesh. While both Arden and

Triven continued to struggle, I stilled. One fact caused me to compose myself.

They had not killed *any* of us.

They wanted something.

"Enough!" I shouted over the melee. Triven's body stilled at my cry, his battered face still smashed to the tar. Only one eye could meet mine and despite the fear blooming there he calmed himself. The shortest woman—the watcher—eyed me, curiosity lighting in her black eyes. The corners of her mouth perked.

Unlike Triven and me, however, Arden continued to thrash. His legs were pinned underneath the upended vent, on which a rather large Tribesman was now perched, obviously enjoying his prey's struggles. Arden howled with rage and the flailing only ceased when the small female pressed her boot on Arden's exposed throat. His long fingers fought to keep the worn boot at bay, barely stopping her from crushing his larynx. The woman's dark eyes flickered my way once more before again falling on the ex-Tribesman pinned beneath her.

"Well, well, what do we have here? Little *Arden* is that you?" The sole of her boot pushed harder against his hands, closing on his bobbing neck. He snarled a string of gargled expletives, his words choked off along with his air supply. The woman eyeballed the knife that had tumbled loose from his grasp in the brawl. A wicked grin split her lips as she leaned down forcing her full weight on the boy. "You never were much of one for killing as I recall. But I must say you have gotten *prettier* in our time apart."

She winked at him, blowing a derisive kiss at his scarred face.

With a shriek, Arden shoved against her foot, but didn't gain an inch until the woman leaned back. With a flick of her hand, the Taciturn pinning his legs slid from his perch, freeing our friend. Arden did not hesitate. With a final thrust, he sent the woman staggering a few steps back while he rolled out from under the vent and to his weapon. Manic laughter erupted from the woman as she regained her footing. Despite the rage emanating from Arden, nothing about her demeanor looked malevolent. On the contrary, she seemed entertained.

"Things change!" Arden howled. The knife scraped the rooftop as he snatched it, ready to attack, but she was ready for him. As his knife tip darted forward it was met with a gun pointed in his face.

"Keep that rage traitor," she cooed. "It will serve you well in times like these."

I watched the fire drain from my friend's face, but his grip on the knife didn't loosen.

"Get it over with already." The words hissed through his clenched teeth. "*Kill* us."

Triven's shoulders twitched, earning him a stomp in his back. The leader's mouth opened but it was my voice that answered first.

"They won't kill us."

The woman's head swiveled toward me, her black eyes shining. She slinked like a cat to stand before me. Stopping with the tips of her black boots kissing mine, she threw her left hand over the lower portion of her face. If not for the fist buried in my hair and cementing my head in place, I would have flinched. The back of her hand created a type of perverse mask, the tattooed skin creating the illusion of skeletal jaw. Despite her now hidden mouth, it was easy to tell she was grinning beneath the tattooed hand-mask. Though muffled by her palm, the words were still clear as she cocked her head to the side.

"And what makes you so sure of that my *Pet?*"

22. AMBUSH

THE KNIFE TIGHTENED against my neck, but did not bury itself further into the skin.

"You want something." I countered, careful to relax my features into something akin to boredom despite my breathlessness. Or at least I hoped it looked like that way.

With an explosive giggle, the crazy-eyed Taciturn bounced back a few steps on the balls of her feet, the masked hand falling away to reveal the lower part of her grinning face again. She continued to bobble in place, clapping her hands like a frenzied child. "I had a feeling I would like you dearest Phoenix."

All three of our bodies stiffened as my name tumbled loose from her lips. I prayed the Taciturn holding me couldn't feel the increasing heartbeat racing in my neck.

"I don't believe *I* have had the pleasure…" My words were covered in frost.

The wicked smile widened as her cocked head, twisting it further to an almost impossible angle. "Well, I don't believe *you* have. Name's Sedia, *Pet*. Sometimes this silly little mind of mine forgets that we never actually met, despite all of the goodies I have stored away in here about you." Wide eyes now serious, she tapped her temple and pursed her lips. The effect made her look utterly unhinged.

"You've been watching us, *Sedia*." There was no question in my tone.

She shrugged noncommittally, winking as the skull mask on her left hand once again hid her stained teeth. While Sedia's fellow Tribesmen watched her with adoration, drinking in the insanity, there was something about the glint in her eye that left the back of my scalp tingling. An Old World phrase crept to mind. *Crazy like a fox.*

Yes, that was what this woman was.

Insane or not—it was hard to tell and maybe a little of both—this black-eyed Taciturn was unquestionably a fox and a deadly one at that.

"You've been busy little rogues, the lot of you." Sedia's eyes glinted wildly as they swept our battered party. Dropping her hand, Sedia's face cracked wide with a cat-like grin as she leered at Arden. Her dark eyes caressed every inch of his trembling body, drinking in his fear.

"Oh, don't worry lovey, we're not here to skin you... *Yet.*" The letter "t" crashed harshly against her front teeth. She chomped her teeth at him before tittering to herself.

In one fluid movement, the fox woman hopped effortlessly onto the now vacant vent shaft, the metal booming under her small weight. Her slim legs swung, kicking back against the tarnished metal with deafening booms five times before she suddenly fell still. Life seemed to slip from her face as she distractedly fingered a hole in her tattered leggings, undoubtedly distracted by voices only she could hear. The awkward silence dragged on until the Tribesman restraining me cleared his throat, loudly. Like the flip of a switch, the manic grin once again beamed mega-watt in the darkness, and her head cocked to the side swiveling in my direction once more. "We hear you're having a party and we have come to *play.*"

Then, with a snap of her fingers, we were suddenly released—the fleshy manacles holding my wrists disappearing along with the biting blade. I spared Triven a glance as he winced to his feet. Possibly a few bruised ribs and a cheekbone, but no major damage. His gaze flew to me making the same assessment. We gave no other sign of affection for each other. Love could easily be turned into a weapon. My Grandfather had proved that.

Despite the urge to rub my tender wrists and check my own neck, I folded my arms casually over my chest.

"And *I'm* supposed to believe you're in. Just like that." My eyebrows peaked. "Nothing comes that easy. Not without a cost, *Sedia.*" I scoured her face searching for tells, but her flashing eyes gave nothing.

The woman picked at her teeth before examining whatever she had dislodged from there. She wiped it distractedly on the man's vest standing nearest. His lips twisted, the snake tattooed on his jaw wriggling in response, but he did nothing to stop her. Instead, she stroked his arm like an obedient pet and surprisingly he relaxed under her touch.

"Oh, I never said that we were in *for sure.* I merely implied that if you set up a meeting of the Tribes, our leader will be there. I'll see to that. *But* after that, it's up to our illustrious leader. He may kill you on the spot to be honest. Zed has never really *played* well with others. Not like me." She winked at me and a dark laugh rumbled through the surrounding Taciturns. Springing down from her perch, Sedia came to stand before me again. Now that my head was no longer being wrenched back, it was surprising to see we were almost the same height, though she carried herself like a much taller person.

"So, Pet, can we come play? *Pretty* please?" Her head tilted sharply toward the other shoulder this time as her dark lashes batted rapidly.

Imaginary spiders were swarming up my throat, trying to claw their way out. I choked them down, trying to keep my voice steady.

I wanted to glance at Triven, to read his face, but as Sedia's wild eyes danced over mine I knew our eye contact could not be broken. One should never break the gaze of a wild animal, lest it attack. I had to make this decision on my own.

This was what we had wanted, but still, gooseflesh rose over my arms. Although she was not their leader, deigning her could mean having our throats slit here and now.

My mouth worked around the words before speaking them. "We'll mark the building the day of the meeting. It will be a place on neutral ground. Look for the white smoke."

She took one of my guns from the Taciturn who had robbed me of it. Shoving her finger under the trigger she spun the weapon with impressive speed. I tried not to flinch, knowing full well the safety was not on. One slip and she could shoot any of us. In a flash the sidearm righted in her hand, the barrel pointed directly between Arden's wide eyes.

My left eye twitched. If she killed Arden with my gun...

But she didn't pull the trigger. Keeping her mark, Sedia stalked uncomfortably close to me. Every muscle ached to move back, but I commanded them to stay as the tip of her nose grazed mine.

"See you in three days, Pet." She purred and then shockingly pressed her mouth over mine in a quick, harsh kiss. This time my foot inched back, but before I could react Sedia was skipping away, waving my gun over her head. "Thanks for the new toys!"

The others dislodged themselves, following the dancing girl. Though none of them carried themselves in the same manner as their deranged spokeswoman. My captor placed a well-aimed shoulder into my back as he passed and a hand clapped loudly on the side of Triven's bruised face. But it was the woman who licked Arden's ear as she left that made me clench my fists. I counted the seconds as they disappeared into the night. a Six buildings away their ink covered bodies dropped over the edge, but not before Sedia turned around and blew a kiss, this time aimed at Triven.

The moment her dark hair vanished, Arden collapsed. Our friend hit the ground, every inch of him shaking uncontrollably. A cross between a sob and a scream burst from deep inside his chest. I moved to his side, but before I could touch him, Arden recoiled.

"Don't touch me!" He screamed. Tears fell in strange patterns down his scarred cheeks. "Don't touch me..."

He said it softer the second time, and somehow that made it cut deeper. Still, I understood.

Triven moved closer, but was careful not to touch either of us. He was scanning the buildings around us, moving his lips as little as possible as he spoke. "We need to get the hell out of here. Now."

My eyes darted up following his. He was right. There was no telling who else knew we were here—who might be watching us now.

"Can you move?" I didn't look down to Arden for a response and he didn't give one. Instead he rose to his feet and began taking shaky steps in the opposite direction from where the Taciturns had just disappeared.

Arden bolted, running, moving faster than I had ever seen him move. We didn't hesitate to follow. I overtook him, making sure to lead us in a roundabout path. It was unlikely the Taciturns knew where our night's hideout was, and I certainly wasn't going to lead them cleanly back to it. Though something instinctual told me they were no longer watching us, it wasn't a risk I was willing to take.

An hour later and now two hours late for our rendezvous with the others, we finally found our way back to the elevator shaft leading to my safe house. As Arden climbed on the cables first, face now dry and hardened, Triven caught me in his arms. The heat of his body enveloped me as he pressed his lips to the top of my head. I hugged back with everything I had, burying my face in his chest.

"I thought we were dead tonight." Triven's voice caught.

"I know." I spoke into his shirt. It smelled like him, sweaty and warm.

It's only going to get worse... neither of us said it. We didn't have to.

"She said *three* days." I said pulling away to look at him. I had always known the Taciturns had spies placed in other Tribes. Tonight was a stiff reminder of that.

Worry filled Triven's eyes as they danced over mine. "I caught that too. They knew everything... But they let us go."

I shook my head, knowing where his thoughts were going. "We can't stay here tonight. We can't risk it."

My sore limbs ached for the mattresses upstairs. But they were not worth our lives. Sedia had let us live, but her other Tribesmen may not be so generous. She wasn't their leader and her word was not law.

"I know." Triven kissed the top of my head again. "Let's get the others."

THE REST OF our unit swarmed the door as we entered and I was greeted by a hard slap to the face from a fuming Veyron as soon as the door closed behind us. Her hair swung out with the force, momentarily revealing her damaged cheeks and scalp. Arden must have told them what happened.

"Veyron!" Triven started next to me as I staggered.

Baxter immediately leapt forward to restrain her, but I waved them both off. I deserved it. Plus, this was the most attention she had given me since our return. Her body vibrated with emotions, bright blue eyes moist. A part of her hated me, I could see it now. But her arms quickly wrapped around me in a painful hug before she once again shoved me away. "I still don't forgive you."

Without waiting for a response, Veyron pushed her way to the back of the group, leaving me dumbfounded. It was a step at least, though forward or backward in our relationship I couldn't be sure.

In Veyron's trail, the questions started pouring out, but I didn't hear any of them.

Otto was consoling Arden in the far corner of the room, the only one of us that truly understood his pain. Arden's back was to us as I watched them, and an ache rose in my chest. Triven's voice hummed in the background as he began answering questions. He paused as I laid a hand over his chest. My eyes never left Arden's shaking shoulders.

"We need to leave." I barely kept the quiver out of my voice. Shockingly no one protested, they didn't even push for more answers. Instead, our band of insurgents snapped to action. Only Archer remained a beat behind. I moved away to gather my own things, but she followed.

In two strides, she caught up to me.

"We aren't safe here." I muttered without looking up. "*He* can't stay here."

"Not arguing." Archer kept her voice low to match mine.

"That's a first."

She snorted. Reaching to her hip she pulled two throwing knives, offering them to me without hesitation. I looked from the blades to her face, not moving to take them. She gave the weapons an impatient shake, the metal clanking together. "You need *something* until we get you more adequate weapons. And as much as I hate to admit it, not many people can throw a stiletto like you."

"Thanks." I snatched the knives, thrusting them a little too forcefully into my holster, one of the blades nipping my thigh. It felt deserved.

Archer turned, hesitating. Then she slapped a hand on my shoulder, making a noise somewhere between a cough and a dark laugh. "Well... that's three Tribes down, one to go, crappy leader. Wins so far."

I looked back to Arden. Otto was packing his things, as Arden stared blindly at the wall.

"Winning feels an awful lot like losing," I breathed.

Archer nodded sympathetically. "Welcome to war P. Someone always claims victory, but really both sides lose."

Triven and Baxter came around the corner. Triven was taking apart and checking the chambers of a handgun I had seen Baxter use on many occasions. I couldn't muster a smile for either of them. Baxter seemed incapable too. His eyebrows rose, unusually serious. "If we're followed tonight?"

I thought of Sedia. Her crazed black eyes, of her desire to join our cause, but mainly her far too accurate knowledge of our movements.

It wasn't even a question in my mind.

"Shoot them."

23. INTELLECTS

A **SCREAM TORE** free. Erupting before I could clamp my lips around it.

I shot upright, the bed of paper crinkled under my feet. The hazy light filling the room blinded me for a second before I smashed my eyes into knees. My arms coiled automatically around my legs, pulling everything tighter, trying to disappear.

Not even Ryker's pills kept away the nightmares last night.

A shaky breath rattled my chest. The bed next to me was empty. Triven's comforting arms nowhere to be found. But I wasn't alone. I felt her eyes watching me before I saw her.

Perched in the corner atop a pile of old rags, Veyron watched me. She was chewing on the corner of her thumb. Oblivious to the fact it had started to bleed. We were the only two in the sleeping space. Based on the rumbling in my stomach the rest were probably in the room next to ours eating.

"Bad dreams?" She paused in the assault on her cuticle.

The lingering effects of Ryker's sleeping pills loosened my tongue.

"I'm sorry we left you." The words were whispered out from behind my knees.

Veyron's face frosted over, every muscle tense—even the scarred ones. She had changed from the girl I met in the bunker. Hardened. "Do you even *know* what you're apologizing for?" She snapped.

My jaw set. I rested it on my knees as I stared back at her.

I didn't know.

Not all of it.

Yes, I had left her in that alley, but it wasn't my choice. Maddox had dragged me away from her, from Arden *and* Archer. We had left them all behind at the hands of the Ravagers. Yet the others had forgiven me. Veyron alone had not, which meant one thing to me. Something had happened to her that hadn't happened to the others. She didn't just hate me for abandoning them, she hated me for something else.

She shook her head at my responding silence in disgust. "I thought not."

"Then *tell* me. What *should* I be apologizing for?" It was rare that I pleaded, but Veyron had once been someone I would have called a friend and those were even more rare.

My heartbeat thundered in my ears as the terse silence stretched. For a minute I didn't think she was going to respond. Then her lips twitched and suddenly she couldn't bear to look at me.

"You left us there to die. *All* of you. Triven, Bowen, you, M-Maddox..." She fumbled over the last name and it made my stomach clench.

I wanted to protest, to tell her *I* hadn't left anyone—*I* hadn't been given a choice. I was dragged away from her. But semantics aside, she was right. When Maddox threw me into the passage and sealed us in, I knew we had left them to die. For over a month their presumed deaths *had* plagued me.

"Why you?" There was venom in her tone. "*Why* did he choose *you?*"

Though her words were meant to lance, they drew confusion not pain. Had I been blind that she had feelings for Triven? A hundred thoughts whipped around in an instant.

"He looked at *me* first. He looked at me, and then he saved *you*. *Twice*." Veyron was shredding bits of paper from her bed stack. When her vibrant eyes whipped up they were filled with angry tears. "Did you even care for him? Did you even flinch when Maddox took that bullet for you?"

Genuine shock slapped the confused expression off my face. *Maddox*... not Triven. Veyron had loved Maddox.

I had never seen them touch, never watched them interact—but had I ever looked?

I had hated the man she loved—and in her greatest time of need, he chose to save me.

There were so many things I could say to her, so many things I *should*, but none came out.

Veyron's gaze fell away as a tear escaped. She reached, fingers stretching to tangle in hair only to find scars. Her hand fell limply away.

"It's not *just* that…" She said to the floor. "*You* of all people know what the Ravagers are capable of."

I sucked in a shallow breath. My nightmare began to replay in my head.

"You couldn't get to me, *fine*. But you still could have saved me. You should have put a bullet in my head that night."

I forced my eyes closed, focusing every fragment of energy on finding my voice. "But you survived."

"Not all scars can be seen, Phoenix."

I shuddered. Archer and the others had not said anything about Veyron being assaulted that night, but in the chaos, it was possible they didn't know. A guilty hole widened in my chest. We had left her alone—in so many ways.

"I'm sorry." There was more meaning behind the words now. I looked up at her, but she refused to acknowledge me.

"I don't care." Slender fingers still busy with the paper shreds.

"I know." I said, but *I* still needed to say it.

"After tonight, I'm out." The paper made ripping noises in the silence. "I won't fight with you. I'm staying behind with the kids." She flashed an aggravated wave around the room in general. "*All* of this was for *them*. To give *them* a future."

None of this was for you. She didn't have to add that last part.

I said nothing, but dipped my chin with understanding.

I stood to give her some privacy, stopping when she spoke again.

"A part of me hopes they blow you up." Her words were choked by tears, not as harsh as before. But honest.

I kept my back to her, pausing before leaving the room. "I know that too."

And I did, I understood. You could love someone and despise them at the same time. The human heart was capable of stranger things. And with that, our conversation—and possibly friendship—was over.

"YOU GOOD?" ARCHER eyed her fellow marksman speculatively, her tone as accusatory as her glare.

"Shut up, Archer." Baxter hissed through clamped teeth.

She held her tongue, pressing an eye back to her own scope. I glared at the back of Archer's head, but the truth was, the slight tremor in Baxter's usually steady hand wasn't doing much to spur my confidence either. He wasn't the only one on edge. After our run-in with the Taciturns, everyone felt less safe, especially in the daylight. We weren't invisible in the city anymore.

But this was not the time to let fear get the better of us, particularly not Baxter. If his shots weren't on point, we were screwed. All of us.

The Adroits were the last on our checklist and so far the only Tribe that had cost us a life. We were approaching from a different side this time, but my eyes still searched for a part of Elin even though there was none to be found. Not that there was much of him left anyway. It was Baxter and Veyron who had laid the groundwork for today's infiltration, though it was clear neither wanted to be here.

Getting in touch with the Adroits had taken more planning than any of the other Tribes. But all the time in the world could not predict their constantly changing minefields. One wrong step and we could explode into red mist or fall into a pit of spikes. I had once thought of the Adroits as the lesser evil of all the Tribes, but standing on the rooftop, heart hammering, they were quickly becoming the most dangerous Tribe in my mind. They were the most reserved and yet suddenly the deadliest. They didn't capture a person, they merely blew you up. There was no fight back against a bomb. One second you were there and the next, boom and you're gone. I had never liked odds that didn't yield much chance of survival.

This plan was well thought out. I tried to remind myself. *Even if Veyron said she wanted you dead.* I pushed that thought away.

The smokestacks of the Adroits' nerve center belched black smoke. Their leader was in there somewhere, hiding safely behind thick walls and miles of IEDs. Wex was the last leader both Veyron and Baxter were aware of, but he was old when both of them defected and in Tartarus, leaders could change overnight. Either way we would not speak to the Adroit leader. We would never be able to get to him. But maybe—if today went as planned— he would come seeking us.

Three Watchmen—as Veyron and Baxter referred to them—were gathered in a building two down of ours. It was a hovel of a structure, with one warped metal door and no windows. But our ex-Adroits warned us not to be fooled. Hidden under the shack was a dug-out storeroom with concrete walls and enough food to surprise even the Ravagers. These people were deadly at building bombs, but they were also skilled at cultivating food. Little did I know at the time, but it had been most of the ex-Adroits who had fostered the Subversive's underground food growth. It also explained why I had rarely   seen the Adroits outside of their own sector. Why hunt for food when you could grow it in secret on your own turf?

That building was our target. Not the supplies inside of it, but the *people*. The three Watchmen in particular. They were the guard dogs of the Adroits, the highest ranking under their esteemed leader. If we could speak to *them*, they were our best chance of getting our word to Wex—or whoever governed the Tribe now.

Their purple and gold stained wraps had disappeared into the door nearly ten minutes ago and it was finally time for us to act.

Veyron's blonde hair tickled my arm as she crouched next to me, but I didn't dare acknowledge it. Since our conversation last night, she had gone back to avoiding me and I in turn did my best to ignore her.

Otto's hand flashed up in a signal. Peering over the edge, my hand mirrored his and without a word Baxter pulled the trigger. I flinched in anticipation but instead of the explosion I had been expecting the bullet bit into the dirt a few inches wide. A stream of curses hissed from Baxter as the group collectively tensed. If an Adroit saw that, we were done.

Two heartbeats passed, however, and Baxter sucked in a tight breath. Then letting go, he fired again. If he cursed again, I never heard it.

An explosion large enough to kill a man charged the air. Then there was another and another, each bullet Baxter sent flying hitting its mark. Many of the bombs he hit caused a chain reaction, but he stayed ahead of them. He had studied the mapped bombs all night. It had paid off.

"Clear!" he barked, finger never pausing.

The ground was still pulsing with the concussions, but instead of ducking for cover, Triven and Grenald tossed the ropes down and we headed straight into the minefield.

Dirt particles swam in the smoke-filled air, making it impossible to see as my feet collided with the ground. I turned in the direction I thought was the street, but a hand grabbed painfully around my bicep, yanking me back.

I expected Triven, but longer nails dug in, holding me in place as Veyron's voice emerged from the smoke.

"Move and die." Her face materialized in front of me, a cloth pulled over her mouth like mine. Giving my arm another jerk, she turned around sliding her grip to my wrist and began to pull. "Step *only* where I step or you kill us all."

Triven's hand wound into mine from behind. "Lead the way."

Each step was like walking through thick mud, excruciatingly slow and near impossible to see. Twice my toes caught the back of Veyron's heels, earning me another wrench on the arm. In another place and time, I would have pulled back and put her on her ass, but this was not the time to let my temper get the better of me.

The dust stung my eyes, tears fighting to keep the dirt out. But Veyron never missed a step. Three times she tugged us sideways, then suddenly she stopped and I stepped on her toe as she turned to face us. Her voice was nearly swallowed by the ringing in my ears, but her crude hand gestures learned from Mouse made her words clear.

Don't move. Behind, bomb. In front, pit. Move and die.

Triven nodded as I stared stiffly back at her, my hands already searching for what we needed. With one last frosty glance, she disappeared in a wisp of smoke and blonde hair. It was then I noticed the explosions had stopped. The air was thinning as the dust settled back to the ground. Shock slowly sank in as the street came into focus and I saw the full extent of Baxter's target practice.

Two steps in front of us, a crater yawned nearly twenty feet across what was once the street. The bombs had given us cover and created a barricade of sorts. Shards of glass winked up at us from the pit, along with rusted steel spikes and what looked like sharpened bones. The edge crumbled downward and I had to repress the urge to step back.

A foul breeze played in my hair, then began to clear the lingering smoke and I saw them.

The door to the food house was ajar and with their heads gleaming, toes brazenly to the edge of the pit, stood the three Adroit Watchmen. I could see now one was a woman, though she was nearly as tall as the men flanking her. A fine dust covered their clothing, catching in their eyebrows and lashes like fine ash. The woman's arm rose, gun pointed at my head. But as the smoke faded around us she hesitated. Her fellow Tribesmen raised their own weapons, but no shots were fired.

Yet.

Their eyes were no longer looking at me, but at the silver oblong hovering above my palm. The red light of the Sanctuary bomb was visible even in the daylight.

Pulling my mask down with the other hand, I spoke too loudly in the aftermath of the explosions.

"I believe we have your attention."

The tallest man to the left pulled back the hammer of his gun and pointed it at my face. His right eyebrow arched.

"I believe you do."

24. TRIPWIRES

A TICKLE IN the back of my throat threatened to undo my bravado. A hacking cough shook my body and the Adroits stiffened in response. The massive crater gave us a false sense of security. Both sides felt unreachable and yet both sides were totally exposed.

The shorter man of the group, with olive skin and eyes black as night buried his hand in his dust covered cloak. When it reappeared, a black box the size of a small brick was clutched in his fingers.

"You have made a grave error coming here." The woman spoke in a flat tone. She wasn't making a threat, just stating a fact.

The olive-skinned man flexed his fingers. Whatever the device was, it wasn't good.

"I wouldn't if I were you." Triven nodded to the small man and the box clutched in his hand. "Yours will do what? Take us out?"

I twisted my palm and the silver bomb moved with it. "*Ours* will take out six blocks. Sanctuary grade titanium bomb. Designed to obliterate everything within your sight."

The slightest flicker of interest piqued the woman, but the men remained skeptical.

"Impossible, no one can breach The Wall." The man holding the box scoffed.

"*We* did. Want to test mine against yours?" Recklessly, I made an upward tossing motion and the bomb lifted higher before settling back to hover an inch off my palm. I couldn't help but smile when they flinched and took a step back. But Triven too stiffened and I sobered up.

"We're not here to make threats." I offered.

No weapon lowered.

"Our streets say otherwise." The tall man countered.

"No damage has been done to anything vital." Triven's voice was a little higher than normal, but they wouldn't notice. "Our intent was never to harm, but to extend an invitation."

"We do not meddle with others." The woman said in her flat tone.

"The Ravagers would say otherwise." I threw their words back at them and the first hint of a smile cracked their stoic facades. They were the epitome of aloof—calculating and emotionally reserved—so like Veyron and so opposite of Baxter.

"They attacked first, we responded accordingly." The smile had left the woman's eyes.

I imagined the tension rising from our friends on the rooftops. The Ravagers had not attacked, but the Subversive members had made it look like they did. Our original plan to divide the Tribes and start territorial warfare could very possibly be the undoing of Ryker's plan. What was that silly old saying? Too many cooks in the kitchen or something like that. Now we had gallons of boiling water and everyone was ready to dump it on each other.

A younger man was shoved from the open doorway. Like the other Tribe members his head was cleanly shaven. A ring of purple paint crowned his skull. But unlike the others' cool demeanor, the young man shook from head to toe. He was followed by a fair-skinned woman with an ample chest that was barely covered by gold plating. She kept a gun pointed at the man's chest. The Watchmen ignored them, and in turn, so did we.

My mind was still doing the math. Five to two now. The younger man sniffled and I spoke to block him out.

"What if I could offer you the opportunity to get back at the ones who trapped you here?" My arm lowered a little, the muscles growing tired. "What if I told you, you could breech The Wall yourselves. Take back what you're owed. *If* you were willing to form a temporary alliance."

"More lies—" The original woman spoke first, but the smaller man next to her eyed my bomb hungrily and cut her off. "What else is in it for us?"

We focused on him—Apple. The nick name seemed to fit his round, red face.

"Weapons. Food. Freedom. It's your choice." Triven flicked a knife between his long fingers. Apple watched the blade roll in his expert hands.

"And we are to *trust* you that this so-called bomb is from beyond?" The tall man—Legs, for now—eyed the silver object in my hand. "Give it to us, let us inspect it for ourselves."

Triven smiled wryly. We had anticipated this.

"We're not *that* desperate for your alliance." I said, "But in good faith…"

Triven flicked his wrist and sent the knife flying over the crater and into the dirt at Legs' boots. "A gift. You will find nothing like that here."

The man bent and picked up the pristine weapon. It was an electrified dagger, designed to stab and fry a person from the inside out. The Adroit marveled at the weight before firmly grasping the knife in his palm.

"Kadence," he said quietly. Without hesitation the busty woman—Kadence apparently—kneed the younger man in the back of the legs causing him to stumble forward. His shivering limbs barely missed colliding with the Watchmen.

"This was your sector, Carell?" Legs asked.

"Yes," the boy, Carell's voice was deeper than expected.

"And you failed to guard it?"

The boy's eyes darted to us. "Yes."

"Penance, brother." The older man said. Then with a swift motion, thrust the knife into Carell's chest and jammed his thumb down on the back of the hilt engaging the electricity. Triven's breath caught as my free hand flexed around one of the knives Archer had given me. If anyone so much as twitched in our direction, I would place it between his or her eyes.

Every muscle in the young man's body tensed. His eyes popped wide while his jaw clamped down undoubtedly on his tongue. Blood burbled from his lips as the boy's eyes slid back in his head. Smoke emanated from his skin, sizzling from the inside out and then he was falling. Away from the Watchmen, away from the knife still clutched in

Legs' hand and into the pit separating us. The ringing in my ears had dulled and I could hear his body hit the barbs below. I blinked slowly, forcing myself not to look down at the dead man.

Legs gazed at the bloody knife with a hint of disgust and admiration. "Not our usual choice, but impressive. This certainly is *not* of our world, sister." He passed the weapon to the tall woman who inspected it, careful to avoid touching the blood.

Killers without a taste for blood. Ironic.

"Join the alliance and there will be more where that came from." I twisted my wrist causing the bomb to glint in the green sunlight for emphasis. "We're gathering in two days, when the moon is high. Follow the white smoke."

"And if we chose *not* to join?" The woman asked.

"Then we'll stay out of your way, and *you'll* stay out of *ours*."

"This is not our decision to make." Legs cut in. Although the woman shot him a sideways glance, she did not contradict him.

"We're not asking you to make a decision now." Triven replied.

I finished his thought. "You have one day to consider. Come or don't. But that choice belongs to your *leader*."

It was a desperate move to bait them into spreading our words. To remind them they had to tell Wex—or whoever the new leader was. There were hierarchies. Rules of the Tribe that must be obeyed. The Adroits' faces remained void of emotion and I had the sudden urge to get away from them. To run. Instead, I shrugged off the tension in my shoulders and licked the roof of my mouth.

The scratching in the back of my throat was starting to feel more like barbed wire now.

"You still owe us for damages." The shortest man took a step forward, the black box still clenched in his left hand as he motioned at the craters the bombs had created.

"Want to collect? Meet us in two days. But for now, we're square."

Triven's hand flashed upwards and Baxter didn't miss the signal. Before the Adroits could so much as blink, there was a whistle of a bullet, then the ball Triven had tossed into the air exploded into a cloud of dust. My fingers fumbled over the bomb as Ryker had showed me, but before I could place it in my pouch, the smoke swallowed us. Two shots rang out from across the pit and we dove. The bullets went wide. I choked on a cough and Triven's fingers searched my face, pulling up the mask to cover my mouth and nose as I stowed the bomb. I could barely see his face inches from my own. There were three more shots, one snagging my hair as it barely missed us.

Panic began to spur my heartrate as Triven's shaking fingers burrowed into my forearms.

Where the *hell* was Veyron?

25. GATHERING

EVERY CURSE IN my extensive vocabulary perched on the tip of my tongue and had it not been for the lingering effects of the dust bomb causing me to cough like a leper, I would have set them free on the ex-Adroit. We were four buildings away now, safely out of range and sight of the Adroits.

"Did. You. Get. Lost?" I managed to get out between coughs. I glared at Veyron and she glared back.

"Baxter put too much powder in the bomb. You're freaking lucky I found you at all!" Her chest heaved and she spat out a mouthful of dust.

"Don't blame me. That bomb was made to perfection." Baxter cut in, temporarily pulling his eye back from the scope. "You asked for cover. I gave you cover."

"Yeah, almost enough to get us killed." Veyron said sourly.

"Enough." Triven cut over our bickering. "Baxter did his job and Veyron got us out alive. We were luckier than Elin." Shame quickly subsided everyone's rage. Triven was right. He placed a comforting hand on Baxter's shoulder and pretended not to notice when Veyron twisted away from a similar touch. Triven turned to me, "How many miles to the next safe house?"

"Ten. We're headed to the heart of the city as planned."

"Then let's get moving." Triven was quick to shoulder his bag and roust the others. I was slower to move. I paused to move the bomb from my hip pouch to a more secure position in the backpack I had left here for safekeeping. The tips of two worn boots stopped next to the bag as I secured the flap.

"Four out of four ain't bad there, crap leader."

I craned my neck to fix Archer with a hard stare.

"At least nobody died this time." She paused and then shrugged, correcting herself. "Well, none of *us*."

"I'm starting to think you'd be a crap leader yourself."

She smiled despite the tartness of my tone.

"Hence why *I* haven't volunteered to lead shit." Archer fell into step next to me as I headed toward the next roof. "You could learn something from me. Number one, don't be an idiot."

I managed a laugh. "I'll keep that in mind next time I have the urge to act like an idiot."

"You're always an idiot."

"*You're* always a pain in the ass."

"And proud!" Archer slowed, letting Otto and Cortez pass us before dropping her voice. "Seriously though, you did good… With all of this. Better than any of us expected."

I eyed the rest of the group. We hadn't lost a single person this time, but spirits were far from high. Arden was lingering on the roof's ledge across from us. His hands twitched, fingers clenching and unclenching in sporadic rhythms. His eyes were wild, jumping at every movement they saw—real and imagined.

I had done that to him.

"It will be worth it." Archer had followed my gaze.

"Not if they all don't show. Not if they choose not to side with us. *This* was the easy part." I picked up the pace again and Archer left me to run alone.

THE CITY WAS silent. The calm before the storm.

It was unsettling.

Only the Ravagers hunted the streets, howling in rage when they could not find any victims. Could they sense it? Would they know we were gathering without them? I hadn't worried about it at first, counting on the fact that most of the other Tribes hated the Ravagers more than any the others. But after our run-in with the Taciturns, obviously we hadn't been as discreet as we thought.

We sent Cortez and Baxter out to watch the Ravagers. To signal if there was movement in our direction. So far, the only thing filling the sky was black smoke from a few Ravager temper tantrums. Still, my eyes constantly flicked to the skyline like the tick of my father's watch. My fingers searched for the familiar smooth metal that usually hung at my chest, only to remember it now rested against Mouse's heart. It was impossible not to think of the little girl—to not worry about the child I would save at any cost. But as Mouse's soft face haunted me, I knew I had to tuck all thoughts of her away. For now. The child had brought out another side of me, the girl known as Prea who had begun to live again, to love. But tonight, the Tribes didn't need a human, they needed a legend—a myth. They needed Phoenix.

They needed a stone-cold calculating killer.

They wouldn't listen to—never mind follow—any less.

The lines between the two parts of me had begun to blur and I needed to sever them. At least for tonight.

Despite the brave front I had perfected, there was a rising panic pulsing in my veins. In a few hours, I was going to intentionally trap myself in a relatively enclosed space with four of Tartarus' Tribes. This was undoubtedly the stupidest thing I had ever done.

There were light steps padding behind me followed by my favorite voice.

"It looks like we're set. There hasn't been any movement in the sector for the past twenty-four hours. Nos reported the huddle of Scavengers moved on this morning and there is still no sign from Baxter and Cortez." Triven stopped next me, his shoulder barely touching mine. I leaned into him, folding in further as his arm wrapped over my shoulders.

Desperation cut suddenly and deeply like a hot blade. Swiveling on my toes, I pressed my body against his and crushed my mouth onto Triven's surprised lips. Our teeth clashed, lips first moving awkwardly then finding their rhythm together. My fingers were wound in Triven's hair, pulling hard but he didn't complain. Instead he lifted me, pulling my legs around his waist. His fingers left a hot trail as they traced my ribs and clutched my thighs. It was the most we had touched since escaping the Sanctuary. It was desperate and reckless—driven by fear. And it was over far too soon.

Triven's broad chest heaved against mine as our foreheads rested together. His skin was flushed, smelling uniquely like him.

"They're going to kill us, aren't they?" His eyes were closed as he whispered against my lips.

I pressed back against his brow, refusing to let him go just yet. "More than likely, yes."

Triven's breathing hitched, but he steadied himself and slowly released me. I slid back down to the floor. Waiting for him to open his eyes. He didn't. Not until my fingers grazed his jaw line. Then smiling weakly, Triven caught my wrist and placed one last kiss in my palm.

"We should tell the others to light the marks."

"Okay." He nodded to himself, trying to muster the courage neither of us felt. "Let's go."

I took one last deep breath and letting him keep hold of my hand, we headed toward the stairs beyond our post.

The next hour would have one of two outcomes.

A hope for a future or our deaths.

THE CHOICE OF building had not been a random one. On the contrary I had been narrowing down the best options since Ryker had first proposed the idea of a Tribal gathering. Many choices fell away without a second thought.

Too exposed.

Too secluded.

Too dilapidated.

Too close to a Tribal territory.

In the end, there was only one place that met my stringent requirements. This building was undoubtedly a far cry from what it was in its prime. The exterior had peeled away in large chunks years ago, rusted metal strewn around the structure like a barricade. It could be navigated, but the paths were clearly defined and easy to view from above. Unlike the building's membrane, the skeleton was rock solid. Even the Adroits would have a hard time leveling the structure. We had inspected every inch of the building finding no signs of tampering. The bags under everyone's eyes told of our meticulous watch over the past twenty-four hours.

Six floors rose toward the sky with few windows. It was here we had spent last night, keeping watch over the city. It was now where Grenald, Nos, Veyron and Arden perched, respective lookouts for each direction. Any sign of trouble and they would set off a micro burst, signaling everyone to run. A pact had been made. If things went sour, all who could escape would head directly back to The Master's hideout. There would be no rescue mission. Each member of our team carried a small knife, sharp enough to cleanly slit one's own throat. If tonight's plans went wrong and we face capture, we would not offer the Tribes any prisoners.

It was vital that at least one of us would survive to carry word back to the waiting Subversive members. The lookouts above had the best view of the anticipated approaching Tribes while the remaining members of our group were scattered randomly on surrounding rooftops.

They could do little to help Triven and me, but they had a decent chance of escape. Archer had put up a good fight before stomping off to her post, practically screaming about hating us forever if we got ourselves killed. At least she didn't throw a punch this time.

While our allies took perch up high, Triven and I burrowed deeper down. The top of the building gave us a near perfect aerie, but it was what lay under the building that had drawn me to it. And it was there that Triven and I now waited for our guests to arrive.

The space was fortified with cinderblock walls and concrete ceilings. Only four oversized openings allowed access to the massive pillar-filled room. One for each Tribe. This was also why micro bombs had been the only choice. We wouldn't see any signal from here, but a pulse big enough to rattle the building without destroying it, that would get our attention.

In addition, the doors were located higher up than the level ground we waited on, giving us a slight advantage. When the Tribes descended the ramps, we could easily fire off a round before they ever laid eyes on us. Any sign of red and black, and I wouldn't hesitate to shoot.

That part of the building's design was ideal. However, once inside, there were also few ways out. What could be a wonderful bunker could also prove to be a death trap. It was why no Tribe had claimed it as a refuge and why I knew it would be perfect. When the Tribes came—*if* they came—it would level the playing field. They couldn't kill each other without high risk of getting themselves killed as well. If a fight did break out, we would all die in here together. Of course, I hoped it didn't come to that, but a vindictive part of me thought it would serve Ryker right if it did. He had asked the impossible of me and deserved my blood on his hands.

Waves of nervous energy rolled off my skin. Smoke was now spiraling from the roof above and the streets were clearly marked with colored stains. Blue for the Wraiths. Purple for the Adroits. Earthy brown for the Scavengers. And grey for the Taciturns. A personalized blood trail for them to follow.

The moon would be nearly at its peak now—the night sky miraculously clear. It was not a full moon, but the light would be enough for our marksmen to see the incoming Tribes.

For the fourth time, I raised my gun, checked the chamber—still full, just like last time—and shoved it back into the holster. We were both laden with weapons. Triven carried three handguns, six knives and had one of Baxter's rifles strapped to his back. I was lacking a rifle of my own, but the ten throwing knives lacing my thighs, four handguns and machete from Grenald were equally impressive. I had twisted my hair back in a wild knot, effectively giving myself a few more inches of height, but also clearing it from my eyes. The slightly iridescent sheen of our synthetic suits from the Rebels completed the look. I hated the weight of the extra weaponry and though Triven had initially suggested coming unarmed as a sign of peace, the weapons were necessary. To the Tribes, lack of weapons meant lack of power. And only power commanded their respect.

Triven shifted next to me and the metal frame below us protested. We had cultivated our spot carefully. Backed up to a solid wall with two doors on either side of us. The room was filled with metal skeletons like the one we stood on. They were once machines like the transport vehicle Gage had imprisoned me in. However, they were long ago stripped bare, the rusting bones exposed, metal, plastic and rubber repurposed into armor and weapons. At some point, there must been have doors enclosing the space— their tracks rusted, but still hanging in place. Now, there were only voids, points of exposure.

My eyes darted to each. Every sound, every illusory movement drawing my attention, spiking my adrenaline. The minutes had ticked by like hours and neither of us spoke. Waiting. Listening.

Nothing.

Triven's fingers brushed mine. I could feel the nervousness through his touch.

Now what? He was asking. *What if they don't come?*

My lungs struggled as panic began to roil in the pit of my stomach. The Tribes should have been here by now. Either to kill us or to hear us out, but they *should* have been here. I had warned Ryker this would happen. I had told him they wouldn't come. But before angry tears could well, Triven's hand shot out, grabbing mine fast and hard. It sent a jolt of pain up my arm, then quickly disappeared as his hand moved for his gun. I mirrored him without thinking. Then I heard it too.

Footsteps.

Someone *was* coming. *A lot* of someones.

I leveled the barrel of my gun at the open door. This was it.

Join or die.

26. CHOICES

THE COLORS FILTERING into the door were not what I had been expecting. No blue or maroon or purple, but brown. The faded earthy colors were quickly followed by the stench—Scavengers. And there were more than I expected.

Thirty-two filthy bodies skittered down the ramp— eyes beady, noses twitching in every direction. The fidgety group was made almost entirely of men, the hordes' leaders clearly at the front. Lips pulled back revealing yellow teeth and rotted gums, but they had come. The group paused at the base of the ramp's slope. None seem surprised to have guns drawn on them, but their keen eyes were on edge, the lack of the other Tribes' presence didn't go unnoticed.

I honestly thought they were going to bail and run. But a tittering voice echoed through another open door and the Scavengers quickly scurried tighter together.

"Damn. And here I thought we would be the *first* to the party."

My second hand swung to the left, pointing another handgun in the direction of the voice.

Sedia's wicked grin flipped into a mock pout as she appeared in the doorway marked for the Taciturns. I had an odd sense of relief. Sedia was the first down the ramp, but the crazed woman was not alone. Though their numbers were less than the Scavengers', the Taciturns' presence was far more intimidating. Sedia swaggered in at ease, closely followed by a pack of fifteen armor-covered Taciturns. And there—at the very center—was a man with eyes as dark as night and an even darker aura. He alone wore almost no protection. In fact, the only thing covering his bare chest was a patchwork vest.

I immediately bristled. Even at this distance, I could make out the stretched tattoos adorning the leather-like material.

Skin.

The entire vest was made of skin.

Sedia watched me, winking when I finally looked back at her.

Zed had come. She had kept her promise.

Zed's eyes swept my body, before jeering, "So *this* is the unstoppable warrior you told me about." He did not sound impressed, despite the desire burning in his eyes.

Perhaps he simply liked my skin.

Triven stiffened, undoubtedly thinking the same thing.

"Well ain't that a proper introduction." A deep raspy voice boomed in the open space, causing everyone but Sedia to jump.

The Taciturns stopped in their progression as hisses emanated from the Scavengers. The oversized group of rats recoiled, converging to the farthest left side of their ramp and Triven's second gun leapt to the newcomers.

I had not heard them enter, but standing proudly on the third ramp was Archer's mother and her best warriors.

Zed's protective entourage suddenly made him look more like a coward than a leader. And Teya, despite her feral appearance, looked one-hundred percent a queen. Wild and dangerous, but a queen nonetheless. Like her Tribesmen, the Wraith leader was clad in matching body armor, but woven into her dark braided hair was a crown of bones. At the center sat a large bird's skull, the bleached beak pressing a dent between her brows. Faces scarred and armed to the gills, seven Wraith warriors flanked their leader. Unlike her Taciturn counterpart, Teya did not hide behind her people, but stood proud at their forefront. A mercenary queen.

There was a shuffling as several Scavengers turned away from their Tribe and disappeared back up the ramp and into the night. Those remaining did not seem to notice or care.

Pulse roaring in my ears, I tried to swallow down the internal noise.

Three Tribes were under one roof. We had almost done it. Part of me was pleased while the other part wanted to blow up the whole damn place. In different circumstances, I might have. But not tonight. Tonight, we needed them. Enemies of fortune. Allies of circumstance.

The momentary adrenaline high singing in my veins quieted as the faces of the final missing Tribe came into view. Cloaks of purple and gold powdered skin emerged from the final opening and my heart sank. The Adroits had come, but not to help us.

Three Adroits stood at the precipice of their entryway. Removed from the group and refusing to come closer. But it wasn't only their body language that worried me, it was their faces.

I knew them.

It was the three Watchmen. No more, no less, and *no* leader.

My second gun moved from the Scavengers to the Adroits. My arms were a perfect mirror of Triven's. Four doors, a gun on each. Not that it would do any good if anyone else shot first. At least fifty various weapons pointed back at us from four sides, but I could probably squeeze out a few rounds before death took me. An eye for an eye and all.

The Adroit at the center, Legs I remembered calling him, moved with surprising speed. A small device appeared in his hand and before any of us could so much as blink, his thumb jammed down on the gadget. There was a collective flinch as it clicked, but nothing happened.

Legs spoke in the same flat emotionless voice as before. "Kill me and I let go. I let go, and this will blow up the entire room."

I didn't lower my gun, but nodded, accepting his terms.

"Oooooo! I like him, he's *fun*!" Sedia giggled, breaking the tension.

The Taciturns ignored her, while the other Tribes drank in the woman's insanity. Teya seemed especially disconcerted by the small Taciturn, though she quickly shook off her distaste and turned to address me.

"Why are we here, ghost girl?" Teya's demanding voice resounded harshly off the concrete. She would be wasting no time.

We had prepared for a hundred different ways the Tribes could react to the gathering. What we hadn't prepared for was *my* reaction.

I wanted to lower my guns, to reach for the device heavy in my thigh pocket as we had planned, but I couldn't. Everything we had fought for, everything we had risked our lives for over the past weeks had been for this moment, and I couldn't open my stupid mouth! I tried to breathe, to lessen the pressure tightening in my chest. Now was not the time to have a panic attack. I knew what was happening, but I couldn't stop the mounting terror. The Tribes were watching me, waiting for me and all I could think of was the cell Fandrin had thrown me in, of watching my parents dying... of Maddox. Why now? I had pushed through my fears for the better part of a week, why were they breaking me *now*? My heart wasn't going to explode, *this is only a panic attack* my mind shouted, but reason wasn't convincing my body. A slight tremor quivered the guns clutched white-knuckled in my hands, and I sucked in a wheezed breath. I desperately wanted to drop to the ground and press my head between my knees, but that would get us both killed for sure. My mouth was filled with sand, the useless tongue sticking to the roof.

Three long seconds had passed, feeling like an eternity. Then Triven took a slight step forward, noticing my hesitation. Could he hear my strangled breathing? Could the Tribes? I stared hard at the skull on Teya's head, counting the seconds as I tried to suppress the storm of anxiety growing in my chest. Triven began to speak, covering for me. I missed his first few words.

Breathe. Breathe. Not now. I clung to the words. *Not now.*

"… We're bringing The Wall down. We're taking back the Sanctuary. With or without you. The terms are the same and you have all been offered the same rewards, but your reasons to fight are your own. Personally, we don't really care *why* you fight, just that you do. Fight or walk away."

"You say *we*. So, you *are* a Tribe." A male Scavenger barked, recoiling slightly as all eyes fell on him.

"No," Triven brandished his next words. "*We* are a revolution."

"Pretty words from a pretty little boy." Teya's round eyes watched me, before pinning Triven. "You're not of our world, *boy*." The statement, while seemingly innocuous, was a threat. The Tribes didn't like outsiders. They *killed* outsiders. I didn't miss that her guards had flexed around her. Ready.

The Scavengers scooted closer, as if sensing a kill.

Triven, however, stood taller, not hearing her words as I had. "I may not—"

Zed's voice scratched out from behind his wall of guards, cutting Triven off. The pitch came out too high, echoing shrilly. The Taciturn leader was quivering from head to toe and there was a manic glint in his eye. "I will *never* bow to another man!"

"I could make you bow to a woman." Teya did not miss a beat, her deep voice overpowering Zed's.

A bark of laughter boomed from the Scavengers, some tittering at Teya's mockery, others at the idea of bowing to a woman. Both the Wraiths and Taciturns prickled instantly. Only the Adroits looked on with mild disinterest.

Teya's cold glare turned on the lowly rat Tribe and in unison her warriors shifted, targeting the Tribes on either side of them. With a nearly imperceptible flick of her fingers, several hand-crafted machetes emerged, hungry for blood. Simultaneously, the Taciturn leader let out a strangled cry. "Shut your mouth, you fifthly RATS!" Zed slammed his body against the guards in front of him, pummeling his fists into their backs but did not cross his line of shelter. The Taciturns quickly raised their own weapons, targeting everything that moved. Even Sedia was snarling at the back of the pack.

The room vibrated with howls and hisses of outrage. Battle cries began to hum with the escalating noise. Bodies crouched, preparing for attack and as a collective the Tribes took a step forward, even the Adroits.

"Stop! Enough!" Triven yelled. The guns shook in his hands as he waved them at the raging Tribes, but his words were swallowed by the din.

The entire room tensed. Make-shift knives and battered guns emerged from beneath the Scavengers' brown rags. One man raised a hand, knife ready, eyes on Triven. A nearby Wraith brandished a sharpened rod, the spikes on the end intended for the nearest Taciturn. The two Tribesmen moved, but so did I.

Instinct snuffed out the terror and my body surged back to life, muscles were once again under my control. My hands moved first, jamming the guns back into their holsters. In the same movement, two knives were pulled free and sent flying.

Then several things happened all at once.

Triven blinked as one blade flew inches from his nose before burying itself into the Scavenger's hand, pinning it to his own shoulder. The knife he had been holding clattered to the ground with his howl of pain and the Wraith preparing to attack froze as my other knife embedded into the broad side of his weapon, narrowly missing the man's skull.

"ENOUGH!!" I screamed. My own voice echoed back in the dead silence. For fifteen seconds, the room was statue-still. All eyes on me. I heaved, legs still shaky, but my lungs were my own again.

The hint of a smile pulled up at Teya's lips, then cracked into a snarl as Zed exploded.

"I WILL *NEVER* FOLLOW A WOMAN!" Zed's crazed screaming was jarring in the hush. The statement seemed less directed at me, but at the room as a whole. Spit flew from his lips as his fists pulled wildly at his hair, ripping a few chunks free as he glared at me. He waved the fistfuls of dark hair at the room around him. "KILL THEM, KILL THEM ALL!"

I braced myself for an attack, but then nearly dropped my guns in shock.

The back of the Taciturn entourage had parted for Sedia. And smooth like the fox she was, she stalked silently behind the hysterical Zed, pressed a gun to the back of her leader's head, and pulled the trigger.

27. SPEAK

THE GUNSHOT WAS deafening in the confined space.

There was a spray of blood and the Taciturns in the front parted, letting Zed's faceless body crumble to the ground with a heavy wet crunch. His words still echoed off the walls, trailed by the reverberating booms of Sedia's shot.

Zed's body had barely hit the ground before Sedia was striding casually onto the corpse's back, unsteadily balancing herself as the body shifted under her steps. Not a single Taciturn looked alarmed by what had just happened, those closest merely side-stepping to keep the ex-leader's blood from soiling their shoes.

"New leader?!" Sedia yelled as she pressed her foot into what was left of Zed's head. In perfect unison, the remaining Taciturns gave a guttural cry I could only assume meant approval. Sedia then tucked her gun—*my* gun, the one she had stolen—carelessly between her cleavage and gestured as if once again giving me the floor.

I blinked at her three times before coming back to myself.

Taking a shaky breath, I lowered my guns and placed them back in their side holsters. It left me feeling naked despite the small arsenal decorating my body. My fingers itched to hold a weapon.

Triven at least stayed at the ready.

What the hell had just happened? Had we just witnessed a coup?

I glared at the Tribes, refusing to look down at the body under Sedia's feet, and gestured to Triven. "*He* may not be of your world but I *am*. I've watched your Tribes war for years. And for what? Better *scraps*?" My voice was getting stronger with each breath. "You want to keep fighting like animals for *caged* territory? Fine. I really don't give a crap which of you live or die here. Me? If I'm going to die, it's going to be for a hell of a lot more than petty Tribe shit. I'm offering you more, and if you're too stupid to take it, that's on you."

"Are we're to serve as *your* army then?" A huge blonde man to Teya's left spoke, his lips pulled back in a growl. "Sacrifice *our* lives, for *you*?"

"Why the hell would you fight for me? That's the stupidest thing I heard." My face twisted into a mask of incredulity as I pulled myself up to full height—which wasn't really that impressive. But the man looked taken aback. "Fight for yourselves."

The man looked like he wanted to say something else, but Teya's hand twitched, silencing him. Her stare was beginning to burn, but snapped away as a soft voice spoke.

"You are missing one Tribe." The female Adroit spoke for the first time. She did not look around the room searching for the Ravagers, but stayed focused on me, already reading my every reaction.

"The *Ravagers,*" a chorus of hisses snaked out as I said their name, "chose their side years ago. And The Minister ruling in the Sanctuary, chose *them. Not you.*" The Adroit stared back clearly unconvinced, so I continued. "Did you really think the Ravagers were able to grow so powerful—with the *best* weapons, the *most* food—because they were *smart* enough to get that stuff?" I let my words linger over the room of killers. "While *your* Tribes fought for food, *theirs* was being handed it. And in return, they killed more people than any other Tribes in this room combined. Do you really want to side with *them?*"

The Adroit said nothing, but her silence spoke volumes. I knew what she was thinking. The word hovering on her tongue.

"Those *rapists?*" I spat the word, thinking of what they had done. To my mother. To Veyron. The Tribes in this room were killers and savages, but even savages have their own twisted morals. In all my years in Tartarus, the Ravagers were the only ones I had seen cross that line. They never raped their own, but they did assault other Tribes and didn't just target the women.

The responses were subtle. Nostrils flared. Fists clenched. Cheeks flushed. I knew I had hit the right nerve. If they couldn't unite to fight for a better life for themselves, then maybe they could unite in their hate for the one Tribe not invited.

"If The Wall comes down and you *don't* fight with us—if we *lose*—The Ravagers will have more power, more weapons than ever before. They will destroy you, *all* of you. And everyone in this room knows what they do to their victims."

The climate in the air had changed. Subtly at first, but I could feel it now. They were listening.

"And if we turn on each other?" A Scavenger man I recognized as an Alpha stepped to the front of his huddle, arms crossed.

"Then kill each other, I don't care. That's between you and yours." I glanced at each Tribe leader and the Adroit representatives in turn. "Just try and take out some Sanctuary guards along the way. When we get inside, aim for the silver uniforms."

"There is only one rule." Triven amended, glancing at me for approval. "If soldiers on the other side surrender, let them live."

"We make no promises." A tall but scrawny Scavenger croaked behind his Alpha, his narrowed eyes greedily looking at the advanced weapons in Triven's hands.

I had expected as much. Especially from the Scavengers. You couldn't release wild hounds and be surprised when they attacked… or turned on you.

"Neither do we." I leveled at the Scavenger before slowly forcing eye contact with as many of the Tribe members in the room that I could. Both Teya and Sedia met my scrutiny with equal intensity. "This is *not* a truce. It's an understanding. But, cross us and we *will* cross you."

"I knew I liked you." Sedia smirked behind her hand mask with a wink. Then she did the thing I was still afraid to. She called a vote.

"Join?" She barked to her people. The same haunting cry as before tremored from the surrounding Taciturns. Her grin widened as the skull-covered hand fell away. "Join."

"Join." Teya barked decisively, looking a little annoyed she did not say it first. Unlike the Taciturns, however, there was no vote in her Tribe. A queen did not ask her subjects' permission. Her Wraiths would fight because she bid them so.

There were sporadic murmurers of "Join" from the Scavengers though their enthusiasm was lacking in comparison and five more scurried back up the ramp, committing to nothing. I couldn't help but wonder if any of them would show at all. Probably not.

All eyes turned to the Adroits, and though I already knew the answer, the words still stung.

"We abstain." They said it in unison, the choice made long ago.

Teya's shoulders pulled back with rage, but I kept my voice calm despite my own boiling anger. "The choice is yours. Go."

Without another word, the purple cloaks swirled and the Adroits were gone, Legs' finger still pressed firmly on his trigger.

"Cowards!" Sedia called after them, earning a round of laughter from her Tribesmen.

I didn't spare the vacant door a second glance and Triven's gun shifted in the Adroits' absence. No one moved, listening for their retreating footsteps. Then a piercing howl echoed down into our man-made cave. Unlike the rest of us, the Wraiths relaxed.

"They're gone." Teya nodded at me. The howl had been a signal for her. "When does The Wall come down?"

"Tomorrow night." I replied.

A shockwave of displeasure pulsed through the Tribes.

"One night is not enough time to prepare!" A Taciturn cried out, an elaborate dagger tattoo started under his chin and ended at a point just above his belly button. Many nodded in agreement, including the woman next to him whose jaw was covered in inked scales like a human snake.

"I know." I agreed. "But one night is all you get."

"And if your precious Wall doesn't come down?" A Wraith warrior, nearly as tall as Grenald, spoke from Teya's side. It was obvious this was her right-hand man. Her Second.

Triven flinched at my response.

Faking all the confidence I could muster, I spoke. "You can shoot *me*."

THE GATHERING DIDN'T last much longer. Tensions were high and feet were edging to escape. Vague instructions were given out, telling them where to gather. But even with their proclamations to join us, I kept the details scant. Minds and loyalties could change and I would not risk being betrayed. Not when we were this close. We had prepared to show them the Rebels' video, but the Tribes needed no further enticement. Whatever their reasons, they were in. It seemed almost *too* easy. Though Elin would have said differently. The remaining Tribes had given their word, but their word meant little without action.

Our recon team had seemed genuinely surprised when Triven and I finally emerged. Though they had supported us, it was clear they had not expected us to succeed. Or survive.

"Are they in?" Archer had been the only one brave enough to ask when we reached them.

"All but the Adroits."

No one had responded. We just gathered our things and took off, racing back to the Master's for our last twenty-four hours of peace.

The clock was ticking down to the final hours and though there were still plans to rehash and sleep needed, there was only one thing I wanted. One person I needed to see.

Xavier was waiting for us a block out from his building. The aging man didn't bother hiding his surprise. His eye darted over us, doing the math. "Well, damn."

"Careful old man, you almost sounded impressed." I muttered walking past him.

He snorted and took the lead. "Careful, *you're* starting to sound cocky."

"That's not new." Archer piped in from behind us and there was a collective chortle from the group. It was a nice sound, something we hadn't heard in weeks. Being back here had lifted a weight in some way. For the next day, anyway, we were free to be ourselves again. Free to hide away and pretend tomorrow would never come.

Though Xavier took us in an entirely new way, as usual, the passage was not empty. People slumped against walls, heads hanging low, some dozing in each other's arms. It wasn't until they saw us and began to cheer, rising to their feet, that I realized they had been waiting. For *us*.

Hands reached out, patting, shaking and gripping as we passed accompanied by shouts of relief and welcome.

Even those who usually gave me a wide berth were suddenly brazen enough to touch me. It had never occurred to me what our return would mean to them. While Triven and the others graciously embraced their friends and family, I pushed through the crowded hall, shoving hands aside as I sought the very back of the swarm.

I had seen her for a split second before everyone rose. I swore I had seen a mop of dark brown hair with blonde curls next to it. My feet stumbled in their haste, tripping over toes. Bouncing on the balls of my feet, I tried to catch a glimpse of brown hair or a round face, but all I could see were shoulders.

"Phoenix!" Someone was calling from behind me. I ignored it.

I rather rudely shoved an older man aside and then I saw her.

Mouse stood back from the crowd, her tiny hands folded gently at her waist. Doc's hand rested on her shoulder but I hardly saw him. All I saw was the sterile white bandage wrapped thickly around Mouse's neck. My mind went blank and then I was rushing to her. Falling to my knees, I grabbed urgently for her throat, inspecting the wound.

Heat burned in my cheeks and my vision went red.

"How?!" I screamed, glaring up at Doc Porters.

Stuttering, Doc yanked his hand away as if my rage had scalded him and Mouse's eyes popped in surprise, but I was already pulling away from her, turning on the person who had been calling my name.

"What the HELL did YOU DO?!" My hands were searching for a weapon. I would *kill* him if he hurt her.

Xavier actually recoiled, his hands snapping up in defense.

"Phoenix, it's okay." Doc had found his voice.

I didn't take my eyes off the Master. "It is NOT okay!"

People were turning to watch us now, backing away. Triven appeared behind Xavier looking confused, but the second his eyes moved to Mouse, his expression twisted to match mine.

Fingers trembling, I had found my gun. My thumb found the catch, but just as I pulled to release it, a small hand pressed over mine, pushing the weapon back down into the holster.

Mouse stepped in front of me, her dark eyes determined but bright. She snatched my hands with a tug, forcing me to look down at her. For a second she flashed a shy smile, then opened her mouth and said in a flawless small voice, "Phoenix."

28. FURNACE

"**YOU PROMISE IT** doesn't hurt?" I was still staring at Mouse in disbelief.

She nodded, beaming from ear to ear.

The shock still hadn't worn off. Not after I had made her say my name three more times, not after Doc had spent nearly an hour answering all our questions.

My legs had given out when she first said my name, the concrete floor leaving angry bruises and Triven had nearly taken out three people reaching us, but none of that mattered.

Mouse had a voice. *My* Mouse.

"Say it again." I grinned at her in awe.

"Phoenix. Triven." Our names came out on clumsy lips and an unpracticed tongue, but they sounded perfect to me.

"And you trust the device?" I asked Doc for the twentieth time.

"My brother always was a genius." Doc blinked back tears.

"Must run in the family." I said. Doc blushed.

"I can't believe you kept this a secret." Triven pushed a stray lock out of Mouse's face and the child smiled at him.

Not sure it would work, she signed.

Despite now having a voice, she still used her hands out of habit. Doc had also mentioned it would take a little while for her body to adjust. Like all muscles, her voice would take time to strengthen. She pressed a finger to the small lump I could see under the healing skin on her throat. Nestled in with her vocal cords, reconnecting the severed ties, was a small device expertly crafted by Doc's brother, Thaddeus. Yet another gift from the Rebels on the other side of The Wall.

Skilled in the ways of technology, Thaddeus had made the contraption while we took refuge with the Rebels. But for all his genius designs, he was not the gifted doctor that his brother was. So, unbeknownst to us, Thadd had sent the miracle package back with instructions for his brother to implant. Worlds apart and the Porters brothers had managed to give a girl back her voice.

Triven and I watched as Doc made Mouse run through a series of vocal exercises. They had been practicing them for nearly a week—the secret surgery taking place the day after we left—but tonight, my name had been her first official word in nearly two years.

I was about to ask her to speak again when there was a knock on the door.

Triven's mother stood in the doorway. Her arms were crossed but there was a hesitation in her movements. As though she didn't want to ruin this moment as much as we hoped she wouldn't.

"Archer led most of the debriefing, we should be set for tomorrow. The weapons are ready and the rations divided—we're as prepared as we can be." She spoke in the familiar sharp tone I had once hated.

"And the rooftops?" I asked, not moving from Mouse's side.

"I helped ready them myself. They are exactly to your specifications."

I only nodded and she shifted.

"I understand you want to be alone and you will have time, but the others are waiting." She looked at her son, thawing a bit.

"Waiting?" Triven slipped a hand around my waist, making it clear he wasn't going anywhere without me.

Doc paused in packing up his things. "We are having one last Subversive party."

"A party now?" I turned to Arstid in surprise.

"Our people came home safely, and after tomorrow we may never get to celebrate that again." Her gold eyes wandered to her son.

This wasn't only a celebration, it was a goodbye.

"Please?" The small voice still made my heart hitch. Mouse was looking at me pleadingly. They must have been planning this for a while, hoping we would return.

I smiled back at her. "For you kid, anything."

THE FOOD WAS a sad showing, not of the usual standards for a Subversive gathering, but it was perfect nonetheless. Friends gathered, told stories, held each other, laughed and cried. The majority of us were leaving tomorrow. We would stand on the rooftops and wait for the rebels to fulfill their part of the deal. And if The Wall came down, then we would plunge head first into a war that would change our world forever. Those not joining us were staying here for one of a few reasons, too old to fight or too young, to tend to the children, or like Veyron, because they refused to fight for something they didn't believe in. But tonight, we were all on the same side. Tonight, these people were not soldiers readying for battle, they were friends. They were family.

I had watched most of it carefully removed until Archer literally pulled me into the mix. It was both soothing and depressing. I sought the faces I knew, and tried not to see ones I had yet to learn. I couldn't look at them. Couldn't memorize more faces that might die because I had asked them.

Triven was taking both Mouse and Maribel for a spin on the dance floor, and I took the moment to excuse myself for some air. I wandered down the maze of halls until I found a deserted one. Sliding down the cool wall, I dropped my head to my knees. It suddenly felt too heavy. *Everything* felt too heavy.

"It's not easy asking people to die for you, is it?" Arstid stood pale as a ghost, blocking the way I had just come.

I hadn't heard her follow me, though I hadn't been listening either. To my surprise, she didn't keep her usual stiff power-stance, but slumped in the floor across from me. It was the first time I noticed how much she had aged since we left. Dark circles rounded her eyes and her lips had grown thinner. Everything about her had grown thinner.

Suddenly, unexpectedly, I pitied her.

"You're not the girl I would have chosen for my son." She eyed me, her left eyebrow raised.

Any sympathy I had evaporated instantly.

"Then it's a good thing he doesn't seem to value your opinion very much." I retorted. If my words stung, she didn't show it.

"My son and I see eye-to-eye on very little these days." Arstid smiled tiredly. "I suppose that does work in your favor."

I stared at her, wondering what she wanted.

"You don't make it easy to like you." Her gold eyes were sharp as a bird of prey's.

"Neither do you."

She tilted her head accepting the insult. "Leaders don't always get the privilege of being liked."

"Like *my mother?*" I threw the words at her and Arstid flinched.

"*Yes.*" Taking a deep breath, she shook her silvery head, trying to clear it. "Leaders ask people to die for them. And people *will* die for you."

I ground my back teeth together. "I know."

"My son may be one of those." Arstid's voice hushed as though if she said it quite enough it wouldn't be true. My chest instantly tightened.

"He will follow you anywhere." Her eyes bore into mine, holding me hostage.

I snarled. "I would make him stay here if I could. Safe. With Mouse."

She studied me for a moment. "I don't doubt that. But my son hasn't listened to me for a long time and he won't listen to you—not about that."

She blinked and I looked away from hers. There was blood on the toe of my boot. I rubbed them together trying to remove it, rubber squeaking in our silence.

"I won't let him die." *He can't die,* is what I meant.

"You can't make that promise. Everyone dies." Arstid's voice traveled, lost in thought, in memories.

Yes, everyone dies. It was part of being human. Part of being alive.

"I will do everything in my power to bring him back to you again." My eyes shot up, trying to force the promise in my words on her.

"For once, I believe you." She cleared her throat in an awkward cough as she rose to her feet. She began to walk away, then paused. Turning her head back she spoke over her shoulder. "He told me what you did. What happened inside... I wouldn't have picked you, but... even *I* can be wrong."

And then she walked away.

I balked. Was that an apology? There was something about her tone, as if she was not just forgiving me, but forgiving my mother as well. Would she feel the same when she found out about our bloodlines? About who my grandfather was?

A beep jolted me out of my reverie, causing me to jump to my feet. Something in my pocket had vibrated. Snatching Ryker's device, I stared at the screen. It was no longer black. Flickering back were white numbers. And they were counting down. Twenty-three hours, fifty-nine minutes and forty-eight seconds. Forty-seven... Forty-six...

Less than twenty-four hours.

Shoving the screen back in my pocket, I set out to find Mouse and Triven. The clock was now literally ticking.

MOUSE DIDN'T CRY when we left her this time. She seemed determined not to. Her brown eyes glistened but not a single tear fell. She only said two words, her hands signing as she spoke.

"Be careful."

The child had spent the night in my arms, her head tucked under my chin as I curled my back into Triven's chest. None of us slept. Three bodies breathing in unison. Three minds racing.

The atmosphere had changed in the morning. All signs of the previous night's festivities had disappeared and a cloud had rolled over the Subversive people. The long day was spent checking and re-checking gear, reviewing maps already memorized. The waiting was almost worse than seeking out the Tribes. At least then we had purpose, we were moving.

That was how we found ourselves spanning the rooftop with two hours still ticking down on Ryker's timer.

The Subversive members were barely recognizable. War paint of every color smeared faces, shadowed eyes, and painted bodies. They were clad in homemade armor, armed with weapons stolen from the Ravagers and donated from the Rebels. A buzz vibrated in the air, surging through us, singing in our blood.

The Wall stood tall as ever. Humming with energy—virile and alive, it showed no signs of failing.

I wondered if this was how the ancient Gladiators I had once read about felt. A fight to the death lying just beyond closed doors, and all you could do was wait.

My hand twitched to my vest tapping the breast pocket. Folded carefully inside was a drawing of a young man and girl, between them a smiling child. Triven's fingers wove in mine, pulling my hand back down to my side with a squeeze.

"We did the right thing. She will be safer with the other children here." He reassured me again. It was what we had agreed on. Even Mouse understood she would be a liability on the front line, but it still felt wrong not to have her with us. To not have her at my side.

"I know, but..." I trailed off. It was selfish. Stupid.

"I know." He repeated.

"How much time?" Otto approached us from the milling crowd. He was not the first to ask this question. We had fallen into a rotation. Someone asking every three minutes or so. Archer the most frequent offender. I had finally set the screen on the roof ledge where everyone could see it. But they still asked.

I glanced first at Ryker's ticker then up at the night sky. We would get no cover tonight. The moon was bright and nearly at its peak. Ryker's clock was true.

"One hour." I confirmed. "Light the markers."

Otto threw up a hand, giving the signal. There were two soft pops and smoke laced the moonlight. He hesitated, watching the smoke grow. "You think they'll come?"

Triven squeezed my hand again as he spoke. "I don't know."

There were only fifty of us. The first wave of attack. We were the battering ram, the ones to clear a path for the slightly less abled. We would enter first with the Tribes flanking us for support.

Support wasn't the right word though.

They were not on our side exactly, they were more like gasoline being added to an already burning fire. We hoped they would fuel the chaos and little more. With the Sanctuary's eyes turned on us and the Tribes, our second wave could enter with less resistance. This is where Triven's mother, Arden and the remainder of our friends and family were. Five miles away, they waited on a roof of their own, ready to launch a secondary invasion. We had no way of communicating. No way of knowing if the other half of our group was safe. Our only hope of finding each other—of finding the rebels—were the two beacons Ryker had given me. Nos currently had ours stowed in his hip pocket, while I had entrusted Arden with the second one. Once we crossed The Wall, the beacons would activate and the rebels could find us.

Arstid hadn't said it out loud, not even as she parted ways with her son, but I knew she understood the truth about her team. They weren't just a second infiltration team, they were our backup plan. The Tribes didn't know about them and if our team failed—if the Tribes turned on us—Arstid's team was our last hope.

I had taken to prowling the roof line as the clock continued to tick, periodically flicking pebbles at The Wall's protective field. Each one hit the invisible shield with a crackle of electricity, turning the rocks to ash. The Wall still stood tall, strong. Twenty feet within our reach and yet completely untouchable. There was no penetrating the iron-clad base—it stood nearly three stories high and was at least a block's width thick. Not even a Sanctuary bomb would put much of a dent in the reinforced barricade. But the dome, electrified with enough intensity to fry anything that touched it, that was the only weak point. Though completely impenetrable from the outside, it *could* be taken down from the inside. If The Wall's power failed, then so would the shield. Thaddeus had warned us that there were backup generators, that once the dome's power was cut, the seconds would begin ticking before it turned back on. The generators would be targeted and taken out next, but there was no guarantee the Rebels could deactivate them all before they powered up. Scattered throughout The Wall's infrastructure, the generators would have to be shut down manually, one by one. If a generator fired on, anyone not clear of that section would be fried.

Salvaged beams and makeshift ladders lined our roofs, ready to drop down and span the gaps the instant the shield dropped. This was the only way in.

At twenty-six minutes, thirty-seven seconds, a shrill whistle cut the night and the rooftop to the left of ours came to life. Bodies slid from the shadows, their silhouettes blurred at the edges, moving in the breeze. White painted faces staccato with blue slashes swam in the darkness and Archer took a step backward.

The Wraiths had come.

There were nearly one-hundred and fifty of them, their numbers alone outweighing ours. A shiver ran down my spine. The whistle rang out again and the foremost shadow raised a glinting blade in the air, tilted the hilt toward me and then clutched it to her chest. A salute meant for me. Teya had been true to her word. They were here to fight next to us.

With a signal from their leader, the Tribe twisted as a unit and in a flowing movement they turned away from us to face The Wall. Only six scouts stayed posted at the other three sides of the building, two to an edge. The two facing us had not drawn their weapons but they were watching me.

They would be the ones to shoot me if The Wall did not come down. I was sure of it.

Ten minutes and seventeen seconds later, a peel of laughter broke the stillness. The Taciturns arrived in an array of organized chaos. Maroon and grey paint splattered their clothing, but unlike the Wraiths, their skin remained exposed. Tattoos proud, many of the Taciturns presented fresh ink and raw skin. I counted seventy-three of them. The Tribesmen were no longer acting as human shields for their new leader, who skipped along the building's edge on light toes. Twice Sedia flipped from her feet to her hands and then back again, nearly slipping off the ledge before covering her face with her tattooed hand mask.

"Did you start the party without us?" She looked up at the looming Wall as if it might be an illusion. "Who am I kidding, we *are* the party."

She giggled again and several of her Tribesmen joined her.

I hated to think what *they* considered a party.

The Subversive members gathered closer together as the Taciturns leered at our band of misfits. We had been right to cover them in war paint of neutral colors. To hide the ex-Tribesmen in plain sight. The Taciturns looked hungry, and I wouldn't put it past them to shoot a traitor on the spot.

At seven minutes, forty-six seconds, there was a shuffling on the Taciturns' roof as their attention moved to their right. The Scavengers were the last to show themselves, but I had a strong feeling they had actually been the first to arrive. The rats were just biding their time. Waiting to see what played out before committing. There were the fewest of them. Maybe thirty-five at the most and nearly half of them looked ready to bolt at any second.

"Damn vermin…" I heard Nos mutter somewhere behind me.

A Taciturn caught my eye. Tilting his head, he pointed two fingers at me, then pressed them to his head, miming pulling a trigger.

Archer snarled next to me. "I'll put a *real* bullet between his damn eyes."

"He doesn't deserve a quick death like that." Otto's grip tightened around his weapon, casting the Taciturn a brief glance.

"Know that jackass?" Archer asked surprised.

"He's my brother." Otto refused to look back at the man staring at us.

With Otto's face covered in paint, little resemblance could be found, but I could see his features in the cut of the other man's jaw, in the up-turn of his eyes.

Archer cast a sideways glance to her left at the Wraiths. "Family is overrated."

"Agreed." I piped in, staring straight ahead.

The seconds that had earlier ticked down like hours suddenly seemed to speed up. Each passing second felt like another bullet aimed in my direction. I could feel everyone's eyes on the clock, but mine stayed resolutely on The Wall.

Less than a minute.

There was a collective intake of breath and I knew the clock had run out.

Nothing.

"Come on, Ryker." I hissed as Triven tensed next to me.

I cast my eyes up to moon. It was at its peak. This was it. This was the moment.

Murmurs buzzed, filling the night and a movement caught the corner of my eye. Guns were pointing my way. Aiming at everyone around me. On instinct, I stepped up on the building's ledge making myself a clearer target. As Triven lunged to pull me back down, an explosion sent everyone ducking for cover. Barks of shock and triumph rang out, but dampened quickly.

It wasn't The Wall.

In the distance, the spindly-legged tower rose in flames. Metal screeched as The Healer's water tower collapsed and a blood-thirsty Ravager battle cry followed. A moment of grief slapped my thoughts for the old woman, then reality crashed back. Suspicion began to fill the air and guns were raising again. There was no mistaking their target this time.

Me.

Desperately, I threw my hands up begging them not to fire and as I opened my mouth to scream—to plead—a deafening crack split the darkness.

Louder than thunder and brighter than any lightning, a blinding blue wave of energy spidered out from a point on The Wall's shield nearly a hundred feet above our heads. The surge pulsed outward before sucking back in on itself with a series of violent crackles. Hexagonal panels exploded to life as the energy pulsed through them. For a split second, a perfect starry sky appeared in the shield, hinting at the illusion projected to the world inside, then piece by piece, the panels flickered out revealing the city beyond.

A city untouched by Tartarus's rot.

A city ablaze with fire.

29. FLOOD

A **BLAST OF** heat slammed into my cheeks, whipping back my hair with its force. The air above The Wall shimmered, hissing and popping as the dome once protecting it sizzled out of existence.

For the first time in *all* our lifetimes, The Wall had come down.

Tartarus and the Sanctuary were one.

No one moved. Not even the Tribes mustered a battle cry. Then a shoulder slammed into mine.

Triven was the first to move, the one to break the spell, and suddenly the rooftops were alive. Shouts broke out instructing hands to take hold, feet to move. My own fingers felt numb as they clumsily snatched the tablet from the ground, stowing it safely back in my pocket and then gripped the dense beam tilting up next to me.

"Release!" Voices were yelling and the makeshift bridges tipped in plummeting arcs before slamming down onto the top of The Wall and connecting our worlds. The beam before me had barely stopped bouncing before I leapt on. Triven was on his too, sprinting toward our goal, side by side. Other planks fell in my periphery and soon the

Subversive members were not the only people careening toward the Sanctuary.

My feet ran the beam with practiced movements and I quickly outpaced those moving with more caution, Triven and I pulling level.

Ten more feet to the iron giant.

I focused on the horizon. The once perfect city beyond was smattered with pillars of smoke and flickering electrical lights. Dampened by the still crackling grid, gunfire mixed with screams echoed somewhere in the distance.

The Rebels' war had already begun.

There was a shriek somewhere to my right followed by a heavy splat. One of the Scavengers had not been careful enough.

My toes fell hard onto the top of The Wall's metal fortification. It wasn't solid as I had expected but perforated. The surface seemed to flex slightly under my steps, but I didn't spare it a second glance. Instead, my focus stayed locked on the other side of The Wall, on the edge thirty feet in front of us and the drop-off looming after it.

One figure far to my right moved with a spring in her step, blade drawn, mouth grinning. Sedia was leading the fray with her Taciturns trailing closely behind, whooping and hollering like hyenas. There was no sound to my left, but the Wraiths were there, surging forward like ghosts. Even their feet seemed to make no noise. Though running a line parallel to mine, the figure in front of the Tribe was gaining on me, her long legs covering twice the ground mine could. Teya's face was fierce and this suddenly felt like a race.

Who would be the first to breech The Wall?

I was not about to be outdone.

Forcing my legs to shove harder, I began counting the steps to The Wall's end.

Twenty-six.

A sharp whistle screeched behind me. Otto's signal. All our people had crossed safely.

I pulled my gloves on.

Eighteen steps.

I raised a hand, letting out a long whistle of my own. Twelve more echoed back. The Tribes to our sides were slowing down, eyeing the edge, but I lengthened my strides further.

Ten steps.

My hand dropped sharply and twelve guns fired from behind. The anchors whistled as they sailed through the air, arcing high over our heads. Black tethers trailed out behind them. The Tribesmen recoiled as the small metal claws embedded themselves into the perforated surface with a series of pops, three in front of each group. The Subversive members surged headlong toward the edge after theirs.

Three steps.

A rope was tossed out over my head, the coiled end disappearing over the side just as I reached up to snag the thick line. On the final step, the very tips of my boots hit open air and I shoved off the ledge. Twisting mid-jump, I kicked out my feet and swung down, back toward the metal barrier. The rope snapped and my feet hit The Wall with bent knees before sliding downward. Triven's body shot out into the open space above me, rope in his hand. There was a grace to the way he fell, then like mine, his boots were screeching against the metal surface as we slid downward. Other people were quick to follow, though more cautiously. The Wall was shorter on this side, the ground of the Sanctuary built up to accommodate the maze of tunnels and safe houses below it. The earth seemed to fly up to meet us. The cushy green surface absorbed most of the impact and I was quick to move aside for Cortez, whose boots were hissing down toward my head. The wisps of smoke from the palms of my gloves was smothered as I grabbed my guns. Then I slumped to a knee, scanning the empty streets beyond us. Triven stepped back, squinting up at the top of The Wall, his lips moving, counting our people as he drew his own weapons. Cortez landed with a thud next to me and quickly moved out in front mirroring my position. This is when we would be the most vulnerable. The most exposed.

Archer hopped down the last two feet from her line, twisting to face the streets too, gun already drawn. There was an unmistakable air of triumph on her long face. But a flurry of white and rattling bones quickly snuffed it. Teya was the first of the Tribesmen to touch ground and the Queen was wearing the same look as her daughter. Her dark gaze landed first on me, then on Archer. For a second, the Wraith leader's face went slack, then the practiced mask reappeared. Archer snarled, her gun twitched in the direction of her mother, but she held true, lunging forward to place Triven between her and Teya. Triven said something I could not hear and Archer gave him a shaky nod, two quick jerks of her sharp chin.

The tense moment was shattered as trilling laughter echoed down the metal wall, and I turned just in time to watch Sedia come to a screeching halt, dangling face-down on her tether, her boots twisted in the rope to slow her fall. The Taciturn's nose narrow missed smashing into the grass before she flipped herself upright and cartwheeled off the rope. She didn't wait for the rest of her Tribe to touch down, instead the crazed woman paused only to give me a wink and then pulled two spiked sticks from her backpack, twirling them as she took off at a prance toward the city. A listless tune whistled from her pursed lips and as the other Taciturns landed, they were quick to follow their pied piper.

The few Scavengers that had made the journey—most seemed to have deserted—were scattering. A group of them were still gathered at The Wall's edge, debating the descent. I craned my neck back to check our numbers and that's when I felt it.

What started as a tingling was now raising the hair on my arms. I glanced down at the rigid hairs, then twisted back to The Wall. Three people were waiting to get on our ropes and two were still perched on the ledge watching the others. Many more of the Tribesmen were still figuring out how to get down.

My skin crawled.

The generators were kicking back on and much sooner than we had anticipated.

The ropes were insulated, designed not to transfer electricity—or that's what Ryker had told us. But that would only protect those *on* the lines. Anyone left standing on The Wall wouldn't stand a chance.

The scream tore loose from my throat. "OTTO!!!"

My warning reached the tall figure just as a blue arc shot across the sky. I recoiled. It slammed into The Wall twenty feet to his right, blowing a Taciturn out into the air.

The body twitched before plummeting into a smoldering heap.

The first spark of the force field trying to come back to life.

Hurried movements quickly turned into panicked desperation. Tribesmen began scrambling over each other to reach the ropes first. Three Scavengers fell like brown birds, flapping to save themselves. The Taciturns began leaping from higher up on the ropes, two undoubtedly breaking ankles as they slammed into the ground and the Wraiths began barking orders. Having the most people, they were in the gravest danger of not clearing The Wall in time. Larger Tribesmen began throwing smaller fighters on their backs, some even shouldering two people at a time as they slid down the insulated ropes. Others at the bottom formed nets with their arms and the bravest members threw themselves down into the waiting human webs. While there were groans of pain with each impact, they *were* catching people.

Our own ropes were lined with the last of the Subversive members—each person falling faster than those before. Feet barely collided with the ground before the next person was tumbling down on top of them. Those of us already down, pulled the scrambling bodies apart making room for others. As I yanked a struggling woman to her feet, my shoulder grazed the cool surface of The Wall and I jerked my head upward again.

The chaos was happening all at once—bodies falling on either side, orders being shouted, but it was the scuffle above us that caught my attention. Two figures shoved at one another at the top of my rope. Not to displace one another, but to force the other on first. Otto had volunteered to be point man, the last across, the last down, and it seemed he was determined to fulfill his role, even if it meant his own death. Nos appeared to have different plans. Grenald, who hung ten feet below the men, appeared to be trying to climb back up toward Otto.

Nos' grey hair glinted blue.

"NO!!!" I screamed, but it was too late.

Nos' arms shot out and with a neck whipping force, he shoved Otto from the ledge. Several others screamed around me, but the crackle of blue electricity devoured their cries. For one glorious second, Nos was illuminated in blue light. His hair glowed brilliantly, then he was gone. Otto fell past three others clinging in shock to their ropes, eyes tracking his fall, barely blinking before he whipped past. For a second Otto looked resigned to his fate. His arms rose as if to embrace death, then suddenly a thick limb shot out.

Grenald's bellow thundered over our heads as his hand slapped onto Otto's raised arm and with a jerk, Otto slammed back against his boyfriend's side with terrifying force. Both men's grips slid, barely keeping hold and leaving angry trails of nail marks on their forearms before catching again at the wrists. The weight of Otto's body dragged Grenald down the rope several feet causing the ex-Wraith to scream through gnashed teeth as he fought to maintain his grip. Every muscle in Grenald's body flexed and the strained arm holding Otto now hung at an odd angle, but he never let go.

Otto was quick to move, winding his legs around the rope to relieve the weight from Grenald's dislocated arm, but the damage was done. Their descent was slow as the men grunted their way down to us. Triven was the first to their side.

Both Otto and Grenald were shaking from head to toe and the second Grenald was grounded, Triven grabbed the huge man's arm. Otto was quick to brace the other side, his face twisted, overwhelmed by a multitude of emotions. A collective wince stirred the onlookers as Triven slammed Grenald's shoulder back into place. The big man barely made a sound, then gingerly working his shoulder, muttered something that sounded like "good enough".

Cortez grabbed his other hand and began smearing a foul-smelling cream over the blistered skin. The friction from catching Otto had torn through his glove. "It will help." She said.

It was easy to recognize the smell of The Healer's salve and the pain in Grenald's face lessened slightly. The old bat was good—*was* being the operative word. I hoped her death had been a quick one. She deserved that at least.

As the last foot touched down, Archer barked, "We got company!"

I could hear them now too, marching feet in the distance accompanied by gunfire.

"MOVE!" I screamed.

30. COLLIDE

I **SURGED TO** the front of the line, nearly knocking over Archer. No one else had moved, still rattled by The Wall's violent return to power.

"Move, NOW!" One hand raised, prepared to fire—though I knew it would offer us little more than cover—while the other hand grabbed a handful of Archer's jacket. With a shove, I forced her in the direction I wanted.

Toward the gunfire.

Toward the marching feet.

After all, it was better to be the hunter than the prey. You only get the element of surprise once.

Rows—mazes—of identical homes stood blandly to our right. It wasn't ideal cover, and if we had to break a few doors down for shelter then we would break down some freaking doors and take hostages if necessary. I hoped it wouldn't come to that.

I spared one last glance for the Tribes, but they were already gone, the unlucky lifeless bodies the left behind. The message was clear, everyone for themselves.

The dome above snapped and popped back to life, and I couldn't repress the feeling of once again being trapped in Fandrin's cage. The air swelled with electricity, both from the sky and from our nerves.

I could practically taste the war and its coppery tang was bitter.

Our pack moved deliberately, quickly matching the pace I set as we would be no match for the Sanctuary's long-range guns. Taking them by surprise was our best option, possibly our *only* option. We blundered toward the protection of the vacant-looking residences. The surface beneath my feet changed as we left green space and found pavement. It was then the smell of charred flesh overwhelmed me and I narrowly missed stepping on a smoldering body. Though his grey hair was sizzled black and the face was contorted, I knew it was Nos. Unexpectedly, my throat clinched as a different kind of heat burned behind my eyes. I had to remind myself he was not the first and wouldn't be the last to die—probably not even tonight.

Hushed sounds of mourning trailed out behind me as the others passed our dead companion. But it was the sob, louder than the rest, that told me Otto had seen him. I knew Nos' face would haunt him, just as Maddox's did mine. When a person gives his life for another, it leaves a mark. There was a shuffle of feet as Grenald forced Otto to keep moving, to leave the body. It seemed heartless, but that wasn't Nos anymore. Just a corpse that would slow us down.

The homes loomed closer as two people flanked me. I didn't have to look to know who they were.

Triven and Archer had barely taken point when my hand flew up again, flashing a quick gesture. What seconds ago had appeared as one chaotic fleeing mass was suddenly organized and fluid. On cue, our pack split neatly into three smaller groups. Dividing into orderly rows, we fragmented off from each other with the precision of a well-trained militia. I would have to thank The Master for that, if I ever saw him again.

Hands full of weapons, Triven's arm brushed mine and for the length of one heartbeat, I pressed back. Then he was gone. I didn't watch his or Archer's departure. I couldn't. I needed my thoughts here with me, not worrying after them. Those assigned to their parties followed suit and those left to me, stayed the line.

The labored breathing of those close behind seemed to press down the back of my neck. My eyes darted between the buildings.

Gunfire.

It was closer this time. The random percussions hammered against my chest. My legs began to stretch, unconsciously forcing bigger strides. We had strategized the plan of attack carefully, gone over it what felt like a thousand times and it suddenly didn't seem like enough.

Fandrin's army was trained for tactical warfare and though they were skilled in a variety of combat styles, these soldiers had never actually faced a Tribe—or much resistance at all for that matter. The Wall, their weapons, and the people's compliance had made Fandrin and his army brash. Still, we wouldn't take unnecessary risks. It didn't matter if we had the element of surprise, they still out-armed us.

Our weapons took precision and skill to use. Despite the rigorous and often brutal training, *their* weapons were designed to simply point and shoot. Well, if you had the properly calibrated chip that is. And even a nervous, shaking hand wouldn't prevent a Sanctuary bullet from finding its mark. If we came at them head-on, we would just be lining up to be mowed down one-by-one. A single line of attack was easy to defend against, but *three*—that would help even our odds. Not even the Sanctuary weapons were that good yet. They hadn't needed to be. Our goal was to disarm and incapacitate. Without their weapons, the fight would be on equal ground. Their child-turned-soldiers could fight, but so could we. I had broken arms before, hurt to keep from killing and I had hated myself for it every day since. The thought of attacking children—even those armed to kill—still turned my stomach. Triven knew this. I had even confided in Archer that I would not go after the kids. They would have to take lead. I only hoped Fandrin had not unleashed his child army yet. I wasn't ready for them, not now. Maybe not ever.

We dodged through the narrow breaks between grey homes, the sound of sporadic gunfire calling us along the most direct path. We ran the straightest line, knowing Triven and Archer would be leading their teams around in a swooping trail. Soon they would be darting sideways and looping back towards us. Encircle, ensnare—that was the plan.

I tried to slow my feet, to pace myself. After all, this method of attack was most efficient if all three parties arrived at the same time. But it wasn't in my nature to slow down. Especially not if there was a chance Triven or Archer would beat me to our goal. I pushed away the haunting visions of the bullet-riddled body I had seen on these same streets. The body I had once thought was Triven's. It wasn't him, not then, but if his team beat us...

it could be. My pace increased. Despite our vow to keep a steady pace, I couldn't risk the chance he or Archer might run into Fandrin's army first.

If anyone was going to draw the first gunfire, it was going to be me. Tension pulsed from the Subversive members behind me, growing with each step—especially from Baxter whose toes were close on my heels—but not a word was said to slow me down. Maybe we were all thinking the same thing. We had to beat the others there.

Every instinct began tingling as we darted out into the third empty street.

Lights in the homes were flickering on and off. Doors were left wide open and streams of light leaked out, illuminating the vacant pavement in sporadic patches. The insides were empty, shells with no occupants. Once I thought I glimpsed the swirls of a matted Scavenger cloak whip past a door, but it was gone before I could even think to care.

I slipped on something and glanced quickly down to see what had broken my strides. In the streaks of light from the open doors I could see them.

Footprints tracked from a puddle behind us to my boots. To our boots.

Red prints.

Bloody prints.

There were fading with each step we took, worn away by the pavement. At least we couldn't be tracked far.

"Where the hell is everyone?" Baxter asked, winded but pulling even with me. His rifle sat butt against his shoulder, muzzle down but ready. His eyes were tracing the same bloody tracks mine had.

I shook my head with a half shrug, not wasting the breath to answer.

I didn't know. But he was right. It felt wrong.

It was far past the Sanctuary's mandatory curfew. If people weren't in their homes then where the hell were they? What the hell had happened since we left?

I hadn't given much thought to what we would find when The Wall came down, but it certainly wasn't this ghost town. People in bunkers yes. But abandoned homes? Bloody streets? No.

Baxter's gun twitched as a fresh round of gunfire echoed around us and my breath caught. Lights danced against the buildings' roofs in front us. Red dots bounced off walls and shouts suddenly began to form words.

We were here.

One particularly narrow alley was the only thing separating us from Sanctuary soldiers now. A spark of pride welled in my chest as those following didn't falter, but instead drew more weapons. Single file we pinched between two homes, the space barely wide enough for my shoulders, but it was broadening. A reverse funnel opening to the streets before us. It was the perfect point of entry.

Silver clothing darted past the mouth and Baxter's rifle jammed into my shoulder as I slowed.

My feet had faltered as a red light danced down the alley sweeping over my chest. Fear clenched my stomach, but as quickly as it appeared, the glowing dot darted away. Sweeping lazily over the darkness covering us. At first I thought we were lucky they hadn't seen us, but in the two seconds that my feet had hesitated, I noticed something had changed.

The night became a vacuum. All sound disappeared. The lights seemed to freeze mid-sweep and the soldiers' faces twisted away from us, their focus pulled somewhere else. To something they *could* see in the darkness.

It was then the screaming began, but it wasn't the sporadic cries we had heard earlier—the tiny bursts, moments of fear. These sounds were different, sounds the Sanctuary had never heard.

These were battle cries. But they weren't those of the Wraiths, the Scavengers or even the Taciturns. They were *our* battle cries. Which meant only one thing. Either Triven or Archer, or both, had beaten us here.

The soldiers standing at the entrance of our alley raised their guns, but their movements were too slow, their muscles hindered by shock.

Fingers inched toward their triggers, but the soldiers wouldn't get a shot off, we would see to that. Quickly holstering my own guns, I had to remind myself we were to incapacitate first and kill only if necessary. The rebels had been firm on this, not all the Sanctuary soldiers were against us, they just didn't know that they had sides to choose from. I would try to abide by their rules, but if it came to my life or one of Fandrin's soldier's, the choice would be easy.

My voice rose, joining the others in the street, not with pride, but as a distraction. Baxter was quick to understand, his voice calling out after mine. A cry rippled out behind us as the rest of our team made themselves heard. Ten voices sounded like a hundred as they boomed off the plaster walls of the alley. The effect was exactly what I had hoped for.

The soldiers standing in our path whipped around in surprise, but had little time to do much else before we collided with them.

I took the man in the middle, knowing my squad could handle the other two soldiers with ease.

As the soldier's gun swung upward, my hands were there. Ready. Waiting. My fingertips curled over the cool metal and I shoved the weapon upwards toward his unsuspecting face. A flash of disbelief flickered in his eyes before I smashed both the gun and my fist into his nose. Using my shoulder, I sent the man sprawling backward into the street. For a second he held tight to his gun and I lunged forward with him. The man slammed down hard onto the pavement, his head whipping back with a crunch. He blinked dazed as I rolled myself over him, yanking the gun away and summersaulting back to my feet. He let go this time and I rose into a well-lit street of chaos.

It had been Archer's team who had arrived first. Silver soldiers fired sporadic startled shots as her team overtook a small group farther down the street. Another pack of armed guards was fanning out to our right, preparing to fire, but their attention was briefly drawn by our unexpected arrival. I lifted my stolen gun to fire first, but immediately lowered it.

A sandy head materialized from an alley behind the distracted soldiers, followed by a dozen more. Triven was quick to engage, his expert hands gentle but commanding as he disarmed and incapacitated two solders before they could react. Silver soldiers were sprawled on the ground unconscious, a few dead, while others were holding up their hands in defeat. Some still fought, but we out-numbered them. I estimated thirty guards to our fifty. No... forty-nine. Still, the gunfire was ceasing, and the wailing screams were fading to whimpers.

It was then I noticed them.

In the midst of it all, a cluster of nearly thirty citizens cowered in the center of the street. Men, women and children. Their white nightwear stark in the darkness. The flickering lights of their homes illuminating the terror on their faces. Next to them was a pile of bodies, a red pool leaking out from beneath white tunics. Dead citizens lay crumpled on top of each other, each corpse showing the signs of an execution style murder.

Most of the people refused to look up at us, their frightened gazes cast downward as if trying to disappear into the concrete. A small girl at the front huddled closer to her mother, inching away from the trickle of blood creeping toward her bare toes. Tears were streaming down her cheeks. But it was one younger man at the front that caught my attention. Unlike the others, his head was not bowed and he was not cowering. Hate burned in the man's glare, but he didn't look at us. He was watching the only seven soldiers still standing in the center of the street. Several were battered and bruised, most already stripped of their rifles and handguns, but each was prepared to fight. We now held most of their weapons, but the soldiers looked at ease assuming their guns would do little in our hands. The small group parted slightly as our three packs converged on them and a smaller figure came forward.

The female soldier stepped in front of me, gun in hand, though it hung loosely at her side. She wasn't wearing silver like the others, but the white uniform of Fandrin's higher ranking officers. The other soldiers may have had the excuse of blindly following a tyrant, but not this woman. She would know who the man she followed was. She would *know* my grandfather was a monster. It was clear she was the one in charge. The woman's thin face was all angles and harsh lines. I would have placed her in her forties, but age was so much harder to guess here. Pure hatred twisted her features and I had to wonder if she recognized me. Ryker's "face of the rebellion", Fandrin's betraying bloodline. Or perhaps she saw nothing more than a savage girl.

One thing was clear. She wouldn't be surrendering and she definitely would not be siding with the rebels. I pointed my stolen gun at her chest—at the Sanctuary emblem glinting on the perfectly maintained uniform.

She smiled lazily at the firearm in my hand, then slowly her own rifle rose as she aimed at my heart.

"Stupid heathen." She smirked, looking at the Sanctuary gun in my Tartarus hands.

I pulled the trigger and the gun fired, my implanted chips were still working. The woman's chest exploded red, but not before a look of shock rattled her smug glare.

"Arrogant bitch." I retorted.

The few remaining soldiers in the street had stopped fighting. The citizens were looking up from their crouched positions in shock. Eyes were jumping from me, to the gun that had just fired, to the dead commander.

They had never seen anyone but a soldier fire a weapon here. No one *but* a soldier should have been able to make a gun fire. What they didn't know was that two universal chips had been implanted in my wrists. The same had been done to Triven and the other rebels. Every gun here would fire for us. The rest of the Subversive members, not so much, but the soldiers didn't know that and that fact was clearly written all over their faces.

I repressed a smug smile. Ryker had been right, they were not expecting us and they had not been prepared for us to fight back with their own weapons.

The soldiers began to drop like rocks, their knees colliding hard with the pavement as fear drained the color from their faces. Some even began to plead for their lives. Only a few remained standing, defiant for what they believed in.

"For The Minister!" A large soldier yelled as he stepped over his dead leader and took aim at my face.

I prepared to fire first, but the young man I had noticed earlier beat me to the punch. With a roar, the boy threw himself out of the crowd of citizens and into the side of the soldier.

The boy attacked with little skill, but what he lacked in training, he made up for with rage. Caught off guard, the soldier went down in a heap, the youth mauling him like a wild animal. By the time the solider had recovered his wits, it was too late. The boy had taken the man's rifle and was pointing it at his head. There wasn't any hesitation in the boy. He pulled the trigger. The soldier recoiled, but as it had for me the first time I tried to shoot Fandrin, the gun merely clicked. Stupidly, the soldier smiled in relief. But the boy flipped the rifle in his hands, hastily turning the highly technical weapon into a mere club. The result, however, was equally effective. The rest of us looked on in horror as the boy's screams tore out and he beat the fallen soldier to death. His cries of rage gradually turned to sobs and still he couldn't seem to stop himself. The soldier's blood splattered the boy, painting him red and pooling in the street.

Eventually, Triven moved to stop the young man, his expression a mixture of disgust and compassion, but he paused. The other citizens were now rising cautiously approaching the young man, hands moving to still their deranged friend.

"And they call *us* heathens."

I started at the sound of Teya's voice. Not sure when she or the Wraiths had joined our assault. She was watching the boy being dragged away from the mutilated soldier.

I was about the ask the Tribal leader where she had come from, when the woman's keen eyes darted to something farther down the street past my shoulder. She snarled, lips twitching up.

My head whipped in the direction she was looking, and I was moving before another word could be spoken.

In a pure white uniform, a soldier was marching down the street towards us. In his arms, gun pressed firmly to her head, was Archer.

31. ENLIGHTENMENT

I COULDN'T SEE the soldier's face. A hat eclipsed it, the brim pulled low. But I could see Archer's.

My feet had hardly taken ten steps before her expression flipped. Archer's tense jaw loosened, her submissive stance shifted, and looking me directly in the eye, she winked.

I slowed, then stopped.

The soldier restraining her paused, noticing the change in her body language, but it was too late. Archer suddenly shifted, grasping his arm in an iron grip and with a throaty roar she ducked, flipping the surprised man first into the air, then slamming him violently to the ground. She snatched a knife from who knows where and aimed it at her captor. Though he had been caught off guard, the soldier recovered quickly. Rolling back onto his feet, he righted himself, stance ready for a fight. He seemed vaguely aware that every weapon in the street was on him, but Archer didn't allow him time to care. She was already advancing, knife thrusting with impressive speed. The man could do little else than fend her off. Archer's skills never ceased to amaze me. The girl was nearly as lethal as I was, and *she* did it with one hand.

"Archer!" Triven's voice called out from somewhere close behind me. A warning. A reminder not to kill unless necessary.

The soldier's head snapped up at Triven's cautioning, then shifting slightly, it seemed he was staring directly at me. That short second cost him however. Greatly.

Though Archer snarled at Triven's reminder, she twisted the knife sideways in her hand and instead of stabbing, punched the soldier square in the face. The force of the blow knocked the hat from the man's head and as raven hair spilled out, I caught a glimpse of blue eyes with a scar above the left one.

I sprang into motion, rushing toward them, arms waving as Archer leapt on the man and began pummeling.

Panic amplified my voice. "Archer, stop. STOP!"

She looked up, puzzled by my tone as the man at her feet let out a groan. Holding his stomach, clearly no longer fighting back.

"What the hell P?!" She snapped, knife tip once again pointing at the officer. Triven appeared at my side with Grenald and Cortez right behind. Both looked equally confused.

"Well, I'll be damned." Triven muttered, crossing his arms.

"You're alive?" I said, shocked. It was in this moment, I realized I had truly assumed he was dead.

The soldier coughed, sitting upright and I was relieved to see his face. Well... until he spoke.

"Seems that way, doesn't it? About time, Princess." Ryker smiled red and spat a mouthful of blood, his tongue probing for loose teeth. There were probably a few, Archer wasn't one to hold back.

I frowned, relief replaced by annoyance. "I *could* say the same to you. Nice of you to show up *after* we did all the fighting for you."

"What can I say, I'm all about good timing." He retorted shaking his head twice as if to rattle a few things back into place.

His usual air of arrogance was there, but Ryker looked different... off. His face had grown thinner in the passing weeks. Dark circles pooled under blue eyes that had lost some of their vibrancy. Something haunted him now. Questions bombarded my mind, catching on the tip of my tongue. Something in Ryker's look told me not to ask. Not yet. Not here.

"Ummm... Hello?!" Archer waved her hand at Ryker's bruised face, glaring at me.

"Oh, uh Archer meet Ryker." I gestured to each in turn, trying to ignore the changes in his face.

Her eyebrows shot up. "As in our *inside* rebel? The big bad traitor to the crown or whatever?"

"Yup." Triven said, suppressing a snort.

Ryker pulled a lopsided smile that didn't quite reach his eyes and straightened, wobbling as he tried to stand. Archer quickly offered her hand, pulling him a little harder than necessary. Ryker jerked upright with surprise and Archer gave him a weighty once-over. Standing toe to toe, the two were nearly the same height.

"Hmm," She pondered him. "I thought you'd be taller."

Ryker frowned, looking us over, eyebrows knitting. "I thought…" He stopped himself.

"We'd be more savage? Grunting? Eating the dead off the street?" Archer filled in the gaps. Ryker didn't need to respond. We all knew it was what he was thinking. We were the monsters outside The Wall. Archer tilted her head looking him over again, then shrugged. "Well, you're not a bad fighter, for a pretty boy. I guess."

And without another word, she walked away towards Baxter who was still guarding the previously subdued soldiers.

Ryker gazed after her, his expression hard to read. "Nice friends."

"The best," Triven replied. I just smirked.

There was a noise like a bird call farther down the street and we all spun, guns at the ready. Ryker, however, refocused. Signaling for us to stand down, he called back in a similar manner and seven shadows stepped out into the streets. As faces came into view I began to recognize them from the training session I had taught here.

Rebels.

But there were so few.

"That's all?" I wasn't sure what I had expected from our welcoming committee, but it was most certainly more than this. And honestly, I hadn't expected Ryker either.

Triven held up a hand, warning our people that these were allies. But none of us relaxed. We may have over taken the guards here, but there were plenty more where they came from.

"That's all we could spare." Ryker gave me a stern sideways look. "A lot has changed since you three left."

Ryker's eyebrows pulled together as he glanced over our rag-tag group. It didn't take me long to realize who he was looking for.

"She's safe." I kept my voice low as if Fandrin could hear us. "She's not here."

Ryker's brows loosened in surprise, but he didn't press the matter. Not out here in the open anyway.

"There's obviously a *lot* of catching up to be done," Triven said, still scanning the streets.

Ryker finished his thought in agreement. "But this isn't the place."

He was right. We wouldn't be safe for long. Especially if the power came back on completely and with it, the cameras.

Ryker touched his ear, nodding to himself. "Sort out the joiners. Mansforth, Hives, Ganes—take care of the rest. We have ten minutes." He turned to me. "Prepare your Tribes to move out."

"They're not *my* Tribes." I retorted, sneaking a furtive glance backward and hoping Teya had not overheard that comment. Fortunately, she seemed unwilling to come too close, but I could tell she was now straining to eavesdrop on the conversation.

"I don't really care whose they are. They can come with or they can stay out here, but their chances are better with us." Ryker eyed them suspiciously. The Wraith leader was certainly listening now.

Teya gave me a sharp bob of agreement and it dawned on me that we might not be rid of the Tribes easily. I should have been grateful in a way since this is what we had wanted. But I couldn't shake the nagging voice hissing inside my head, or the wary glare on Archer's face.

The Tribes were not to be trusted.

I HAD WANTED to press Ryker about what the hell had been going on—what the hell we had just walked into—but he shook me off, moving to help clear the streets, a litany of unanswered questions trailing out behind him. *What had my grandfather done to him? How had he escaped? Who was dead? Could I still trust him?* Each question spurred a hundred more. And each would have to wait. So much had happened here too. And obviously, not just to the city, but to *him*. The swagger in his step had faded. I tried not to think about it, whatever *it* was.

The rebels moved fast, rounding up the citizens, taking over our guard of the remaining soldiers. They were like a machine made of well-choreographed parts. It dawned on me then, this wasn't the first time this situation had happened. The night's gruesome event we had stumbled upon had become a norm in our absence. Ryker was right, things had changed here.

Unsure of what to do with myself, I stood back and watched. In fact, most of us from Tartarus did. The Wraiths damn near disappeared into the shadows as I sent a few scouts to keep watch. It was suddenly obvious we were outsiders in a world we knew little about, a world that feared us. A few Subversive members had offered to help, but the citizens had recoiled in fear. Even the rebels seemed leery of us. Triven, Mouse and I had been people they knew, we had a history with them. But decked out in war paint, clad with weapons, the citizens of Tartarus were not given the same trust. We were here because they had requested our help. And, we had just saved their lives. Yet somehow, we were still the monsters. It was hard not to resent their fear.

So instead, we tended to our own. We had lost a few more of our people to the guard's startled shots, and though they were not anyone I knew well, the lack of their presence could still be felt. Our survivors now wore makeshift bandages and smelled of The Healer's touch. I had been right to seek her out and, in an odd way, it felt as though her legacy lived on with each person's pain eased, each potential infection stopped.

Ryker's rebels had shot six more guards before offering immunity to the rest of the frightened civilians and the remaining soldiers. In the end, five citizens chose to join the ranks of the rebel army of their own accord, while the others only wanted to remain neutral. The few lingering soldiers were quick to remove their silver uniforms, but refused to meet anyone's eye. I had to wonder if their surrender was sincere or just an act of self-preservation. From the contemptuous looks and twitching fists on the civilians, they were thinking along the same lines.

The group of civilians wanting no involvement were escorted to a safe house, where Ryker assured they would be safe until this was over. Two of his guards took them to another tunnel access, separate from the one we were to take. As they watched us suspiciously, eyes shifting from the access tunnel back toward what had presumably been their own homes, Ryker promised it would not be for long, that they would be home soon. I had to control my expression.

I had read history books of the Old World, wars could last for decades. We all wanted this over quickly, but the reality of the matter was, it might not be and probably *would* not be. Any promise of that was most likely a flat-out lie.

The surrendered soldiers were taken toward another access point by the three guards Ryker had called to earlier. Triven's brow furrowed as we watched them.

"We don't kill them." A short rebel with thick black hair and a narrow frame had been watching us. "But we can't put them in with the civies either. Wouldn't last the night."

He nodded to our right, at the blood-smattered boy lingering hesitantly next to Grenald and Cortez. Unsurprisingly, the boy had been one of the ones to join the rebels—the first in fact. Though calmed now, anger still contorted his face as he watched the stripped soldiers being forced into line. I was positive if he had a gun in hand that could fire, he would have used it. I thought of the Ravagers. Given the chance, this same situation, I would have killed them too. I stared at the boy, not looking away when his fiery eyes met mine. I knew that look of hate. His father was in the pile of bodies behind us.

Yes, I would have killed them too.

The short rebel was right. Lock the oppressors and the oppressed in the same room, and things would get ugly. Fast.

It didn't matter if the soldiers had been under orders or not. Following orders is still a choice, it just gives you an excuse to do terrible things in someone else's name. But at the end of the day, it's *your* hands covered in blood. The fear in the soldiers' eyes showed that truth.

I watched as the pile of dead bodies dressed in white, our friends added to the top, was lit on fire. The few lingering citizens mourned their loved ones, knowing there was no time for ceremony and across from them, our people did the same. The bodies burned, dark smoke filling the air, but their blood on the streets remained. A reminder.

"*What* was happening here?" Otto whispered next to me, his gun pointed aimlessly at the stained street.

Baxter answered. "It was a culling."

"A culling?" Grenald's deep voice questioned, fixated on the flames.

Otto answered, his gun lowering as realization hit him. "A purge… they were hunting for—"

"For us." A tall woman dressed in grey with a beaky nose and sharp eyes had turned away from the burning bodies and was walking toward us.

My body reacted angrily—muscles tensing, heart pumping—but part of me also felt strangely relieved. I hadn't seen her before now, but her presence didn't surprise me.

"Fiona." I acknowledged her with cool reverence. The slender woman pulled herself up to an impressive height, stopping a few paces shy of our group. Though her uniform was gone, she still looked like a solider, square shoulders, rigid back, head held high.

She nodded at me, but her thin mouth twisted as though the idea of saying my name soured her tongue.

"They're hunting for rebels?" Triven stepped toward her and offered her his hand in greeting. She took it with a firm shake. Her issue was obviously still only with me then, nice to see some things hadn't changed.

She shook her blonde head, chin lowering. Even Fiona's hard features couldn't hide the disgust and shame. "Most of us had already gone underground, Fandrin and his little army couldn't touch us. He knows that. So, this is his way of flushing us out. Killing those we love, killing innocents. The old man executes a few people every raid, claims they had joined our cause. Then promises he'll take care of anyone who is found innocent, who is *loyal*. The worst part is, people are turning on us. Blaming the rebels for *his* cruelty." Fiona snarled, then sighed staring at the fire again. I realized then how tired she looked. "We can barely keep up. This was the seventh raid *tonight*. Thirty-five citizens dead in the last three days. We can't get to all of them."

Ryker's short tone earlier made sense now as a forgotten thought clicked into place. We didn't have the beacon any more. It had died with Nos.

"You weren't coming here to find us." I stepped next to Fiona. She was watching Ryker as he set fire to the soldiers' vehicle.

"Not everything is about you." She said curtly. I turned away from her to start rounding up our people when she added quietly. "Thank you for getting here before we could. For stopping them." Her sharp eyes narrowed as Ryker picked up a small child and placed her safely into her mother's shaking arms. They would be joining us. Though my own arms ached for another little girl, I was grateful Mouse wasn't here. That she was safe. I pressed my hand on her drawing, still securely stowed over my heart.

"Like you said, it's not all about me anymore."

32. WALLED

IT **WAS HARD** to keep my claustrophobia in check as we moved through the tunnels below the city. The barrel walls seemed to breathe as the light from the rebels' torches cast long shadows around us. Like the rest of the city, the power down here was patchy. A rebel woman I recognized but hadn't bothered to learn her name, said they had to take out most of the Sanctuary's power to bring down The Wall and the generators were designed to focus solely on getting that back up before powering the city again. They estimated we had almost an hour left before the Sanctuary's full power system was once again back under the Ministry's control. And though they seemed confident in their assessment, it did not go unnoticed that their steps seemed to speed up with every passing minute. Throats cleared tensely behind me. Fingers drummed on weapons. No one was at ease. And with good reason.

Everything down here was familiar and yet I knew none of it. I hated how everything was the same here. I wished this war was in our territory, on *my* turf. I felt vulnerable here. The walls breathed closer again and I had to shut my eyes for a few paces. To distract my mind, I began doing the math of where our numbers stood.

The events this evening had left us with only three weary rebels at the helm and two at the rear, forty-six tense Subversive members—as three more were lost to our cause while taking over the street—and twenty stoic and intimidating Wraiths sandwiched in the middle with a healthy gap on either side.

Fortunately, Teya had split her Tribe into parties, the smallest one staying with us. It was a relief not to have the entire Tribe shadowing us, their collection of rattling bones haunting our every step. But she had not done this for our convenience. It was purely a move of self-interest. It was something I would have done. Hell, it was something I *did* do.

My heart sputtered, thinking of those we had split from. Had the others made it over? Was Arstid able to keep them alive? I wanted to ask Ryker if there were signs of them, how he had managed to survive and about a million other questions, but this was still not the time. Too many unwanted ears were listening. I glanced at a dead camera on the tunnel ceiling. The light was out, but I could still feel the press of its eye.

Was *he* watching us?

I started as a smug voice broke the tense silence.

"Sorry about the face." Archer, who had placed herself as far from her mother as possible, cast Ryker a sideways glance. He was pinching at his still bleeding nose.

He shrugged it off. "I've had worse."

"I've *done* worse." Archer smiled demurely, an obvious act, as it broke into a full-blown grin. "Good thing I didn't hit you very hard. I might have damaged a lot more than your ego, Pretty Boy." Part of me wanted to slap a hand over her constantly moving mouth, but then again it was better than the silence broken only by anxious footsteps and the clattering of bones.

Ryker stared at her blankly for a moment, then a slow smile crept to his own lips. "Wow, Prea, and I thought *you* had a smart mouth."

"Please, my wit makes her look like a princess." Archer teased, giving me a particularly saucy look.

Ryker's face was blankly innocent, but his eyes danced with a hint of the old Ryker again. "Funny you mention *princess*, I've been calling her that for years—"

"Shut up Ryker." I cut him off.

Archer's mouth popped wide, but I shoved a finger in her face before she could say another word. "Don't even think about it." I warned, "You call me that, I will cut out that smart tongue of yours."

She shrugged unoffended, knowing I wouldn't follow through, but also knowing this was a line she shouldn't cross. Still, she and Ryker shared a glance and I fell back from the two of them, trying to shut out their incessant banter. It surprised me that the rebels weren't *more* on edge, especially Ryker. His steps had purpose and he seemed more himself down here in the tunnels. Archer's was a forced her ease. The chatter with Ryker was her way of keeping nerves in check, but Ryker usually stopped talking when he was anxious. Now he stood tall, gun loose in his grasp as if he had forgotten it was there.

Triven's hand brushed mine and I instantly felt my swelling irritation and anxiety quiet. It was a gift to be able to calm me, one unique only to him. I took Triven's fingers, claiming them before he could move away, not caring who saw.

I needed it.

A tiny celebration we were both alive.

A redheaded rebel at the lead touched his hand to his ear and muttered something I couldn't catch. I watched the other rebels as they too tilted their heads, listening. They were talking to someone. I strained my own ears, as if I too could hear the voice on the other end. But there was nothing. A hand appeared under my nose, two small bean-shaped devices resting on the palm.

"Thadd's latest." Ryker offered as I took one of the gadgets. "Unhackable frequency and can pick up a response barely above a whisper."

I rolled the contraption between my fingertips. It was oddly flesh-like in texture. Triven took the second, examining his with equal suspicion as Archer watched with an air of curiosity. Ryker tapped his ear and I could now see the small device nestled in his canal. I popped mine in, pulling a face as the cool plug slid into position with a squelching sound. The instant the device had settled in, a voice began to speak as though standing right next to me. She wasn't speaking to me directly, just spewing out information about the power outage, last reported whereabouts of Fandrin's guards, and ETA callouts. Ryker's team was not the only one out tonight. When I blurted out her name, the deep voice stuttered.

"Mae?"

There were two deep breaths. "Damn, it's good to hear your voice kid."

"Never thought I'd hear you say that." I murmured.

"Yeah..." She hesitated. "See you soon. Going silent."

The line cut out. I was about to ask Ryker how far out we were, when the lights flickered to life, blinding us before once again plunging back into darkness. My body tensed. Ryker swore and another familiar voice popped over the line.

"Cameras flickered on." Thadd's deep voice whispered in my ear. "One hundred and sixty-seven seconds before the next surge. I was able to cover you this time, but teams need to seek cover *now*." There was a static pause. "Falcon Team, how far out are you from the retrieval point?"

"Five minutes, site cleared." Fiona's voice echoed up the tunnel to me as it also spoke in my head.

Ryker cut in, curt and serious. "Why?"

"A second squad of soldiers arrived on site, I caught glimpse when the power surged. It's Fandrin's Beta team. They're tracking you."

Ryker picked up the pace to a jog. Shoulders squaring, his fingers anxious around his weapon again.

I fell in step next to him as the footsteps behind us matched the new pace without question. I asked, already sure of the answer. "Beta team?"

"Gage." Ryker spat through his teeth, flushing crimson at the name. His gun shook in his hand.

I nearly stopped—ready to turn back, ready to shoot the sadistic boy myself—but Triven's hand caught my shoulder, forcing me to continue moving.

"How many?" Triven was doing the math, making calculated choices, not the emotional one.

"I can't be sure, the feed cut out too fast, but maybe about a hundred strong. Heavily armed. It's the largest party he's sent out." Thadd's disembodied voice answered. "They might be in the tunnels already. The safe house, your location, might be compromised." Simultaneously, the rebels began to move quicker, running now. Triven flashed a signal and our team fell into quick succession. The Wraiths made no noise now, their bones tucked away, but I could see Teya's face in the crowd, many of her warriors a head above the rest.

Ryker let out a string of curses that seemed to impress even Archer. "Plan B?" He asked.

"Plan B." Thadd agreed.

Archer stared at me, not fully understanding the half of the conversation she could hear, but clearly getting the message. The rest of the Subversive members seemed equally in tune.

"Running or fighting?" She asked, pulling her rifle, ready either way.

"Run!" Ryker barked the order.

The tunnel surged as our group burst into a full sprint. Before we had moved slowly with caution and stealth. Now it was an all-out dash, noise be damned. After two turns, however, our noise was irrelevant.

Fiona's voice began counting down from five, screaming both in my head and from the back of the pack. I had a sinking feeling about what was going to happen when she finished. Her final number was nearly lost as a pulse of heat and shear power surged up from behind us. The explosion rattled the walls, raining dust and debris down over our heads.

Startled cries rang out as many ducked down in a covered run.

I choked on the cloud of dust swallowing us like one of Baxter's smoke bombs, managing only two words. "Us? Them?"

"Plan B." Ryker sputtered back.

Reeling back, I aimed to punch Ryker for his lack of warning, when a door suddenly screeched opened ahead. Weapons sprang up, but quickly fell away as a round face with unruly black hair and a streak of silver emerged in the settling dust.

"Fifty-four seconds, hurry your asses up." Mae barked. Ryker moved to follow her orders, pushing Archer in ahead of him, but his aunt caught his arm as we passed. Though her grip was firm, she was quick to snatch back her hand. Triven, Ryker and I stepped aside, urging the others in. People bumped us as they pressed past into the doorway, eager to get out of the smoky tunnel.

"We have a problem." Mae's dark round eyes darted to each of us, then settled on me. "Another group came over from Tartarus during the power outage. We just caught sight of them—"

Triven grabbed Mae's hand. "My mother?"

The strain in his voice struck me and I felt like an idiot. Of course he had been more concerned than he had let on. But Mae shook her head, eyes going wide and darting to me again.

"Ravagers?" Dread yanked my heart down. Had they too seized the opportunity? Yes, Fandrin had used them to dispose of people, had been supplying them, but he wouldn't have let them in surely. Not willingly. Teya had paused behind us, lingering with the pretense of ushering her Tribe in first. I tried to ignore the prickling of her presence.

"No," Mae's lips trembled. "Prea, they were being led by someone with white blonde hair. I didn't know her... I couldn't be sure before the power cut again, but I swore there were children with her. I... I could have sworn one was... that I saw her... I thought she would be with you if anything... but she's not here." Mae glanced down at my empty side.

My heart stopped.

Impossible.

She wasn't here. She was safely away from all of this. That's why I had made her stay behind.

"Mouse?" I whispered the name, afraid to say it out loud.

No. NO...

Mae nodded and my knees gave out.

33. TRESPASSERS

I **BLUNDERED THROUGH** the crowded rooms. Limbs knocked me as I rushed past, but I didn't see a single person. I was following someone, the broad shoulders clearing me a path, as he pushed his way through the maze of people. It was Ryker, maybe? Or Triven. There was a tug on my hand. No, *that* was Triven. I glanced up at the dark head leading me. Definitely Ryker. I could see that now as the world around me was coming back into focus. He was asking something of his aunt, shouting questions, but all I could hear was the blood rushing in my ears.

Mae had been wrong. She *had* to be wrong.

Mouse was safe. She was back in Tartarus, under Veyron's care. Xavier's lair was impenetrable. The safe house of all safe houses. They were untouchable there. She wasn't here. It was a mistake.

Ryker slammed through a door into a closet-sized room, startling a skinny man perched in front of a wall of translucent monitors. Frozen images illuminated most of them, while a few others flashed to life then extinguished as the city's power grid struggled back to life.

Mae barged in behind us, barely squeezing past the door frame into the crowded room. "Drake, pull up the video from before, the one I flagged."

The startled rebel began typing at a screen, only to be shoved away by an impatient Ryker. The discarded Drake crammed himself into a corner trying to disappear as Ryker's fingers pounded the key.

Triven was searching the screens. "How are these working while all other power is out?"

"Present from Thadd. Our own personal generator." Ryker distractedly toed an oversized black box I had assumed was a piece of furniture and that took up most of the small room. I could hear it humming now. The screen directly in front of his face changed. "There."

The footage was grainy, distorted in the darkness, but you could make out buildings, sidewalks, dark lamp posts. It was an empty street. Storage facility buildings lined the perfectly paved road, each one dark without power. It almost seemed like a still image, but then there was movement. It was almost unnoticeable in the gloom. A slight quiver in the shadows. One might have missed it at first, but then a woman emerged. Her face was hidden, but a long plait of silvery golden hair swung out behind her. A man was quick to follow, his dark shaggy head low as if avoiding the cameras. My chest began to ache. Then a slight form stepped out next to the woman, a hood pulled low over her face and I stopped breathing. Triven's hand latched down painfully over mine.

Ryker was squinting at the screen, slowing the footage. His nose was nearly touching the monitor.

I didn't need a better look.

The girl looked too tall, too old. But there was a knife clutched in her hand, and she held it perfectly. *Exactly* the way I had taught her. I let out a gurgle of despair.

Mouse was in the Sanctuary.

Triven recovered first, "Where are they?"

Drake peeled himself off the wall and began rambling as he took back control of the monitors from Ryker, searching for other images. "I saw them once more in the power surges. It looks like there were maybe twenty-five of them. Mostly kids based on the size, a few adults—"

Drake cut off as I grabbed a fistful of his collar and slammed him back into the wall. He was nearly a foot taller than me and still the man recoiled as I snarled Triven's question again. "*Where* are they?"

Drake blinked, startled by my sudden outburst. "Th-th-the last place I saw them was in the food preserve district, not far from here."

I dropped him and started to the door, but Mae blocked my way as Ryker assumed my position in Drake's face.

"Did you cover their feed?" Ryker's head pivoted between Drake and his aunt. When they hesitated, he tapped his earpiece. "Thadd, I know you're listening. Did you cover their feed?!"

"We were focused on the teams. On you." Thaddeus' voice was quiet, apologetic even over the line. "We've wiped the feed now, but I didn't see them until it was too late."

Ryker looked ready to explode but his fuming dampened as he looked at his aunt. The usually brazen woman looked close to tears.

Triven broke the uncomfortable silence, "Get us to them. Now."

I didn't wait for Ryker to take lead. Instead, I barged from the room past the stricken Mae ready to bolt toward the door we had come in, but was immediately nearly knocked flat as I ran into a hulking body. Grenald steadied me as Archer's head popped out from around his bicep. Otto, Baxter, and Cortez were huddled close behind.

"We heard." Archer waved a hand in Triven's face before he could speak. "We're coming with you."

Ryker appeared already shaking his head dismissively. "No way. We can't cart your entire team. Maybe seven people max and a few of those are going to be mine. We know these streets better than you. The cameras are going back up and we can't safely move fifty some people. Rescue mission or not. If Fandrin doesn't know where they are already, we risk leading him straight to Mouse."

I wanted to protest, but there was logic to his words.

Archer, on the other hand, pushed past Grenald, inserting herself in Ryker's face. "You are not in charge of me."

Ryker didn't back down, but it was Triven who spoke. "He's right. A small party would be best. We have no idea what we're up against out there."

"This is taking too long. I should just go alone—" I began to push my way through our friends. My hands were already running inventory of my weaponry, but I was met with a swam of harsh replies and blocking hands.

"Absolutely not."

"Don't be stupid."

"That's a terrible idea."

"Do you have a death wish?"

"Idiot!"

I paused, but my legs were itching to get moving. I took in the surroundings—a warehouse of sorts, similar to the laundry facility we had hid in our first time here—I realized how many blank faces were looking to us for leadership. Mouse needed me, but these people needed someone too. "Okay, okay! Ryker's right, we need someone to stay here. To fill in our people and to watch the..." I tilted my head toward the Wraiths. "A high-ranking rebel should be the one to stay. We need as much information as possible."

I glanced at Ryker, who snorted immediately. "Don't even bother Princess, I'm going."

"Fine." I snarled back. "Any volunteers?"

Archer chewed her cheek, looking anywhere but at her mother who stood dead center in the crowded room watching us. "Shit." She heaved an exaggerated sigh. "I'll stay to watch her. To make sure she doesn't turn on us."

Archer's voice quivered and Baxter's hand fell quickly on her shoulder. "Go. I'll stay and watch her. She so much as looks at me wrong and I will put a bullet between her eyes."

Gratitude painted Archer's expression and for the first time she seemed lost for words. Merely nodding with gratitude, she clutched his arm fiercely.

Mae spoke from behind us. "I'll stay and brief your people." She pointed at Baxter. "Gather your most trusted, we will convene in ten."

Baxter nodded before disappearing into the warehouse already signaling for others to follow.

Ryker tapped his ear, "Fiona, you're with me. Thaddeus, you're going to be our eyes and ears." Both confirmed as Ryker turn to address us. "We leave in five."

"We leave *now*." I corrected him.

Ryker's gaze searched my face. He tapped his ear again. "Fiona, get the guns and meet us at the east exit. We're leaving now."

THE TUNNELS WERE out of the question. Fiona's bomb, while effective, also created a dead end we didn't want to find ourselves trapped in. As the power grid began to come back on, Thaddeus had also gained better visual of the city. On my request, Ryker had procured three additional earbuds for Otto, Grenald, and Archer before we left. Otto had tried to make the still injured Grenald stay, but he refused simply saying, "I go where you go." I couldn't argue that sentiment.

To our benefit, The Tower—Fandrin's colossal hideout—was the first to boot up. A giant silver beacon in the night. After that, the civilian areas were next. Sections of homes began to glow with light, illuminating the areas around them with an unnatural radiance. The service districts would be the last. Which fortunately for us, was where we were. Thaddeus' soothing voice walked us through the city streets, guiding us toward Mouse. Twice he forced us to take cover, barely giving us warning before a power surge spiked in the area. I was tempted to start shooting out cameras, but feared damaging them would give away our location faster, not to mention we might need to save the bullets.

Every passing second felt like agony. Each a precious moment stolen from me that I wasn't with Mouse. That she might be dead. Fear swirled with rage.

I could feel the tension escalating around me too. All of us thinking the same question.

What they hell were they doing here?

"If Fandrin doesn't find them first, I'm going to kill Veyron and Xavier." I muttered to no one in particular. No one answered.

We had cleared nearly three blocks of eerily abandoned streets when a mechanized screeching pierced the air. Those of us from Tartarus recoiled, pressing ourselves against buildings and searching for the source. Ryker and Fiona, however, ignored our caution and waved us onward with an air of irritation.

"What the hell is up with the freakin' racket?" I could hear Archer's voice in one ear, though the other heard only the caterwauling. Her face was screwed up against the sound.

"It's the city alarm." Fiona smiled. "It means the Tribes have breached The Wall."

"Status?" Ryker snapped. He was leading the pack, keeping us close to the shadows, skimming the still dark buildings. Twice I rammed the barrel of my gun into his spine to push him faster. He obliged but the truth was, a sprint would not have been fast enough.

Thadd's voice answered. "The Tribes are doing exactly what we had wanted. Their mere presence is creating total chaos. They're pillaging homes, it looks like some have even stolen military vehicles and are terrorizing the city."

"Body count?" I asked.

"Surprisingly low." Thadd replied, clearly astonished. "They've done a lot of damage, trapped some people in homes but they seem to be mostly targeting soldiers."

I breathed a little easier. They were holding to their promises. For now.

Thadd continued. "Civilians are fleeing into bunkers, soldiers are retreating to The Tower, it looks like the city is going on lockdown."

"Good." Ryker said.

"Good?" Otto retorted. "Lockdown doesn't sound good to me."

Surprisingly it was Triven who answered. "It means most of the citizens will be locked away safely in secure bunkers. Fewer people will be on the streets and less innocents will get caught in the crossfire."

I often forgot how much Triven remembered of this world.

"It also means we and the others will be easier to spot." I added. "How far?"

"Four more blocks." Ryker lowered his voice. "Radio silence. Be on your toes. We might not be the only ones out here."

The sky above us was black. No simulated moon or starry night sky could be seen, it was like staring into a void, signaling the grid was undoubtedly back up. Blue hexagonal shapes flickered occasionally, as if to remind us that we were trapped inside the electrical cage.

My eyes darted around the streets, to the rooftops, to alleys hidden in shadows. Nothing moved. This should have been reassuring, but the absence of anything or anyone set me on edge. Ryker slowed, gesturing to a small warehouse across from us. It was the one Drake had mapped out for us. The last place he thought he saw them. I scanned the roofs again and then shoved past Ryker. Someone hissed behind me, but I didn't care. I sprinted across the street, fully exposed for ten seconds before melding back into the shadows. One by one the rest of the team followed, Ryker issuing a fierce glare of disapproval. I glared back. We weren't shot. He could be mad at me later, when I knew Mouse was safe.

Fiona was quick to take lead, winding us around the concrete block walls to a nondescript grey door. She pushed on the handle and found no resistance. Flashing me a warning look, Ryker counted down from three on his fingers. As the last one disappeared Fiona shoved the door with surprising force and we poured into the vacant cavernous room. Every nerve in my body sang, ready for a fight. The room was dark and smelled heavily of starch. Three torches flared to life, casting the space in soft light. Massive vats towered on either side of the room, surrounded by stacks of white crates filled with silvery pouches. Our guns searched every corner as we sprawled out in the space. But nothing moved around us. The room was completely empty. Our guns slowly began to lower. They weren't here.

I nearly choked on a sob threatening to break free, when a small voice came from behind me.

34. MORTALITY

"**P**HOENIX?" MY GUN rose instinctively still not accustomed to the gentle voice, but dropped instantly.

Sliding out from an impossibly tight crack between two stacks of crates, came a small girl. I threw myself the last few steps, pulling Mouse into my arms. I squeezed so hard it had to hurt, but she didn't complain. When I finally pulled back she was white as a ghost and trembling from head to toe. A gash across her forehead had swelled alarmingly turning the skin there an angry purple. Blood crusted in her eyebrow.

"*Why* are you here? What happened?" My tone came out harsher than I meant as I gave her a little shake. She looked terrified, but I needed to hear it from her first. She wouldn't lie.

Ravagers. She fell back into sign language, as if the words were too terrible to say out loud. *They got in, they attacked us. So many dead.*

Triven made a horrified sound behind me, before whispering what she said to the others. Tears were streaming down her face. The blood drained from mine.

"What were you doing outside of the safe house?" I said fiercely, but she only shook her head, tears falling faster. I would never forgive myself for this. I pulled her in close again. "I should have never left you."

There was shuffling around us and people began emerging from their hiding places. Fourteen kids ranging in age from four to early teens had appeared, looking just as scared and nearly as battered as my Mouse. There were ten people large enough to be adults, but I could only see one of them. Shoving Mouse protectively behind me. I hurled myself at the slender blonde woman with the scarred face.

"How dare you?!" I screamed, shoving Veyron hard into one of the huge vats. It boomed as her head slammed into the round metal surface. "How *could* you?! We trusted you! You could have gotten them all killed!"

To my surprise, she shoved back with a snarl. I staggered backward, immediately hunching, ready to pounce. To kill her.

Two strong arms wound around my chest, effectively pinning my arms down. Someone was speaking, but I couldn't hear him through my rage. I thrashed wildly, throwing him off. Pulling my handgun free, I spun on Veyron and stilled. Two guns were suddenly pointed at me.

Veyron's entire body shook as her handgun quivered, aiming at my head. But it wasn't her aim that had made me stop, it was the cold metal of Xavier's muzzle against my temple that froze me in place.

Our rescue party raised their weapons in response and the rest of the room recoiled.

"Easy," Triven spoke, raising his hands calmly to the room. He was breathing heavily, but kept his voice low. He moved slowly, inserting himself between Veyron and me. I quickly lowered my gun, not wanting to accidently fire at him. Veyron did the same, but Xavier didn't budge.

"Xavier." There was a warning tone in Triven's voice.

"I'll lower my weapon once she hears me out." The Master replied.

"What happened? Why were you outside of the safe house?" I shot him an accusatory glance. "Speak quickly or I will have Ryker drop you."

On cue Ryker stepped forward taking closer aim. Mouse stood in shock behind Archer, clinging to her leg. Maribel's blonde curly head peeked out from behind them. The child's ringlets shivered in the darkness.

"The Ravagers *infiltrated* my building." Xavier spoke clearly, slowly, as if explaining to a child.

"What?" I snapped sideways to look him in the eye.

"Bullshit," Archer barked simultaneously. "That place was a freaking fortress."

"Yeah. I thought so too." Xavier's jaw worked, his nostrils flaring as he leaned back. Despite the rage boiling under his skin, he pulled the gun away from my face and I got a good look at him for the first time. Blood coated his shirt and matted his dark hair. It was hard to tell if it was his or someone else's. "*Apparently*, we were both wrong. Someone figured out how to get them in." My eyes shot suspiciously back to Veyron as he continued. "And since you ruined my safe house, we had *no choice* but to come here. Lost six more getting over the damn Wall. The Ravagers showed up barely half an hour after the rest of you lot departed. Like they *knew* we would be less protected." His snarl turned up into a wicked smile. "Fortunately, your little traitor didn't know about all my security measures and that this gal here is quick on her feet." He motioned to Veyron, "Or we'd all be dead."

Veyron stood up a little taller, but her glare didn't soften. Neither did mine. It suddenly seemed too coincidental that she had escaped not one, but *three* attacks on the Subversive.

"How many of you made it out?" Otto asked interrupting my speculations.

"You're looking at it." Xavier gestured to the room.

Archer let out a startled sound and then saluted in mourning. Everyone in the room save Ryker, Fiona, Xavier and me, mirrored her. There were twenty-four of them. We had left nearly sixty.

"What about my mother? Have you seen them?" Triven pressed, not looking hopeful.

"We came over on their lines, so they must have made it in, but you're the first souls we've seen. The kid damn near has the city memorized." Xavier indicated Mouse, but he was frowning. "But I'm guessing if you found us—"

Fiona cut over him impatiently. "Yeah exactly. So, not that this little family reunion isn't great and all, but either kill each other quick or shut up and save it for later." She leaned cautiously next to a hazy window, watching the street.

"Later then." I muttered. Careful to keep Veyron in my peripheral vision, I headed toward Mouse.

"Status?" Ryker barked. Those of us with earbuds paused, waiting for Thaddeus' response.

"Cameras are still down. Most of the patrols have been accounted for. Beta team headed back to The Tower." Thadd said over the line. "If you're going to move I suggest doing it now. The grid will come back on in less than ten minutes. Your section is the only one still out of power."

Ryker was quick to start barking orders, calling for reallocation of weapons to anyone big enough to hold one. After sacrificing three guns of my own, I knelt by Mouse and Maribel. The girls clung to each other, both holding knives I was sure came from Xavier.

"You stay with me. Whatever happens, you stay with me." I waited for both girls to confirm they understood. I leaned in and placed a swift kiss on Mouse's forehead. "Together?"

"T-together." She agreed.

"Together." Triven grabbed Mouse around the waist and swung her up into his arms for a hug. Maribel made a frightened chirping noise and I gathered her hand in mine pulling her closer. She was alone. The tall brunette woman I knew to be her mother was not here, which meant only one thing. Maribel was now just another orphan of Tartarus. A victim of our cruel world. I smoothed her cheeks, wiping away the tears. "You're with us now, okay? You're safe with me."

She gave a shaky bob, but the light in her had extinguished. Gone was the bubbly child who had once been Mouse's voice. As Triven set Mouse down, I placed Maribel's hand in hers. "Don't let go of each other."

We moved to the door, Fiona and Ryker taking the lead with Archer bringing up the rear, eye already pressed to her scope. She was muttering something about higher ground. I noticed then that the formation Ryker had planned was not careless. While Xavier was lined up at the back, Veyron was two people ahead of me, two older and more capable children flanking her. As Fiona pressed a cautious ear to the door, Ryker cast one last sweeping glance over us. His eyes lit on mine and though his lips barely moved, I could hear him clear as day. "Watch her."

He hardly looked at Veyron, but the message was clear—he didn't trust her either. What surprised me more, was that Triven shifted closer to her too, his chin lowering slowly. Clearly, I wasn't the only one making connections. The mutual understanding was clear. *If* Veyron was truly our traitor, we needed to know what she had leaked before we took care of her. Which meant for now, we needed her alive.

"On my count." Fiona pressed one hand to the knob while cradling her gun with the other. "Three. Two." She signaled the last number then made a fist.

Slowly Fiona cracked the door and slid out. No one moved. No one breathed.

"Clear." Her voice spoke in our ears.

Ryker signaled for those closest to follow, while the rest of us urged them forward from behind. Quietly as possible, we snaked from the open door into the dark alley. At the mouth, we pressed tightly into a group. Mouse's hand slid into my belt, tugging gently to let me know she was there. Despite Fiona's assessment, I scanned the streets, searching for anything, everything. But there was nothing to be found.

"Single file. Three to four at a time. Move quickly. We need to reach that building five down on the left. There is an access there we can use. Thadd, can you cover us in the tunnels?" Ryker hissed orders, slipping back to soldier mode, the focused military leader I had once detested.

"I can buy you time there, but you need to get there quickly." Thaddeus was typing on something in the background, the clicking of his typing too loud as I struggled to hear noise in the deserted street.

Fiona grabbed the arm of a little boy, tugging him behind her as they jogged out into the open. They were headed to the alley across from us, nearly in the shadows when Thadd's voice came back on the line. Alarm slurred his words. "Run! All of you, now! The grid is coming on. I'm locked out. I can't stop it! RUN!"

"RUN! GO!" Ryker echoed Thadd and we shoved the scared group forward. We burst from the alley and the streets flared to life in a brilliant outpouring of white lights. The people in front of us reared back, recoiling from the beams, but I rammed them forward. My arms rose and bullets began to fly. Archer and Triven were the first to catch on, and they too quickly began targeting cameras and street lights. One by one the lights exploded to black and the cameras powered down.

"GO!!" I screamed as loudly as I could, pushing on the bodies around me again.

Toes stepped over mine as we thrust toward the building Ryker had pointed out. I slammed a hand over the fingers on my belt. Mouse was still there clinging to me, her other hand tight around her best friend's.

We were two buildings out when a harsh buzzing filled the air. Five silver orbs descended around us, closing in on all sides. They stopped hovering eye level above the streets, blocking the alleys, obstructing our paths.

Fiona staggered to a halt as the sphere closet to her glowed a brilliant green. The light shimmered and from it grew the image of a boy. But the projection wasn't just from the orb nearest her. It was all of them. Five identical boys surrounded us, looking smug.

A woman near Archer bolted for a gap between the devices. She barely made it three steps outside the circle when one of the orbs spun. Tiny muzzles lifted from the smooth surfaces of the two spheres closest to her, and in the blink of an eye, riddled her with bullets.

I snarled as the perfect likeness of Gage grinned wickedly. I fired a shot at the boy closest to me. The image wavered, only to re-form undisrupted. The projection of the young man glared at me—not guessing my location, but staring *directly* at me. Gage clucked his tongue.

"Thought that was you *prodigal*. Won't Fandrin be so glad to see his precious progeny is back." I could feel people around me flinching, those who didn't know pulling away. "Oops," Gage smirked. "Looks like not everyone knew darling Prea's little secret. Still, your blood means nothing. *I* am his only heir now. Especially now that you're all about to be dead."

The orbs began to hum louder and we pulled tighter against each other.

Another shot fired, this time hitting an orb directly. The sphere sparked, knocked momentarily off course before righting itself. Ryker was seething, gun still pointed at the globe nearest him. Gage shifted his gaze toward Ryker, but paused. Distracted. Then his eyes lit up, widening like a predator's.

"*Sooo* nice to see you, *sister.* How is that neck, found your voice yet?" He purred. Mouse said nothing, but a small whimpering noise of pure fear quavered up from behind me. The hand on my waist trembled as he drawled on. "I *had* hoped to do this in person, but then again I wanted to try out my new toys. Besides, why send a man when a machine can do the job. Who knows, maybe I'll get lucky and you'll survive. Then I can finish what we started in person. Be seeing you soon little sis."

The projection raised its hand and with a wink, snapped his fingers.

The images of Gage snuffed out as all five orbs shot down like bullets. They shattered the concrete, embedding themselves deep into the earth. And then, they exploded with a force worthy of the Adroits.

The ground bucked beneath us as the world filled with fire and pain. I grabbed the small hand still clinging to my waist and with a tug, folded myself around Mouse. Another arm wound over me and I could feel Triven's day-old stubble on my cheek.

This was it.

We were going to die together.

35. REVENGE

THE RINGING IN my ears was deafening.

While I ground my teeth against the mind-splitting sound, it meant only one thing.

I was alive.

It hurt to breathe. Heat and a chemical tang soured each breath, burning my nostrils. I coughed, trying to inhale through my mouth.

Slowly my body came back to me, not in soft movements, but in stabbing pains. My legs and arms felt as though they had been shot through, and my spine screamed, sending shockwaves out to my fingers and toes. But none of it compared to my head. The left side of my face was on fire. Pain shot from my jaw to my temple like lightning. Each beat of my heart like another strike.

It took me a minute to remember where I was. Who I was.

We had been thrown, torn apart…

Slowly, painfully I raised my head.

I stared blankly, trying to put the pieces together. The ringing was *so* loud. For a second I thought I was back in Tartarus.

The street was obliterated. Buildings were missing entire sides. The ground had buckled, throwing bodies like rag dolls. The power had gone out again, the only light cast was from a series of small fires. A few took on human shapes and I stopped looking.

Something moved in my arms.

I squeezed tighter until a soft groan purred against my chest.

Mouse was still with me. Alive! I tried to whisper her name, but nothing came out. So I squeezed again. A small hand pressed into my stomach. The fist opened slowly, forming a symbol.

Okay.

I hugged her again, relieved. Mouse was alright.

Then she was wiggling away. I tried to hold her, but my arms barely moved. There was a fuzzy memory. Someone had grabbed me before, but they were gone now, ripped away by the force of the explosions. As Mouse pried herself free, I groaned and rolled over trying to get my bearings. Instead of a city street, I found a body. Two dead eyes stared back at me. I shot bolt upright. Blood covered the face and though I knew it well, mercifully, it wasn't Triven's.

Veyron's eyes gaped blankly. A small boy lay in her limp arms. Neither one moved. I scrambled away searching desperately for Mouse who had disappeared, for Triven, for anyone. Bodies littered the street. Many moving, writhing, but most were motionless. A figure farther down began to move and I recognized Fiona's short hair in the firelight. I wanted to move to her, to help, but my feet were rooted. Her body flopped sideways strangely and I realized then it wasn't her moving, but the person buried beneath her.

Ryker sat up in a cloud of dust and then froze. He was staring down at something. I didn't remember blinking, but suddenly Archer was there, yelling at him. He didn't look at her. Using her good hand and her teeth she was securing something around Ryker's thigh. He didn't scream, or move much. He just stared down toward his legs. There were others now, moving through the debris, searching. I didn't hear him calling my name, but Triven's face unexpectedly loomed over mine. I watched his lips, trying to focus on the words forming there. But there was so much blood on his face running down his neck. I reached up to touch the space where his ear used to be, but he swatted me away then shook my shoulders.

I heard him this time. He was inspecting my face, my body.

"Can you walk?"

I nodded dumbly.

"We have to get the survivors out of here. Prea, I *need* you to focus." His eyes were wide with fear. "We need to move them. Can you help do that?"

I bobbed my head again.

He kissed me briefly, tasting of blood and then disappeared. I watched him check two dead bodies before turning away.

Though my brain was still struggling to function, my body began to move. Twice I had to remind myself what we were looking for. Twice I vomited as I pulled rubble away from limbs, finding little else. Then I saw them. Two girls were at the edge of the firelight distanced from the rest of the group, barely visible in the darkness.

People were racing around, shouting to each other, pulling those screaming from the wreckage. As the world around them scurried in chaos, the girls were motionless.

Mouse's hair clung to her face, concealing her expression. But she was looking down. Staring at the body at her feet. A cascade of curly blonde hair spilled out like golden ribbons on the broken ground.

I blundered forward, staggering over chunks of cement and shattered buildings. Desperate to reach them. Maribel was alive, she had to be alive. I had promised her she would be safe with us. That I would protect her. My toe caught on something, sending me sprawling as I reached the girls. Fingers stretching out, they wound in the silken curls. My hand came away sticky and the pulse in my cheek escalated.

Blood stained the perfect ringlets, dying them a copper.

Dragging my legs under me, I crawled over to the girl. Large chunks of debris covered Maribel, pinning her legs and smothering her torso. Her face alone remained untouched. The porcelain skin shown under a thin layer of dust. With her eyes shut, it looked as though she was merely sleeping.

"Maribel?" I whispered as if gently trying to wake her. I pressed my hands to her face patting it lightly. Then harder. "Maribel?!"

Her skin was warm, but I couldn't find a pulse. The child's head lolled when I let go and panic began to rip a hole in my chest. "Mouse, help me. We have to get her out." I bumped into Mouse, desperately shoving the large pieces of debris off her friend, but she didn't move to help. She only stared.

A huge piece of concrete pinned the child's chest. Screaming with the effort, I pried the slab off, my hands already moving onto other hunks as the large piece clattered away. Rubble cut my hands as they flew over Maribel and as the last piece of brick was cleared, a new heat began to stream down my cheeks.

She looked nearly perfect. Tiny purple smudges swelled on the girl's pale skin, but nothing looked broken. She was fine. I grabbed wildly at her face, shaking it harder this time. "Maribel?"

She wasn't breathing. She was… She was…

A voice crackled in my ear. Words popped in and out of the static.

"Deployed… coming… ten minutes out… Gage…" It cut out.

My mind snapped back to reality with painful clarity.

Gage was coming. For us.

For Mouse.

Twisting, I grabbed for Mouse, but for the first time since coming into my life, the girl withdrew from me. Surging back to life, Mouse threw herself down over Maribel's body. Her small hands latched over her friend, refusing to let go. The harder I pulled, the harder she held on. An inhuman noise filled the air and it wasn't until her tearstained face twisted sideways that I realized it was coming from Mouse. I yanked harder and this time Mouse lashed out, her bony elbow slamming into my temple. White spots popped into my vision as she continued to thrash. I could barely keep a grip on her. I didn't realize I had started screaming Triven's name, but suddenly he was there. Stumbling over bricks and snatching Mouse from my arms. I sat back stunned, no longer recognizing the girl in Triven's arms. Her little fists beat against his chest as he picked her up, but he ignored them. When her attack didn't work, she flipped in his arms, reaching back for her friend.

"Not dead!" Mouse screamed, her voice cracking. "Not dead! NOT DEAD!"

I could see the panic swelling in Triven's expression, as he tried to murmur soothing words to her. It wouldn't work. Mouse would never let her go. So, with the little strength I had left, I scooped up Maribel's body in my arms and rose. Mouse quieted, her hand still outstretched. I stood just out of reach.

Tears were flowing down Triven's face as he held tighter to our little girl. I could barely choke out the word, "Go." But he did, carrying Mouse who watched us over his shoulder. Maribel was gone, her body limp against mine. But it only made me hold her tighter. I was vaguely aware of arms offering to help me. Of people saying things, people who weren't with us before. They had come to help maybe? The world was too fuzzy. Filled with static. I refused their offers help and clung to the girl. For six miles, I carried her body back to our hideout, cradled to my chest. It was another hour before I would let anyone take Maribel away from me. Away from Mouse. We sat in the middle of a crowded room while other people rushed around us. Maribel's head lay in my lap, my fingers absently stroking her hair as Mouse held her hand and wept.

I had failed her.

I had failed them both.

THE NEXT FEW hours passed in a blur. I remembered someone prodding at my slashed face. Someone finally taking Maribel from my arms. It was like watching the world through a series of flipping book pages. Seeing the snippets, but not retaining the information. Children screaming. Mothers crying. And the Wraiths helping us. None of it made sense. So much blood. At some point my brain shut off and I passed out or maybe fell asleep. But that short lived.

Someone shook my shoulder. Lightly at first, then more aggressively when I did not rouse. I started grabbing for the knives that were usually on my thigh only to find smooth scaly fabric. My weapons had been removed, probably with good reason. A voice was hissing at me, trying not to disturb the others sleeping around us. We were in the large warehouse again, cots were staggered amid crates, both being used as makeshift beds.

A familiar face floated over mine, a rebel I knew. "Zeek?"

"Prea. We found them." His lips split into a triumphant smile. I stared at him through the haze of sleep, then jolted awake as his words crept in.

Triven stirred next to me. Then seeing Zeek, he shot up too, bleary eyed but suddenly alert. There was a sizable bandage covering his ear, but he still managed to hear Zeek's words.

"The beacon?!" Triven asked, kissing me quickly on the good cheek first, he was already rolling off the cot, careful not to step on Mouse asleep below.

"We found them." Zeek's smile widened.

Triven scrambled through the crowd toward the surveillance room. Many were still tending to the wounded. I paused to check Mouse. She was fast asleep, though clearly it was not restful. Her forehead pursed, pink lips twitching. I wanted to follow Triven, to help bring the others back, but how could I leave her again?

A large hand reached out, patting my arm.

"They gave her a sleeping pill. She'll be fine. Go. We'll watch her." Grenald sat on the ground next to our cot. Tears left a steady trail down the man's face, but he smiled comfortingly through them. I lowered my gaze to his lap. Otto's head rested in the crook of Grenald's knee. A bloodied bandage covered the left side of his face. He looked horribly pale, but Otto was breathing.

"Grenald…" I placed a hand over his.

"Go." Grenald said again.

Thanking him, I took off after Triven and Zeek.

My head felt heavy, but the pulsing in my cheek had stopped. They must have used something on me. Healed me when I was sleeping. My fingers searched, finding the skin raised and hot beneath a freshly healing scab. It wasn't perfect, but it wasn't bleeding any longer either.

Rounding the corner to the room filled with screens, I nearly collided with a mass of bodies coming toward me. Hands shot up, catching me as I came to a screeching halt. I stared at the startled face, utterly lost for words. Then Arden was pulling me into a hug.

The rebels hadn't just *found* our other half, they already brought them back to us. People were swarming now, pushing past to greet their friends. Many were crying with a mixture of grief and relief. So many had been taken from us in the past twenty-four hours, but now others were being returned.

"How? When?" I pushed back from Arden, studying him in shock. "The beacon?"

He pulled the small device from his pocket, examining it. "Never worked. We tried to turn it on, but nothing."

I frowned as he pushed the button a few times. "So how did they find you?"

Arden looked equally perplexed as Baxter stepped out of the group, laying a hand on Arden's shoulder. I started counting heads as I listened. "Mae found them almost an hour ago on the feed. Thadd covered them immediately and we went out to get them."

"Why didn't you tell me. Why didn't you wake us? We would have gone!" I glared at the serious amount of weaponry Baxter was carrying, he had clearly been part of the recon mission.

"Exactly for that reason. You've been through enough in the last twenty-four hours. We all have." Baxter looked away. "We agreed it was better not to get our hopes up, not after…" He trailed off.

Not after Gage killed fifteen of our men, women and children.

This should have been a victory, a happy reunion. But a celebration felt wrong, not in the wake of losing so many innocents.

I felt raw. Salt still burned my eyes, but I couldn't cry any more. It was as if I had run dry. Baxter and Mae had been right. If this mission had failed like ours, it would have been devastating. I stared at Arden, unable to speak.

We still had to tell them. My mouth gaped as I searched for the words I didn't want to speak.

They were all dead...

Arden spared me. "We know. They told us on the way back, and Phoenix—"

I could guess what Arden's next words were going to be based on what happened next. A woman shoved the two men speaking to me aside and in that instant she reeled back, I caught a glimpse of Triven's horrified face as he chased after his mother. But he was too late. With enough intensity to knock me sideways, Arstid slapped me across the face.

36. ABSOLUTION

I STARED AT the closed door I was too cowardly to open.

The screaming on the other side had been minimal today, but I could feel him seething behind the thick metal. It had been three weeks since the night we came over The Wall. Since the night Maribel died. Since the night Arstid slapped me.

I traced a finger over the jagged scar running from my eyebrow to jaw. Yet another souvenir from Gage. His generosity with scars knew no bounds.

Only sixteen of us survived Gage's attack. And not one of us was unscathed. Most of the wounds were gruesome at best. Not even the newly returned Doc could have fixed them with his best serum, which he was eagerly working with his brother Thadd. The two were inseparable since their reunion.

Otto lost his left eye, leaving him to sport a wrap of sorts that concealed most of his face. Grenald said it made him look more ruggedly handsome, but both men laughed a little too hard for it to be true. Even after some healing, Triven was missing the majority of his right ear. It gave him a strange unbalanced look, but changed nothing about the way I saw him. Even battered, he was still the boy who read to me in the darkness. Though he said it wasn't bad, I could hear him whimpering in his sleep if he rolled to that side. His hands would search in his dreams, pulling at the damaged flesh, only calming when I took his fingers in mine.

Dearest Mouse had taken to picking her nails until they bled. At nights, she was sleeping underneath our bed again. And though she never went far from me, Mouse also hardly said a word. At first I thought maybe the blasts had damaged the device Thadd had given her for a new voice, but then she stopped signing too. On the surface, it seemed she had reverted into a frighten silent child. But I knew her. I read more in her round eyes than anyone else. There was something darker in her now. Angrier. Her brother had taken so many things from her already, and now her best friend. Mouse knew what war was, had seen many terrible things in her young life. But watching your best friend die, seeing the gruesome destruction of war—no one is ever ready for that. At any age.

Worst was Ryker. Fiona had leapt to shield him, sacrificing her life for his. But Gage's bombs had still managed to take Ryker's right leg from just above the knee. It was clear in the following days that it took so much more. The bombs in the food district had blown wide open the underlying fissures I had seen in Ryker.

I had once told him I was no longer the girl he remembered, that she had died long ago. It seemed now, he would understand what that meant. The few times I could meet his eyes since the bombing, gone was the boy I had known. Gone was our once playful banter. He had become darker, introverted. The once confident and arrogant leader did little else in meetings than fume in the back of the room staring at his missing limb. And that was if we could get him to come at all.

We had moved from two safe houses since our arrival. Each time Ryker had to be carried or hauled, unable to walk on his own. He was both infuriated and humiliated by the process. After each move, his outbursts became more frequent, more violent. He would scream at anyone trying to help him and throw whatever was in reach. I tried to be encouraging at first, then screamed back at him, but nothing seemed to work. We needed him. With Fiona gone, he was the rebel's most skilled leader now. But he didn't seem to care. He only flipped between catatonic and livid. Occasionally, tears would mix with his yells.

I toed the ground uncomfortably just thinking about it.

Grown men crying did strange things to me. My chest would ache. My eyes burned and I was always quick to turn away.

For the first time, I truly appreciated what Triven had gone through when I came back broken. He had pulled me through. Saved me. But Triven had been my rock before the damage was done. We were connected. He was my person.

Ryker didn't have that, and I couldn't be that person for him. I *wasn't that* person. Fiona might have been at one time, but she was dead.

It was Ryker's door I stared at as I slumped against the hallway. I *had* given up on him, or I wanted to. But here I sat. Again. Too cowardly to go inside. Too guilty to leave. I jumped as a crash emitted from inside the room, followed by slew of screamed curses. Ryker was awake. Mae was in there with him, trying to get him to eat. From the sounds, it wasn't going well. I rested my head on my knees and stared at the floor.

Everything seemed to be falling apart.

The attack took something more than just our loved ones. It was the first domino in a series and the chain of events triggered was inevitable. The bombs had intended to kill us, but they had also wreaked irreparable damage even Gage had probably not foreseen.

The explosives took out half of our people—yes, but they had also taken out most of the Sanctuary's food district. The inhabitants that made it to the bunkers would have enough food to last them a while, but all the citizens left topside would be running out in a week. If the rebellion persisted much longer, Tartarus wouldn't be the only city starving. The moment we got back, Mae had begun running the numbers, portioning the food, underfeeding us. With Tartarus' numbers added to the mix, she estimated we had maybe six weeks of supplies left—that was three weeks ago.

Small parties went out to forage from abandoned homes, but most were already picked clean. The same Tribes we brought with us to fight in our war, were once again our competition for food. Though Teya—who shockingly was still with us—maintained that her people would share their plunder, I knew it was a lie. Sure, she might share *some*, but she would protect her Tribe first. Just as I would my own people.

Truly though, if not for them—for all the Tribe members who had come with us—the war might have been lost already. When the Tribe's presence became known, Fandrin called his soldiers back to his silvery Tower to protect him. Clearly saving his own hide was more important than protecting the hundreds of citizens still exposed on the streets. The catch to this turn of events, was that the old man was practically untouchable now. We knew it would be hard to get to him initially, but with Tribes on the loose, Fandrin had become even more paranoid. This city was practically ours with the soldiers' withdrawal. But their lack of presence didn't guarantee our safety. Gage's bombs didn't need soldiers to deliver them. They could deliver themselves.

Shockingly, despite the easy prey, all the Tribes had held true to their word for the most part. They kept the slaughtering to a minimum and for a group that was not used to hiding from ever-watching cameras, they did an astonishing job of keeping themselves scarce. Only twice we had glimpsed a crazed woman with her skeleton tattoo, and the Scavengers had gone so completely off the grid, I could only surmise Fandrin's soldiers had taken them out.

This seemed like progress to some, yet so little had been done to win our rebellion. It felt like we were always waiting. Waiting to be attacked. Waiting to attack. Waiting for plans. Waiting on the tides of war to change. It was killing me a little every day. I don't know what I had expected to happen after we crossed The Wall, but it wasn't this. It wasn't hiding from my grandfather and waiting.

I hissed, my palms stinging as my fingernails dug into the skin. I hadn't realized I had been clenching them so hard.

I wished Triven was here to say something wise and calming. To give me the advice I could only hear from him. But he was needed elsewhere—where I *should* have been—talking strategy and rehashing last night's fruitless raid with the newly assembled council. There was nothing I could add that he didn't already know. They were a motley crew comprised of an odd mix of rebels, Subversive forerunners, and Wraiths.

Word had spread fast among the Subversive members about the news of my birthright and Arstid was quick to denounce me. Her once frosty tendencies became outright frigid. After the slap that left my cheek purple for a week, she hadn't spoken to me since. And the instant she struck me, the rebels stopped trusting her. Lines were being drawn between the very people we had only weeks ago fought so hard to unite. Those still loyal to Arstid were quick to blame me for Gage's attack. They thought me a traitor. *I* knew I wasn't, and Mouse at least still seemed to believe in me. A few others drew away from Arstid in support of me as well. But the damage was done. The members of the Subversive looked at me differently now. There was no point telling them I thought it was Veyron. Accusing a dead girl would look like a desperate attempt to shift the blame. Even Triven—whom they had loved and trusted—his words seemed to carry less weight with his people after they found he helped cover the truth about my bloodline. He was trying desperately to hold them together. And no one talked to the Tribes. The Wraiths constant presence was building like a pressure bomb. Teya was becoming restless, and I began to worry if they would soon turn on us for trapping them here. Things were being whispered in dark corners, and though we went out side by side, it was clear there was no trust. Fear and blame were being passed around like sweets. It was a dangerous combination and mix in the lack of communication, things were about to get ugly. If I hadn't been so caught up in my own mind, I might have realized it sooner. But instead I chose to sit here in the hallway alone, plotting my own revenge.

I wanted my grandfather and his protégé dead.

The less the rebellion listened to us and the more Ryker coiled into himself, the more a half-cocked idea of a suicide mission started percolating inside me. What if I went to the Tower alone? If I offered myself up to Fandrin. Alone. Unarmed. It wouldn't be hard to slip away, too many people were caught up in their plans to notice one girl slipping out. The old man might just take me in. Let me get closer. The man had once been so desperate for his blood legacy, that desire might sway him. All I had to do was get close… maybe hide a bomb on my person. Let him walk right up to claim me and then—

The door sprang open and I jumped as Mae bustled out. There was grey food splattered on her shoes and a broken dish in her hands. Her eyes were red with tears. She slammed the door behind her before noticing me.

"Oh, hi…" she stammered. "Sorry. Bad day today, Prea."

"I noticed." I stared at the food on her feet.

Mae's strong chin quivered. Every day was a bad day. The woman let out a resigned sound between a laugh and a sob. Falling back against the door, she slid to the floor sinking to my level. Tears were welling in her eyes again. She stared at the broken plate in her hand.

"I wish Inessa were here. She was always better with this stuff. More patient, more nurturing." Mae swiped the tears angrily from her face.

My heart sank lower in my chest and I asked the question, not sure I wanted to know the answer. It was barely a whisper. "What happened Mae? The day we left, what happened to her?"

The dark-haired woman closed her eyes, shutting me out. "Fandrin went after her, because of her connection to your mother. He thought she might be helping you. That's why they brought Ryker in that day. Not for questioning, but to interrogate *her*."

The color drained from my face. I remembered all too well what it was like to be tortured at Ryker's hand. That's why he wouldn't tell me about her. That's why Ryker could no longer meet my eye. I knew the answer but I hoped Mae to prove me wrong. I swallowed back the rising bile. "He did it?"

Mae's face twisted as she turned away, and I had my answer. I wanted to get up, walk away and never look at Ryker's face again, but Mae's words held me in place. "It's killing him you know. Every day. I think that's why he's taking the loss of his leg so hard. He's treating his own misery as penance."

"But how *could* he? My situation had been different. He had tortured *me* to *protect* me. But to have tortured Inessa, he would have been only protecting himself, like coward." I felt sick.

"She told him to." Mae covered her mouth, smothering a sob. "He was refusing, and on the pretense of fighting back she tackled him and whispered for him to do did. That he was more valuable than her. She told him it was the only way, that she forgave him. They would have come for me too if they'd known about us."

Mae, the love of Inessa's life, wept. For nearly two decades the women had to hide their love, and still, Fandrin had managed to tear it away from them.

"Could she still be alive?" I asked gently. It was a possibility. The Minister had a bad habit of liking to play with his victims instead of killing them.

"We don't know. She was when Ryker left." Mae looked up, pleading with me to understand. "Is it terrible to say I hope not. You know better than any what The Ministry is capable of. Would you wish that on her?"

It was my turn to look away. "No. I wouldn't."

"THAT'S IT!!" ARCHER exploded from her chair, nearly unseating those closest to her. "What the *hell* are we doing here?" She threw her hands up dramatically.

Arstid, Petra and Zeek, who had just been outlining our next line of attack possibilities, looked affronted.

Archer blazed on, ignoring their looks. "Let's be honest. That plan is crap. *All* the plans we've had are crap! Our two best strategists have pretty much gone to the shitter and you all let them!" She rounded on Ryker. His unshaven chin tightened, eyes narrowing.

"Yeah, you lost your leg," Archer waved her stump of an arm in his face. "Sucks doesn't it. But you know what, you're alive. You're here. And if you spent less time pissing and moaning about all the things you can't do, maybe you'd realize all the things you *can*. Everyone gets a pity party now and again pretty boy, but not a whole damn parade. Your people need you. Suck it up."

Ryker's mouth opened, but instead of shouting back as I expected, he snapped it shut again. He crossed his arms, flexing them over his chest. But for the first time in weeks, he continued to glare at Archer and not down at his missing leg.

Archer's finger then swung wide, seeking me out at the back of the room. "And you!" Still pointing at me, she glared down everyone else in the room. "So she's Fandrin's granddaughter… Big freakin' deal! Teya's my mother," she gestured at the Wraith leader with her missing hand. Both mother and daughter recoiled from this admission. "That changes *nothing*. Does it? So, I'm the descendant of one of Tartarus's most fearsome Tribe leaders. Big whoop. *You're* still listening to *me*." She wheeled back in my direction. "So, *you* better start speaking up again and you *all* had better start listening!"

A few shamed faces cast downward, but a strange look passed over Teya.

Pride?

"Now. Let's make a *real* plan. I'm not dying of starvation down here sitting around waiting, talking pointless strategies. I want an end game."

"We can't just—" Mae began to protest, but Archer cut her off with a look that made me cringe.

"Don't want to hear it. Say it with me. END GAME." She turned on Petra, who sat up straighter. "Petra, your husband got what I asked for yet?"

"Yeah, I think so, but it hasn't been tested." Petra spoke confidently, there was even a smile playing at her lips. Unlike most, Archer didn't intimidate her. I had the feeling Petra even liked Archer.

"Well, no time like the present." Archer barked and began marching over to Ryker.

"I agree." Petra got up from her chair with an air of excitement and headed toward the door. "Doc's room in fifteen?"

"Yup!" Shockingly, Archer stooped, snagged Ryker's right arm and began hauling him to his feet. She shouldered most of his weight as he wobbled on the one foot, dragging his arm over her shoulder. Ryker's face went beet red and I honestly thought he was going to punch her, but Triven slipped quickly under his left arm. It looked like he was helping, until Triven's knuckles went white around Ryker's wrist. He *was* supporting the man, but Triven was also restraining him. If Ryker hit Archer, she would hit back, missing leg or not.

"P, get them headed in the right direction, then grab Mouse and meet us at Doc's." She paused halfway through the door causing Ryker and Triven to stagger. Archer glanced at her mother. "It's time you started speaking up too, we didn't bring you here out of adoration. You're essential to this rebellion. Start acting like it."

Teya bristled, but her daughter was already leaving.

Arstid sat back appraising me, her arms folded. "Fine, *Prea*, what's our next move?"

"Arstid." There was a warning in Baxter's tone. Mae shot her an equally disdainful look. While I appreciated it, I didn't need their protection.

I cleared my throat. "We come out of hiding. If Fandrin won't come out of his Tower to meet us face-to-face, then we'll bring the war to him."

Arstid snorted, her thin lips practically disappearing. "And how exactly do you propose we do that? The Tower is a fortress. And I don't need to remind you about their new bombs." No, she didn't need to remind us. "We won't get within ten blocks—"

"That's not necessarily true." Teya's voice echoed in the room, a smug smile crept to the woman's lips.

Apparently, I wasn't the only one holding out.

37. GIFTS

MOUSE WAS TRAINING in the main room with Xavier when I found her. Her thin arms were looking less childlike these days. Muscles had started to stretch under her pale skin. Skin that was covered in tiny white scars. The marks from her brother's bombs were miniscule in comparison to most of us, but they were still there. Each nick cut at me. She had refused to let us heal them.

As I approached, the two of them had attacked quite the audience and though Xavier was clearly restraining himself, she was not. It was frightening how much of myself I saw in her. It took a significate amount of focus to rearrange my face before calling to her. When she looked up, the distraction earned her a cuff to the ear. Staggering away, she cursed. A strange sound in her newly sweet voice. I frowned. I was going to have to give Archer a lecture about her colorful vocabulary around Mouse.

"Sorry to interrupt," I approached them slowly, keenly aware that their onlookers were now watching me. Xavier stepped back and it pleased me to see he was panting. It was maybe wrong to be proud, but I was. Mouse was getting better—not that I ever wanted her to use those skills.

What's up? Mouse signed pausing to take a sip of water from the cup Xavier had handed her.

"Archer wants us." I replied.

She frowned, glancing back at Xavier, clearly unwilling to cut her training short. Then her face went slack as a thought stole her attention. Mouse's face lit up for the first time in weeks. "Doc!?"

"Yeah something about—" I stopped talking as Mouse ran past me. She came to an abrupt halt and turned back to grab my hand.

"Hurry!" She commanded, dragging me behind her.

Doc's room was an old janitorial closet. Our most recent hideout was something Zeek had called a TAC—Technological Advances Center. Mae and Thadd had tried to convince me that securing this place was a "big win". I knew there was value in it, that all the wires, screens and scattered mechanical parts were good for something. But personally, I would have preferred an armory. I was much better with knives than technical crap. Doc seemed to be the only one of us who was as excited as his brother. The two could been seen at all hours, heads touching as they worked over something. Normally Doc's closet felt welcoming, abuzz with his enthusiasm, but today it felt downright moody and hostile. Mostly due to its current inhabitants.

Triven was near the door when we entered. Mouse was quick to touch his hand as she passed. I took up the space next to him, letting our shoulders touch. I shot him a curious glance, but Triven only shrugged his wide shoulders. At least I wasn't in the dark alone. Archer was holding up the wall diagonal from us, tapping her toe impatiently.

Wood creaked as Ryker shifted his weight. He sat on a makeshift table made of crates and a door, surrounded by glass jars filled with blue liquids and scattered mechanical fragments. Shockingly, Mouse hopped up next to him, rattling the jars as she settled herself in. Ryker barely seemed to notice. He was picking at the folds of fabric creasing his right pant leg. Prodding the place where his leg had been.

"I thought we were supposed to be planning. *End game* and all." Ryker's glare moved sluggishly up to Archer who stood cross-armed on the opposite side of the room.

"You're not fit to plan anything. Not unless we can *scream* The Minister to death." She sniped back.

"Pfffft. Please, and what are you going to do, *fix* me?" He waved a hand around Doc's impromptu lab, then slapped what was left of his right leg instantly wincing in pain. "I'm freaking useless!" Ryker's voice rose and Mouse scooted away from him. He seemed to take notice of her for the first time, almost startled to find the child sitting next to him. "Sorry..." he muttered, dropping his voice. Mouse signed, *it's okay*. But didn't move closer. The room was so completely silent I could hear the ticking of my father's pocket watch under her shirt.

"Yeah well, you're way beyond fixing anyway. Your momma probably dropped you when you were a kid—" Archer paused, scrutinizing him further. "Twice."

Ryker glared back angrily, but at least he didn't throw anything. In fact, he sat up taller.

"Maybe three times." I added, taking advantage of his momentary lapse back to humanity. Triven let out a stifled cough that sounded close to a laugh.

"Yuck it up lover boy. You're not so pretty yourself anymore." Ryker smirked for the first time in weeks.

Triven's mouth ticked up, recognizing the same hint of the old arrogant soldier, but he kept a cool facade. "I'm sorry, what did you say? This ear seems to be deaf to bullshit lately."

Mouse covered up a giggle that quickly turned into a snort and the five of us burst into a smattering of laughter. It felt a little tense, forced even, but there was a genuine flash of teeth in Ryker's halfhearted smile.

As the laughter died off, Ryker took a shaky breath. "If you can't fix me, why are we here?"

He was pleading with Archer this time, he wanted to be fixed, to feel whole again. She stiffened at the pain in his voice. "We're *improving* you, not fixing."

"And how do you plan to do that exactly?" Ryker pressed. I was genuinely curious myself. Losing the ability to walk had killed something in Ryker. I couldn't see a quick fix.

A chipper voice cut in from the doorway. "It's all about *who* you know."

Petra glided into Doc's makeshift office, twirling a small tool in her hand. Her stunning megawatt smile lit the room. Like most of us, she had lost weight since our first meeting when I had borrowed her face, but she was still beautiful—sienna skin glowing, green eyes vibrant. And still a hugger. I usually avoided getting too close to her for that reason.

The brothers trailed her, both men wearing an expression of excitement and apprehension. Doc clutched his black bag while Thadd carried something heavy looking, bundled up in a grey blanket. Mouse jumped down from the table, making space for whatever it was the men were carrying, but didn't go far. She ran to Archer, throwing her arms around Archer's thin waist, sharing a look of excited knowing. It irritated me that they had a secret I was not privy to. Placing the blanket carefully next to Ryker, the brothers began unwrapping its contents. Triven and I stepped closer to get a better look as the men worked. Ryker watched them warily. When they stepped back, Petra winked at me while Archer and Mouse beamed.

The metal contraption was made of silver piping, multicolored wires and what looked like repurposed body armor panels. It was a compilation of metal and mechanics. And the shape was unmistakable.

Ryker's jaw went slack, his eyes swimming. "You made me a leg?"

Thaddeus smiled at his rebel leader, glowing with pride. "A leg for you, and..." Carefully pulling something else from the folds, he held it up for Archer to see. "A hand."

"**HOW DO YOU** know this is going to work?" Ryker poked at a wire protruding from the leg's insertion point.

"Mine worked." Mouse said, accentuating the fact by speaking a little louder than necessary. Petra leaned down and kissed the top of her head.

"Plus, my husband is a genius." She added, giving Thadd a look that made me want to gag and flush at the same time.

"Archer?" Triven asked, hovering over Doc's shoulder.

"Seems to work fine to me." Archer pulled her new hand out of Thadd's grip and flexed the mechanical fingers then contracted all but one to flip Ryker a rude gesture. Mouse giggled as Petra disapprovingly tried to cover the little girl's eyes. I stifled a laugh as Triven clapped Archer on the shoulder approvingly.

Ryker snorted, a ghost of a smile playing around his lips. But it slipped away as he eyed the leg meant for him. "How long will it take me to learn to use it?"

Thadd leaned back against the stack of crates Archer sat on. "It could be a few hours or a few weeks. It all depends on how well it maps to your system. We calibrated them to your genetics, but I can't guarantee there won't be a learning curve."

As he said this, Archer picked up a knife from the table. She flipped it twice in her new hand before the fingers went limp and the blade clattered to the floor.

"Damn." She shook the hand, then slowly wiggled the fingers, testing them as they came back to life. They made little clinking noises with each movement.

Doc picked up the knife and handed it back to her. "Our point exactly. It will take time, same as Archer's arm and Mouse's voice box."

"Will I be able to fight with it. Run?" His voice quavered.

I understood the frightened reserve in Ryker's words. He didn't want a band aid—a mechanical crutch that did little else than remind him of all the things he couldn't do. He wanted his old life back. His quality of life hinged on being able to get back into the fight. He was a rebel and a soldier. He wanted—no *needed*—to be able to fight for himself again. To defend himself. To move like a free man.

I understood that.

"How bad?" Ryker was staring at Archer, daring her to lie. His long fingers massaged gently over the tip of his amputated leg. Archer had mentioned to me, if his loss was anything like hers, the skin around the severed area would be sensitive and that he would experience something called phantom pains. How strange that a leg that was no longer there could still itch or worse yet, ache. We had all watched as Doc fitted the hand onto Archer's arm. She had slipped what remained of her forearm into the tube-like structure of Thaddeus's hand, like putting on a very heavy and shiny glove. That part wasn't so bad, but when the cuff around the glove's rim unleashed a dozen spider-like legs, each tipped with a needle that clamped onto her arm, even tough-as-nails-Archer couldn't hide the pain completely.

Archer squeezed the fingers again, still mesmerized by their movement. She traced the skin around her new hand, touching the points where the mechanical legs had buried themselves into her skin. She made a point to look Ryker in the eye. "It wasn't as bad as losing it."

Ryker brushed the smooth metal hesitantly like it might bite him. He closed his eyes, taking a deep breath. Then turned his sunken gaze on Doc. "Screw it. Put the damn leg on."

"And if it doesn't work?" Thadd stared at the leg he had made. Nervous.

Ryker responded with no mirth, staring at me. The one person in the room who might understand. Who might carry out his request. "Shoot me."

38. COMPASSION

MERCIFULLY, THADDEUS'S MECHANICS along with Doc's medical knowledge had worked a minor miracle. Ryker complained about the weight of the leg, the lack of perfect mobility. But after Petra told him chipperly to shut up, that it was a prototype, Ryker began to act like the boy I had once cared for as a brother *and* despised. Like many of us, he was just a ghost of that boy, but a version of him nonetheless. That's what war does. It strips away the layers that make us whole, leaving the core intact but changed forever.

The following two weeks flew in contrast to the tedium of the previous three. Archer's outburst had set gears into motion. The Tribes, rebels and Subversive members were not only talking, but listening to each other. It was strange. I would be lying if I said there wasn't still tension hanging in the air. There was. Nearly palpable and thick enough to choke on at times. Case in point, Arstid. But we were talking again, not always cordially, but we were agreeing.

We had a plan again. A real one.

One that might work.

We had spent the last two weeks training, plotting and sending out small parties to gather intel and supplies. Though they refused to come back to our base, the Taciturns had reappeared to join our cause. I had seen the crazed woman twice since our strategy was set in motion and neither sighting did much to improve my opinion on her sanity. I couldn't prove it, but I also had the feeling Teya and Sedia had been talking since we crossed The Wall. Maybe even before that. It was a crazy idea, but I couldn't shake it. The idea of two Tribe leaders—one *severely* unbalanced—holding private meetings didn't exactly thrill me. Truthfully, it was more a cause for concern than celebration. But it was a relief to know the Taciturns would fight with us. The last thing we needed was a Tribe to turn on us now. Words of loyalty aside, I still wasn't going to risk another Veyron-like incident. Even Triven, who was gifted with finding the good in all people, seconded my request to have Zeek monitor the Tribes as closely as possible.

Little by little the cameras were becoming ours again. Zeek and his team wore the circles under their eyes with pride. Every sleepless hour was a minor victory for us. The Tower's security was the only thing we could not hack and if we had to go in blind, it seemed fair Fandrin should be sightless too.

Two weeks had rapidly dwindled down to two days. Forty-eight hours and everything we had sacrificed for would come to an end. In forty-eight hours, I could be putting a bullet in my grandfather's head.

I spent most nights curled in Triven's arms, but had kept our promise to Mouse. Though both Triven and I left on hunting parties, we never went together. Not since the night of the bombing. One of us always stayed with Mouse. I didn't know what was worse, leaving them behind, or watching Triven leave without me. I hated all of it.

Today was a rare day, both our teams were at the base. Everyone was. With only two more days to prepare, we were all on edge as the last details had to be put into place before leaving our base.

Half of the main room had been converted into a training space during the days. Beds were pushed to the sides making room for training and doubling as spectator seats. Circles formed as people honed skills like hand-to-hand combat, weapons handling and Doc's contribution— in field triage. There wasn't enough serum to go around and even with what we brought from The Healer, there was only so much that could be done without some medical knowledge. Many of the citizens who had joined the cause since our arrival were not willing to fight, but they were willing to help save lives and Doc's trainings had become vastly popular.

The Wraiths rarely showed off their own skills for the rest of us to witness, but it was nice to see that Teya and her warriors appeared surprised if not impressed by what the rest of us were capable of. Only when Grenald or Archer practices, did their expressions change from admiration to resentment. I made sure to stay close to those training sessions, weapons ready. What was it Astrid had said once about me? Even trained dogs bite?

It didn't take long for me to notice that any time I taught or practiced, the Wraith leader was always nearby, watching. There was satisfaction in training the others and watching them get better, but I always claimed to need a break whenever a younger kid wanted to train. Twice Jeric, the vengeful boy who had joined the rebels on our first night, had stepped in eager to spar with me and twice I had excused myself. I never sparred with anyone younger than me and was grateful when Xavier took my place without so much as a word. He didn't know the gory details, but he knew enough. He had no desire to help with our planning, but had taken to training others like oxygen.

Today, the vaulted ceiling echoed with the grunts and smacks of combat. I had tuned them out. Instead, I was straining to hear a different voice, a familiar one. Triven sat cross-legged on the opposite side of the room with a small audience of his own. In his hands, he cradled my favorite weapon of all. A book. The group surrounding him was growing with each page turned. There were kids and adults alike, every one of them rapt with his words. Mouse curled up at his side, her head leaning against his shoulder as she listened. From the snippets I could catch, it sounded like a classic. Possibly from Inessa's banned collection. Maybe Mae had brought it as a little piece of her soulmate. Her way of keeping Inessa alive without having too much hope that she really was.

I was trying so hard to pick out Triven's words, that I nearly didn't hear the rattle of bones until she sat next to me. Teya was calm and reserved, but my hand still went to the knife at my hip.

I stared at her, reading her every movement. However, she wasn't looking at me. She was watching Triven and Mouse.

My fingers tightened on the hilt.

"Do you know why I decided to join you?" Her voice grew deeper when she spoke quietly.

"I stopped trying to make sense of anyone's decisions a long time ago." Keeping my hand on the knife handle, I turned away to continue watching Triven.

Teya continued unperturbed by my sharp reply.

"The night you first came to me, you threatened me with the life of my youngest daughter. I was going to skin you alive for that. Literally. And I would have. But then you left her." She turned to face me. I stared resolutely ahead. "Any other Tribe would have taken her as leverage. *I* would have. Yet, you left her unharmed where she would be quickly found… It was a stupid decision."

"So, you joined me because I'm an idiot. That doesn't sound very intelligent on your part." I tilted my chin toward her with a side glance.

Teya smiled in her strange wild way. "It *was* stupid. But it was also the first act of humanity I had seen in many years. You spared a child." Teya paused. "We don't harm children. We have taken some, yes. But they are then raised as one of our own."

So that was how their numbers had gotten so big. Teya had turned the Wraiths into a Tribal version of the Lost Boys. It was like another of my favorite books, filled with abandoned children who fought off wicked pirates to survive. Teya's words painted a nice picture, but I didn't believe them. She hadn't always been a rescuer of abandoned children. She had left at least one for dead.

I held her gaze, forcing Teya to face the truth in my words. "I doubt *all* your children would agree with that statement."

Teya sighed, looking away. I didn't need to follow her gaze to know who she was watching now. Ryker and Archer had teamed up and were taking on Xavier together at the far end of the room. Ryker was slower than before, which was to be expected. His new leg was heavier, but he was doing well. Archer had been right. He wasn't fixed, but he was improving. Archer too was excelling with her new hand. She still favored the right, but her dexterity with the metal appendage was getting better.

Teya's gaze would be on them—on *her*—rightfully so.

It should have pleased me to see the hint of guilt on the Wraith's face, but it only stirred confusion. Monsters didn't have regrets. Did they?

I pushed her. "So, it's true? You took your own daughter's hand to gain the throne?"

"Yes." Teya admitted, but she shook her head. The long dreads woven with white feathers swayed around her face. "But it was a kindness."

She glared at me when I scoffed at her words.

Her upper lip quivered in anger. "Don't judge what you don't know, child. Archer's father, Drek, was leader then but he wasn't supreme like I am now. He had people to answer to. He wore the crown, but he was a puppet, every string pulled by the Tribe's elders. Even at a young age I saw the rebelliousness in my daughter. Archer was never one to be controlled, her smart mouth alone was cause for concern. Archer talked of ruling differently, of change. Of trying to work with the other Tribes. And the younger generations were starting to listen. The elders saw her as a threat. They wanted her dead, to make an example of my child.

"Drek was weak," Teya spit at the mention of his name. "He couldn't see what needed to be done. The elders were going to have our daughter killed. So, I made a move before they could. I slit the Drek's throat in the bed we shared and then, *yes*, I lured my daughter into the city and took her hand. *Yes*, it gave me the throne. But do not forget. I took her hand, *not* her life."

"You left her for *dead*." I said with disgust.

"I left her *alive*. The Wraith elders assumed she would die, bleed out. But a mother knows her daughter. She's a survivor, I knew she wouldn't give up so easily..." Teya trailed off, watching Archer hold her ground against Xavier's assaults. The Wraith's hands caressed the bones decorating her slender neck. "I wear my daughter's bones as a reminder of her sacrifice, of what her hand cost and what it gave our people. The Wraiths have never been more powerful than they are under my rule." Teya's lips twisted into a wicked smile. "There *were* a series of unfortunate accidents after the elders gave me the crown for 'killing' my daughter—missions gone wrong, people falling asleep and not waking up again. But the elders were old after all and accidents happen."

A chill swept the back on my neck.

Teya twisted a well-worn bone between her fingertips. It was smoother than the others, one she must have worried every day for years.

There was a boastfulness to her words. "It wasn't long before there were no longer elders to answer to. I made the decree to never harm children as a way to grow our numbers at first. But it was much more than that. You see me as a monster, but even *I* have my standards. I don't harm the innocent. Not if it can be avoided."

"Why are you telling me this?" I pressed my palms together to keep them from shaking. This not my secret and not one I wanted to be a part of.

"I have listened and watched. I know the stories. You too never harm kids, not unless it's to save their lives."

My stomach curled as she drew the comparison between us. I had never gone as far as to cut off a child's hand, but I had broken a few and worse.

"We *are not* the same." I snarled.

Teya studied me. "Perhaps not."

Then without a second glance, she left, bone still twisting in her slender fingers.

Across the room, Archer took a heavying swing at Xavier, crowing when she made contact. I hated Teya for burdening me with her secret, for being too cowardly to tell her daughter herself.

But maybe it didn't matter. In two days, our world would be changed forever and most of us probably wouldn't live to see it.

39. FACADES

ARDEN STOOD RIGID as a pole in the corner of the vacant home's living room, rubbing the place on his arm where the rebels had inserted his firearm calibration chip. Nearly every Subversive member had one now and a few Tribesman as well. A peculiar hiccupping noise had started emitting from him. Otto eyeballed him with his good eye, stepping away in case Arden vomited. Again.

"You need to breathe." Grenald relaxed calmly against the wall next to him. The large man was the picture of ease. The calm before a storm.

Arden was fixated on the only photograph hanging in the room. I had done my best to ignore it. The younger version of Fandrin glared down at us. Judging. Threating.

"You don't have to come." I quieted my voice, leaning in so only he could hear, offering my friend an escape. There was still time to back out. Arden could choose to stay behind, to join the second wave or go back to guard those choosing to abstain. I doubted anyone would blame him. It had surprised me when Arden volunteered to be part of the first wave. But since getting here, he had become a possessed man, like he needed to redeem himself. For what, I didn't know.

Slender fingers trembling, he traced the burn scars covering his cheek and neck. Arden's glare hardened as he stared at Fandrin's portrait, but it softened when I nudged him with an elbow. "Really. No one would blame you."

Arden let out a long sigh.

"A bit late for that." He gave me a nervous smile. The shaky grin did little to instill confidence, but it was better than the hiccupping noise. Or vomiting.

Phase one was complete. We had taken over one of the abandoned homes. I tried not to think about what had happened to its inhabitants. Hopefully they were holed up in a public bunker somewhere and not buried in one of the rotting piles Fandrin's raids had left behind. It had been weeks since any soldiers had come out of their precious Tower, but that didn't mean the killing had stopped. Gage's bombs needed little guidance to find a target. Coordinates were set and they were deployed. Simple really. They were an ingenious weapon. Obviously lethal, but they were also prototypes, new toys that had not yet been perfected, and that meant two things. They were in limited quantity and there were still kinks to be worked out.

His bombs were effective, but they had a range limitation. With Fandrin refusing to let his soldiers leave the confines of his Tower, Gage's bombs could only go so far.

This was what the Taciturns had been doing over the last few weeks. While we were spinning circles, and going nowhere, Sedia had been testing the Ministry's reach. Like a true Tribesman, she had been pushing the boundaries of her territory and marking it.

The house we hid in now and twenty-eight others just like it loosely encircled Fandrin's silver fortress. There were three ways into the massive building on ground level and if our plans went well, there could be five by the end of the night.

Night was a relative term these days. Since The Wall's breach, the dome had re-engaged, but its surface remained black. It was eerie, like looking up into an abyss.

Tartarus' sky was almost always brooding, but even those green swirling angry skies were better than this. If you stared too long, it felt like you might fall up and the blackness would swallow you whole. I shuddered thinking about it.

Voices echoed up the stairs from the hidden doorway. This house didn't have the safe rooms below like Ryker's had, but it was still connected to the tunnels. All the homes were.

Arden began wheezing again and I gave Otto a meaningful look.

"How about we go upstairs to check on Triven and Archer?" Otto clapped a hand on Arden's back, already guiding him off the wall and toward the steps leading upward. With one last glance at Fandrin's photo, Arden went willingly. Otto cast me a look over his shoulder. Subtly, he pointed at his eye and then at Arden's back with a smile. *I've got him,* the gesture said.

Light feet hopped up the stairs from the subfloor, skipping steps as they approached. A dark head with fathomless eyes came into view. Tensions in the room instantly rose as Sedia bounced up the last step. She was grinning as always, humming something to herself that carried no tune.

She was quick to pick me out in the crowd, her face lighting up. I didn't return the grin and she didn't seem to care. Seven other Taciturns sporting an impressive number of tattoos appeared behind their leader. Unlike Sedia, they showed no sign of being happy to see us.

"Your Adroits are fun, even if they no longer wear their colors." Sedia purred.

I looked past her.

The breath I had been holding released as a pair of tall, dark-haired men brought up the rear with two other ex-Adroits close behind. I had seen the round-faced woman and the squat man many times before, but it wasn't until a few weeks ago that I learned their birthright.

We couldn't get the Adroit Tribe to join our cause, but that didn't mean we didn't have *any*. It had been Arstid's idea. And a good one at that. Getting into a pissing match with explosives was dangerous. But using smaller bombs to *trigger* other bombs—*that* could be useful.

Ryker touched his ear, looking me directly in the face. "Maroon team, back. Confirmation on deployment. Everything is in place."

A chorus of "Confirms" replied before the line went silent again.

"How soon?" Grenald rolled his shoulders, coming to my side. Sedia's head craned back to get the full view of him. She looked like a child next to our giant. Her head fell sideways, eyes stretching wide—a *demented* child. Grenald didn't step away, but it was obvious he wanted to. Sedia had that effect on a person.

"Thirty minutes." Ryker confirmed checking his watch. He shifted his weight to the good leg.

"You're big." Sedia cut in, clearly not listening to anything that had just been said.

Grenald stared down at the tiny woman. "You're short."

She twirled with a peel of laughter. There were singe marks in the Taciturn's hair and her face had suffered what appeared to be a shrapnel assault. Little scabs flecked her neck, cheeks and forehead. Consequences of testing bomb ranges, I supposed.

With the grace of an acrobat, Sedia vaulted herself over the couch. She flounced onto the grey cushions. What I hoped was mud flecked off her boots as she ground the heels into the tightly knit fabric.

"Has anyone raided the kitchen yet?" She patted her stomach, "I'm always starving before a good kill."

Her Tribe members chortled. A large dark-skinned man at the rear barked out a laugh. Lust was clear in his expression as he stared at Sedia. "Damn, crazy looks good on you woman." One side of the man's head was shaved and embellishing the exposed skin was a giant spider, a grinning skull its oversized body while the legs cascaded over his brow and down his neck. It was hard not to stare.

Sedia blew him a kiss as he headed toward the kitchen, dragging along a smaller man with flames covering his bare back. Grenald and another rebel, whose name I hadn't learned, followed casually.

"Thank you Levo," she purred. Tucking her chin into her shoulder, Sedia batted her eyes at me. "Insanity does suit me, but *we are all mad here*."

I froze. Sedia's eyes sparkled mischievously.

That was a quote from a book. *I* knew that, but did she?

"*Or you wouldn't have come here.*" I spouted the next part of the line. Testing her. I didn't remember all of the book in great detail, but that quote had stuck with me.

The change was barely perceptible. If I hadn't been looking for it, I might have blinked and missed that split second when the insane woman suddenly looked stone cold sober. But it passed so quickly, I thought I might have imagined it.

Sedia clapped her hands and began laughing. "Awe. I love it when people play." She threw her arms over the couch, propelling herself up onto the back. She stood there, balancing on the edge. "Now, this mouth isn't gonna to feed itself."

Quick as a whip, the Taciturn leapt down and snatched my arm, pulling me close. "My brother always said you were smart. I see why he liked you." Sedia pecked my cheek and loped into the kitchen to find her own food.

I stared after her, utterly baffled.

"She's something else." Ryker whispered behind me.

"Definitely something else." I turned toward the stairs leading up to the bedrooms. Someone had just called my name. "Keep an eye on her."

Ryker nodded. Sedia might indeed be crazy, but she was also a hell of a lot smarter than she let on.

TRIVEN WAS STANDING at the top of the stairs waiting for me. He had grown his hair longer in the past month, letting it fall over his missing ear. I reached up and brushed it back from his forehead. He leaned into my hand, then took it in his own. Our fingers intertwined as he began to lead me down the narrow hall to the room at the end. Archer would be posted there, eye on her scope watching the streets, The Tower. If anyone so much as sneezed within a five-block radius, she would see it. Otto and Arden were talking about something quietly, it sounded like they were comparing weapons. On one of my raids, we had managed to break into a Ministry bunker and it had been stockpiled with an impressive amount of weaponry. It was not an armory by any means, but it evened the odds a little. We took everything we could carry. From the sound of it, Arden must have gotten an amplified knife.

I moved toward the doorway, but was tugged back. Triven had stopped one door down from our friends. Backing into the dark room, he paused in the doorway and gave my hand a gentle tug. I didn't need any further encouragement to follow.

Sliding past him, I walked into the empty bedroom. It was the same as all the other rooms in the house. White walls, white furniture, white sheets. The single bed was mussed. Someone had either been crashing here, or was pulled from their bed in the middle of the night.

"This was my room in our house." Triven shut the door quietly behind us. With a sigh, he leaned against the door and stared at the rumpled sheets. His breathing was steady but fast.

Closing the space between us, I forced my way into Triven's arms and pressed my ear to his heart. It hammered against his ribs. His hands slid around my waist pulling me close. His cheek rested on my head. There was no flare of passion, no need to get lost in each other this time. We simply stood there, holding each other. Neither of us wanted to talk about what lay ahead, to say out loud what might happen. So, I talked about something else. Anything else.

"Mouse?" I asked. She was always in my thoughts.

I could hear Triven's smile in his words. "She's fine. They made it to their hideout and Petra is keeping a close watch over her. We can com her before we go."

"I want to, but maybe it's better we don't. It was hard enough leaving her this morning. I'm not sure I could handle another good-bye." Mouse had cried this time. Even though they were soundless tears, she clung to me when I tried to pull away. It nearly undid me. Sucking in a gulp of air, I changed the subject to something else that was nagging at me. "Triven, Sedia said something downstairs. She was talking about her brother, as if I knew him…" I trailed off, there was only one person I could think of. It was impossible, but who else could it have been? Their eyes, the Tribe lineage. But how would she have known about me? They couldn't have talked, not since he left the Taciturns. They would have killed him for being a traitor. But who else could it have been?

"Is her brother…" I struggled to say the name, but his face was clear.

"Maddox?" Triven finished for me.

"It's not possible, right?" I asked leaning back to look up at him.

"I had my suspicions the first night we met her. When she attacked us on the rooftop." Triven's chest expanded in my arms, then let out with a heavy exhale. "They have the same eyes. The same jaw."

"She said *he told* her about me. How? Was he selling us out to the Taciturns?"

Triven soothed my cheek, brushing back a loose strand of hair then lightly tracing the scar. "I don't think so. I knew he had a sister. One he trusted explicitly. For years, Maddox had tried to get her to join us. To leave the Taciturns and avenge their brother, but she refused. I guess she had revenge ideas of her own. The night we met her, it seemed to fit."

"Well, she got revenge." I pressed my face into Triven's shirt, blocking out the memory of Zed's face being blown off. A hollow feeling filled my chest. "I didn't know Maddox had a sister. He died for me, and I hardly knew anything about him."

"You two weren't exactly on the best of terms." Triven didn't mean it as a jab, he was stating the facts. "What Maddox went through before he came to us, it changes a person. Twists them from the inside. In his own way, I think he loved you."

"He had a crappy way of showing it." I muttered. I owed the man my life and still, I hated him.

"He didn't exactly have the best role models." Triven hugged me a little closer.

"Do you always have to be so level-headed?" I asked, both annoyed and in awe.

He laughed and kissed the top of my head.

I had a knot in the pit my stomach. A premonition. No—a certainty that something bad was going to happen.

This was the battle we had been waiting for. The reason we were here. The reason we had fought so hard and lost so much. This war had started a long time ago, sparked by our parents' generation, but *this* was the hard part. Wars were easy to start, but *never* easy to finish. And it was up to us to finish this one.

"Don't die." I whispered into his chest.

"You either." Triven replied.

Our lips touched briefly, but no promises were made. We wouldn't make liars out of ourselves. After all, people die every day.

There was only one promise I needed from him. One we *had* to keep no matter the cost.

"Gage can't live. For Mouse's sake." I pulled his face down toward mine, searching his hazel eyes.

"For Mouse's sake," Triven agreed.

Triven's lips brushed mine again as there was a soft knock on the door. I pulled away from the comfort his arms as the door shifted, pushing us apart. Archer's face appeared in the crack, backlit by the torch Otto held above his head.

"It's time." She said quietly. I took a shaky breath. Palm open, I gestured for her to lead the way.

When we reached the bottom of the landing, Ryker tossed something at Archer. She caught it with ease in her new hand, but didn't seem to know what it was. I recognized the small device, but it made no sense. Another flew toward Triven, who grabbed it with a similar confused expression.

"What are these for?" I asked, plucking the gadget from Triven to examine it closer. "This looks like the face shields we used."

"An improved version." Ryker said. He stepped forward, taking the apparatus from Archer's metal fingers and clipped it over her ear. She watched me warily. I narrowed my eyes. Archer knew something I did not.

"*What* is this for?" I pressed again, shaking the shield at Ryker. "These weren't part of the plan."

"It was. We just didn't tell you." Archer looked guilty now.

"Or me." Triven frowned taking the device back. The fact Triven was also in the dark did little to dissuade my anger.

Arden stiffened next to me as Sedia swaggered in from the kitchen. She was licking a powdery substance off her fingertips. Tucked around her ear was the same apparatus.

In fact, *everyone* in the room had one.

Everyone, but Ryker and me.

"Whose face?" I snatched the shield from Arden this time and practically shoved it up Ryker's nose as I thrust it at him.

Ryker turned, staring down at me. He chewed the inside of his cheek.

"WHOSE FACE!?" I yelled again.

"There are only two people Fandrin will want to personally see suffer. Who he will hesitate to have killed on sight." Ryker leaned over me and I shrank away as if he had just slapped me.

Triven clipped the projector over his ear and quickly tapped it. In the blink of an eye, there were two identical Rykers glaring at each other.

"Oooo! Me next!" With a gleeful screech, Sedia tapped the side of her head and an image appeared shielding her own features. Gone were the dark eyes that matched her brother's, gone were the tattoos and wide smile. The Taciturn vanished, and staring back was my own face.

40. INCURSION

I GLARED AT the backs of my own head. It was surreal. The facial features were impeccable except for one missing feature. The new scar courtesy of Gage. That alone was mine. Still the bodies were all wrong. Too tall, too broad, mismatched skin tones. Tattoos. Rebel uniforms. Wraith colors. Subversive war paint. My face on a hundred different physiques. It was all wrong.

An ache radiated from my jaw, my teeth clenched tight. This was a stupid plan. A reckless and stupid plan.

A dark head moved at the front of our unit. There was a slight limp to his steps, more effort made every time he lifted his right leg. This was the real Ryker. I glared, hoping he could feel it boring into his skull.

This hadn't been some last-minute scheme, an impulsive notion. No. The rebels had scanned my face the day I wore Petra's. For months, they had been preparing to use my likeness to get them close to Fandrin. I felt foolish not to have seen it coming, to have assumed we were going to attempt the invasion with pure force. While I was preparing to fight my way in, the rebels had been banking on *my* face to open the gates.

Ryker was right not to tell me. I never would have agreed to letting *anyone* wear my image. True, Fandrin might not kill me outright, but the same could not be said for Gage. My face could just as easily be a target as a shield. And Ryker's visage was equally as dangerous.

It was eerie seeing myself multiplied. Their smiles and scowls twisted my features in foreign ways. A select few kept their own faces—some out of choice, others because we didn't have enough shields. Thadd was talented, but not even he could make supplies materialize out of thin air, so the number of shields were limited. I tried to focus on those people, the ones who still looked like themselves.

"Fifty-seven projectiles were deployed. They're on track." Thadd spoke over the line. He was our eye in the sky.

"Hold positions." It was Arstid's voice now.

The people in front halted, obeying orders, but I pushed through them. My feet only stopped when no one else blocked my way. The Tower soared above the other buildings in the distance, a pinnacle. A beacon. We were five blocks out. Poised. Ready. And I would be the first in. I burned with anticipation, gun in hand. The rebels wanted Fandrin alive, I had other plans.

One of the Rykers brushed elbows with me.

Triven. He hadn't left my side since the facial shields went up. He had refused to wear Ryker's face at first, but the rebel leader made a good argument. If Fandrin saw Triven, he would know the real me was close by. Triven's face could spoil the entire ploy and risk all the other groups. In the end Triven donned the mask.

I pushed against his arm in reply. *It's me,* we were both saying.

The first tremor pulsed underfoot. Fiery fingers stretched up over the buildings ahead of us.

"Initial intersection successful." Thadd's voice crackled as another explosion detonated farther away.

"Hold." Ryker reminded everyone. If we charged in now, we would be running head-long into a minefield.

The concussions were sporadic, each one causing a spike in my heart rate. Bits of plaster sloughed off the white walls of the buildings we were gathered near. The small chunks flecked my hair and shoulders. The falling pieces shattered the illusions of my face, momentarily disrupting the projectors' feeds. For a brief second I caught a glimpse of Archer's ear.

Sweat was collecting along my hairline. A bead trailed down my spine. *We're out of range.* I reminded myself again.

Another explosion. I gripped my gun tighter.

Our diversion bombs were working so far. The small team of ex-Adroits had compiled their knowledge to create a series of trigger bombs. Through a string of tests—and close calls—the Taciturns had discovered most of Gage's explosives were heat-seeking. The weapons' deployments were initiated by general coordinates being set, then the bombs would hone in on their targets based on heat signatures. With Thaddeus' guidance, we had created a series of our own bombs that not only set off the heat stamp of a human, but that could also be triggered at a safe range. Our bombs went pop, theirs leveled a street.

The bombs were Baxter's idea. Alone, they were practically useless as bait, but combined with Zeek's genius hacking skills, phase two of our plan was almost complete.

Fandrin had kept most of the sectors outside of The Tower without power. He wanted to keep us hungry and in the dark. It was a smart tactic. Scared and hungry people tended to make poor decisions. What he was too arrogant to realize, was that those of us from Tartarus had been scared and hungry for generations. It was what drove us. Yes, Fandrin had cut our power, but he had kept the cameras alive. This was his second mistake.

If the cameras had power, Zeek could hack them. And hack them he did.

All of the feeds outside The Tower had been under our control for nearly a week. And we were using it to our advantage. Contrived sightings had been leaked into the feed to let the Ministry think they had the upper hand, but they only saw what we wanted them to. Right now, they saw hundreds of us bearing down on their precious Tower. What they didn't know, was that the feed placed us blocks ahead of our real location. Gage's bombs were being deployed, exactly as anticipated, but instead of finding us, they were met with our trigger bombs. There was no way to know how many Gage had managed to make, or how many he had left, but Ryker brought up a point I had to agree with. Gage was foolish, impatient and arrogant. If he thought we were coming for him, he would throw everything he had at us. I hoped we were right.

I was counting the explosions, ticking off the numbers. Three more and we could move in. The toe of my boot inched forward. Each explosion was bringing down a layer of defense for the Ministry.

Two more.

I leaned forward, preparing to launch into motion.

"Prea?" A hesitant voice popped in my head. I twitched, looking around. No one else had heard it. The feed had been spliced to my headset alone. A prickling sensation stirred at the base of my neck.

"Petra?" I whispered. I could hear her breathing. Another bomb went off, closer again.

"Petra?" I hissed, pulling upright from my crouch. I half turned to Triven. The panic on my face registered immediately. He lowered his gun, trying to read me. "What—" He started to ask, but I waved him off, listening.

"Tell me she's fine." I closed my eyes and grabbed Triven's arm for support.

"Prea, I'm sorry. I-I don't know how she escaped. She just slipped out… I think she's heading to you." There was a tremor in Petra's voice. "Prea, she took my tactical gear."

There was no doubt in my mind where Mouse was headed, and it wasn't to me. She had been muttering his name in her sleep, training like she intended to kill. Training for revenge. I should have seen it for what it was. I should have known. I whipped back to scan The Tower, staring at the illuminated glass windows that stretched toward the sky. She wouldn't need a map to find her brother. Mouse was headed this way, I was sure of it. She was coming for Gage. And there was no way I was going to let her arrive first, alone.

I surged forward, breaking the line. Shouts erupted, people calling me back, but I ignored them. Ryker's face was right behind me, shoving aside startled people to follow. He was quick on my heels and there was only one person it could be. Triven huffed next to me.

"Mouse?"

"She's going for Gage." I panted.

We both picked up the pace. A series of expletives broke over the line and I could hear Archer following us. Arstid called for her team to hold, but our team began to break rank.

A handful of people hesitated, but soon they were following us. I ran straight at The Tower. Mouse couldn't make it there first. I wouldn't let her. If she found Gage before I could, if he hurt her… My vision went red.

The smoke grew thicker as we neared one of the blast sites. I barreled toward the destroyed streets. My eyes danced ahead, picking my path ten paces in advance. One misstep, and I would break a leg. Bricks, mortar and broken concrete littered the ground, but there were no bodies.

"Cover!" Thadd screamed over the coms.

Triven hurled himself over me. We slammed into the ground as an explosion pounded the air.

"ENGAGE!" Ryker barked over the earpieces.

The last bomb had detonated. Gage's toys were obliterated and now everyone would be charging. The blast was close, but not close enough to slow me down. Bits of rubble rained down around us but I was already pushing to my feet, springing out from under Triven's protective weight. He grabbed a fistful of my jacket, shoving us forward.

A sulfuric stench burned my eyes. Tears began to blur the streets, making the lights emanating from Fandrin's Tower sparkle. I swiped them away with the back of my hand. The crackle of flames and crashes of crumbling buildings faded. Hundreds of running feet shook the ground and battle cries rose. We hit the final clearing. A band of grass encompassed the massive building, but the once green lawn had soured, turning it brown. We would be exposed here, but there were no other choices. Screams rose louder as we closed in on our mark. Hundreds of people swarmed from the damaged buildings surrounding The Tower. Weapons were held high and the mass of people charged like water overflowing a dam. My feet carried me toward The Tower, but my eyes were everywhere. Searching for threats, looking for Mouse. The open ground flooded with versions of Ryker and myself.

Gunshots boomed from above. A woman to my right with her own face dropped like a stone. Her body was swallowed by the crowd, trampled by those behind her. I searched the top of the building, but couldn't see their snipers. Four more bodies in our unit hit the ground before Arstid made the call. "NOW!"

I yanked Zeek's black box from my hip pocket and jammed a thumb onto the trigger. Scattered around the building, fifty others were doing the very same thing. The box clicked and I could feel the pulsation in my bones. The night shivered with the surge of power. Then The Tower's lights wavered, the electronic masks flickered and then, as anticipated, the snipers' shots ceased.

I tossed the box discarding the carcass. The EMP—electromagnetic pulse— devices only packed enough juice for a one time use per unit. They weren't enough to take out the entire building's power grid, nor were they meant to. But they *could* fry specific smaller devices for a short period of time. Zeek's frequency targeted Sanctuary weapons alone. For the next twenty minutes, all Sanctuary-grade weapons would be little more than fancy clubs and ordinary knives. The short gap of time was all we needed.

The Sanctuary's weapons were superior in every way, except one. They needed power. Tartarus guns ran on hammer-action, gun powder and Old World mechanics. And better than that, our homemade weapons needed no mechanical engagement at all. If you could swing a bat— throw a knife—no power was needed, just a little skill and a whole lot of anger. We were well equipped with both.

Our warriors carried weapons from both of the two worlds. Our ancient weapons would get us inside and when the power finally returned to Sanctuary's arsenal, our stolen weapons would level the playing field.

The structure rose above us as we closed in on our team's target—the transport doors. The massive doors shuddered and then rolled upward.

A mob of people surged out. Silver suits shone in the mass, but these weren't just soldiers pouring from the doors. Black and red war paint mingled with the uniforms.

My entire body went numb as a familiar battle cry rose against our own. Fandrin's pet dogs had been let out of their cage.

The Ravagers had joined the fray.

41. POWER

I **DREW MY** guns, firing a line to clear our path. The soldiers slowed, realizing their guns were no longer working. A few stopped, eyes widening as they considered our numbers and their useless weapons. Several hung back, unsure of what to do. The bold rushed forward, flipping their firearms into clubs. I targeted those soldiers.

Colors ceased to exist, and I stopped thinking about who I was shooting. In this moment, anyone in my way was the enemy. We had agreed to wound most of the soldiers, not kill. But unlike Triven, I shot them with no remorse. This was not the time for mercy, not in the throes of battle. A spared life now could be a knife in the back later.

There was no time to waste. I had to find Mouse.

The gap separating the side was narrowing quickly and at ten feet away, my chambers emptied. Holstering one gun, I freed a knife. I could see the whites of the Ravagers' eyes, smell the stench of their yellowed teeth. They took in our matching faces in surprise, but didn't falter. Only the soldiers took pause. My face meant little to the Ravagers.

But it would after tonight. How appropriate that my mother's eyes would be the last thing most of them saw.

Two steps before we clashed, I lunged and flipped the other handgun in my grasp. Grabbing the muzzle, I kicked off the ground and launched myself into the mob of Ravagers. The butt of my gun smashed down on a skull as my knife plunged into another.

The world around me swirled. Knives slashed, guns swung brandished like clubs, and fists flew. Years of training took over and my movements flowed naturally. The few blows that landed slid off, and no blade so much as kissed my skin. Triven fought at my side, our backs grazing each other as we moved in unison.

I caught a glimpse of one of my lookalikes bludgeoning anyone who came within reach. She wielded a huge mallet laced with spikes. A skull tattoo covered her hand and she was laughing maniacally with each swing. Like their leader, the Taciturns were taking violence to a new level with every Ravager. And the sentiment was returned. The Ravagers fought with no restraint, and the savagery was quickly escalating.

Weapons and bodies clashed brutally. Metal sang against metal. Bones broke and the mortally wounded fell. My feet trampled the dead littering the ground. Slowly the mass of bodies began to thin. A small team burst though The Ministry's line. Triven and I were among those at the front. I hurtled toward the open bay doors. Five people sprinted ahead of us.

Voices were shouting in my ear, calling out orders. From the sounds, we were advancing. Then an explosion rocked the ground. My feet staggered but I kept them moving forward. There were screams of pain over the earpiece. Apparently, Gage hadn't sent out all his bombs. But the heat from them never reached us. The bombs must have detonated on the opposite side of the building. The yelling escalated in our ears, but we ran on. There was nothing we could do from here. Nothing but get inside and hope to stop the battle from within.

With a loud screech, the bay doors began to close. Once shut they would be damn near impossible to reopen. A huge man leading the assault slammed himself into the closing door. He caught the bottom as it reached his thighs and pulled with all his strength. He screamed with the effort to hold it. As the man struggled, his face smashed against the metal surface and the shield clipped to his ear fell free. Grenald's face appeared, red and sweating. Veins popped in his forearms and neck. Triven rushed forward to help him. Stooping, I snatched a soldier's discarded rifle from the ground and hurled myself under the door. I slid past the Grenald's legs and as I passed underneath, I wedged the rifle in the narrowing opening.

A body slid in at the other end. When she popped up, her spiked mallet jammed the opposite side of the door. Sedia grinned through my borrowed face, then twisted sideways. The door clanged as a knife slammed into the thick surface. The tip narrowly missed both Sedia's head and Grenald's fingers.

The knife flew from my hand as I rolled to a crouch, quickly reloading my gun. There were scattering footsteps and then bullets began to fly. I screamed at those coming through the door to wait. A bullet hit Grenald's leg and he crumpled. Triven dove out of sight. The wedges Sedia and I had placed held, for now. Fifteen Ravagers squared off in the center of the garage, their piercings glinting in the dim lights. The huge room held a few transport vehicles lining the walls and offered little cover. Cat calls screeched out as Sedia and I lurched to our feet, fresh weapons drawn. The Taciturn ripped the earpiece from her head and let out a horrific battle cry. She wanted them to know who they were fighting, who was going to kill them. We opened fire at the same time and I charged at the Ravagers. Our people on the outside of the door only needed a few seconds of cover to get in. Several of the Ravagers scattered, while others took the bullets. Several fell, but they weren't dying, not even bleeding. They grinned up at us. Fandrin had given them body armor.

"Head!" I screamed at Sedia. She didn't miss a beat, shooting a woman between the eyes. People were streaming in behind us and my clip emptied. I dove behind a pillar as a round of bullets riddled the opposite side. I pulled the clip to reload but dropped the gun as a nail-laced bat swung at my face. I ducked, rolling away just as the bat smashed into the column. One of the nails grazed my scalp. Twice more the club swung down on me and I barely missed getting crushed. From a distance my suit could somewhat protect me, but blunt force trauma at this range and I would be dead. As the man swung upward the third time, I spun, kicking his feet out from under him. He slammed into the floor, both club and head cracking on the ground.

I wanted to search for Triven in the fight, to see if he was okay, but the man I loved had disappeared into the sea of replicated faces. Maybe that was part of Ryker's plan. With the masks in place the enemy couldn't see individual faces, but neither could we. Our loved ones had disappeared from sight, making it impossible to worry about them. To get distracted. It was horrible and genius.

The Ravager on the ground groaned. A bullet exploded the Tribesman's head and a shadow slipped out from behind a transport vehicle. It wasn't one of ours, but another Ravager. Metal spikes protruded from his face, nose and ears. Even the red eyepatch covering his right eye was decked out with metal thorns.

There was no mistaking that face. It was in a dark alley. His taunts had turned to screams as my dagger took his eye. It appeared I wasn't the only one recalling that night. The Ravager snarled, advancing on me. A huge rusted blade twisted in one of his hands, a gun pointed at me in the other. I took a few careful retreating steps. The fight behind him was intensifying. Both Ravagers and rebels alike were squeezing through the door. No one paid attention the two us. No one would notice I was cornered. My gun was still by the pillar behind him. I could see it, lying just out of reach, utterly useless. I pulled two knives free from under my vest and flipped them in my hands. The Ravager stopped. His eye flickered from the knives to my face.

If he didn't recognize me before, he did now.

I grinned, spinning the knives again. "You know, it's all fun and games until someone loses an eye—oops! Too late."

Roaring, he did exactly as I wanted. The Tribesman threw down the gun, and went in for the close, personal kill. He hauled his blade high overhead, winding up. Instead of drawing away, I hurdled toward him, slipping under his arms just as they reached their peak height. Pushing up as hard as I could, I buried my knives under the left side of his ribcage and thrust skyward. The Ravager made a terrible wheezing sound as I punctured his lung. The heavy blade clattered to the ground. His grubby hand pushed against my shoulders, grabbed weakly around my throat, but I held him tight against me.

He gasped desperately, then spit in my face. I snarled, pulling him closer with the knives. "For my parents."

Ramming my knee upward, I dislodged my knives and let the dead Ravager fall to the ground. I stood there staring at the battle raging by the door. My hands were shaking, skin hot with his blood. For years, I had dreamed of revenge for my parents' deaths, but now all I felt was empty.

I started when a voice spoke in my ear.

"Garage level taken!" It was Ryker.

Thawing to life, I snatched up my fallen gun and ran for the entrance, the dead Ravager already forgotten. People were sliding under the door in masses, but they were *our* people. I snagged a Ryker who stumbled in. He was covered in blood and shaking. A small backpack rested on his shoulders under layers of Wraith furs and war paint.

"Get us online. Fast." I hissed at Zeek. "Find her."

His disguise was perfect, a Ryker mask with a Wraith costume. Looking at the man, no one would suspect the Sanctuary's best hacker was hidden in plain sight. We needed him to blend in. To disappear from The Ministry's radar and get to a security room. From there, he could hack The Tower's feeds and we would no longer be fighting blind.

Though I couldn't see his real face, I was sure he was in shock. Zeek didn't say anything but began stumbling to his right toward a discrete door in the wall. I whistled and five more lookalikes appeared, encircling the hacker.

Without further instruction, they hustled Zeek away. Three other teams split off, disappearing down halls and through doors.

I ran through the garage, letting memory guide me to the main floor. We had scoured the blueprints the rebels had drawn for us, the layouts flickering through my thoughts, guiding my feet. I remembered shooting my guns, thrusting with knives, but it passed in a blur. Stranger yet, we met little resistance. It was *too* easy. The stairwell thundered with our footsteps and then the door was flying open and we poured into The Tower's main lobby. The space was blindingly white, and covered in blood. The front doors had been blown wide, the white surroundings singed black.

It was bedlam.

I tried to pause, to assess the scene, but the bodies pouring out from the stairwell shoved me forward. As I got closer, I could see the fighters. Ravagers, Wraiths, Taciturns, rebels and soldiers battled for every inch of ground.

A hand caught my elbow and yanked me sideways. I followed the broad shoulders without hesitation. As we skirted the fight, I reached up and yanked the projector from his ear. Triven's face instantly returned and I took an easier breath. I needed his face. Needed to know he was okay. Ryker's plan be damned.

Triven pulled me around a corner away from the battle. I searched the crowd, looking for Mouse. Shockingly, we outnumbered them. With their weapons rendered unusable, we were overtaking the Ministry's militia. We had assumed a few of his own soldiers might turn on the oppressive leader, but more than anticipated seemed to be switching their allegiance. Soldiers were changing to *our* side, some were even taking out the Ravagers, their intended allies. I wanted to feel hopeful that we might win, but as I searched for Mouse, the rising terror cause by her absence was all consuming. What if she was still outside? What if she never made it this far? Panic flared and then Triven grabbed my arm. He was pointing up to the back of the room. Instead of the child we loved, we found her brother and my grandfather.

Watching from a balcony two levels above, Gage stood shaking a useless gun in his hand. Fandrin stood next him, a controlling grip on the boy's shoulder. They were fenced by a collection of the smallest cadets imaginable. Each child held a handgun. I was ticking through the math. The EMP surge would be obsolete soon and the kids would be able to fire. A few more minutes and they would become a threat we would have to subdue. We expected this, that Fandrin would use them as a buffer. Tribes, rebels and Subversive members had all agreed to hurt as few children as possible, but there would be casualties. The instinct of kill or be killed doesn't always take into consideration the age of the shooter. I avoided thinking about it. There was only one boy I would kill without hesitation. And he was standing across the room.

Shaking off Triven's hand, I sprang into the fighting mob to get a clearer shot. My bullets were gone, but there were still two Sanctuary guns strapped to my back. *Please*, I thought as I yanked them loose and rounded on the exposed balcony. The crowd parted and I took aim. Fandrin saw me then. Our eyes connected and a rush of rage burned, swelling in my heart, more painful than ever before. I wanted him dead. I pulled the trigger. Once.

Nothing. I fired again and the gun came to life. Bullets exploded from the muzzle straight toward Fandrin's face. I pulled the trigger again and again, but the bullets stopped before reaching him. A perfectly translucent shield quivered with each shot, but it did not give. Pock marks studded the surface, distorting the people standing behind it. The old man's lips pulled back as he smiled wickedly down from his behind his bullet proof glass, tipping his cane in salute.

The gun faltered in my hand as I realized my mistake, too late.

The Sanctuary weapons were working again, and I had just alerted his entire army.

42. END GAME

"**WEAPONS ARE UP!**" Ryker shouted over the coms. I hadn't seen him, but he had seen me. Both sides scrambled to extract guns, to pull amplified knives free.

Fandrin waved a limp hand mockingly. The sharp lines of his suit accentuated his broad shoulders as he turned away. The children soldiers moved with him, his living shields. Only one boy remained behind. Darkness consumed Gage's expression as he watched the massacre below.

"Fandrin!" I screamed and unleashed another round of bullets. They were useless at this range. But if I got closer… maybe then they would penetrate the barrier. I began shoving people out of my way as I searched the walls, looking for any surface that could provide some kind of purchase. There was a ledge tracing the third story. It wasn't wide, but I could run it. I just needed a way up. Fandrin's head disappeared from view and desperation gripped me. He was *so close*. Both he and Gage within reach yet untouchable. If they left our sight, if we lost them… "Zeek? Cameras!?"

"Working on it!" He responded.

"Work faster!" Archer screamed back. It was a relief to hear her voice.

Someone seized me from behind and I was wrenched backward into a broad chest as a machete swung down where I had been standing. Triven's cheek brushed mine and he shot the Ravager wielding the blade.

"GO!" He shouted, shoving me.

I dove forward, continuing to search.

"Baxter," Triven bellowed over the escalating gunfire. "Glass!"

"A little busy right now!" Baxter growled over the coms.

A woman came out of nowhere, and I lurched backward. The tip of her knife slid past my nose. I could hear it crackling with electricity. Grabbing a fist-full of her red mohawk, I twisted around, yanking her with me. I spun and then released the woman into a waiting Wraith's knife. The Wraith roared victoriously and then tossed her body aside, creating a gap in the crowd.

My heart jumped. Then stopped.

I threw an arm wide, digging my nails into Triven's bicep.

On the far side of the room, pipes rose from the floor, crisscrossed, forming mismatched geometric shapes. They varied in size, but they were definitely climbable, a proven fact since someone was already scaling the feature. A slight-framed girl was working her way up the angled pipelines with ease. She slid from rafter to rafter, walking the lines with grace and sure feet, pulling herself up with surprising strength. Her eyes were watching the ledge I too had spotted. Like so many others tonight, the girl wore my face, but I knew who was under the mask.

"Mouse…" I breathed her name at first. "MOUSE!!!"

Cries and gunfire swallowed my screams. The girl was nearly halfway to the ledge already. I glanced back at the balcony. Gage was watching her too. A sharp grin splitting his face. Mouse's foot slipped and for a terrifying moment the girl dangled from her hands. I raced toward her, not watching my steps. My toe caught, throwing me down. The ground slammed into my chest, knocking the wind from my lungs. Triven was there, quickly pulling me up, but not before I caught sight of what had tripped me. Grenald's body sprawled face up, his eyes wide and blank. Otto was laying across his body, caressing the giant man's face. A knife protruded from Otto's back, and still he clung to Grenald in his last moments. Otto's lips were moving, saying something over and over again, but the words didn't register until I was already running, eyes back on Mouse. And when they did, his words hit like a blow to the stomach.

I go where you go.

I swallowed back the agony. *Focus.*

Mouse was moving again. Her legs swung high, pulling her back to safety. At this pace, she would be on the ledge soon. Triven and I reached the perimeter of the huge room, and I finally had a clear lane. I increased my speed, eyes still on the girl.

Seventeen more steps and I would reach the structure. I could climb faster than Mouse. Overtake her—

A huge body exploded in our path. I hadn't seen the corridor he emerged from, but the soldier was suddenly there. Chest heaving. Rifle pointed at my head. I tried to slow, but there was too much momentum. My feet slid on the polished floor. I freed a knife ready to throw it, but a hand stabbed out, grabbing the muzzle and shoving it upward just as the soldier pulled the trigger.

Blood sprayed the white wall—splattered my face. The soldier staggered and I wasted no time slitting his throat. I didn't pause to watch him collapse. Instead, I turned to the man huddled against the wall. Triven twisted around and I let out a startled cry. He was cradling what remained of his hand. Blood poured down the front of his suit, dripping on the ground. At least two of his fingers were missing.

I stared, unsure what to do.

"Go." He said, trying to tuck the mangled hand out of sight. "You have to get Mouse..." He winced.

I retreated a half step from him, but couldn't move any farther. Triven's face was going white.

"DAMN IT, GO!" He screamed, clutching his hand tighter. There was so much blood... "PREA, GO!"

Triven slammed his shoulder into mine, knocking me sideways.

I stumbled with the force of his blow, but kept moving. I cast one last pained look backward. Triven was slumping against the wall, his hand shaking as he held it to his chest. But I did what he told me, and I ran at Mouse.

She was at the ledge now. Her legs stretched as far as they could go, fingertips reaching for the lip of the outcropping.

I dodged chaotic violence around me, keeping watch on her. My hands snapped out when necessary, knives slicing at anything that got too close. The pipes were almost in reach when long limbs crashed into mine. I moved to attack, then stopped. The face was familiar. Arden was covered in sweat, but his expression was hard. Gone was the fearful young man.

Instantly, he fell to a knee offering me a step with interlaced fingers. I flipped the rifle behind my back, holstered my knives and stepped into his hands. Arden thrust as I jumped, launching me in the air and past the first three rungs. The metal pipes clanged as I slammed my hands on them. Sweat and blood made my grasp slip, but I held on. The toes of my boots landed hard, but barely touched the surface before I was climbing. Twice I screamed her name with no response. Mouse had hauled herself on the narrow ledge. She balanced there finding her center, eyes on her brother. Gage was watching her with fascination. Mouse groped her ear and with a jerky movement, ripped the shield free. The deranged boy practically salivated as his sister's face appeared. Deliberately, he threw aside the gun he had been holding and withdrew a large knife. Palm open, teeth showing, he beckoned her forward.

I yelled Mouse's name again as I pulled myself recklessly upward.

I was almost to her.

Mouse's toes straightened, aiming at her target, and then she was running. A knife glinted in one hand, the other was clenched in a fist. The structure vibrated and I knew people were climbing up after me.

I could only hope they were on our side.

The ledge caught under my fingertips and I pulled, swinging myself upward. I hit the mantel and as I stood, the wall next to me exploded into tiny pieces. Reflexively, I dove to my stomach, barely clinging on. Ahead, Mouse had done the same. We were both horribly exposed.

"I need cover!" I shut my eyes as another bullet hit.

"On it!" Archer yelled over the earpiece and instantly the bullets stopped. By the time I had my feet back under me, Mouse was already running again. When did she get so fast?

The girl was screaming as she ran, barreling at the glass wall. When she hit it, the shield would not give. It would toss her backwards and down a three-story drop.

Gage danced on the other side, his grin widening. I whipped my rifle around and jammed down the trigger. Bullets flew, spraying the glass as I ran. Spider webs burst on the surface, but the glass held. The rifle clicked and I tossed it aside, full out sprinting. Mouse was twenty steps away from the shield. Maybe, if she hit it hard enough, I might be able to snag her on the rebound.

In a sudden movement, Mouse's closed fist reeled back then shot forward. A silver ball no bigger than an eyeball soared out and hit the glass partition. Unlike the bullets, this device stuck, clinging to the pitted surface. Gage stared at the orb, then began backing up. There was a pop and the glass shattered.

She had timed it perfectly.

Mouse launched herself through the breaking glass and directly onto a startled Gage. The boy soldier flinched away from the flying shards, his hands moving instinctively to shield his face. Mouse came down on him, her knife plunging into Gage's chest.

Brother and sister fell, disappearing behind the balcony's rail.

I vaulted the last six feet, throwing myself through the broken opening. Glass crunched as I crashed through, drawing my weapons.

I had jumped too far. I rolled the length of the narrow room, slamming to a halt against the opposite wall. Whipping around, I searched for immediate threats. There were two sets of doors, one at each end, and I eyed them both suspiciously. But the room was empty expect for the three of us.

A strangled cry escaped when I saw her.

Propped against the low wall we had broken through, covered in glass and cuts, Mouse sat staring down at the boy's head resting in her lap. Gage was clawing at his sister's arms, reaching for her throat with weak hands. Blood bubbled from his lips. And for the first time since I had encountered him, Gage looked scared. Mouse sat taller, keeping her face from his reach. In her hands, she held one of Xavier's prized knives. She had hit the target perfectly. A river of red pulsed from the hole in Gage's chest. Mouse had hit his heart, probably severed an artery. Each weak heartbeat pushed out more blood from Gage's wound. When she had pulled the knife out, Mouse had sealed her brother's fate.

Tears were trailing down her cheeks. Mouse glanced up then, surprised to see me. The rage that had possessed her was gone, the only thing remaining was the void left behind. I knew that *too* well. Slowly, Mouse's gaze fell. Dropping the knife, she grasped one of Gage's hands. He clung desperately to her. Something passed between them. Something I would never understand. After everything, they were still brother and sister. Then with a last shudder, Gage died in her arms.

Mouse's tears were turning into sobs. My heart splintered. This is what I had desperately wanted to keep her from. There was blood on her young hands now—and her life would never be the same.

Abruptly, three people flew through jagged opening in quick succession and I dove, snatching up the gun Gage had thrown aside. Arden's landing was less than graceful, but he righted himself quickly. Like me, he swept the room, surprised to find it empty. Two Wraith warriors soared in behind him, both carrying Sanctuary assault rifles, the scarred markings on their face highlighted in blue.

Before I could react, the door to our right burst open. We turned in unison, but the Wraiths quickly held up their hands to call us off. Showing her true face, Teya charged into the room from a stairwell. Blood covered her white furs, making it look like she had just skinned the animal.

I was shocked at the sight of the two women following her. Archer and Arstid both looked worse for the wear. Their masks too were gone. Triven's mother had a nasty gash across her forehead and looked equally surprised to see me alive.

"Secondary pathway clear." Arstid said, obviously not speaking to us.

Archer stood in the doorway, staring down at Mouse. Her expression mirrored my own. We all remembered our first kill. It haunted you the rest of your life. I moved to Mouse then, unsure of how to comfort her. I was nearly to her side when the doors opposite swung in and bullets began to spray the room.

43. DYNASTY

ARDEN TOOK ONE to the chest, laying him out flat, but he rolled to his side coughing in pain. Five inches higher and he would have been dead. I threw myself over Mouse, shielding her. Several ribs snapped as bullets hit my back. The suit absorbed most of the shock, saving my life, but the pain of the broken bones still blurred my vision. I kicked Gage's body on its side to give us more cover.

Arstid, the smaller Wraith and Archer dropped, returning fire while the other warrior dove to protect his queen, taking the bullets meant for her. He knocked them both to the ground and without a suit like mine, he was dead before impact. Teya ducked behind his body while she too fired back.

Soldiers poured into the room. Silver cadet uniforms mixed with officer white. Fandrin had been holding out on us. The soldiers fighting below had been lower ranking. Pawns that could be sacrificed. These were his prized possessions, his strongest line of defense. A perfect balance of deadly and innocent—the highest-ranking officers in the Ministry and the children brainwashed into following orders.

We were dead.

We had walked into the hornets' nest and now we were dead. As the morbid thought crossed my mind, suddenly the soldiers began to scatter. More people were filling the room, but this time they were wearing fur, rebel grey and tattoos. His limp more pronounced, the real Ryker James barreled into the room with his own army in tow. Their returning fire gave me enough cover to think clearly.

Mouse was completely still beneath me and for a moment I thought I had been too slow. But her warm breath tickled my ear. Not dead, in shock.

Scooping her up in my arms, I rose to my feet. The room was packed, battling figures pressing us back against the balcony. Children soldiers were being subdued where possible, but their own officers had begun to use them as shields. Some of the children surrendered, their small frames curling in on themselves, trying to disappear. Others fought harder than any of the adults, trying to prove themselves. These tiny soldiers were the perfect weapons. Trained to kill and yet monstrous to harm. The masks of my likeness had begun to disappear, the power sources finally dying and I realized how many faces I didn't recognize. Mouse clung to my neck, eyes closed. I pushed us back against the broken partition and stole a glance down. War was still raging below us. I thought about jumping out, about trying to make it back to the ledge, but it was impossible with Mouse in my arms. I looked down, contemplating the fall, but the notion vanished immediately. A tall man with dark hair was crumbled directly below us. Doc... A Ravager stood over him, still swinging his club. I didn't remember throwing the knife, but it flew from my hand, embedding in the Ravager's skull.

Unexpectedly, I was knocked against the wall as a white-haired woman was thrown into us. Both Ryker and Archer called for backup. The officers were overpowering us. I knew I had to get Mouse out. Arstid rose, heaving to catch her breath. I was about to force the child on her, to tell her to get out of here, when Arden's yell emptied all other thoughts from my mind.

"Fandrin!" He roared.

I looked up through at the door the soldiers had come through, and there he was. White hair, copper cane, walking toward an elevator. No glass between us this time. Arden was barreling toward him. I shifted Mouse in my arms, nearly dropping her as I yanked my gun out of its holster. I fired. Two officers were hit as they stepped in my line of fire. I shot again. The bullet clipped Fandrin's ear and he ducked away. For a glorious second, I thought Arden had him. His knife rose above the cringing man, but as he plunged downward, Fandrin was ready for him. His cane punched up, smashing into Arden's nose. Blood spurted down his face and he staggered. With a speed I didn't expect from an old man, Fandrin snatched Arden's hand and spun him. Arden was whipped around and I took my finger off the trigger. His own knife was pulled against his throat as Fandrin hid, untouchable behind my friend. To kill him meant shooting them both. Forcing Arden to move, the two stepped backwards into one of the open elevators. I fired a shot, hitting the back wall of the metal box, and the doors slammed closed.

"Shit!" I stammered. There was a second lift, its doors wide. I had to get there, to follow them. "Zeek, the elevators?!"

"I'm almost in." He sounded more confident than before. "Cameras are mine!"

"Take her." I tried to pass off Mouse to Arstid, but she was already moving, rushing toward the elevators where Fandrin and Arden had just disappeared.

I moved to follow, gun raised, unsure of what to do with the girl in my arms. Fandrin was mine, *I* was going to be the one to bring him down. But Mouse...

Arms reached out to me as a deep voice offered salvation.

"Give her to me." Teya stepped closer, slipping her hands under my arms. "I'll take her to safety. You, go after him."

She pulled on Mouse, but I held her tight. "If *anything* happens to her—"

Teya cut me off, "You kept *both* my daughters safe. I will protect yours."

She pulled again and this time I let Mouse slide into her arms, snarling. "*Protect her.*"

"With my life." And the Wraith disappeared, running for the stairwell.

I plowed in the opposite direction toward the elevator, following Arstid. Shoving my way forward, I punched two officers and flipped a kid without slowing. Another bullet hit my back and the already broken ribs blazed, but I kept moving. When I finally reached the hall beyond, I was less than ten steps behind her. Bullets chased us down the corridor, but their aim was wild. Arstid dove into the open elevator and I slid in after her. The doors didn't move.

"Zeek!?" I screamed looking for a button to push.

"I'm in!!" He whooped with joy.

"Get us moving?" Arstid stood back as I fired a few rounds out the door at the officers trailing us.

"At least close the doors!" I barked. Three more officers were advancing and my clip emptied. I castoff my handgun, snatching for Arstid's. A female officer hurdled in front of the open doors. A gun unlike any I had seen before swung up in her hands. Arstid lunged across the elevator, shoving me hard as the officer fired. With one squeeze, the gun shot off eight rapid rounds and the doors slammed shut. Arstid's push had slammed my head into the wall, the mechanical screech deafening as my ear collided with the elevator panel. I yanked the com from my ear, watching it spark as I threw it to the floor. Useless. It bounced, then landed in a pool of blood.

"Arstid?" I stammered as I crashed to my knees beside her. My hands flew over the bullet holes. The officer's gun had been armor-piercing, seven rounds penetrating the suit.

Arstid frantically began fishing in her pockets and pulled out a vial of healing serum. I stared. It was green. Not the good stuff, not the perfected serum Doc had lost in the fire, but it was still better than nothing. She tried to pull the stopper, but it slipped in her trembling hands. How had she gotten it? Our supplies were so low a vial like this was a rare find. I had thought only our medics had them.

"Where did you get this?" I eyed the green liquid.

When Arstid didn't answer, I snatched the vial. She had been so terrible, showing me little other than hate and disdain since the day I came into her life. I could take the vail, kept it for myself and she knew it. I thought about it, for one instant I considered keeping it. But as her breathing hitched, I pulled off the top and poured it over her chest.

Arstid hissed in pain, her back arching. The skin sizzled, trying to stitch itself shut, but it wasn't enough. Three wounds had scabbed over, but the other four were still bleeding. I groped in her pockets searching for more, but Arstid grabbed my arm, stopping me.

There wouldn't be any more, there was only the one. Understanding, Arstid's throat began to work around her words.

"Tell Triven..." she coughed up a mouthful of blood, spitting before speaking again. "Tell him... I wasn't always a good mother... but I loved him." Tears leaked out, sliding into her white hair.

"He knows." I took her hand holding it to my chest, comforting her. "He loves you too."

Arstid smiled weakly. Then she took a deep inhale and stopped breathing. My hand shook as it slid her eyes closed. I had never liked the woman, but I had respected her in some ways. And Triven loved her.

The doors slid open with a hiss, making me jump. I had almost forgotten where we were. Who I had been chasing.

The elevator led to an empty corridor. Moving quickly over Arstid's body, I took any useful items—a half-empty handgun, two clips and a knife. The elevator next to mine was open, vacant. I was halfway down the corridor before I realized I should have taken her earpiece too. I was cut off from everyone. Alone. But I didn't need guidance. The white hallway was not long, and there was only one set of doors. They stood slightly ajar at the end of the hall. Light was coming out, beckoning me.

There were no guards, no children soldiers. Fandrin was unguarded. The arrogant bastard hadn't expected anyone to make it this far. He hadn't thought we could hack his elevators.

I hesitated outside the door, listening for sounds of movement. Red spots dotted the marble floor. Blood. Arden's or Fandrin's? I could barely make out the room beyond, but already knew its layout. I had seen it before, large windows, clear furniture and monitors. Lots of monitors... Holstering Arstid's gun while keeping her knife in the other, I straightened from my half-crouch and pushed the door open with one hand. It swung wide without resistance.

Standing behind his translucent desk, framed by windows filled with fire and smoke, was Fandrin. He smiled coolly around Arden, knife still held to his throat.

"Welcome home."

His eyes flickered the to the monitors on the wall. Half of them had gone black, but there was one showing the hallway—showing me. I was right. He had been expecting me. I glanced at the monitors again. No screen showed the inside of this office. A quick sweep of the room confirmed it—there weren't any cameras in here. Once I stepped inside, Zeek's watchful eyes would not be able to follow.

"Let him go." I took a step inside, the door closing behind me. Fandrin's hand tightened and the knife dug into Arden's throat. I snarled. "It's over old man. Your soldiers are dying. Gage is dead. And we have control of your elevators. *No one* is coming to save you. This city is ours."

His expression twisted at the mention of Gage, but he brushed it off. "Casualties of war."

Arden stared at me pointedly, the scars on his face whiter than usual. His hands were held up at his chest in submission. I kept my eyes on Fandrin, but was focused on Arden. His fingers were twitching, counting down from five.

"Did you think you could just walk in here and take everything from me?"

Arden's fingers curled.

Four... Three...

"That this little war of yours could stop me? These people *love* me. They will *always* love me—"

Two... Arden's thumb twitched last and I flung out my arm.

The knife flew high, launching a good three feet above the men's heads and to their left. Exactly as I had planned. Fandrin's head tipped backward, following the projectile and the slight movement caused him to lean out. I let a second blade fly. Arden ducked sideways as the second knife drove into The Minister's shoulder. Fandrin roared in pain, easing his hold on Arden, who was quick to react, shoving against the restraining arm and he grabbed the knife. Twisting, he broke free of his captor's grip and ran to stand behind me, panting.

Fandrin bellowed, yanking the small throwing knife from his shoulder. He slammed a shaky hand down over the bleeding gash. I moved forward, Arstid's handgun re-drawn.

I growled at Arden, "Com the team. Tell them The Minister has been..."

What? Taken? Killed?

The latter sounded better.

My gun leveled at the Fandrin's chest, the tip wavering. Ryker wanted him alive—the rebels wanted to pass their judgment—but the rebels weren't here now. As if by its own accord, the barrel steadied. With a feather-light touch, I squeezed the trigger and a tiny red dot flickered to life, illuminating the furrow between his greying eyebrows. One twitch and he would be gone. One bullet and I would be the last in our line left standing.

Pull the trigger. I goaded myself. *Pull it!*

My finger remained frozen.

The Minister leaned over the top of his self-proclaimed throne. His bloody hand smeared the clear backrest.

"Do it." The wrinkled face unexpectedly distorted with rage as Fandrin clutched the back of his translucent chair throwing it aside. Flecks of split spattered the desk as he screamed, glaring at me. "DO IT!"

The veins in his neck pulsed angrily as his chest heaved. Not a single muscle in my body had moved, until now. Carefully, deliberately, I took two steps forward and squared my stance to fire.

It was then, as I shifted, that I realized he wasn't looking at me. He had *never* been looking to me.

Perverted triumph flashed in my grandfather's expression and I looked down.

Arden's arms wrapped around me as he plunged his knife into my stomach.

44. DEATH

THE BLADE CUT through my suit with ease. The Sanctuary grade weapon was designed to slice through anything.

Fandrin smiled. "Were you really so stupid to think I wouldn't have any protection?"

I stared at the handle protruding from my abdomen. The arms holding me let go and I twisted away to face my attacker.

"*You?*" I could hear the hurt in my own voice, the betrayal. Clutching the knife's hilt with trembling hands, I stumbled away from Arden, backing up until I hit something solid. The Minister's desk rattled as I collided with it.

Arden said nothing. He just stared at me and at his own hands as if surprised by what they'd done.

"Since when?" I snarled. It was getting harder to stand. My entire body was collapsing. The pain from my stomach was pulling the rest of me into it. A black hole of agony.

Arden stammered.

"WHEN?!" I screamed, doubling over.

"Since the night we took you in!" Arden's face contorted as he screamed back. He frothed at the mouth, then wiped it away. "While Triven was saving *you*, he neglected the rest of us. There was another pack of Ravagers hunting that night. And they found *me*." He shuddered. "They offered me a choice and I took it. I did what I needed to *survive*."

I gaped at the stranger standing before me, my blood painting his hands. No—not just mine—*so* many people's blood on his hands. It was never Veyron. Never Arstid or Maddox. I had been wrong. This entire time, I had been wrong. "You were the traitor… All of it? The Ravagers attacks? The fires? The beacon? The attacks?!"

Hot tears burned down my cheeks.

Arden's chin rose in defiance. "*You* should understand better than anyone, *Phoenix*. Sometimes a few must be sacrificed for your own survival. It was me or them. I chose me."

It sounded like he was pleading with me to understand. To absolve him.

"And *what* did you get out of it? *What* was killing your friends worth?" I sneered, trying to stay vertical. The room was starting to tip.

Arden at least had the grace to look ashamed. He glanced behind me to my grandfather. Then back. The tip of his tongue wet his lips anxiously as he stared at the knife. There was so much blood. My hands were slick with it. Finally, he answered. "Freedom. For loyalty, Fandrin offered me freedom."

I roared, screaming until I couldn't breathe.

Fandrin had seemed amused, watching our exchange. "And so I did, young man. Congratulations son, you've earned it. You're free."

The gunshot reverberated painfully around the room. I flinched as Arden's body crashed to the floor, gore spewing from the hole in his neck. The bullet had pierced straight through. A clean shot. Arden's hands clawed uselessly at his throat. His eyes were wide with fear. He thrust up a bloody hand, reaching for me, pleading for help.

Holding the desk for support, I turned away.

Fandrin was inspecting his gun, counting the bullets. He didn't give the dying boy on the floor a second thought. With a flick of his wrist the old man snapped the chamber closed and pointed the barrel at my forehead. One faded blue eye shut as he checked the sight.

"One bullet left." Fandrin leaned a little closer, waving the gun, taunting me.

I took the bait.

Screaming through the pain tearing into my lower abdomen, I lunged, reaching desperately for the handgun. Despite my best efforts, the Fandrin easily stepped back and pulled the weapon aside, away from my outstretched hand. I managed to catch the front of his lapel, smearing a bloody handprint down his white coat before collapsing sideways against the desk. I groaned as I slid slowly off the glassy surface down to the floor, a bloody streak trailing out behind me. The futile attempt had taken my last bit of strength. Everything was giving out and shutting down.

I crumpled into a heap at the foot of Fandrin's desk. Barely managing to roll onto my back, I stared up at the man, holding my stomach. At least he would have to see my face when I died. The face that looked so much like my mother's.

Fandrin watched me. A cat considering his prey. He pointed the gun at me again, though his aim lacked any real conviction. Even after everything, after I turned his world against him, he still couldn't shoot me.

"Coward." I wheezed.

"Why waste the bullet? You're not worth it." Walking out of sight, he grunted. There was a thump followed by a dragging noise. The legs of his throne grazed the edge of my vision. Purposefully, he perched in his chair. It was the perfect place to watch both the door and his only granddaughter die.

"I'm sure your friends will be here soon to rescue you. Who do you think it will be first? Lover boy perhaps? Or our solider friend? Or maybe the child?"

I couldn't see him from this vantage point, but I knew where his weapon would be pointed and someone *was* coming. Their footsteps were hammering down the hall.

Tears began to stream down my cheeks as my jaw locked in pain. The only sound of warning I could give was a guttural cry. I twisted my head toward the corridor.

The hinges swung wide and Archer burst through the open door. Fandrin's trigger finger was fast, but Archer's was faster. Her shot clipped The Minister's hand causing his to go wide, shattering the door frame. Fandrin pulled the trigger again and it clicked.

Empty.

There was an uneven gait and Ryker appeared, blood covering his uniform, but he seemed unharmed. One quick glance of the room and he was charging inside. To me.

"On him!" Ryker managed to order, pointing at Fandrin as he ran. Archer moved quickly. Concern warped her expression, but her attention never left the man behind the desk.

Every inch of my body had begun to convulse, a slow twitch at first, but now a steady tremor.

The ground shook as Ryker's metal knee hit the floor. I tried to force words from my mouth, but the tremors were so bad I was more likely to bite off my own tongue than utter a word.

I knew what was happening to me. My body was in shock. Cold crept into my fingers and toes. I had lost too much blood. The pain that had been excruciating at first, was dulling. This was a bad sign. But it wasn't until I saw Ryker's face, that I knew the truth.

I was dying at the feet of my monstrous grandfather. Literally cut down by a hand I had trusted.

In a moment of panic, Ryker grabbed for the knife, ready to pull it out. I sputtered, drawing it further into my body.

"Nnnn-nnnn…" I couldn't get the word out, but he immediately stopped tugging. Archer glanced down, her rifle still on Fandrin.

"Shit." Her breathing hitched. "Okay… don't pull it or she'll bleed out." There was a movement of fabric beyond my vision. "Don't freaking move!" Archer's hand shook as she looked back at The Minister. Her face towered above Ryker's shoulder, gaze darting around— from me to Arden and back to Fandrin again. She was trying to put it together. It didn't matter, not really. The traitor was dead. But I knew that look in Archer's eyes. She needed answers.

"Tttttt—rrrrr—aaaaaaiii—ttttt—." Even I couldn't understand myself. I gave up on words and let my head roll sideways toward Arden. Then slowly, I floated one hand over the bloody knife, trying to show them.

Message received.

Archer hissed at the same time Ryker's lips twisted into a snarl.

"It wasn't Veyron?" Archer said in disbelief.

My head lolled side to side. Regret creased her features. We had hated the wrong person. What was worse, we had *trusted* the wrong person.

A cold chortle came from behind the desk. "He was so eager to please too, stupid bo—"

Crack!

Archer's rifle flipped backward as she slammed the butt of her gun into The Minister's face. The man sputtered, spitting blood. She had broken his nose, maybe even knocked out a few teeth.

"Next time it's a bullet in your crotch." Archer growled. The tip of her gun dropped, aiming lower. "The rebels want you alive, they didn't say shit about being whole."

Fandrin settled, but something was off. Almost as if he *wanted* her to shoot him.

Ryker's fingers brushed over my arms, my neck, distracting me as they searched for something. Probably a pulse. There was so much blood on his hands. As if he had dipped them in paint. Was it all mine? The copper sent toxified every breath. I focused all my energy on making words.

"Ttt—tell, t—them I—I lllov—"

"No. Don't you dare say it." Ryker pressed his hands over mine with a fierce look. "Keep your hands here. Keep pressure. Don't. Die. Got it!?"

He took one of my convulsions for a nod.

"Get Doc." He said quietly.

Archer shifted next him, unsure if he was speaking to her. He said it louder and this time she was clearly torn between taking her gun off Fandrin and running for help.

"GET DOC!" Ryker screamed this time. Snatching something from the ground, he thrust it sideways and pointed at what I could only assume was Fandrin. A shimmer of tears was gathering in his blue eyes, but he held them back. "GO!"

Archer bolted.

There was another sound of movement and Ryker shot upright. Keeping a hand pressed to my stomach, he glared over the desktop. His finger squeezed, stopping just before the hammer would engage.

"You know you want to." Fandrin's words were slurred after Archer's attack. "Or have all those years of being my puppet made you soft."

Someone was running down the hall again. Multiple people by the sound and moving fast.

Ryker bared his teeth. "You would like that, wouldn't you? A quick death?' The trigger eased under his touch. "You don't deserve it. Better yet, maybe I should let the cadets' parents tear you apart. Why not throw the master to his dogs? I'm sure the Ravagers could get creative, even with an old man like *you*."

A bubbling noise erupted from deep inside me. It pressed between my clenched teeth, out my nose, asphyxiating me. Panicked, Ryker's gun clattered back to the ground. Careful to keep pressure on the wound, he turned me on my side just as I heaved. Agonizing pain tore through my stomach, spearing straight through to my spine. I both screamed and vomited. Stars flickered, blinding me. Ryker was shouting something again, but I couldn't hear him over the roaring in my ears. There was something else, something shining along with the stars in my eyes.

Polished shoes gleamed against the white floor. But that wasn't what I had seen. A gun shifted in Fandrin's lap, catching the light again. It wasn't the weapon that had caught my eye. It was the single bullet rolling between his fingertips. As I retched again, Fandrin took advantage of Ryker's distraction. Wrinkled but expert hands slid the bullet into the chamber. The gun rose and I clenched Ryker's hand in warning.

A shot rang out.

Fandrin's hand went limp and the silver gun clattered to the floor. The barrel was still smoking. Chunky red specks sprayed the white walls. A smattering of gore was cascading down the glass windows.

Ryker had managed to raise his own weapon at my warning, but it wasn't his bullet that killed The Minister.

Fandrin was dead of his own hand.

Ryker's voice was husky with adrenaline. "Coward..."

I sputtered again and Ryker lowered his firearm, turning his attention back to me. Tenderly, he rolled me onto my back again. There was a commotion at the door. The cursing announced Archer before I could see her. My hand automatically stretched out for the man who was with her. I would know his footsteps anywhere.

Triven slid to my side, his good hand quickly finding mine as he assessed the damage. There was a makeshift bandage wrapped around his injured hand. It was stained completely red, but he had more color in his cheeks now.

"Doc?" Ryker pleaded with Archer.

Holding her gun limply, she shook her head.

Of course she hadn't found him. Doc was dead. I saw it with my own eyes. The one man who might have been able to save me was gone.

"Serum?" Hope was fading from Ryker's words.

"There isn't time. She'll be dead before the other triage team gets here." Triven said.

Archer screamed and kicked Arden's dead body. Repeatedly.

It was getting harder to keep my eyes open. Everything was cold.

Pulling myself from sleep, I squeezed Triven's hand, trying to tell him it was okay. I knew what was going to happen and I accepted it.

I wanted him to lean in and kiss me one last time, to hold me and promise I wouldn't die alone. But a spark lit in his eyes.

His uninjured hand found Arden's knife, still buried in my abdomen. It hovered over the handle thoughtfully.

"This is Sanctuary grade."

"And?" Ryker stared at him.

"It could cauterize the wound." Archer whispered, seeing where Triven was going.

"You'll fry her!" Ryker protested.

"Not if we calibrate it to a lower setting." Triven looked to me for approval. I blinked slowly.

Let me go. I wanted to say. But my tongue refused to work. The pain was ebbing again and I wanted so badly to sleep.

There was a tugging around my stomach. People were talking, but the words made no sense. It was like listening to muffled voices in another room. I closed my eyes and was treated to the sweetest face of a little girl with brown hair and round doe eyes. The Mouse of my past, innocent, happy—unscarred by loss. Why wasn't she here?

My eyes fluttered open, searching for her, for the reason I had risked so much. What would she say if I gave up now?

A female voice came back into focus. "This could kill her."

There was a pause, a hesitation.

Warm hands pressed over my stomach and I slid mine over them, guiding them to the electric knife. Then with a shaking hand, I signed. The movement was slow, but the symbol was clear. *Phoenix.* Triven would understand, only he knew the reason behind my chosen name. What it meant—that I was a survivor.

I might die, but at least Triven could tell Mouse that I fought until the very end.

Hands wrapped around the knife, but moved as another set replaced them. The blade shifted as Ryker took hold. "Better she hates *me* if she lives. Ready?"

I took what might be my last breath and braced myself.

EPILOGUE: REBIRTH

A **BREEZE PLAYED** in my hair, tossing it gently. My bare toes curled over the edge of rooftop. The streets below were full of people. The city was still slowly being rebuilt, though it would never again be what it was. A fact I was grateful for. The aftermath had not been easy, it still wasn't.

Citizens continued to withdraw when a Tribesman came too close and opposing Tribes still carried bad blood even if their children played together. Fighting a war side-by-side hadn't changed that.

But they were here, sharing this new world, and I supposed that was a start. I stood on our roof's ledge, relishing in the fact that no one could see me. It was a gift from Ryker and Thadd. The privacy shield that had once cloaked Ryker's roof, now protected ours. There weren't cameras watching our every movement like before. But since Triven and I had chosen to stay in The Sanctuary, claimed a home for our own, people continued to view me as Fandrin's granddaughter. I had wanted nothing to do with the new council, with the government Triven was spearheading, but still people were leery of me. That was one of the reasons I loved it up here. It was nice to disappear.

I sighed as a fake cloud drifted overhead. The dome was back up, once again painting happy pictures of a sky that didn't exist. Nearly a year later and I still wasn't used to it. The Wall stood again between our two worlds. It no longer acted as a barricade, but a gate. Peaceful people were allowed to come and go as they pleased, but the level security was still high. The Sanctuary's citizens never left their boundaries, but some Tribe members eagerly crossed over, seeking a new way of life here.

Most Tribes had stayed in Tartarus, claiming the territories of the dwindling Ravagers. The few Ravagers that had escaped the war were being hunted. Tribal justice I suppose.

The rebellion had changed a lot, but world would not transform overnight. Tribes still warred, citizens still sometimes cowered in fear and our worlds were still trying to figure out how to live together.

Teya was one of those who chose to remain in Tartarus. She had refused to relocate her people, but she did sit on the new council. I always wondered how the meetings went when mother and daughter had to sit across from each other. Teya never told Archer the truth about her arm, and neither did I. Triven assured me the two women were civil, but Ryker painted a different picture. I tended to trust his rendition as he was usually the one to calm Archer down these days. The two had become nearly inseparable. They both swore it was only friendship, but they were both lying idiots. They were good for each other and I hoped they would realize it soon.

The strangest and most shocking Tribal relocation was Sedia. After the war, she became the first Taciturn leader to willingly step down and the first to announce her migration to The Sanctuary. Many of her Tribesmen attributed the choice to her insanity, but it was more than that. Though her tattoos were hard to ignore, and the manic glint in her eyes never completely dulled, she had changed. Sedia took to natural food cultivation. While she worked the land, the crazed veneer calmed and I found myself drawn to her. I would volunteer to work with her although the other citizens gave her a wide berth. Slowly, she began to talk about her brothers. The shared stories seemed to heal us both.

I smiled, stepping down from the ledge. "How was the council meeting?"

Triven laughed, "I still can't manage to sneak up on you."

My laugh mixed with his. "You drag your right toe when you're trying to walk quietly."

"Hmm... guess I will have to work on that." Triven's arms wrapped around my waist as he buried his face in my hair. I leaned into him.

"Teya and Archer butted heads about the weapons regulations, again." He said.

"Tell me something new."

"Petra is going to head the new schooling programs. Sedia and Teya offered to escort her and a few others into Tartarus to raid the library. Thadd hated the idea, what with the baby on the way. But Petra told him to stuff it and then kissed him a little too enthusiastically, as usual." His tone was disapproving, but I would tell he was smiling. Triven and Thadd had become close in the past few months. What started as shared grief became friendship.

"They do realize most of the good books have already been stolen, right?" I grinned, thinking of my stash in our room downstairs.

"And *who* would do such an atrocious thing? Damn those rogue book nerds." Triven kissed the side of my neck and I batted him away laughing.

"*You* should know." I shot back. After all he had stolen plenty of his own.

Triven's hands wrapped over my stomach as our laughter slowed. They fell over the scar, his thumb unconsciously tracing the raised skin. Fandrin's last gift to me. It was ironic really. The man who had so desperately wanted to strengthen our bloodline, was the one who snuffed it out. The knife's shock had saved my life, but ruined any chance of Triven and I having children of our own. I knew it saddened him, but secretly I was relieved. My family had been tainted for generations, almost as if violence was in our genetics. Somehow it seemed right that the line would end with me.

Besides, I had Mouse.

As usual, we were of the same mind. "How was *your* day? Did you and Mouse go see Inessa?"

I took a heavy breath, thinking of my mother's best friend. We had found her locked up in one of Fandrin's cells. The once loving and kind woman was completely catatonic. Mae swore the woman she loved was in there somewhere, but Inessa had become a shell, an empty vessel gone long before we got to her. It was cruel. She was here and yet Fandrin had killed her. I tried to smile, but couldn't. "Yeah, it was a good day. Mae said she's started humming to herself. I guess that's something. Mouse is still there. She wanted to stay and read, so I left her. After all, it's the most she uses her voice since…"

She killed her brother.

Mouse had developed nightmares that rivaled my own and though I spent most nights calming her down, she barely spoke anymore. Reading to Inessa seemed to help, so I always encouraged it. But it worried me. Mouse had lost so much.

"Give her time." Triven whispered, but there was a hint of despair in his voice. "We all heal in our own way. We'll be with her every step and when she's ready to talk, we'll listen."

I turned in his arms and stepped up on the ledge so I was taller. Leaning down, I took his face in my hands and pressed my lips to his. I pulled away just far enough to speak. "You're a good man Triven Halverson."

He smiled against my lips. "For you Prea Mason, always."

I leaned away from him, looking down at the pavement below. It had not been that long ago when I had thought about throwing myself off a rooftop. Triven's arms surrounded me, pulling me down into his embrace, his lips claiming mine again. It was true, death was easier, but life was worth the pain.

ACKNOWLEDGEMENTS

PHOENIX IS ALL the things I wish I could be, the traits I am not so proud of and a reminder to let others in and love them in return. From the day Prea first graced my pages, she and the other characters of the New World Series have continually taught me that nothing is black and white, not everyone is good or bad, and how surrounding yourself with the right people, can make you a better person. There is a fabulous and bittersweet moment when a series comes to an end. And I would be lying if I said there weren't both tears of joy and sadness upon typing my final words. For nearly six years, Phoenix has not only been an integral part of my life but of so many others as well.

I must first thank my biggest supporter. The man who has kindly shared his wife with a slew of unruly characters, gone to bed alone while I stayed up all night writing and gave up weekends with his best friend so I could disappear into the dark streets of Tartarus. Auston, this series would have never seen the light of day without you. I can't give you back the hours it stole me away, but promise to find a balance with my next book. Our adventures will once again be epic, and I will always be happy sneaking in new chapters between shuttling you from mountain peak to mountain peak. You are my rock, my best friend, my hero. I love you.

Mom, where do I begin? My fans need to know how essential you were to the completion of this series. After myself, no one has poured over these pages more, re-read them as extensively or put as much time into this as you. You helped me take Phoenix's story to the next level, you have grown with us since that first rooftop scene to the final one. There is no one else in the world I would have wanted to go through this incredible journey with, but you. I owe you another adventure in Moab with life changing hikes and wine under the stars. Many children fear becoming their mothers, but I am honored to be so much like you. You're truly one of my best friends, and even though I am no longer a child, I still look up to you every day. Both you and Dad raised me to be adventurous and to peruse my dreams. Like all humans, you may not be perfect, but you were the best parents a girl could ask for. Thank you – for everything.

Hidden in the depths of these pages are some of the most amazing people I have ever had the pleasure of knowing. Annette Meyerkord, Dawn Faller, Cerri Norris, Kimberly Karli, Cameron Walker and Amie Bergeson—you ladies rode this rollercoaster with me since the beginning. Not only am I grateful for your insight and support, but to have you in my life. Like Triven and Mouse with Phoenix, you make me a better person. I must also give thanks to Andy Meyerkord, Eric Faller, Sophia Hanson, Dela, Freedom Mathews, Jackie Fix, Juliana Waltz, the amazing OwlCrate and all my other cheerleaders, supporters, and friends.

At the top of that supporters list is the entire Oftomes family. Ben, thank you for reaching out to me nearly two years ago and loving my books as much as I do. I gave her a voice, but you gave us a platform to stand on. You are genuinely one of the most supportive and inspired people I have had the honor of calling not only a friend but a loyal publisher. Kim-G you made my covers come to life, enticing fans before they ever turned a page. You are amazingly talented, thank you! A huge thanks to Eight Little Pages for the beautiful interiors and Xina Hailey for your sharp editor eyes. Also, I must acknowledge all the other authors in the Oftomes family. I am honored, humbled and inspired by all of you.

Last and never least, thank you—my fans. You have made me cry with joy, touched my heart and reminded me why I write. Thank you for loving Phoenix and taking this crazy ride alongside us. You inspire me. Thank you—each and every one of you—for your continued support. You have forever changed my life.

CPSIA information can be obtained
at www.ICGtesting.com
Printed in the USA
BVOW08s2236061217
501840BV00002B/63/P